Praise for *All the Stars and Teeth*

"Adalyn Grace's captivating magic and lush world-building brings *All the Stars and Teeth* to life. You'll fall in love with her cast of **FIERCE** and **UNRELENTING** characters, and their thrilling sea adventure will keep your heart pounding until the very last page. Do yourself a favor and get lost in this beautiful book!"

—TOMI ADEYEMI, #1 New York Times–bestselling author of *Children of Blood and Bone*

"Adalyn Grace has delivered a **PHENOMENAL** debut, filled with unexpected magic and a fiery female protagonist. **READERS WILL FALL HARD** for this high-seas adventure."

—ADRIENNE YOUNG, New York Times–bestselling author of *Sky in the Deep* and *The Girl the Sea Gave Back*

"**VICIOUS** and **ALLURING**, *All the Stars and Teeth* is a force to be reckoned with."

—HAFSAH FAIZAL, New York Times–bestselling author of *We Hunt the Flame*

"**BEAUTIFUL** and **BLOODY**. Vicious and charming. Dark and romantic. Let *All the Stars and Teeth* ensnare your heart and soul."

—ASTRID SCHOLTE, author of *Four Dead Queens*

"*All the Stars and Teeth* is a debut jam-packed with swashbuckling adventure, **SWOON-WORTHY** romance, and dark, lush magic. Amora Montara and the crew of *Keel Haul* will drop anchor in your heart and refuse to leave until you've turned the last page."

—CHRISTINE LYNN HERMAN, New York Times–bestselling author of *The Devouring Gray*

"*All the Stars and Teeth* is a **DELICIOUSLY TWISTED** fantasy that keeps your heart jumping from page to page. Grace's epic storytelling is a blend of fantastically creepy blood magic and lush island world-building, and brings an exciting new voice to the YA scene. **RICHLY IMAGINATIVE** and full of political intrigue. I loved every moment of this fast-paced adventure!"

—AKEMI DAWN BOWMAN, author of *Starfish* and the upcoming *The Infinity Courts*

"Grace crafts a romantic and bloody nautical adventure featuring a fierce, but deeply flawed heroine governed by loyalty and justice for her people. This book is a **THRILLING, MAGICAL WORLD** I didn't want to leave."

—ISABEL IBAÑEZ,. author of *Woven in Moonlight*

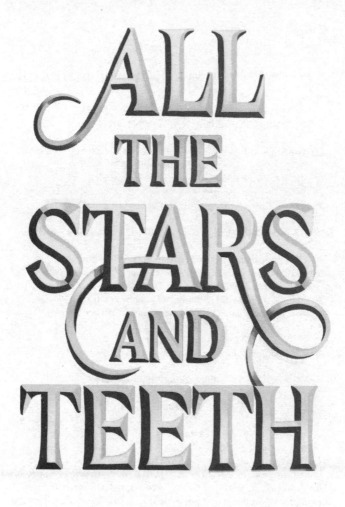

ALL THE STARS AND TEETH

ADALYN GRACE

{Imprint}
MAKE YOUR MARK

NEW YORK

[Imprint]
MAKE YOUR MARK

A part of Macmillan Publishing Group, LLC
120 Broadway, New York, NY 10271

Library of Congress Cataloging-in-Publication Data is available.

ISBN 978-1-250-30778-1 (hardcover) / ISBN 978-1-250-30779-8 (ebook)

Our books may be purchased in bulk for promotional,
educational, or business use. Please contact your local bookseller
or the Macmillan Corporate and Premium Sales Department
at (800) 221-7945 ext. 5442 or by email at
MacmillanSpecialMarkets@macmillan.com.

Book design by Natalie C. Sousa
Imprint logo designed by Amanda Spielman

First edition, 2020

3   5   7   9   10   8   6   4

fiercereads.com

There was once a mermaid who loved nothing more than a beautiful
conch shell she brought with her everywhere. A sailor, noticing her affection
for the conch, stole it. He believed he could trick the mermaid into
thinking she'd lost her prized possession, and that she would fall in love
with him once he returned it to her. But the mermaid was too clever for
his tricks. She shed her fins in favor of feet and went ashore to hunt the
sailor down. Upon finding him, she ripped out his heart, ate it, then returned
to the sea with her conch in hand. This book is protected by mermaids.
Steal it, and you best watch your heart.

Map art by Dave Stevenson

To Mom and Dad—
For your love, eternal support,
and for waiting in the hot sun every time
I dragged you to a million book signings.
I wouldn't be here without you . . . literally.

To Taylor—
Because we finally did it.

THE KINGDOM OF VISIDIA

ARIDA
Island of soul magic
Represented by sapphire

VALUKA
Island of elemental magic
Represented by ruby

MORNUTE
Island of enchantment magic
Represented by rose beryl

CURMANA
Island of mind magic
Represented by onyx

KEROST
Island of time magic
Represented by amethyst

SUNTOSU
Island of restoration magic
Represented by emerald

ZUDOH
Island of curse magic
Represented by opal

CHAPTER ONE

This day is made for sailing.

The ocean's brine coats my tongue and I savor its grit. Late summer's heat has beaten the sea into submission; it barely sways as I stand against the starboard ledge.

Turquoise water stretches into the distance, stuffed full of blue tangs and schools of yellowtail snapper that flounder away from our ship and conceal themselves beneath thin layers of sea foam. Through the morning haze sits an outline of cloud-shrouded mountains that shape the kingdom's northernmost island, Mornute. It's one of the six islands I've not yet seen but will one day rule.

"Where are we headed?" I ask. "To the volcanos of Valuka? The jungles of Suntosu?" The weather is gentle enough that my words carry to the bow where Father stands, overlooking the water.

Years at sea have wrinkled his tanned olive skin, making

him appear older than his forty years. The wrinkles also make him look stern, which I like. Arida's High Animancer, the King of Visidia, should always appear stern.

"The sea is a dangerous beast, Amora," he says. "And you are too precious to lose. But prove your strength to our people tonight, and I'll know you're capable of braving it. For now, focus on earning the throne." His deep brown eyes flicker to me, and he grins. "And on announcing your engagement."

My throat thickens. Ferrick is a fine enough man, if one dreams of settling down with a childhood acquaintance. But I prefer my daily suitors, and their gifts.

Amabons, ginnada, and dresses from the finest fabrics, all to woo the impressionable princess they believe I am. Boys in the kingdom think they can buy my love and title, and I let them believe it. Nothing can compare to the lavish trinkets of hungry suitors, and I'm not keen on ending their generosity.

"Are you ready?" Father's words are low but firm; something in his eyes shifts. He's not talking about my impending engagement.

Instinctively, my hand goes to the leather satchel resting on my hip. The contents inside clatter as I touch their rigid edges.

"I am," I say, though the words are bolder than I feel. Because even as the king's only child, my people will not simply hand me the crown and let me lead out of birthright. Here, in the kingdom of Visidia, I must first prove myself to them if I'm to earn the title of heir. And I'm to do it by showing them a proper demonstration of Aridian magic; the magic shared only through the blood of the Montara family.

Tonight, I've only one chance to prove I'm fit to claim the title of Animancer—a master of souls. But my people won't settle for a *good* performance. They demand excellence, and I'll give them just that. By the end of the night, I'll prove to them there will never be anyone better suited for the throne.

Sprawling mountains of ripe green and lush cliffsides stretch before us as the sea tugs our ship toward the docks of Arida, my home island. The cliffsides are thickly shrouded with bioluminescent flora, which, while beautiful in the daylight, will steal a person's breath when they spread their brilliant purple and pink petals beneath the moon.

It's magnificent, yet a thick knot of bitterness constricts my chest as we approach. I try to ignore it, but it sinks into my gut like an anchor.

I love Arida, but gods, what I wouldn't give to turn this ship around and keep sailing.

Our sails bloat as wind hauls us toward the harbor, and Father readies himself to dock. I may be expected to run the kingdom one day, yet Father still refuses to teach me something as simple as sailing *The Duchess*. As I'm one of only two potential Montara heirs, he tells me travel is too dangerous. Despite my years spent begging, arguing that I should be able to set sail and see my kingdom, he hardly lets me touch the helm.

But that just means it's time to try harder. Today is my birthday, after all.

I shoo my worries away with the seagulls that circle the main mast and join him. Father's lips pucker as I smile; he knows exactly what I want.

"Please?" I rest my smooth hand beside his rough one on the helm, craving the sun-kissed glow and sea-roughened calluses he wears with pride—the telltale signs of a voyager.

There's not much time left before we dock. The waters are growing shallow, beating angrily against the ship as we near Arida. A small crowd of servants and royal soldiers wait for us on the red sand, ready to whisk us away in preparation for tonight.

"No." Father squares his shoulders to block me out.

I duck around him to claim his stare. "Yes. Just this once?"

Father's sigh makes his broad chest quiver. He must sense how badly I want this, because for the first time in my life he steps aside and offers me the helm. My free hand grips the smooth wood without missing a second, and I suppress a shudder at how it feels between my palms.

Natural. Like my hands were built for this.

"You must go slowly," Father says, but I'm only half listening. The ship feels every bit the beast I wanted it to, able to take on the sea's promise of adventure and conquer anything in its path. It's strong, fearless, but I sense its reluctance to listen to me. This ship is like my people; it demands only the most deserving captain, and will accept no less.

I scrape my nail gently against the wood and twist the helm, just an inch. The ship shudders in response, considering me. Father lingers close, his hands twitchy and ready to take over should something go awry. I won't let it.

I am Amora Montara, Princess of Visidia and heir to the High Animancer's throne. There is no ship I cannot sail. There is nothing I cannot master.

The wind shifts with a gust of air, disturbing the sails and pushing the vessel an inch or so to the left. It's not a big shift, but the ship is challenging me, and I'm not one to lose. I adjust my grip on the helm to correct it.

I don't need to look up to know we're coming into shallow water. I can feel it in the ship's behavior, in the way its steady back-and-forth lulling stiffens into something rigid and fierce.

"Tighten the grip of your left hand." Father's voice is distant, but I do as he says. The ship creaks in response.

I am Amora Montara. I dig my nail into *The Duchess* again when the ship quivers. *The power of Arida is within me. You will obey.*

The Duchess groans as we hit the sand, and the impact rattles my chest. I lose my footing and scramble to get a better grip, but the helm is slippery from the ocean's mist, and my face slams into it. Jagged wood scuffs my cheek, causing the ship to laugh as it settles into the sand. I pull back, running a finger along my skin. It comes away dripping blood.

The ship has won, and she knows it. I can't remember the last time anything made me bleed.

"Amora!" Father's voice cracks in horror. Anger swells in my belly as I glare at the hands that have betrayed me.

Blasted ship. All it had to do was listen.

"By Cato's blade, you're bleeding."

Tonight, I must be perfect. There's no room for ugly injuries that signal weakness.

"It's just a scratch." I shoo him away. "Mira will be able to cover it."

Father wears guilt in the wrinkles between his pinched brows. The sight of it makes anger rip through my veins like poison. It's not his fault I'm bleeding. It's not his fault I cannot command even a ship to listen to me.

I take Father's arm before he can say anything else.

We descend the bridge of *The Duchess*, to where Mira waits upon sand the color of fresh blood, standing between several rigid men and women who sport light blazers with rose-gold trim. She wears loose black trousers and a matching top that billows from her small frame, fastened by tiny pearl shoulder straps that shimmer beneath her hair—a thick stream of waves as dark and sleek as a raven's feather. The solid rose-gold trim along her outfit matches the royal emblem she wears proudly on her chest; it's the same as the others wear—the skeleton of an eel wrapped around a crown of whalebone.

Though she's hardly older than I am, Mira's sharp face is prematurely wrinkled from constant anxiety. In her five years as my lady-in-waiting, she's taken every moment possible to fuss over me, as protective as my parents. When she catches sight of my cheek, she gasps and draws me forward.

"Today of all days." She fishes a handkerchief from her pocket and rubs it across my cheek. Fierce disapproval lingers in the backs of her squinted blue eyes, and as I await the verdict, she frowns. "The wound's fresh, so we may be able to conceal it if we act quickly. Come, let's get you ready."

I glance back at Father, seeking his smile of encouragement. But it withers into a frown as the officials draw him in, whispering secrets not meant for unproven successors. I take a step toward him, silently begging him to turn and seek my counsel or invite me into the discussion, but Mira grabs hold of my hand.

"You know they won't tell you anything." Though her voice is soft, the words feel like claws. "Not until after your performance."

I shake Mira's hand away, letting the ship steal my attention. Its wood creaks with laughter as it settles onto the sand, mocking me.

The sound sinks into my bones, and I wonder: If I cannot rule one ship, then how am I ready to rule an entire kingdom?

CHAPTER TWO

Ikaeans have enchanted the torchlight, blanketing the crowded path beneath my balcony in dazzling shades of pinks, blues, and purples.

Hundreds of Visidians climb the steep cliffs from the beach's shore up to where the celebration begins below the palace, some of them using paved pathways while those more adventurous weave in and out of rainbow eucalyptus and up the switchback, choking on jeers and quick breaths as they race one another. A group of Curmanan soldiers wait at the shore to help those who can't or prefer not to make the climb. They lift children and families into the air and high up the northern cliffs to where the celebration awaits. They're skilled enough with their levitation magic that it comes as easily as their breaths.

The steady thumping of the drums is more intense than it was earlier; every beat clatters my bones while the hollow rattling of percussion fills my chest. The air pulses with energy and laughter, warm with the scent of richly spiced pork and roasted honey plums.

Every person—young and old—is out tonight. When the time comes for my performance, there will be no hiding from the eyes of Visidia.

"Isn't it magnificent?" Yuriel asks. "It's better than the theater out there, with all those fashions and magics. We should get the kingdom together like this more often." My cousin sits on the corner of my canopy bed, lounging against a duvet of goose feathers as he picks at a platter full of lavish desserts. Sitting there, he looks almost like a goose himself, careful to keep anything that resembles chocolate away from the dyed pink peacock feathers that make up his eccentric suit, but sipping deeply from a crystal glass of plum-red wine all the same. I keep finding myself distracted by the startling brightness of his lavender eyes and the beautiful fluorescent-pink makeup that wings out from them.

"When I rule, I'll bring the kingdom together for plenty of celebrations." I step away from the balcony and draw the velvet curtains shut behind me. Saying it aloud heats my blood, making my skin prickle with anticipation for tonight.

In just a few hours, everything I've spent eighteen years working for will finally be mine.

My title as heir to Visidia. The opportunity to set sail and see my kingdom. The right to not only learn its secrets, but to command it.

"I'm glad to see you're confident," Yuriel says between gooey bites of frosted fudge. "I'll hold you to that."

Though Yuriel and I are both Montaras, our similarities end at the blood in our veins. With a father who is pale as powdered snow, my cousin's skin is several shades lighter than my own copper brown. And while my hair is a mass of dark curls, his, like all things in his hometown of Ikae, is extravagant. It's the starkest shade of white, pure even at the roots. Where I'm tall and curved with muscle, he's soft and delicate—a poster child for Ikae.

But our most distinctive difference is that despite his royal lineage, Yuriel cannot learn soul magic. He gave up that right when he was five years old and accidentally used enchantment magic to turn Aunt Kalea's hair fluorescent green.

Though he was too young to be held responsible for this choice, it's now a duty Aunt Kalea and I bear alone. If I'm not deemed a fit heir, then my people will move on to Aunt Kalea; the only remaining Montara left who has yet to claim a magic.

But that won't happen. No one in my family has ever failed their performance, and I've dedicated too much of my life to be the first.

"Amora?" Mira appears from the connected parlor. Her irises are white and glazed over; the look of a Curmanan using mind speak. "Your parents are ready for you." She blinks the blue back into her eyes. "When you're ready, Casem will escort you to them."

Yuriel wags his brows as I turn away to steal a final look at myself. The scratch on my cheek is hardly noticeable under layers of creams and powders. My crepe gown is made to be eye-catching—royal blue with a tight, structured top embroidered with thin gold whorls that accentuate my curves and illuminate the warmth of my copper skin. It's tight in all the areas I can appreciate, and with my dark brown curls bundled loosely at the nape of my neck, the created effect is fierce.

Mira offers me a cloak that looks as though it's been drenched in melted sapphires and dusted with starlight. She hooks it to my gown, just below the shoulders, and my breath catches. It glistens like the sun reflecting off dark water and stains my fingertips with shimmer as I brush them across the soft fabric.

"You've truly outdone yourself," I tell her, catching the proud smile she tries to mask.

"Ferrick's a lucky man," she says. "You look beautiful."

My excitement shatters. With as much time as it took to fit me into this gown, I certainly ought to look beautiful. And I felt every bit of it before Mira mentioned Ferrick.

"Thank you," I say briskly, trying to snuff out the thoughts of my soon-to-be fiancé. "I'm ready to see my parents."

"Good luck!" Yuriel cheers as he pours himself another glass of wine. I leave him behind in my room, boots clicking against the marble floor as I follow Mira out the door. My guard, Casem, waits with his head tipped back against the wall.

As a Valukan, Casem's able to manipulate the air around him. But Casem prefers weaponry over magic, and doesn't often practice his skills. He proudly wears the uniform all royal guards and Visidian soldiers wear, regardless of which island they hail from: a striking royal-blue blazer and a shimmering sapphire cape threaded with silver stitching along the trim. The royal emblem of the skeletal eel gleams brightly on his cape as he dips into a bow upon spotting us, though his pale blue eyes linger on Mira longer than they do me. He's like a walking honeycomb with his suntanned skin and sandy blond hair, and I swear that's what he melts into every time he looks at her.

Perhaps one day they'll work up the nerve to kiss and put an end to their constant longing.

"Do you two plan to enjoy the celebration?" I ask as we walk, thankful to have someone sober to talk to. "Or has my father put you both on duty?"

Their momentary silence is enough of an answer.

"I doubt I'll be needed." Casem looks over his shoulder, grinning at us. "But watching over you tonight is a privilege. Though, I admit . . . the roasting pork smells like it was cooked by the gods. I wouldn't be opposed if you managed to stow away some extra food—"

"Casem!" Mira gasps, but the guard laughs and I smile at his gusto.

"I'll tell the kitchen staff to set something aside," I assure him as we ascend the stairs, my heart skipping beats as we approach the throne room.

The colossal double doors stare down at me, a looming presence that chills my bones. I pause before it, drawing a long breath as I take a moment to steady myself. Eighteen years, and this is finally happening.

Ornately carved with the map of the land we command, the entire kingdom of Visidia unfolds across the golden slabs, portrayed by a collection of islands inlaid with shimmering jewels. The island of soul magic and the capital of our kingdom, Arida is represented by a bright sapphire that sits proudly in the middle of the map.

My skin warms as I brush my finger across my home island, trailing straight above it to Yuriel's home—Mornute, marked by rose beryl. A lavish, affluent island, full of stylish denizens who use their enchantment magic to have purple hair one day and pink the next. Mornute is well-known for not only its magic, but also for its lush mountainside vineyards. The island of enchantment produces and exports most of Visidia's alcohol. Though their ale's delicious, their wine is by far my favorite.

To the left is Casem and Mother's home island of Valuka. Marked by a ruby, it's where elemental magic is practiced. While Mother chose for her affinity to be water, those with Valukan magic may pick between wielding either earth, fire, water, or air.

Below Valuka is an island more elusive to me—Kerost, the island of time magic, portrayed with an amethyst. Though it's impossible to manipulate time itself, those with this magic are able to change how bodies interact within time, slowing them down or speeding themselves up. We have soldiers and staff here at the palace who hail from all the islands, but it's been ages since I've seen time magic in action. Father's told me stories of how taxing that magic can be for its users, which is why it's Visidia's least practiced magic.

To the far right of Arida sits a thick emerald stone that marks the center of Suntosu, the island of restoration magic. Skilled healers often come to work for the kingdom, where they're dispatched to healing wards all over Visidia, tasked to care for the sick and injured. But Suntosu is also the home of Ferrick, my fiancé, and for that reason I skim over the island quickly, not wanting to think about having to announce our engagement. I trail my finger upward instead, to the onyx that marks Curmana, the birthplace for many of our royal staff, including Mira. I think of the Curmanans I watched earlier, helping others up the cliffs.

But not all are skilled at levitation; some, like Mira, are skilled mind speakers who can communicate directly into another person's mind without ever having to use her lips. Father's employed several of them to work with the advisers on each island, and their magic is how we communicate with one another so swiftly. It's also a great resource for the kingdom's latest gossip.

When I go to pull my hand away, my thumb brushes over a tiny hole in the map, to the far south of Arida, and I bend to examine the hole that was once filled with a beautiful white opal.

Zudoh. An island that specializes in curse magic, banished from the kingdom when I was a child. I don't know much about their magic—just that it was used for protection. They could create barriers and charms that, when touched, would make people see strange things. But mostly the island was known for its advanced infrastructure and uniquely engineered wood that lent itself to producing our homes as well as our ships. As the southernmost island, its climate is the coldest of any. Winters in Zudoh are said to be harsh and full of snow and blizzards.

I don't remember much about their banishment, as it happened when I was only seven years old. It's a tender subject of conversation around the kingdom, often spoken of in whispers behind shut doors. Even Father doesn't like to discuss it. Whenever I've pressed for details, he's been quick to turn his shoulder and say that Zudoh doesn't agree with the way the Montaras rule, and that they never will. Beyond that, everything I know about Zudoh's banishment has been gleaned from keeping an ear to the kingdom's gossip network.

I've heard that Zudoh's advisers turned on Father during one of his visits to their island, and a fight ensued that left him severely injured. I vaguely remember a brief period when Father took a break from training me and I wasn't allowed to see him. Back then I'd assumed he was busy; it wasn't until years later that I connected the dots.

It's infuriating, being expected to one day rule this kingdom, yet being treated like a child by having so much information kept secret "until I'm ready."

That's what I'm looking forward to tonight, more than anything. The moment my performance is over and I'm officially recognized as heir to the throne, I'll demand to know everything there is to know about my kingdom. No longer will I have to wonder. No longer will Father be able to keep me holed up on Arida, telling me to keep practicing my magic. He'll have to treat me with the respect the future queen deserves. I may be one of the few possible heirs left, but I am not the fragile, breakable thing he believes me to be.

"Amora?" Mira's voice draws me back.

Two palace guards flank my sides, each with a hand resting on the thick handles of the door, waiting.

I draw a breath. "Open them."

The doors bring a rush of air as they part, knocking a few loose strands of curls free from their coil at my neck and into my eyes. My chest grows tight as my breaths quicken. I glance back at Casem and Mira, both of whom are on one knee with their heads bowed, then step inside.

The doors slam shut behind me.

There's no need for light in the throne room. Torch- and starlight sneak through the open back wall and flood the cavernous space. Like everywhere else inside the palace, the floor is a striking white marble, though in here it's partially covered by a thick sapphire rug laced with golden trim. At the edge of it, three thrones made from pearl and whalebone sit at the top of six black marble steps.

There will be four chairs, soon. Once married, Ferrick will sit beside me every time I hold council.

My palms sweat, but there's no time to dwell on the invisible fourth chair. My parents stand before the two front thrones; the exposed panoramic balcony that overlooks Arida spreads out behind them. The enchanted torchlight that filters in illuminates their profiles and turns their bright smiles into miniature glowing moons.

"Amora." Father speaks first. "You look beautiful." There's a table behind him, though I can't see what's on it.

The reality of what's finally about to happen turns my legs into stone. Shakily I force them forward, step-by-step. Marble pillars loom tall beside me—there are four more between my parents and me. I count each as I move.

14

One.

One more hour until I prove to Visidia that I'm meant to be their heir.

Two.

Two more hours until I'm engaged to a man I'll never love.

Three.

Three more hours until I give the command to ready a ship to set sail tomorrow, and demand to know every secret about this kingdom that's ever been kept from me.

Four.

Finally the nerves come, burrowing into me. Making me sweat.

At the bottom of the stairs I bow, and Father chuckles.

"Come, Amora," he says. "Come sit."

I swallow a lump in my throat and climb the steps too quickly as I start toward my chair—the one in the back. Mother grabs hold of my shoulders and turns me around.

"Not that one," she whispers, pointing me instead toward the largest chair—the one meant for the High Animancer.

My heart is a monster that rages against my rib cage as Father takes hold of my arm and guides me into his seat.

The room looks massive from here. There are no stars from this angle, nor any windows to overlook the island. It's just me and a stretch of empty space that feels too large.

"One day, when the gods take my soul or the island no longer sees me fit to rule, this is where you'll sit. You will rule this kingdom, as the gods created you to do." Father's voice is distant; my thunderous heartbeat pounds in my ears, louder than his words. "I know your magic, your control, and your strength. For these past eighteen years I have watched it grow within you every day, and I could not be prouder. The power of Arida is strong within your blood, and yet you've conquered it. Now it's time you prove that to our people. Show them that when my time ends, they may put their trust in you." Father reaches behind him, drawing two elegantly vicious epaulettes from the table.

The ornamental shoulder pieces are alarmingly tall, encrusted with thick gemstones to represent the various islands of Visidia, and form jagged and dangerous spikes that will surely slice my own cheek if I turn too quickly.

Desire swells, nearly choking me. I never realized how cold or how light my shoulders were until this moment.

"Amora, do you swear to accept this position the gods have offered you by wielding your magic with honesty and fair judgment?" he asks as he hooks the first one on.

"I do." I grip the arms of the chair to steady myself.

"Do you swear to uphold the laws of soul magic, knowing that every time you wield it, it must be with finality?" Father hooks the second epaulette.

"I do."

He draws a step back to look me over. "And, most important, do you swear your dedication to protect the people of Visidia by upholding this magic for the duration of your life? Even knowing the consequences?"

I look at Father firmly, my chin high. "I do."

His eyes beam as the torchlight catches them. "Then may your training end here, and may you be Animancer by sunrise. You have my blessing."

The gemstones graze my neck and ears, forcing goose bumps across my skin. When I shiver, Mother presses a hand to my arm, her presence steadying me.

"Happy birthday, my love. We're proud of you." Mother's beautiful brown skin glows as radiant as the seaside cliffs at sunrise, the warm amber shade nearly a perfect match of my own. Her brushed-out auburn curls are voluminous beneath her elegant crown—a series of brilliant shells and coral, with several dried starfish woven in and inlaid with dainty sapphire gemstones. It matches her royal-blue gown, loose and seemingly understated, but woven with rich detail. Ruby-red threading lines her cape and marks her as someone originally from Valuka, and a smattering of tiny diamonds are dusted along her bodice. Her jewelry is what truly shines—fat pearl-and-diamond earrings, sparkling rubies and sapphires that adorn her dress's collar as it fans out around her neck, and thin rings that make her fingers shimmer as she moves.

Something in her other hand catches the light and gleams. When she notices me staring, she smiles and opens her palm.

"This belonged to your grandmother," she says, dangling a necklace from her fingertips. The chain is solid gold. It winds around a heavy sapphire that hangs in the middle, teardrops of diamonds dangling beneath it. It's one of the most beautiful things I've seen. "She entrusted it to me when you were a child. These jewels are worthy of the future Queen of Visidia."

Before I know what's happening, the necklace is hooked around my neck. Mother kisses my temple, but my parents aren't finished yet.

When Father draws a crown from behind the throne, all the breath in my body escapes.

The giant headpiece has been constructed from whalebone and plated in ivory. Sixteen pillars of bone spike from the base and spiral at least a foot and a half into the air. They're sharp as icicles, ready to impale, and are softened only by the indulgent white and blue flowers Mother tucks behind my ear and weaves through the bones.

If there's one thing I know for certain about this night, it's that I am meant to wear this crown.

When I present myself tonight, there will be no question of whether I'm the one meant to be Visidia's future High Animancer, once Father's time has passed. When my people see me tonight, they will know, just as I do.

I stand and hug Mother first, then Father. Both hold me tight, but are careful not to knock the crown or cut their cheeks on my sharp epaulettes.

"Put on a terrific performance out there." Mother adjusts the flowers in my hair, giving me one final look-over before smiling her approval.

"Show our people the power of the Montaras is strong," Father says.

"I'll do more than that." I trace my finger along my crown, my breathing easier and my muscles relaxing with each passing second. "I'll show them *I'm* strong."

With the comfortable weight of the satchel on my hips, I'm ready.

Father cuffs my shoulder gently, just once, and offers his hand to Mother.

It's time.

CHAPTER THREE

Every head turns our way as Casem escorts me from the palace and into the thick of the celebration. Heavy vines tangled with glowing pink flowers hang from the cliffside, brushing my shoulders and attempting to snake around my crown as we scale the mountainside, upward to where I'll perform my ceremony later this evening.

Casem leads me through a sea of people who part for us as we pass, not letting me linger in any one place for too long. As we walk, he breathes deeply through his nose and groans. "By Cato's blood, I wish my birthdays smelled this good."

Dozens of vendors are perched along the mountain's path, offering everything I could have imagined and more—roasted pork, sticky-wet honey cakes, rich banana pudding and sweets from Ikae, raw fish and sugar-glazed mango slices, chicken, fruits, *everything*. There are even some who sell toy crowns, or sabers inlaid with bold sapphire stones.

Two Aridian women have situated themselves near the wine barrels, laughing boisterously as a royal guard tries to usher them away and to the food stands. One of the women shoos the guard's hands away with another laugh that's almost contagious. Behind them, pink and blue torches light the night, shimmering with Mornute's enchantment magic. They illuminate the figures of both performers and civilians who dance and sing to the beat of the drums, joyous and carefree. Wine-coated laughter bubbles in the air and layers itself on top of the music. On the beach below, others are still arriving on their ships, grabbing food and greeting one another merrily before they begin their ascent.

"It's the princess!" A Valukan girl's sharp whisper draws my attention. She stares at my crown with a slack jaw, and those who surround her are no different. They gawk at my adornments before they remember themselves and bow.

Before them, I keep my neck tall despite the weight of my crown, and my shoulders back even when the epaulettes fight me. Though part of me wishes to wave away their formalities, the truth is I crave them. Seeing my people dipped in respectful bows sets my shoulders straighter as my chest swells with pride.

All my life I've trained to protect these people, and now they'll finally see just how capable I am.

As I make my way through the crowd, most Visidians step nervously aside, side-eyeing my crown and epaulettes with awe, while others rush to greet me with offered handshakes. While I recognize the faces of some, hundreds of strangers have flocked to my home to watch their princess secure her title of Arida's Animancer, heir to the throne. They wear the colors of their home islands, creating a sea of various hues and fashions.

Like Yuriel, citizens of Mornute are adorned in feathers—today's current fashion trend. One woman has enchanted her gown to look like it's a single swan feather, with a sparkling gossamer top that billows out at the waist until it fluffs around her. The man beside her has vibrant blue makeup that wings out from the bottom of his matching eyes. He wears a peach cape with shoulder pads of feathers that flare from his neck. Every few steps he takes, the cape shimmers with the passing image of a flamingo flying over it.

Children of Valuka are dressed simpler, wearing loose shawls and beautiful skirts or linen pants—light clothing that frees their movements. They play around one of the torches, stealing its flame and tossing it back and forth. A little blond girl loses control of the flame and singes the edge of her ruby shawl. Her mother catches what's happening and swats the girl's hand. She shoos the children away from the flame and relights it with a wave of her palm.

Magic in amounts I've never before seen is happening all around me, and I crave it. A woman with rich violet-brown skin and a soft face framed by cloud-like curls dons a Suntosan emerald cape as she uses her magic to heal the fire-wielding Valukan child. Behind her, a Curmanan man in black robes floats two glasses of wine beside him and carries full plates of food for his family.

In the midst of these people, children and their parents flock to watch a puppet show, one of the dozens of various street performances happening tonight.

"Come, one!" a voice trills dramatically from behind the booth.

"Come, all!" a crowd of children respond automatically, watching with buggish eyes.

Only after their response does the narrator continue. "Come, gather to hear the story of the great Montaras—conquerors of magic, protectors of the kingdom!"

Parents pull children onto their laps, and I wonder if they think this display as wonderfully over the top as I do.

21

I take hold of Casem's sleeve as the dark velvet curtains of the booth open for the start of a show, and pull him back into the shadows to watch.

"Really?" he asks, sighing as I hush him.

"Once upon a time," the narrator whispers, "a vicious monster sought to destroy Arida with its magic." Lights flicker on in the booth as one of the performers jerks his hand up—it's covered by a crudely made puppet of something meant to resemble a monster. "This beast was vicious and sought to corrupt those with multiple magics. Back then, you see, no one knew the dangers of it. They were exhausting their bodies, leading to slow, painful deaths as excess magic ate away at them.

"Magic has a way of making a person greedy," he continues. "The more someone has, the more they tend to want. The beast preyed on this greed by offering others the chance to learn its magic—the most powerful magic the world had ever seen, it claimed. People jumped on the opportunity, never expecting what the monster really wanted from them: their souls!"

Gasps sound from the audience, and beside me, Casem stifles a laugh. I nudge my elbow into his side, stopping him before anyone notices.

For Casem and the onlookers, this is simply another ancient story of our history that we grew up with. For me, this is my blood. My ancestry.

"—the magic was a dangerous, wicked thing," the narrator continues. "Today, we call it soul magic. It bound itself to soul after greedy soul of those who wielded multiple magics, killing them! But even with half of Arida's population destroyed, the beast wasn't content. As its hunger grew, it sought to spread its blight." The beast chases a series of screaming puppets around the tiny stage before swallowing them. Casem presses his lips together tightly, forcing back a smirk. I let him have this one.

"When all hope seemed lost," the story continues, "one person took a stand against the monster—Cato Montara!" A regal-looking puppet of my great ancestor jumps onto the stage, drawing applause from the children and adults alike. Many of them lift fake replicas of Cato's skinning knife into the air and cheer.

"Cato hadn't yet established the monarchy; he was but a humble, magicless man who sought to protect the people he loved. He made a deal with the beast—if he could convince everyone to be content with practicing only one magic forevermore, then the beast would have to give Cato its magic and leave Arida alone. The beast laughed in Cato's face and agreed, for it believed people were too greedy for such terms. It didn't expect Cato could ever convince others to stop practicing all but one of their magics—and yet he did.

"Cato then vanquished the beast with nothing more than a single skinning knife, and because of their agreement, its magic was forever bound to the Montara bloodline!" Children gasp in awe, looking at their toy knives.

The narrator's voice rises dramatically. "But if we were to go back on our ways, the beast could one day return. So to protect our people from ever being tempted by multiple magics again, Cato ruled that people pick only one type of magic to practice, and go to live on the island that would now represent that magic. He stayed on Arida, with those he chose as his advisers from each island, and created the kingdom. King Cato made Visidia what it is now, but"—here, the narrator lowers his voice in warning—"we are not the only ones responsible for keeping the beast away. The Montaras protect us, keeping it locked away within their blood. Should it ever break free from the Montaras, it will seek vengeance on all of Visidia. It will destroy every one of our souls."

The children start to shift with worry, and the narrator's voice evens out again, perfectly timed. "But don't fear; as long as we don't break our vow to practice but one magic, and so long as we have a capable animancer who's strong enough to maintain the beast's power and master its magic, Visidia will forever remain safe."

Pride warms my skin and peppers it with goose bumps. It's an incredible show, designed perfectly to preface the performance I'm about to give. I'm so invested in it that I jump as a little boy shouts from the audience, "If the magic's so dangerous, why do the Montaras still practice it?" He earns a sharp *shush* from a woman I assume is his mother, though others offer a few quiet sniggers.

The narrator is prepared for the question. His voice is coy and smooth as molasses. "It's not quite so simple. Magic is a strange thing, my boy; it's not something that simply disappears when neglected. And Aridian magic is particularly dangerous, for the beast who gave the Montaras this magic is constantly fighting for control over its user's soul. The magic must be used and exhausted, otherwise it will fester and grow until the beast becomes strong enough to take control.

"When King Cato locked it within the Montara bloodline," the narrator continues, "he made it his family's mission to master and contain the beast. Those who do are given the title of Animancer—a master of souls. That's the reason we've gathered here tonight, to watch Princess Amora solidify her position as heir to Visidia by proving herself capable of becoming Animancer. May she one day rule as well as her father, King Audric."

Nerves seize my chest. I take Casem's arm to pull him away before anyone notices us, but a snort from the crowd halts me.

"Right, because another lazy ruler is really what we need."

My hold on Casem's arm slips.

A frivolous soprano responds with a laugh. "Lazy? Please, you're babbling like a clueless Kaven supporter. The islands are *thriving*."

"Perhaps *your* island is thriving. But hardly anyone's been visiting Valuka since the hot springs ran dry. Not to mention Kerost, which is barely keeping afloat."

Several palace guards stand nearby, their eyes sparking with curiosity. They make no move to stop the slander.

From my position behind them, those watching the performance don't notice me until I step forward to make myself known. "Excuse me?" Silence ensnares the conversations as one by one, faces turn to me in horror. The guards straighten at once. "Just what lazy ruler are you referring to?"

They stare at my crown. At the epaulettes. But their eyes are missing the same awe I noticed earlier. Fear sits in its place.

"We should get moving." Casem takes hold of my arm and tugs me away from the audience. I let him.

"What was that woman talking about?" My blood burns, heating my ears and neck with annoyance. "Who's Kaven? What did they mean about Kerost barely staying afloat?"

Casem waves me off with a flourish of his hand. "I wouldn't worry about it. Clearly she has no idea what she's talking about."

"But it's like they were afraid of me. And the palace guards just stood there!"

His forehead wrinkles. "Amora, you're wearing a crown of bones, and knives for shoulder pads. Don't misinterpret their respect as fear. And what would you expect the guards to do? Even fools may speak freely."

But the words don't settle me; there's something more. "I should speak with my father."

Casem's lips press into a thin line. "You should be relaxing. If you get too worked up before the ceremony, you're going to get your magic all riled—"

"This isn't a debate," I snap. "I need to speak with him. Don't make me fight you, Casem."

Casem's eyes drop to my satchel, then to the dagger at my side. I've trained with Casem and his father, the weapons master for our soldiers, since I was a child. Mother and Father insisted I learn to protect myself, so Casem's been my sparring partner for years. But he favors the bow, and I can count on one hand the times he's bested me with a sword.

"Fine," he huffs, tempering himself with a long breath. "But the king isn't going to be happy."

We find Father near the top of the mountain, lingering in a secluded area near the garden's edge with advisers from all over Visidia flocked around him. Despite the drinks that several of the advisers hold, they're anything but jovial. When I push past the guards, I see their bodies are taut and expressions serious.

Casem's father, Olin Liley, is among them in a pristine sapphire blazer with golden trim. The royal Aridian adviser straightens as his son approaches, eyes narrowing in what I can only guess is a warning.

Casem was right—Father doesn't look happy. But there's a young man across from him who looks even angrier.

The adviser is younger than the others, in his early twenties at most. His garb is expensive—finely tailored breeches of a soft khaki, an unwrinkled linen shirt, and leather boots that nearly reach his knee. His frock coat is the bright shade of a ruby, and as his cuff links catch the light, I see that they're embossed with the royal emblem. The trim that thinly lines the coat is a bright gold—he's a royal representative from Valuka, then.

"We need to figure out a way to stop this," he argues, face pinched as if thoroughly exasperated. "Please, just *listen* to me, would you? Everyone can believe what they want about Kerost, but Kaven won't stop until he's—"

"Kaven's nothing more than talk." Father's harsh dismissal causes the Valukan to bristle. But before he can say anything more, Olin sets a hand on Father's shoulder.

"We have company, Your Majesty." He nods to me, and Father's brows lift in surprise as he turns.

"Who is Kaven?" I demand. The advisers snap to attention as I step forward. Their focus shifts to Father, whose fierce expression is amplified tenfold beneath his crown. It's not quite as tall as mine, but it's incredible—an ivory-plated skeleton of a Valuna eel. It's a deep-sea creature of legends; a ten-foot-long beast with rows of dagger-sharp teeth—each the size of my index finger—that our ancestors were rumored to have fought nearly a century ago. Its mouth is so large that Father's face sits within it. The upper jaw curves around his head, and the bottom half sits beneath Father's chin, as if eating him. The eel's jewel-encrusted spine stretches down his back and curves upward at Father's tailbone.

I wonder if I look half as terrifying in my crown as he looks in his.

"You shouldn't be here, Your Highness," Olin answers. "You should be in the gardens, readying yourself for your performance." His attention lifts to Casem, who wilts behind me.

"And I will be, once someone tells me what's going on." I look around him and at the Valukan adviser who now stands tall behind Father. He said something about Kerost, and as I look over the representatives surrounding him, there's one color in particular I don't see: amethyst.

"Where are the Kers?" My chest tightens as Father's placid expression slips. The more I look around, the more startling their absence is. It's not just a Kerost representative who's missing.

In all the excitement of the night, I hadn't noticed an entire island of my people was missing. "Are they all right?"

"They're fine," Father says at the same time the Valukan adviser says, "They're revolting against Visidia."

Father groans, turning over his shoulder to glare at the Valukan. The young man glares back at him while the surrounding advisers shift uncomfortably.

"I'm trying to help you," the adviser presses. "The least you can do is hear me out—"

"You're all dismissed." The anger in Father's booming voice causes the adviser to flinch back. He opens his mouth as though to protest, but screws it shut when his hazel eyes find mine. I try not to stare back as Father says, "I'd like a moment alone with my daughter."

Olin and the other advisers bow before they push the Valukan boy's shoulder to get him to move. "Fine! But don't say I didn't warn you!" He growls a few choice words as the rest of the advisers apologize for his ignorance and steer the Valukan away.

Eventually only Casem remains, though he excuses himself to a spot several feet away, out of immediate hearing range.

"Strange that I haven't met him before," I say to Father. "I could have sworn I knew all the advisers."

Father grunts. "Lord Bargas was apparently too ill to make the journey, and sent his son in his place. Charming boy, that one. Stormed in here and demanded a meeting like he himself was king."

Though I don't want to, Father's blatant annoyance at the Valukan makes me laugh. It eases the tension in his shoulders, and clears the air between us just a little.

"I wasn't aware Lord Bargas had a son," I say, though the adviser certainly looked like the son of Valuka's lead representative—smooth brown skin, a strong square jaw, and an almost annoyingly straight nose. He was built similar to the baron, too. A little stocky, with broad, muscular shoulders and arms that the rest of his body hadn't quite grown into, and the cocky look of someone with wealth to flaunt. "What did he mean when he said the Kers were revolting?"

"No one's *revolting*. The Kers are only trying to make a statement; it's nothing you need to worry about."

"Then tell me what they're protesting," I argue, igniting a twitch that eats Father's jawline. "Surely it's something, if they're trying to make a statement."

"By Cato's blade, you're as stubborn as your old man." He steps forward, and it's impossible to determine whether it's anger that lights his eyes. I steady myself, prepared to argue, but he drops his hand on my head, just before my crown, and the fire within me fizzles out.

"They want something I can't give them." Father's voice lightens from the powerful baritone he used with the advisers and into the soft and quiet voice he uses at home. "Kerost has always been plagued by vicious storms. It's why we employ groups of Valukans with a water affinity to live there, to help calm the tides and prevent the storms from destroying the island. But the Kers don't like being dependent. A few seasons ago, I started to get reports of the Kers bribing the Valukans for training. They wanted the Valukans to show them how to control the water."

His words snatch the air from my lungs. "They wanted to learn multiple magics? But that's suicide!"

Father grunts, dropping his hand from my head. "If enough people were to practice multiple magics, our hold on the beast would eventually fall. Souls would be ruined, and the beast would run rampant. That's why I had to remove the Valukans from Kerost, to end the temptation. Unfortunately, they fell victim to a bad storm early last season. And without the help of the Valukans, it destroyed part of their island."

It's as though a thousand leeches suck the blood from my veins, making me cold and nauseous.

"What about the Suntosans?" I press. "Did you at least keep healers there to help them?"

"I had to remove them from the situation, too," he says, and I'm glad to see that there's at least a hint of shame reddening his cheeks. "It was only meant to be until they agreed to stop trying to learn multiple magics. But then the storm happened, and the timing was . . . unfortunate."

How could he have kept this from me? And not just him, but Mira, too. As closely as she's connected to all the kingdom's news, surely she would have known.

I'm to be the ruler of this kingdom, and I intend to be a great one. But how can I be expected to protect Visidia if I don't even know what's happening within it?

"I needed to ensure you didn't lose focus," Father says, as if reading my thoughts. "Remember, Amora, until you or Yuriel have children, you are but one of two possible heirs left for the throne. Right now, the most important thing you can do for this kingdom is perform well tonight and claim that title."

I squint my eyes shut as frustration swells within me, trying to quell it enough to see the situation clearly.

I know tonight is important. And it makes sense that the Kers are angry. But if Father let them get away with practicing multiple magics, Cato's agreement with the beast would be voided and the kingdom would fall.

However, without the help of the Valukans, the Kers' homes are being destroyed. We can't let that happen, either.

"We need another way to help them," I say. "We can strengthen their understanding of the potential dangers of practicing multiple magics, but we also need to give them stronger materials for their buildings and help them repair. We can't take away their only source of protection."

He sets a hand on my shoulder. "And I don't intend to. But as the King of Visidia, I have to protect *all* our people. Keeping the Valukans there was a death sentence on our kingdom. But trust that we're figuring it out, Amora. Trust that I'm going to fix it."

Of course I want to trust that Father will make things right, but what I don't understand is why he isn't already in Kerost, helping them rebuild. If the storm was last season, why are we still standing around trying to figure this out?

"Just where does Kaven fit into this?" My head feels thicker by the second. How have I been so clueless? How has everyone managed to keep this from me?

Clearly wishing the discussion over, Father's sigh is long and annoyed. "He's a man who doesn't agree with some of the decisions I've made," he answers flatly. "But no one can agree with everything I do, can they? He's no threat to us. Now settle your thoughts. All will be fine for one more night."

Thinking back to the Valukan's angry face, I'm not sure I believe his easy dismissal. I want to argue with Father and tell him I deserve to know more, but as I open my mouth, Aunt Kalea comes clambering up the hill with a grin. My aunt doesn't wait for permission to approach, or even stop to think for a moment that she might be interrupting something important. Carelessly, just barely avoiding my epaulettes, she throws her arms around me with a hearty laugh.

"Oh, my beautiful girl! What a vision you are!" When she pulls away, she bats Father lightly in the shoulder. "How did an oaf like you manage to raise such a radiant woman, Audric? She's stunning!"

Father laughs. "She gets all her charm from Keira. I'm afraid all she gets from me is her stubbornness."

"And your sense of adventure," I add, which makes Father still, his eyes softening. It's a strange moment; a slow one where he trails his eyes over me, then onto the crown, as though seeing me in it for the first time. When he smiles again, it's warm with pride and heats my blood.

"And my sense of adventure." He turns to his sister and claps her on the shoulder. "If you'll excuse me, I should find my wife before the ceremony, but bring Jordi and Yuriel by and we'll celebrate with some wine afterward. I've three barrels reserved just for us." He grins toothily, looking like the silly older brother I only see him be when my aunt's around.

"And Amora?" he adds quietly. I turn, nearly flinching back when he bows his head to me. "I love you. Remember that after tonight, won't you? Once you're officially the heir and are off on all those grand adventures of yours."

"Don't go getting all sappy on me now," I tell him, trying to hide my embarrassment. "I love you, too."

His smile is soft as he bends to kiss my forehead. The teeth of the eel crown graze my cheek.

And then Father's gone, leaving my aunt in his place.

She's lovely in a gown of soft blue. It's a statement gown—a mix of Arida's sapphire and Mornute's soft hues. It says she understands her roots are with Arida, but that it's no longer her home. She's a small woman with olive skin similar to Father's, deeply tanned and brushed with gold from so much time spent in the sun. She's plump and youthful, with only the soft wrinkles around her eyes hinting at her age.

"I'm so glad I found you before the performance," Aunt Kalea says. "How do you feel?"

For as long as I can remember, Aunt Kalea's hands have always been the softest, warmest ones I've ever known. She cups them around my arms, holding me close so she can inspect me with molten eyes. They're the same eyes as Father's, but significantly less stern. And though she does well at masking her expression, worry rests in the tightness of her breaths and the hitch of her words. If she's to keep her lavish life on Mornute, she can't afford for me to make any mistakes tonight. And I can't afford to, either.

Should I fail to demonstrate control over my magic and prove I've tamed the beast within me, I'll be held until Aunt Kalea's proven she can become the throne's successor. Given that the law dictates a Montara without fully controlled soul magic cannot remain free, I can't ignore the possibility that I could even be executed if I'm deemed too much of a risk. Our magic is too dangerous to not be fully controlled.

"Like I've been training my whole life for this," I say. Aunt Kalea searches my eyes for another long moment, and there's a flash of concern before she pulls me in for a firm hug.

"You can do this," she whispers, her thick curls tickling my neck. "No one's more ready for this than you."

Though I know she's right, the anxiety that's been gnawing at me since the puppet show is building. I force myself to smile at her, trying to snuff it out.

Only after Aunt Kalea draws back does Casem hesitantly step forward. "I don't mean to rush you," he says, "but it's time for Amora to get going."

"Of course." Aunt Kalea nods, tucking a soft brown curl behind her ear. I try not to stare at the lines of concern crinkled between her brows, or think about how both our futures hinge on whether I deliver a proper performance.

She kisses my cheek before peeling herself away. But before she lets go of my hand, her eyes capture mine, and I'm not prepared for what I see within them. No longer are her eyes the rich brown that match Father's—they flash a bright, piercing pink, there for one moment and back to brown the next.

"Do your best." Aunt Kalea's smile trembles. "Please. For the kingdom."

The anxiety doesn't snuff out; it surges until it's like hands around my throat. The noise I make as her hands slip from mine is hardly human. The ground beneath me is like the sea, swaying as her words sink in.

Aunt Kalea's learned enchantment magic.

I am no longer one of two possible heirs; I am the *only* possible heir. Should I fail, there will be no one left to protect Visidia from the vengeance of the beast within the Montara bloodline.

Aunt Kalea showing me this was a warning—should she be forced to accept Aridian soul magic, it'll be her second magic. The bond with the beast will be severed.

"You were supposed to wait." My words are as shaky as my trembling hands. "How could you do this?"

"It was an accident." Her eyes are wet when she reaches back out for me, but I refuse to look at them for another second. I take Casem's arm. His eyes are narrowed with uncertainty, not having seen her use enchantment magic.

"Take me to the gardens," I tell him, needing to get away from her as the magic within me stirs. "Now." Casem obeys without hesitation.

It's only a short walk to the gardens' entrance, and my head is still swirling with a thousand thoughts when we arrive. I have to try my hardest to push them to the side and focus on the task at hand, just as everyone has been telling me to do. I can't let myself be distracted by her betrayal.

Tonight, I must be perfect.

A place of worship, the gardens sit atop the tallest peak in all of Arida, about two miles north of the palace. The entrance is through a cavern that's covered by heavy vines and thick ivy that Casem pulls back so that I can enter without snagging my adornments.

"You've got five minutes before others arrive," he says as I duck into the cavern, greeted by the bioluminescent flora that coats the walls and helps guide my way into the gardens.

The moment I step into it, the sight steals my breath, as it always does.

These gardens are beautiful in the daytime, but their true magnificence shines beneath the stars.

A field of untamed flowers stretches out before me, some of them tall enough that they brush against my satchel, while others drip from trees in perfect spirals. Much of the flora is bioluminous, petals and bulbs glowing in brilliant shades of greens, pinks, blues, and purples.

I brush my hands across the bulb of a flower that's taller than my hip, and it rocks back as if in surprise, its petals unfurling at my touch. They shimmer as they open, stretching awake.

Behind them, at the back of the garden, rests a small waterfall that glows as brightly as the flowers, creating breathtaking scenery that many travel from all over the kingdom to see.

At the base of the waterfall, a flat stone slab with a fire pit carved into the center has been erected as a stage for my performance. I take a seat on the edge of one side as voices begin to stir behind me. From the corner of my eye I see my parents enter the gardens, but I don't turn to them in case Aunt Kalea is there, too.

I press a hand to my chest and draw in a long breath to steady my heart. It doesn't help much, so I run my finger across the lip of the satchel and bow my head, praying that the gods steady me. It's a familiar feeling, one that reassures me even as anticipation nips at my skin and buzzes around me. More and more people enter the gardens, heating the air with their chatter and creating a space that's so full of different colors and styles that it's dizzying to look at. Before them I make myself stand tall, refusing to let anyone see just how deeply my nerves run.

I can't think of Ferrick, somewhere in this crowd with a ring I'm to receive the moment this performance is over.

I can't think of Kaven, trying to start a rebellion within my kingdom. Or of Kerost, broken and suffering from the storms.

And I refuse to think of Aunt Kalea, who will be Visidia's demise should I fail tonight.

But I won't let that happen.

I unhook the satchel from my hip and ready the teeth and bones that wait within.

CHAPTER FOUR

I've spent weeks preparing the contents in my satchel, ensuring every tooth and small bone is ready to be wound with a hair from the prisoner I'm to work my magic on.

Because while this may be a demonstration of magic, it's also an execution.

I hear the rattle of chains before I see the prisoners they belong to. Ten of them—seven men and three women—and all branded on the neck with two bold *X*s, the mark of someone tried and convicted for murder. Tonight, some of their brands are fake.

The guards drag them through the crowd of onlookers and to the base of the stone slab I'm perched upon. Then the guards back away, leaving the prisoners standing below me with fear and rage warring in their eyes.

My magic works in two ways—the ethereal soul reading, and the physical ability to end a soul through death. These prisoners are here to test the first side of my magic; I'm to determine whom I'm to execute by finding the irredeemable soul among the group.

Never in my life has an execution been public. Father and I perform them annually, late at night and deep within the underground prison, taking only the souls of Visidia's most unforgivable prisoners to satisfy and quell our magic. For a person to have been selected for this demonstration, their soul would have to be beyond redemption.

The first in line is an older woman whose dark eyes catch mine sharply. I find my magic waiting in my belly and pull small pieces from it, waking the beast. Its warmth licks my skin, inviting me deeper into it by connecting me to this woman's soul.

Magic spreads welcome heat through my veins and across my temples, and I sink into the power, relishing it. My vision fogs before quickly sharpening to reveal an entire garden of souls before me. They're the colors of clouds—some like a threatening storm and others the clearest day—and they dance with the wispy motions of smoke. I press my nails into my palms for focus, and home in on the soul of the woman before me.

It's like a dead starfish—faded, graying, rough, but ultimately still something that was once beautiful. She's older, and with her age there's been pain and hardships, enough to muddle and crack her soul.

This woman's a fake. Someone only here to test me.

I step past her and move to the next prisoner, assessing his misty soul. It's clouded by greed and wrath, and stained with the signs of murder. But he has remorse for the wrongs he's committed. He feels his guilt, which means he's not the one.

Swiftly but carefully moving through the line, magic scorches my core as I search soul after soul.

I know he's the one the moment I find him. On the surface his gaze is cool, but the deeper I dig, the more rotted his soul becomes. It's jagged and purpled like a bruise, peeling away at the edges and on its way to fading entirely. The wickedness of it chills me to the bone.

This man's soul shows the tarnish of someone who has committed the foulest crimes imaginable, worse even than murder. Empty white space shines bright behind the peeling edges, telling me that there's no going back for him. He holds no remorse for his choices, nor any sympathy for his victims.

"Him."

Two guards step forward to lift the man onto the stone slab, while the other prisoners are pulled back. A few of them sigh in relief.

Beneath my lashes I peek up at Father. He nods, just barely, and I relax in knowing I've already succeeded with the first half of this performance. I picked the right prisoner, and now it's time to prove mastery over the physical side of my magic.

"What's your name?" I draw my dagger from its sheath on my thigh and use it to cut a handful of the man's hair.

His answer comes in a voice so hoarse he has to cough to get it out. "Aran."

"Aran," I echo, "I have looked into your soul, and I have seen not only its corruption, but the pleasure you feel from the chaos and pain you've caused. You have no remorse for the crimes that have led you here, and I've found your soul too far gone to be repaired."

Chills roll through my spine when he tips his head back and smiles. I try not to wonder who he killed, or if his family is watching from the crowd. As the future ruler of this kingdom, I cannot pity that family, and they know it. Aran certainly didn't pity the families of his victims.

Silence builds as I steady my nervous breaths, strike a flint, and let the flames of the fire pit flare between us. "Do you have any last words?"

Aran spits at my feet, but I don't flinch. Instead, I wrap the sheared hair around one of the teeth in my pile and skim my nail across it. His jaw twitches as he instinctively runs his tongue along the top of his teeth, and I know the magic's working when I see the very moment fear settles into his bones.

"All right, then." I hold the tooth above the fire. "Let's begin."

I toss the tooth into the flames and the man seizes violently, spitting up a puddle of blood. In the middle of that blood is a tooth that I crouch to pick up, my body pulsing as the magic blazes within me. I sink into the power.

This physical side of my magic is based on equivalent exchange. If I want to hurt someone's bones, I need to offer a bone first—any bone, but soul bound by part of the person who I want to use my magic on. Tonight, I use Aran's hair. For everything that's taken, an equal payment must be given, which is why no one will die until I use their blood.

I could end him slowly, if I wanted to. I could break bone after bone, or drain his blood until he's nothing but a sack of flesh.

But I get no pleasure in these deaths. It's my duty as a Montara to use my magic, or the beast within me will get stronger and try to take control. And so Father and I choose one prisoner a year each—the worst of the worst—to help contain our magic.

I make their deaths quick and as painless as I can; but in order to do so I need several ounces of their blood, which is where the teeth come in. Though I could use anything to get the blood—an arm, a leg, an eye—making someone lose a few teeth is the most humane way I know to get the amount I need.

As I work, I know without a doubt that no one will be able to question my skill. I'm in full control of the beast and its magic that rips through my veins. Aran's blood flows steadily from his mouth as I offer the fire another tooth, and his eyes bulge with fear.

Confident, I peer sideways at the faces of my people and stand tall, wanting them to see me. To see their heir to the throne; their princess, who has spent the entirety of her life mastering this magic not for herself, but for them.

But as my focus centers on the crowd, they don't watch me with the pride or awe I expect. Horror plagues their faces.

I catch sight of a man covering his daughter's eyes, face twisted in shock. The replica of Cato's knife trembles in her hands.

And then I see Aunt Kalea, her lips curled with disgust for a magic she's never wanted. In my imagination, I see her eyes flickering colors, and have to still my trembling hands before anyone can notice.

I'm doing everything that I am meant to do to fulfill my duty, and yet there's no respect or love in the eyes of Visidia. There's only fear and revulsion.

My hands hesitate over the fire as the confidence I built like armor around me shatters. Everything I've done has been for *them*. And yet . . . my own people fear me.

I clutch my chest as the realization buries me, breaths tight. I watch each drop of blood splatter from Aran's lips to the ground. I hear the sharp intakes of breath around me, and feel the weight of my people's terror pressing down on me, so heavy that I can't breathe. Panic climbs from my stomach to my throat, rising and building and clawing.

My attention slips from my magic as I take in the reaction of my people, and the magic within me lurches. This is what it's been waiting for; my control slips, and the beast springs.

The magic sinks its fangs into me deeper than ever. The once comforting warmth now burns up my fingertips and spreads through my body like wildfire, tearing me apart. It's as though I'm breathing through a reed, hardly able to find enough breath to fill my lungs. I shove my shaking hands against my sides and try to center myself against the hundreds of fearful faces that look back at me.

But I can't do it. The magic consumes me.

Raw, urgent power thrums through every crevice of my being as I smear my blood-coated thumb across the prisoner's tooth, feeling the heaviness of his life force pulsate beneath the tips of my fingers. I toss it into the flames, then take a bone from my satchel and do the same. Aran screams as the bone in his finger twists and snaps. But I don't so much as flinch as I find another bone and a handful of teeth. I toss them into the fire and rip my way into and through the prisoner's body, tearing it apart inch by inch.

More gasps sound from the audience, along with indiscernible yells of protest as Aran chokes on the teeth that fall from his mouth. But the noise hardly reaches me through the haze. I don't feel the heat of the fire against my cheeks, or smell the flame charring my hair as I take those teeth, blood and all, to replenish my satchel.

"Your soul is wicked," I hear myself telling Aran as he digs his nails into the ground and gasps for breath. "You don't deserve a quick death."

The beast whispers mercilessly in my head, telling me to rid the island of this tainted man, and then to find others. Wipe his soul from the earth, and destroy the rest of the prisoners, too. And then why stop at the prisoners? Every soul is wicked in some way, so why not take them all?

Breathless, I'm drawn to the pile of bones at my side. Beads of cold sweat trail down my neck as I snatch one, wind it with his hair, and dip it into his blood. The fire lashes before me, fervent and seething with hunger. I offer the bone, and it splits and cracks as the flames gobble it up.

Aran's scream grates against his worn throat as each unbroken bone in his finger snaps one at a time. Even with the pounding of the waterfall behind us, his sobs carry through the gardens.

"Mercy." He spits up blood with every garbled word. "Please, by the gods, mercy."

"The gods do not listen to the pleas of the wicked," I hear myself say. "And neither do I."

Somewhere in the distance voices shout, but I don't care what they say. I let my magic eat its way through him, throwing bone after bone into the fire until Aran is nothing more than a heap of mangled limbs on the stone slab. His contorted body lies broken, limbs impossibly twisted. He's misshapen clay I've molded to my will and painted with blood.

I prepare for another strike when a hand grips my shoulder. I turn, snarling at the molten brown eyes that stare back at me. It takes me a moment before I realize they belong to Father. His eyes are wet, and my skin itches with discomfort.

"Amora." It's a desperate plea that settles into my bones and quenches the fiery magic. I sway as my vision flickers, the haze fading. "Please, you have to stop."

The crowd surrounding us roils, screaming distorted sounds that make my brain feel as though it's being pinched together. I focus solely on Father instead, using him as an anchor to drag myself back into reality. The magic within hisses its protest, baring fangs as it fights to maintain control. I suffocate within its hold, choking as I rein the magic back.

Father holds me tight, strong fingers digging into my skin harder and harder until my vision clears and I gag on the stench of blood. I begin to shake as I take in the stains on my palms and fingertips, the smoke scalding my lungs. The stones beneath me sway as the realization hits: I lost control of my magic.

Dizziness makes my weight betray me, and I collapse to my knees.

I let loose the beast, and it stole my senses until it claimed me entirely.

Aran lies before me, dead. He no longer looks human, all shredded flesh and mangled limbs. I clench my hands to the dirt as I try to recognize him, but it's useless. When used correctly, my magic is meant to give someone a swift death. But there was nothing swift about this; Aran was tortured and maimed.

And I'm the one who did it.

I press my forehead against the dirt, eyes stinging as I bend before his body. "I'm sorry. By the gods, I'm so sorry."

But my apologies don't matter. As I hear the words Visidia's people scream, I know even the gods can't help me now.

"It's the beast!"

"She'll destroy everything!"

"She's the one who should be executed! She'll kill us all!"

I spot Mother's face at the front of the crowd. Her body goes rigid while Aunt Kalea's face falls with horror. Yuriel is between them, his hand clenching his mother's arm tightly. His once wine-flushed face is now ashen with panic. Father stands before me, back turned to the crowd so that only I can see the terror in his eyes or the raggedness of his breaths. When his hands begin to shake, he presses them tight at his sides. My own hands are coated with blood, and I'm not the only one staring at them.

"I can't protect you from this," Father whispers urgently, almost as if the desperate words are meant for himself. Then he says it louder, in a harsh whisper that cracks his voice. "By the gods, Amora, I can't protect you from this!"

I've no time to compose myself before arms yank me up from behind. Two guards slide their hands under my arms, narrowly avoiding slicing their faces on the spiked bones on my crown and the jagged epaulettes as they pin me tight.

"I'm sorry." Father's chest heaves. "I'm going to try my best to fix this."

The world is spinning. Spinning. Spinning. A vicious coolness spreads deep into my bones. It starts in my stomach and spreads to my legs, then down my arms. Prickles of darkness plague my vision and threaten to overwhelm me as the aftershocks of too much magic make their move.

If not for the arms around me, I wouldn't be able to stand. It's taking everything in me to rein the beast within me back. To keep it tamed.

I try to keep my eyes open on Father, steadying my vision enough to see him turn his face away and clamp his eyes shut in disappointment. It's a look that cleaves through my chest and leaves me aching.

Hundreds of Visidians stare back at me without mercy, and I shut my eyes against their yells, wishing I'd let the magic consume me fully.

I barely let myself hear Father as he speaks, his words like a thousand knives.

"Take her to the prison."

CHAPTER
FIVE

I steady my trembling vision on the cell bars, using it as a focus point to anchor myself.

Hugging my knees tight, I try to conserve my warmth against the bitter cold that rips at my skin. Though I've been in these prisons many times before, it's never been like this— stripped of my weapons and left forgotten in a cell.

I was five years old when Father first brought me to the prisons, late one autumn night. I'd been bleary-eyed and half-awake as we traveled down the switchback, watched by only the stars as the rest of Arida slept unaware. It wasn't until the moonlight winked out behind us and my eyes were forced to adjust to the sparse torchlight of the prison that he told me it was time to claim my magic.

I'd been excited. But there'd also been a pervading chill in my bones that bloomed the deeper into the prisons that we traveled. The sense of realizing something significant was about to happen, but not truly understanding what that meant.

Centuries ago, Valukans helped build the prison at the base of the mountain, hollowing it out to form three long tunnels that each formed a unique prison.

The first tunnel is for petty crimes and short sentences. Security in this sector is fairly minimal, with palace guards posted outside the entrance.

The second is reserved for more offensive crimes, such as assault, or even murder in some cases. The security there is stronger; all the guards are highly trained magic-wielders from the various islands.

The third prison is for the most dangerous criminals, and is reserved only for those with souls that Father or I have deemed the most dangerous. It's a prison for those who didn't just kill once, but would kill a hundred times more. Those who have assaulted their victims in the most despicable ways, and have no remorse. Its security is some of the best in the kingdom; there are no cells, but sealed rooms protected by guards I'd never want to go toe to toe against in a fight.

It was deep into the third tunnel that Father and I traveled. Nerves gripped my neck, making the hairs stand as the walls surrounding us grew tighter and darker. With every step forward, the metallic tang of blood grew denser in the air.

We didn't stop until we'd reached the farthest sealed room, pausing only so a guard could use three separate keys to let us in.

I don't remember much about what happened next, but I remember the prisoner's face and the chains that shackled her. She was a woman hardly older than I am now, with blond hair and panicked blue eyes. I remember I couldn't stop staring at them, wondering what she did to deserve this fate as Father pressed a dagger into my hands—the same one I use even now.

"This is how it has to be, Amora." Father guided my trembling hand to the woman's arm and helped me press my blade into her skin.

The woman cried all the while, but the moment her blood coated the steel, the beast within me sprang to life, and I no longer needed Father's aid. The shadows of the prison walls and the screams that careened off them stopped seeming so overwhelming as I sunk into the beast's power and let it filter through me. Let it feast on the blood of this prisoner until she fell to the earth, lifeless. Only then, when the beast was satisfied, did I come to my senses.

But it was too late to go back.

Father held me tight as the beast within latched onto my soul. It's never let go, since.

It took only a season to quell the beast and recover physically, but years for the nightmares to stop. Since then, I've had to visit the prison annually in order to exert my magic and keep the beast within me at bay.

I've never *enjoyed* executions, or having to watch a soul fade to death by my hands. But I've come to realize that someone has to do it in order to keep Visidia safe, and the gods chose me.

But I'm no fan of these stuffy tunnels, and I kick the heavy iron bars of my cell to tell it as much. I hiss when it does nothing but send a shock of pain to my ankle, and tuck my forehead to my knees. The guards need to hurry and bring me food so I can stabilize.

Since my magic is useless without my satchel or a fire, they stuck me in the first prison—a small luxury, and perhaps a fleeting sign of respect as this prison is the cleanest and most maintained. But poor ventilation this far underground makes the place reek with a mixture of must and human excrement that does nothing to help the nausea that fights to best me.

"Looks like we've got ourselves a fresh catch," a prisoner across from me taunts, squinting through the haunting red glow of torchlight to peer into my cell. In the darkness, he's one of the few others I can see. "Never thought I'd see you all locked up, Princess. How about you give us a little show?" The man makes smacking sounds with his lips while another joins in, venturing into elaborate detail about all the ways she'd like to slice me up and feed my body to the Lusca, a sea beast of horror stories, meant to scare disobedient children.

"Try, and see what happens," I growl. My hands itch for the satchel or dagger that were stripped from me, wishing I had a proper way to shut them up.

Because although I don't let them see it, their words eat me alive.

I would never have thought I'd end up on this side of a cell, either. But that's Visidia's law: if a Montara cannot control their soul magic and is deemed too dangerous, they'll be held until a trial can determine their fate—another chance at best, an execution at worst. Since the possible Montara heirs are so low in number, I doubt they'd kill me. I'm too valuable for that. Still though, it's not something I want to risk.

I need to get out of here. Eat some food. Get my strength. Find a way to make things right.

But instead I'm stuck in this blasted cell, leaving my fate to be determined by whether Father's able to sway our people into believing I'm still somehow worthy of their trust, and meant to be the next High Animancer. To be their future queen.

He *has* to convince them; there's no other option. Since Aunt Kalea's been secretly practicing enchantment magic, she'd run the kingdom straight into the ground if she tried to learn a second magic.

I want nothing more than to protect Visidia and show my

people that I'll be a worthy leader. Yet, in the moment I've been training for all my life, I failed to prove that.

I can't be angry that they've locked me behind bars, though the weight of it suffocates me. My people were right to strip me of my belongings; they're right to be afraid of me. Aran's death may have been Visidian justice, but *how* I killed him was nothing short of monstrous.

When Father had me sent to this cell, it wasn't by choice. He had to adhere to the law. But that doesn't mean it hurts any less.

I hold my head in my hands, pinching my eyes shut to cast away the spinning image of Aran's body.

The sharp squeal of the prison doors echoes through the tunnels, piercing my skull so fiercely I have to fight down a bout of nausea. Despite my swimming vision, I force my eyes open to see if it's Father here to tell me everything will be okay; to tell me that despite how badly I messed up, my people have decided to give me another chance.

"Amora?"

My stomach drops. I recognize the voice even before Ferrick makes it to my cell, each footstep slow and hesitant.

Bathed in the dim glow of torchlight, he looks like a frightened fox with his fair skin, slicked back orange-red hair, and sharp cheekbones hollowed by the fire's shadows. His nose is scrunched and his green eyes wide and anxious, as though he expects a prisoner to break through the bars and attack him at any moment. When I notice the three trays of food he balances on his hands and forearms, I groan and drag myself closer to the cell bars as he carefully lowers to his knees and sets the trays on the floor.

He's brought everything—pine-steamed amabons, rolls stuffed with fat pieces of spicy prawn, coconut curry and sweet rice pudding, three skewers of freshwater eel, caramelized Curmanan milkcakes, and several whopping servings of ginnada. Another tray holds four bowls of Valuka's signature stew—wild game smoked atop volcanic coals, with potatoes and onions that melt in the mouth like sugar.

"This wasn't what I had in mind when I found out we'd be dining together tonight." Ferrick takes a seat on the dirt floor, tensing from the jeers and flirtatious whistles of other prisoners, and pushes the trays toward my cell. "Are you okay? What can I do to help?"

"Where's my father?" I ask, slipping my hand through the bars to take a serving of ginnada. "He should be here by now." I try to push the smell of the prison away as I shovel the food into my mouth. The moment the sugary almond pastry melts on my tongue, my dizzying vision begins to stabilize. I groan contentedly before I notice that Ferrick's forehead is pinched and his eyes squinted.

"He's . . . doing damage control. I'm going to try to help, but I wanted to bring you some food, first. Those guards were only going to bring you bread." He scoffs, bitterness seeping into his tone. "I knew you needed more than that."

I do. Most magic is fueled by a life source, meaning that bodies will hit a point where they get too tired to perform magic. But Aridian magic is unique in that it's bound to the soul; when I use it, that's where the source of my energy is drawn from. And if I use too much, I don't just risk exhaustion like those with other magics—I risk death.

Ferrick can understand this to an extent. His Suntosan magic draws from the energy in his own body, as well. It may not be dangerously bound to him in the way mine is, but we both need food for fuel. I'll eat every bite of what he's brought me, at least.

"Thank you for this," I tell him between mouthfuls of stew, already on my second bowl.

Ferrick nods before hesitantly reaching a hand through the bars of the cell, careful not to touch any of their grime. I still as he presses a hand against my cheek, unsure of what he's doing until his skin warms against mine and I feel the sharp sting of his restoration magic; the Suntosan magic he uses to heal both himself and others. I hiss a breath and jerk away from it in surprise. But when I lift my hand to my cheek, the scratch from this morning is gone.

Ferrick smiles and rises to his feet. "I should get going, but I'll be back. I'll see if I can find your—"

The prison doors squeal open again. I bolt to my feet automatically thanks to the burst of energy the food's given me, expecting Father but instead finding the Valukan adviser from earlier sauntering toward us.

Ferrick tries to be discreet about the subtle way his chest inflates like a bloating pufferfish. "Who are you? Who gave you permission to be down here?"

The Valukan stills at the sight of Ferrick. I scan him for weapons, noting the broadsword sheathed at his side. But he doesn't reach for it. He straightens himself instead, holding his chin high.

"My name's Bastian Bargas. I'm the son of Baron Bargas, and am acting as Valuka's representative for the night. I need to talk to the princess."

Ferrick's hands twitch at his sides. "Baron Bargas is a friend of my father's," he says slowly. "I've spoken with him numerous times, and he's never mentioned having a son."

Bastian's momentary hesitation dissipates. His smile morphs into a confident, wondrous thing as he draws a folded sheet of paper from his coat pocket and flashes it at us. The seal of Valukan nobility is embossed in wax at the corner of the page—it's similar to the royal emblem, but rather than one skeletal eel wound around a crown of bone, there are two eels, and they wind around a smoking volcano. Only the Bargas family uses that seal.

"Aye?" Bastian asks. "Well, when you've earned the reputation I have, you'll find your father often neglects to mention you in conversation."

Ferrick snatches the letter from his hands, reading over it with a pinched expression. "And why couldn't the baron make it, exactly?" He runs his finger over the wax emblem as if to test it.

Unfazed, Bastian says, "You read the letter; I'm afraid he's been infected by a rather nasty stomach bug. Let's just say that my father didn't want to risk making a fool of himself from both ends." He plucks the letter from Ferrick, folds it neatly, and tucks it back into his coat pocket with a little pat. "Now, if you don't mind?"

Ferrick folds his arms across his chest. He's thinner than Bastian, lanky where the Valukan is broad. And with only a rapier at his side, Ferrick would never win the fight he seems ready to initiate. "Apologies, but I'm afraid I can't let that happen."

I sigh, not about to watch him lose. "You hold no rank here, Ferrick. Stand down." When he turns to me in protest, I fix him with a dangerous look. "I may be behind bars, but I still make the decisions. Stand *down*."

The shadows on Ferrick's face darken as he looks between the Valukan and me. "I need to find the king, anyway. But I'll be back shortly." He doesn't spare me another look before he pushes past Bastian, making the Valukan's brows bounce curiously.

"Was I interrupting something?" Bastian muses.

I try not to roll my eyes at his easy demeanor. "Why are *you* here?"

His amusement dims as he reaches beneath his coat, to

something hooked onto his hip. I jerk away from the cell bars, anticipating a weapon. I've no way to protect myself here; the cell is too shallow to hide within, and offers only a single bed-roll and an empty metal basin as protection.

My fingertips itch to use magic, but I've no way to summon it. Everyone wields their magic a little differently, and for mine to work, I need fire. The torchlight, however, is too far to reach. I'm defenseless.

But when Bastian draws his hand back out, it's not a weapon he holds. It's a large ring of worn copper keys.

Dread grips my stomach. "How'd you get those?"

Bastian shoves the key into the lock. "Does it matter? Listen to me, Princess—they're going to execute you if you stay here."

The conviction in his words causes my heart to slam into my throat.

"They wouldn't," I say. "At least not until they have a trial." They'll want to ensure Kalea's able to control soul magic, first. They'll want to make sure they have another option.

When Bastian's eyes catch mine in the torchlight, the pieces holding me together begin to dissolve. I press a hand to my throat, clammy and sticky with sweat despite the dank, pressing coolness of the air. Because it's not anger in Bastian's glance, nor is it annoyance. Though his mouth is a hard line, his eyes have softened with sympathy. They hold me tight, chilling my bones.

"Sure, they'll have a trial, but things aren't looking good for you. Do you really want to take that risk?" His words are a whisper spoken soft and gentle, under his breath. "They're planning for your aunt to move here at the end of the summer, to accept her magic and begin training. Your father's trying to sway them, but the people think you're too much of a liability; they want to keep you locked up."

As much as I don't want to admit it—as much as I want to believe my parents are well loved and influential enough to stop this, and that Visidia wouldn't want to get rid of a potential heir when there are too few of us—deep down I expected this.

There's no way I should expect people to overlook what I've done. I maimed a man right before their eyes, and I smiled as I did it.

Bastian grips a bar tight. "You might be as good as dead if you stay here. But if you come with me, right now, I can help you. We can help each other."

I hate not having a weapon. I'd love for him to say that to me again when I can press a blade to his throat for the blasphemy. "You want me to abandon Visidia?" I ask at the same time another prisoner across from us calls out, "How about I go with you instead, handsome?"

Bastian rolls his eyes and leans closer into the cell, dropping his voice so that no one can eavesdrop. "Listen to me. I don't want you to abandon Visidia." He pulls back his coat to reveal my dagger and satchel tucked into his belt. "I want you to save it."

Before I can protest or demand to know how he got his hands on either, he tosses both into my cell. I don't hesitate to scoop them up, feeling whole the moment my fingers brush the burnished leather and slide around my blade's worn hilt.

"I'm not here to fight you." Bastian yanks the cell door open, and I ready my dagger to strike if needed. But he doesn't come closer.

"What do you mean you want me to save Visidia?" My voice is weaker than I will it to be, my thoughts scattered a million different ways.

Ferrick could return any minute with the palace guards or even Visidian soldiers in tow. My cell could be slammed shut again, with Bastian thrown into the one beside me. And then what? Locked in this cell, what are my options?

I must find a way to earn Visidia's forgiveness. To prove myself to my people. All along, Aunt Kalea was Visidia's backup plan. But now I'm all they have.

Either I can wait and hope that Father's able to come through, or I can find a way to earn my own second chance.

"Listen, these are stolen keys." Bastian motions to the cell door with an exasperated huff as I linger. "And let's just say that the guards are taking a little nap right now, courtesy of some of Curmana's finest herbs. I tucked them in a cell, so they should be perfectly comfortable, but they're not going to stay asleep for long and I imagine there will be some shouting once they're awake. I'll explain everything once we're on my ship, but I swear to you that if you don't come with me right now, Visidia as we know it will be gone by winter's end."

The world spins, but this time it's not from nausea. I grip the bars to keep myself steady, thinking.

This man has a ship.

Ships are good. A ship will get me off Arida and give me enough time to prove to my people that my head is worth sparing. That I can lead them. It will give me a chance to save not only Aunt Kalea, but all of Visidia.

And if what Bastian says is also true, and Visidia truly is in danger, then what choice do I have but to help? To prove myself. Change my fate.

It's like there's a current behind me, pushing me toward the Valukan whose eyes hold the same earnestness now as they did when he tried to speak with Father earlier. He'd been trying to warn us of something then, too. Of Kaven.

Bastian has answers. He's got a ship, and offers me a chance for redemption that I can't risk leaving up to fate.

This man, whatever his true motives may be, is the best chance I've got.

I don't second-guess what my gut tells me. Ignoring how wildly my blood pulses, I remove my crown and the flowers Mother wove through my hair, then undo my epaulettes and let them drop to the dirt like discarded trophies. I pull my hair from its loose bundle at my neck, letting the thick curls fall past my shoulders. Though I wanted nothing other than to show off these adornments earlier, I feel light as air now that they're gone.

"You saw what I did to Aran," I warn him, thumbing the lip of my satchel, comforted by the clacking of bones inside. "One wrong move, and I'll do the same to you."

When he doesn't argue, I slip around him and bolt to the exit. Now that they see the glint of my blade and hear the rattle of bones and teeth as I walk, the prisoners no longer jeer.

I take off down the tunnel with Bastian in tow, certain I know the way better than he does. Being in the first tunnel, we don't have far to go to reach the entrance. Yet nervousness prickles my skin as we run, our footsteps echoing off the walls. Each one sounds like the shot of a cannon, too loud and too jarring. Darkness stretches around us, eerier than ever without the gossip of the guards. When Bastian points to a cell I squint my eyes, trying to make out shapes in the shadows. Eventually my vision adjusts, and I see the distinctive outline of three large figures slumped into the cell.

"Curmanan herbs?" I flash him a look, and he grins.

"Aye. Potent when inhaled, but not as long lasting as when they're ingested." Even as he says it one of the guards begins to stir, murmuring words of confusion under his breath. I grab hold of Bastian's hand and pull him along, dragging him up the stairs and to the exit.

The moment fresh air smacks against my skin, I'm forced to squint my eyes shut, taken aback by the sudden brightness of the moonlight and the luminescent flora that lights our path.

Because the prisons are built at the base of the mountains, we're far from the celebration happening in town. The only voices are still distant, though I know better than to get comfortable. If there's one thing I know about Ferrick, it's that he's smart. He likely noticed the prison's lack of security and is already on his way back with reinforcements; we need to hurry to the docks.

"What's your affinity?" I peek over the cliffside—it's about fifty feet down to the docks, and while I know every step of this island and am confident I can get there quickly, I don't trust Bastian to keep up.

"Earth?" Bastian says, though it sounds more like a question than an answer.

"Perfect. Hurry and build some stairs into the cliffside. We'll collapse them once we hit the sand."

But instead of grounding himself into a proper stance or making any motion of using his magic, Bastian draws a step back. "I think it's best if we walk. We wouldn't want to cause a commotion."

When he presses his lips together, I can practically feel his anxiety. I turn to him fully as understanding dawns, and I look at his hands—they're calloused and a little sandy, but otherwise pristine. No dirt under his manicured nails. And his stance is all wrong; he's lighter on his feet than any earth-affinitied Valukan I've ever known.

I draw my blade and, before he has time to react, press it firmly against his throat.

"You're no Bargas." I use my free hand to grab him by the hair, keeping him steady. "You don't have an affinity, do you?"

Bastian's eyes flicker down to my blade as he sighs. "Well,

this certainly isn't very polite of you. I'm the one who gave you that back." I press the blade closer. "Ouch! Fine, no, I'm no Valukan! I'm a sailor. Now put that thing down and I'll explain—"

I tighten my grip on his hair and yank him toward the edge of the cliff, letting the dagger nick his skin. Bastian grabs hold of my arms to steady himself, his breaths quickening. One push, and he's as good as dead.

"Tell me what you did to the baron," I press. "You have his seal!"

Bastian's eyes flicker to the corner, grimacing at the drop behind him. When he hesitates to answer, I lower him farther off the ledge until his knees begin to shake.

"He's fine! Stars! I promise you, he's fine. I snuck aboard his ship before he left Valuka and dumped a pouch of sleeping herbs into their wine and water barrels. What I used on these guards was the last of my supply; that's why they're already waking up. But the baron and his crew ingested enough that, if I had to guess, they're about halfway to Arida, napping in the middle of the sea."

I clench my teeth together. "I know better than to trust a man who's stolen not only his clothing, but also his name." I scoff. "You're nothing more than a thieving pirate."

Bastian throws his hands up in defense. "As I said, I prefer the term 'sailor.' And really, this whole thing is a big misunderstanding. So, if you put that thing down . . ."

The once distant voices grow closer, and I hesitate to press the blade any deeper. If I'm going to leave, it needs to be now.

I find my magic waiting and tentatively wrap it around myself—just enough to warm my skin—and focus on reading Bastian's soul. With my magic still weakened from the performance, there's a missing piece I can't read. I see only a misty veil of light gray, and the spirit of adventure lingering in his soul. It's enough to tell me he's not a threat, but I don't let on that I know that just yet.

"If you're no Valukan, then where are you from?"

Though his face darkens, he slackens his body and lifts his chin. "That's the reason I lied." His words are quiet but confident, daring me to challenge him. "I'm from Zudoh, and my people need your help."

The words cause my blade to go slack. I withdraw it from his throat and take a quick step back.

"Tell me why I should help a banished island." I try to keep the fear from my voice when I ask. If Bastian notices, he doesn't let on.

"Because it's not just about Zudoh. Kaven wants to destroy the entire kingdom. And if you don't come with me right now, he's going to succeed."

There's that name, again. Kaven.

It's like fire to my throat and lead in my stomach; a name that, deep in my gut, I know is somehow wrong. Bastian has the answers that Father won't give me. Answers that I'll need if I'm to properly rule Visidia.

Bastian may not be telling me the whole truth, but he's not lying about this. And for now, with the voices of the guards growing closer and the future of Visidia on the line, that's enough.

I sheathe my dagger and nod to the switchback that carves our way down the cliffside. "Keep close, and get me to your ship."

CHAPTER SIX

When we make it to the sand, breathless and dripping with sweat, there isn't one ship in the bay that's manned. I search for Bastian's crew, but they've likely all been given leave to view my performance and enjoy Arida's festivities; if Bastian plans to sail us away, we won't get far without them. Yet he doesn't stop moving. A rope ladder dangles from the side of a brigantine and he latches onto it, ascending with ease.

It's a ship that snatches my breath, smaller than Father's, but far from simple. While our ships are made from oak, this one is a magnificent shade of white I've never before seen—made from aspen or birch wood, perhaps—and outlined with rich gold trim. Older, it reeks of charm and adventure.

At the bow, a brilliant figurehead of a sea serpent stares back at me, its forked tongue out like it's hissing. Half its face and whiskers are covered in sculpted barnacles, which make it look as though it's just emerged from the depths of the sea. The sight of it quickens my heart and makes my throat thick with desire. It's the loveliest ship I've ever seen, and though part of me knows that this is far from what I should be feeling in the midst of fleeing my home, I can't ignore the surge of excitement that heats my blood as I clutch the fraying ladder and pull myself up after Bastian.

By the time I throw my legs over the side of the ship, he's already got his sleeves rolled up, halfway through hauling up the anchors.

"Welcome aboard *Keel Haul*!" he grunts. "Make yourself useful and help me get this thing up."

"What does it matter if we've no crew to sail us?"

Bastian rolls his eyes. "I'm afraid we don't accept pessimism aboard this ship, Princess. Come help!"

I wipe the sweat from my brow and move to join him, wishing my dress wasn't half as heavy or nearly so tight as I help him raise the anchors, surprised by how easily they move with just the two of us. But I'm half distracted as I help, squinting my eyes shut to hone my magic and see what other souls it can sense.

Even below deck, Bastian's is the only soul I can feel. I drop my hold on the anchors at once, ignoring the pirate's exasperated sigh.

"Who is this *we*?" I demand. "The two of us are the only ones on this ship, and there's no way we'll be able to sail it on our own."

"Now what did I say about pessimism?" Bastian chides. "If you don't trust me, then feel free to jump off the plank and swim back to your kingdom right now."

"Well, I wouldn't really have to swim, now would I? Considering *we can't sail*."

Bastian's lips quirk as he finishes reeling in the anchors. "Oh? You sure about that?"

I follow Bastian's finger as he points behind me, and I'm dizzy again. I swear I've been here for no more than two minutes, yet the shores of Arida are at least a hundred feet away. When I turn back to Bastian, he takes a seat on the deck and pats the space in front of him.

"Before we get into specifics," he says, "I need you to tell me something—did you truly have no idea what was happening with the Kers? Not even a suspicion?"

"Of course not!" I slam my hand down onto the deck, and he frowns in offense at the spot I've hit. "How dare you even imply—"

"Why wouldn't I imply it?" Bastian argues. "The majority of the kingdom knows."

The words are claws to my soul, tearing its lining to shreds. If Bastian's telling the truth, then just how much has Father managed to keep hidden from me?

"Yeah, well, I didn't. If I'd known they were suffering, I wouldn't have stayed silent. I would have found a way to help." The words don't feel like enough. They're quiet and painful, but they're all I have to offer. "I swear it."

I can't be sure Bastian even blinks when he stares at me. His face is so stern and assessing, as if waiting for me to flinch under the pressure. When I don't, he leans back on his palms, the hard lines of his face eventually softening with belief.

"The *king* is a fool to not take Kaven seriously." He spits Father's title. "The Kers are done begging him for support he refuses to provide. They've turned instead to Kaven, a Zudian who's had enough of the same thing. He's been raising a rebellion of like-minded individuals, all who believe that learning multiple magics is a necessity for Visidia's survival. But the issue with Kaven is that he doesn't know when to stop. In building a name for himself and forming this rebellion, he destroyed Zudoh, helping support only those who sided with him while leaving anyone else to rot. Now he's aligned himself with Kerost, where he's doing the same thing." Bastian's voice tightens in anger. "I came here to warn your father that Kaven's expanding his reach to the other islands, though I shouldn't have wasted my time. I knew he'd never listen."

Disbelief and worry war within my skull. We've had nothing to do with Zudoh since I was a child—so why now?

"What does this rebellion want, exactly?" I have to dig to find my voice. It's raspy from the salty air, scratching my throat with each word.

Bastian doesn't hesitate with his answer, though my world freezes when he says, "They want the end of the Montaras. They want to abolish the monarchy, and practice however many magics they'd like. Soul magic included."

I nearly laugh as fear swells within me. There's no telling whether the dampness of my skin is due to the ocean, or my own sweat. "They're asking us to let them destroy Visidia!"

Bastian leans forward and says, "Aye, so let's not let them win. Kaven's the brains behind this rebellion. If we take him down, the rest of it will crumble. He doesn't have the support he needs to wage a true war. Right now, the Kers are divided. Only half of them support Kaven, while the others are focused on rebuilding their island on their own. And the Zudians . . ." He takes a moment to consider his next words, face darkening. "Most of them want Kaven gone, too. But we have to get to him before the other islands join his cause."

"And you expect us to do this on our own?" I press. "Two people, against a rebellion?" A thousand questions war in my mind. What are Kaven's tactics? How long do we have? What are the numbers like? But this ship is moving fast, and there's little time to make my choice—turn back and hope Father's able to convince Visidia to give me another chance, or put fate in my own hands and earn my chance.

"I'm not looking to start a war," he corrects me. "I'm looking to end one man, which will put a stop to all of this. You said you wanted a chance to help your kingdom, so here it is. Will you take it?"

My chest seizes. Not with defeat, but purpose. The ocean's brine is a perfume that steadies me as I press my fists against my lap so that Bastian can't tell how deeply his words resonate.

"And what role do you play in all this?" I ask, because I want to glean every bit of information I can before I let him know I've made my decision. "Am I to believe that a pirate has no ulterior motives and is doing this for the good of the kingdom?"

The ocean pounds into the ship, but Bastian doesn't flinch. He watches me with the thoughtfulness of a particularly clever feline. "I want my home back. And so long as Kaven's there, I'll never have it. That's my only motive, and with my ship and your magic, I believe we'll make quite the pair. So how about you and I strike a—"

"For the honor of Arida, I will not stand for this!" The voice comes from behind.

I whip my head around and see Ferrick, soaked and dripping water onto the deck. His skin has taken on a greenish hue. He sways slightly, barely managing to hoist a rapier out in front of him.

"You have kidnapped Princess Amora," Ferrick says, "and I'm prepared to sacrifice my life to save her. I hereby challenge you to a duel!"

He looks like he's about to throw up.

"Ferrick," I groan. "What are you doing here? This isn't necessary."

But Bastian's already on his feet. "Code of conduct, Princess—if you don't want stowaways, be sure to draw up the ladder once you're done climbing it." He sighs and crosses the deck, looking over Ferrick's ill-fitting emerald garb with a grimace I fully understand. "I'm guessing you're a Suntosan?"

Ferrick squares his shoulders and tries to stand proud despite the seasickness that colors his skin. "I knew there was something off about you. Thank the gods I trusted my gut and turned back; I saw what you did to the guards, pirate. Let Amora go."

Bastian draws a sword from his belted sheath and taps Ferrick's blade with it, as if in greeting. "Ferrick, was it? I suppose it has been long enough since I've had a proper duel." There are stars in Bastian's eyes and amusement brimming in his words.

Ferrick thrusts with his rapier, but Bastian parries it without looking. Show-off.

The clanging of steel bounces off the deck before the ocean devours the sound. The sea is less gentle than it was this morning. It's angry at the ship disturbing it, rocking it fiercely as we venture out of the shallow waters.

Bastian wields his sword as though it's an extension of his own body, unrivaled by a swaying, seasick Ferrick. He moves effortlessly, stepping with the to-and-fro sway of the waves. I've no doubt he's a practiced pirate. His tongue and wit are as sharp as the blade in his hand. He's been doing this for many years, but I've never heard any stories of a pirate who sailed the seas without a crew.

"Ever lost an arm in a duel, mate?" Bastian asks as he effortlessly weaves around Ferrick's next strike. There's no time to consider his words before he half jumps forward and brings his sword down on his opponent. The sound of Ferrick's surprised yelp fills the sky. His rapier clatters to the ground, and his right hand thumps down alongside it.

CHAPTER SEVEN

"**B**y the gods!" Ferrick peers down at his hand with more annoyance than pain, and Bastian looks at the blood that now coats the deck of his ship in the same way. "Was that really necessary?"

Drawing a handkerchief from his coat pocket, Bastian wipes the blood meticulously from his sword. Once it's sheathed, he steps forward to examine Ferrick's severed hand, cut just below the elbow.

His blood is already congealing. New skin grows around the wound, forming a small nub of flesh and muscle. When Bastian pokes at it, Ferrick jerks back.

"What in the stars?" my soon-to-be fiancé growls. Weaponless and with one arm rendered useless, he's still trying to feign toughness. Though I'm used to his magic, it's always alarming to see how little pain he feels.

I stare openmouthed at the arm, embarrassment for the

Suntosan sinking my gut. To be fair, he was the one who challenged Bastian, but no one should have to lose so decidedly.

"That was a cheap shot," I say.

"Relax, Princess. I knew it wouldn't hurt him. He scraped his hands climbing *Keel Haul*; I saw the wounds healing." The look Bastian flashes me is nothing more than a brief roll of the eyes, unwilling to yield from his absolute delight. Much to Ferrick's dismay, the pirate closes the space between them once again and prods at the redeveloping ligaments. "How marvelous are you Suntosans! I've always heard restoration magic is impressive, but people who can regenerate themselves *and* heal others? I had to see it with my own eyes."

"Glad to help with your fantasies," Ferrick huffs bitterly. "I should never have expected a fair sword fight from a *pirate*." He says the word like it's poison on his tongue, but even in the faint glow of moonlight, the flush on Ferrick's pale cheeks is clear. I know I should feel bad for him, but every second I'm forced to spend with him, knowing we're to be forever tied, my frustration grows.

It's unfortunate our magics are so well suited. If I need a tooth, I can take one of Ferrick's. If I need an arm, he has plenty to spare. He's a rare breed of Suntosan; whereas most only have the ability to regenerate or heal others, he's mastered both skills. With Ferrick at my side, I would be the strongest animancer that Arida has ever seen.

"Enough bickering. Swords down, boys." Both turn to look at me.

"Don't engage with him, Amora." Ferrick's face is pinched and angry as he glares down at his arm. "Blasted pirate, take us back to Arida this instant."

Bastian ignores him by stepping closer to me, and I notice for the first time how tall he is. Confident, too, but a fool. When he takes another step forward, I unsheathe my dagger and press its point against his chest. Bastian's smile fizzles away at once, and he sours his lips in offense.

"Really? Again?" He lifts his hands into the air. Beside me, Ferrick exhales a relieved breath.

I press the blade against his skin, enough for the steel to bite. "You've given me enough information, already; I can figure out the rest on my own. Give me one reason why I shouldn't toss you overboard and make the journey myself."

To my surprise, Bastian laughs. Though he stops short when it makes the dagger press deeper into his chest. "So this is the thanks I get for helping you out? Stars, I wouldn't have guessed you'd be so charming. Throw me overboard if you'd like, but as you've noticed, I don't exactly have much of a crew for you to command. Throw me off, and you'll lose your ship. Besides, you're no captain. You wouldn't even know how to navigate."

"Zudoh's straight south," I argue, but Bastian only bats his eyes and smiles.

"It sure is. But I'm afraid it's a little more complicated than that, love."

I press the blade forward until I feel his muscles flex beneath it. "And why's that?"

Though he tries to maintain his easy smile, his jaw tenses. "If this is what I get for sharing information freely, then I suppose you'll have to keep me aboard to find out."

I sheathe my dagger, never having intended to actually stab him. It's just good form to ensure he knows who's in charge.

"Amora, I really think we should reconsider this strategy—"

I cut Ferrick off swiftly. "There is no *we* here. I'm not holding council."

Bastian brushes his chest off as though I've dirtied his coat with my blade. "Then I take it you're still in?" The sea tries to steal his whisper but I latch onto it tightly. Warmth replaces the coolness in my body as a strange, enigmatic tension electrifies my skin and fills the space between us as I consider those words. The hairs along my arms stand on end.

And as my heart beats, I know there's no way for me to say no. I saw Father's blatant dismissal of Kaven's threat earlier, and I heard the whispers. I saw Kalea's shifting eyes myself, and know that she'll never be able to take on the crown.

If Visidia's truly in danger, I will not leave its fate to chance. Nor will I leave my own fate up to Father's persuasion. I'll take it in my own two hands, and use this as an opportunity.

I draw in a breath and lift my chin toward Bastian. "I'm in," I tell him, much to Ferrick's protest.

"But they're forcing Kalea to move to Arida by the end of the summer," Ferrick argues. "You'd give the throne to her so easily?"

"Of course not. I know what I'm doing." I make my voice firm enough that both boys freeze from the harshness of it. My aunt knows the stakes as well as I do; she'll buy as much time as she can on her end, and I'll use it to stop Kaven and earn another chance at becoming my people's animancer.

"You said they wanted to bring Kalea here by summer's end? Then that's when we'll be back. And on our journey, you'll explain this ship to me, pirate." This marvelous ship. My gaze circles around the deck. How is it sailing so effortlessly without a crew? "And you'll teach me to sail it."

Only then does Bastian show frustration. He draws his bottom lip halfway in and bites down on it, gnawing as if ironing out his thoughts.

"You have to understand, a man views his ship as one might view their child. Letting anyone sail it is . . . sensitive."

Between him and Father both refusing to teach me, I'm sick of excuses. "If you want my help getting your home back, you'll teach me to sail *Keel Haul*."

He perks up slightly, as if pleased I've remembered its name, then bites at the corner of his lip as if to conceal whatever true expression he feels. "Fine, but only after you have a feel for her. Get to know her, take her to dinner. I've found ladies don't respond well when you try to control them." He pats the ship and it groans beneath his hand, the full sails propelling us farther and farther into the sea.

I bite back my grin, not wanting Bastian to see. Something tells me he already knows and understands my excitement. His home is the water, and while I love my island and my role in it, part of me envies his freedom. He's no one but himself to look after; what must that feel like?

"Fair enough." I nod. "Though we do have one more thing to discuss."

He already knows. Bastian turns to Ferrick, who draws a defensive step back and readies his rapier. His right arm twitches and stretches a little farther. I try not to stare at the forming flesh, endlessly mystified by the strange magic.

"I'm not leaving," he says firmly. "For as long as Amora remains with you, I'll stay to accompany her. As her fiancé, it's my sworn duty to protect her."

Bastian's lips twitch upward as he lifts a brow. "Fiancé, huh? Pardon my ignorance, I've no idea how I overlooked the gushing chemistry between you two."

Ferrick's chest shakes as he draws in a long breath and stares Bastian down.

The pirate remains perfectly at ease. "Regardless, you're another mouth to feed, and are not part of the bargain. Tell me why I shouldn't drop you off now and let you swim back to Arida." Every one of Bastian's words hinges like a question, unabashedly curious. And yet there's something about his presence that unnerves me. He has the same spark of life—the same knowledge of the world—that Father has. It's because he's a voyager. Jealousy pits itself with me, spreading its roots.

"You know why I should stay." Ferrick straightens his spine and tries not to glance down at his severed hand. The pirate peers down regardless, and I stoop to pick up the limb, grimacing at the way it hangs limp in my grip. His fingers will make a fine addition to my satchel once I break them off; anything else can be fed to the fish.

The majority of Ferrick's body is painlessly disposable; there's no denying the power I might wield with it. But Ferrick is selling himself short; he's also an incredibly skilled healer. And if we're to fight a man who has a following of people who all want me dead, having a healer around might not be the worst idea.

If he's to join us, however, I've conditions to make clear, first.

"Stay with me and lend your help," I tell him. "But should you break my command and act on your own—if you try *anything* behind my back—consider yourself thrown overboard. This is bigger than you or me, Ferrick."

Ferrick's throat bobs as he swallows. He shares a look with the smug pirate. Bastian happily points to *Keel Haul*'s plank and walks his fingers in the air while whistling a tune that mimics falling.

Ferrick's cheeks burn red when he drops his head in a bow. "As you wish, Princess."

A twisted knot in my chest unravels as tension I wasn't aware existed is drawn from my body. This is happening, then.

"So it's settled?" Bastian unfurls himself from where he leans on the main mast. "We have a deal?"

Ferrick and I share a look, though it's mostly me silently daring him to disagree. Eventually he nods, and with a smile I extend my hand to Bastian. He accepts it with delight.

"Welcome to the crew." His words drench my skin with

72

warmth. I soak them into myself like a sponge and feed them to my hungry, eager soul.

I am Amora Montara, Princess of Visidia, and I will be the future High Animancer.

I am the right choice. The *only* choice. And I will protect my kingdom.

CHAPTER EIGHT

Bastian leads us to the ship's hull, and though I knew already there were no other souls aboard, I'm still unnerved to see for myself that there truly is no crew. It's a small ship, but *Keel Haul* is still a ship, and I've never known a ship to sail without a crew.

Just what did he mean when he said that, without him, the ship would stop sailing? Somehow, magicless though he is, Bastian has a ship that can sail entirely by his sole command. And though I know he won't tell me how, during our journey together I intend to find out how that is.

At least the lack of a crew means Ferrick and I each have our own cabin. They're tiny rooms with only a hammock hanging from the ceiling, but I don't mind; surrounded by the sea, I can hardly think of sleep.

"Have you anything for me to wear to bed?" I ask Bastian, who frowns from his position in the doorway.

"I'm not accustomed to bringing princesses aboard *Keel*

Haul." He's hardly apologetic. "Can't you wear what you have on?"

I lift a brow. "This is a ceremonial outfit I just killed a man in. So no, I won't be wearing this to sleep, thank you. And all I have beneath this dress is skin I'd prefer to keep covered, considering I'm on a pirate's ship."

While Ferrick's pale skin darkens to crimson, Bastian's expression contorts into feigned horror.

"*Keel Haul* may be ferocious, but she is still a lady. I would never dare plague her sensitivity by having you parade around *naked*." Bastian says the word as though it sours his tongue, yet amusement twists the undercurrent of his tone. "I'll find you something suitable for now, and you can grab something more fitting when we reach Ikae. It's a port town off the coast of Mornute."

"I know where it is." I try to ignore how my stomach flutters with the same eager anticipation I feel when the palace chefs bake fresh ginnada. Of course I haven't been there, but I know all about that town from Yuriel and Aunt Kalea. Home to the finest jewels and fashion, it's a tourist town I've always wanted to visit. My aunt brings me gowns from there each year, and they've quickly become my favorites. The items they produce are lush and wonderful, though it's not a town known for being affordable.

I give Bastian the once-over: his scarlet frock coat is impeccable and the fabric thicker than any you can find in Arida. It's even finer quality than I'd originally thought, with tiny slivers of golden threads stitched around the cuffs. He would have had to pay off a royal tailor to get a coat with golden trim and the royal emblem embossed into the cuff links—that, or he stole the coat. But his tan pants are also hemmed and tailored to perfection, and though he lives on a ship, his scruff is meticulously trimmed and styled. It's no wonder he managed to pass himself off as an adviser—his aesthetic is commendable. Especially compared to Ferrick, whose emerald blazer, along with his shirt, is far too loose, and his pants too tight. It makes his shape that of an upside-down triangle. He's dressed like he's taken his clothing straight from a shipwreck.

But as much as I'd love to parade around Ikae shopping with Bastian, the late summer air already cools with the threat of the changing season. We've only until the end of summer before Aunt Kalea's to move to Arida and accept soul magic.

"We shouldn't waste time," I say. "Let's set sail straight to Zudoh."

Leaning against the wall, Bastian flourishes a hand, moving it as he talks. "Trust me, Princess, I'd love to do that. But remember when I said that getting to Zudoh wouldn't be so easy? They erected a barrier around their island when they were banished. We need a way to get around it, first."

Beside me, Ferrick frowns. "And we'll find that in a town known for fashion?"

"You'd be surprised." The light in Bastian's eyes never seems to dim, and his crooked smile is far too bright for a pirate. "Every town has an underbelly. You just need to know where to look. Now, if you'll excuse me a moment, I'll be back."

The moment he's gone, I feel Ferrick's presence as heavy as an anchor. "Do you truly trust him?" he asks.

I nearly snort. "Of course not. He's a pirate." I move around him to exit my cabin, searching the hall for somewhere to clean up, but he follows.

"Then why do this?" Ferrick presses, his voice an urgent whisper. "There has to be some other way. We can sail back to Arida and tell your father—"

"I may not trust the pirate, but I never said I didn't believe him." I saw Bastian trying to warn others about what was happening, and it was useless. Father thinks that he's protecting

Visidia; if I want to take hold of my fate and protect this kingdom, I have to act against him by going to Zudoh and finding Kaven myself.

Returning to Arida now, after breaking out of the prison, would be a death sentence. And not just for me. If I can pull this off, no one else will ever know about Aunt Kalea's betrayal.

I'm forced to sidestep my way through the tight quarters of the ship's head to reach the single washing basin. Though the age-worn ship creaks with every step, Bastian's spent time maintaining it. The brilliant white wood shines with fresh lacquer, and the rooms are neatly organized and swept clean, as though the pirate was expecting guests at any time.

I lower my face toward the basin and scrub my skin clean. The water turns cloudy from rouge and creams as I wash away the memories of the night. Ferrick continues to stand there with a sour face and worry in his eyes all the while. Finally, when I can no longer take his insistent staring, he says, "So much for our engagement, huh?"

I drop my focus to the basin. "Now's not the time."

"Well, when is the right time? I've been trying to talk to you about this for weeks."

"There's nothing to talk about—"

"There is!" The words are so exasperated that they take me by surprise. My mouth screws shut as his face turns from pale to pink, cheeks flushing. Drawing a deep breath, he says more calmly, "There is. I know neither of us asked for this, but you've known how I feel about you for years, Amora. I know I've never been more than a passing thought for you, but I truly believe you're the right heir for Visidia, and I'll help make that a reality in whatever way I can. Then, once we're home . . . I want you to know that I plan to be good to you. I didn't have the chance to say it before, but I really want you to know that."

The concentrated way he looks at me would be enough to

make most people shrink back, but I don't. I can't tell him I love him, or act like I'm pleased by his words, because he knows how I feel—there will never be anything between us.

"For now, I need you to focus on the task at hand." I know it's not what he wants to hear, but it's all I can offer. "We need to protect Visidia."

His lips press together and he dips his head in a small nod.

I'm thankful when Bastian's footsteps fill the hall, sparing us any further awkwardness. He carries pieces of clothing draped meticulously over his arms, taking care not to wrinkle the fabric.

"These no longer fit me," he interrupts, "but I had to keep them anyway, because . . . I mean, look at them." Bastian sets the clothing in my arms. The shirt's linen is smooth against my skin.

"The stitching on this is phenomenal." I lift a ruby coat from his arms to admire.

Bastian makes a noise of appreciation in the back of his throat. "Isn't it? It cost two black pearls and a full pouch of sea glass, so I'd hope it's perfection."

"There's no way a pirate can afford that," Ferrick grumbles.

Bastian's chin lifts with defiance. "A pirate's salary is as infinite as they want it to be. But if you must know, I wooed a very lovely girl for it. The daughter of Mornute's finest tailor." He rolls his shoulders back with initial pride before realization strikes. "Speaking of which, we'll have to avoid that shop."

"You're horrible." I press the clothing to my chest. Earlier, I'd thought my outfit and adornments lovely. Now they suffocate me with memories of being consumed by my magic. Nothing would be better than ripping them away, changing into something light, and crawling into the hammock.

I brush past both boys and start toward my cabin.

"We're set to sail to Ikae?" I ask, not looking back.

"Aye," Bastian says. "With *Keel Haul's* speed, we'll be there before sundown tomorrow."

I nod. "And tell me again how stopping there is going to help us find Kaven?"

Tipping his head back against the wall, Bastian's arms fold across his broad chest. A lazy smile spreads across his lips as he says, "You know, Princess, the wonderful thing about my owning this ship and you needing to borrow it is that I'm the one who gets to call the shots—something you must not be used to, I know, how *awful*. But we're going to stop in Ikae to get information, and that's all you need to know."

Hand on my cabin door, I shoot the boy a dirty glare. "Fine, keep your secrets. But remember that if you try anything, I'll stab you without a second thought."

"Are you flirting with me? It's a bit hard to tell, considering how terrifying you are."

I turn away from him as my neck and cheeks warm, not about to let him see me flustered. "You're insufferable. Once we've found Kaven, know that I plan to throw you overboard and make this ship mine."

"Well, no one can say that you're not honest." I don't see him laugh as I let myself into the cabin, but I hear it. "Rest well, Princess."

I slam the cabin door shut with a huff. What an awful, arrogant oaf. The day I'm able to commandeer this ship as my own and kick him into the sea will be a fantastic one, indeed.

Casting aside all thoughts of Bastian, I set to work tearing off my clothing. I remove my necklace and bundle it inside my cape, tucking it and the lovely sapphire gown into a corner for safekeeping, my neck and shoulders cold in their nakedness as the weight of my adornments disappears. The bundle of Ferrick's severed hand draws my attention, but I'll deal with it tomorrow.

For now, I change into the linen shirt and loose cotton pants. I wrap my satchel even tighter around my waist to hold them up as I climb into the hammock.

This low, the waves sound more ferocious than they are as they beat against *Keel Haul*. The ship rocks gently against the ocean, and the rhythmic lull makes my eyes heavy. Against the low creaking of wood, the moans of wind, and the sloshing of waves, I find sleep easily.

I'm more comfortable on this ship than I ought to be.

CHAPTER NINE

I've never slept better than I did my first night on the ocean. I didn't dream of my execution as I'd feared, nor did I dream of Aridian magic or Aunt Kalea's color-changing eyes. For the first time in longer than I can remember, I didn't dream of my magic or ruling Visidia.

In fact, I didn't dream at all. I slept through the entire night, despite the hammock.

My cabin is dark and windowless. When I press my hand against the wood, coolness nips at my skin. There's no way to know the time, yet I'm well rested and my mind already races. This small cabin is no longer comforting, but claustrophobic. I crave the briny air in my lungs.

I tighten the satchel so it holds up my pants, stuff on my boots, and throw Bastian's scarlet coat over myself before I climb the creaky wooden stairs up to the deck. My blood pounds with excitement I hardly understand—I should be focused on getting to Zudoh and finding Kaven before summer's end. Not getting distracted by the joy of waking up aboard a sailing ship.

Frigid air floods my lungs the moment I step outside. It's coated in a thin veil of mist that wraps around my skin and sweetly strokes my face, greeting me like a forgotten friend. The odor of brine and seaweed is thicker than I've ever known it. It tells me we're farther from Arida's bay than I've ventured, and while my skin crawls at the thought, it's not from worry.

It's excitement. Perhaps excitement that would be best experienced under different circumstances, but still. I've craved this for years.

I make my way to the bow, lean over the ledge, and suck in a breath until my lungs nearly burst. The gulls above me cry out as they dive into the water, scooping frenzied fish into their beaks and gulping them down before soaring back into the sky and rejoining their flock. The day has barely broken through the hazy gray skies, and the droplets of water that splash onto my cheek are still cold.

Still, a relaxed warmth fills my chest and I sink into its comfort.

"Good morning, Princess." Bastian stands behind me, a loaf of bread in his palm. He cracks it in half and hands a chunk to me. "There's some dried meat as well, though I'm afraid the food on *Keel Haul* is nothing as exquisite as the food on Arida." The ship groans against the tides, and Bastian pats the edge of it gently. "Sorry, love. You know it's true."

I've never seen Bastian in the daylight, and am surprised to find he looks even more like a seasoned voyager than Father. While the sun has bathed itself in his skin, casting gold beneath his warm brown complexion, his eyes hold a brightness that can only come from being drenched in starlight. They're a striking hazel with brilliant flecks of yellow, and he's got a smattering of freckles dusted below them. He's not like anyone I've seen before—he's molded by the world, crafted by travel and adventure. There are stories in those eyes, but I don't fall for them so easily.

I take the offered bread.

"Good morning, pirate." I bite into the loaf, surprised to find it's still soft. As if reading my expression, Bastian turns rueful. Slowly, making a show of it, he draws something from his breast pocket. It's wrapped in an emblazoned handkerchief, and I'm too curious to be amused. Palm flat as he holds it out, he uses his other hand to slowly unfurl whatever is inside.

It's ginnada, and I'm salivating.

"You stole that from Arida," I say, only posing it as half a question.

"I don't think of it as stealing." He makes a motion to rewrap the dessert but stops with a laugh when he notices me staring. "I think of it as diligently restocking *Keel Haul* before a hungry princess and her extra-mouth-to-feed fiancé join me. You're lucky I did, too. Otherwise, we'd be having stale bread and wine until we find somewhere to restock." He runs a hand through dark chestnut hair, and I notice it's speckled with sandy pieces the sun has latched onto and bleached.

"You mean somewhere to swindle?" I ask with a smile.

Bastian snorts. "Just take it. I saw the way you scarfed these things down last night."

"You were watching me all night, then?" Bastian rolls his eyes when I ask this.

"You flatter yourself. In that crown of yours, you were hard to miss."

This pirate's tongue is too clever for its own good; I don't bother trying to best it with a response. Instead, I snatch the ginnada from his hand and take a bite, groaning as the sugary almond and buttery crust melt in my mouth.

"I'm glad I *stocked* several more." Bastian laughs as I cram the rest of the ginnada into my mouth. "It's not often you happen across a giant festival with free food. It's best to take advantage of such fortunate circumstances."

Another gull wails before it dives for its meal. I watch it, finishing off mine while Bastian leans against the ledge of the ship and stares out into the sea. He may have been handsome beneath the glow of the stars, but here in the sun he's glorious and comfortable. He must know every inch of *Keel Haul*.

"*Keel Haul* is a magic ship," I say. "Isn't it?"

His shoulders stiffen as he keeps focus on the gulls. Two of them fight above the water for a fish, their wings smacking angrily against the waves as their squeals fill the air.

"I suppose you could say that," he admits. "It's not the type of ship that requires a crew."

Magic, then. But none I've seen before. Even the most talented Curmanans have to travel in groups to steer heavy ships, and this is nothing like the protective curse magic I was taught Zudians practiced.

I watch him from the corner of my eye, waiting for him to elaborate, but he doesn't. He takes a small hunk of his bread and tosses it into the sea. A fish larger than any I've seen floats to the surface and sucks it up before the seagulls can steal it.

I take another bite of bread. "Well, if you won't tell me about that, will you at least tell me how familiar you are with Kaven? If Zudoh's barricaded off as you said it is, how'd you get off the island?"

Tension knots his shoulders. He chucks another bit of bread into the water before finishing his off. "I left ages ago, before the barricade. I knew Kaven back then, when this mess was first getting started. He stole my magic from me, and I intend to take it back."

The fog must have finally made its way through my coat and into my bones. The chill of it touches my core.

"What do you mean he *stole* your magic?" I wrap my arms around myself, words nearly catching. Magic is part of a person's being; everyone has it. You can learn it, study it, grow with it, but you cannot make it disappear once it's yours. Even if you never use it, it's still forever with you. "There's never been a report of someone being able to do that. It's impossible."

"There's never been a report of a magical ship, either. Yet, here we are." Bastian waves his arm behind him to gesture around *Keel Haul*. "The world doesn't work with only your eyes, Princess. There's truth in more than what you can see."

I settle into my position leaning over *Keel Haul*. The sun is beginning to break through the thick layer of clouds. Hints of it warm my hands as I close them into fists.

After seeing part of his clean soul last night, my gut says Bastian's telling the truth—at least, why would he lie about something so personal?—and if I've learned anything in my eighteen years, it's to follow gut instinct. If Bastian *is* telling the truth, and if magic can really be stolen, then Kaven's a bigger threat than I ever could have imagined.

Why didn't I know about this? Why doesn't *anyone* know?

"How did Kaven steal it?" I ask. "And if you've no magic, then how is this ship sailing?"

Bastian shakes his head. "Do remember that I just watched you kill a man." His words are more matter-of-fact than they are cold. "*And* you threatened to stab me—multiple times, might I add—and steal my ship. So forgive me if I distrust you as much as you distrust me."

"He's truly that dangerous?" I ask quietly.

A shadow crosses Bastian's face. "Do you know anyone else with the power to steal another person's magic?"

I shake my head. I can't even imagine what it might be like to have someone steal my magic—it'd be too invasive. Like they were stealing part of my very soul. But I relax in knowing that not only is my magic tied to my soul, but also my very blood-line. I doubt something like that could ever be stolen.

Bastian lifts his gaze to focus on Ferrick as he approaches, dressed the same as he was last night. His arm has regrown a little overnight, though he's still missing everything from the forearm down.

"Good morning, fair fiancé," Bastian bellows, swiftly changing the subject. "There's bread and dried meat in storage if you're hungry."

At the mention of food, Ferrick presses a hand to his stom-ach and groans. He looks even worse than he did last night. His green skin rivals the color of his blazer. With one of Bastian's handkerchiefs wadded tightly in his hand, he wipes sweat from his forehead.

"No, thank you." Ferrick's voice is pinched. "How anyone can live on a ship, I will never understand. I felt as if I was float-ing on the sea the entire night."

"That's because you were," I say.

Bastian laughs and moves to pat Ferrick on the shoulder, all charm and smiles once more. "Not quite the sailor, are you, mate? No worries, it takes some people days at sea before they adapt. Stick around and you'll have your sea legs in no time. But in the meantime, if you're going to throw up, try to avoid doing it on my ship."

Ferrick sways. Hurling on *Keel Haul* is precisely what he looks ready to do.

"How are you, Amora?" he asks, eyeing the bread in my hands. When I take the last bite, Ferrick looks even queasier.

"It doesn't bother me," is all I say, because how am I sup-posed to tell him the truth? How do I admit being on this ship feels as natural as breathing? That when I woke up this morn-ing, it wasn't the possibility of my execution I thought of first. It was the excitement of travel. Of sailing.

It's not the way I imagined it, but I'm living a dream I've had since the first time I saw the ocean.

"You're a natural," Bastian says. "You even woke with the sun."

I accept his compliment with a smile. Though there's still the tension of curiosity between us, I let it go for the time being. Perhaps some memories are too painful to share. "Does this mean you'll begin teaching me how to sail?"

"Nice try, but being a natural on the sea doesn't mean you're a natural with *Keel Haul*. Your enthusiasm is charming, but not quite yet." The amusement laced in his voice is like a honey cake, warm and sweet. "Besides, you should probably do something about that little amputated gift in your room. Before it starts rotting, please."

Ferrick takes a seat and holds his head between his knees. He's not too ill to snort.

"It'll be bloody," I tell Bastian, who turns up his nose. *Keel Haul*'s deck is spotless, meaning he must have spent hours scrubbing the mess he made the night before.

"Drain it into the ocean and then we'll head below. I've a few burlap sacks you can work on."

I nod, instinctively setting a hand upon my satchel. After everything I used for the execution, it's almost empty of bones. I'll feel better once it's heavy again.

"And you're fine with these clothes getting stained?" I ask.

Bastian takes a long moment to consider it. Eventually, and probably only because they no longer fit him, he relents. "Just . . . take the coat off, first." He turns to Ferrick. "And you'll feel better if you stay on deck. Try to go below as little as possible. Lift your head and keep a watch on the horizon. Sound good, mate? Eyes on the horizon."

Ferrick slowly lifts his head, and instead of ducking it between his knees, he props his chin atop one, forces his eyes to the horizon, and groans.

Bastian takes this as a dismissal. He turns to me. "How about you show me what you plan to do with that arm?"

My fingers twitch at my sides as I hesitate, thinking of the horrified faces from last night. Of the terrified screams of my people.

Though my magic was meant to impress them, my performance only solidified my people's fear.

For years I've done this part of my work in private, training for the day I'd be able to claim my title as heir to Visidia's throne. But now there's no joy in showing off my magic. Nerves writhe within me as I think of Bastian watching.

Will he think my magic too messy? Too brutal? Or will he understand that what I do is necessary for Visidia's survival?

He follows me to my cabin, where I scoop the hand from the floor before heading back to the deck to unbundle it. My nose curls at the rancid odor of spoiled meat tinged with sweetness, as though someone has tried to mask the stench of death with awful perfume. The skin has blued overnight. It's vulgar, yet Bastian can't stop staring as I draw my dagger.

Hands aren't unusual for me to work with. They're small enough and easy to extract from. I draw the blade across the radial artery, and thick, jelly-like blood congeals beneath the blue skin. Not wanting to get any on *Keel Haul*, I'm careful when I hold it over the ledge and scoop out the oxidized blood with my dagger. Splotches of red paint the water the color of a dark bruise.

When we eventually move below deck, Bastian fetches two burlap sacks from storage.

"Help me understand something about your magic," he begins as he spreads them out on the wood floor. "Why is it that, even if you're using Ferrick's bones or—gods forbid—his entire hand, your magic doesn't hurt him? Why would it hurt someone else, instead?"

"Fair question." I crouch above the burlap, then shift to my knees to maintain balance. This far below deck, the waves are fierce and jarring. "I *could* hurt Ferrick, but I choose who I bind my magic to, and binding requires a conscious effort. I first have to be near them and be able to look into their soul while doing it. Using Ferrick's bones as a base for my magic, and not as a binder, is a choice." I try not to think about how much trust Ferrick has in me to let me keep this severed hand of his as I lay it across the burlap and cut open the palm. The blood is minimal as I stretch the skin away from the thin layer of fat, then cut my way through the muscles beneath.

Though I've drained as much blood as I can, that doesn't prevent my hands from becoming a mess of tissue. Bastian chokes, halting his own vomit.

I freeze at the sound.

"That's very . . . interesting," he starts to say, though his words are strained. Brows creased, I look up just in time to see him take one look at the dissected limb and pass out on the floor.

My body ignites with shame. It comes in a heat that fills my belly, and a rush of nerves that makes my movements sharper. Quicker. I move to cover the hand, but the ship quivers as *Keel Haul* hits a fierce patch of water. It wails a ghostly sound, full of splintering and creaking wood, and I'm tossed back to the floor. I latch onto a heavy barrel of wine to steady myself, waiting until *Keel Haul* stabilizes, then say a silent thanks to Ferrick, who must have taken the helm while likely puking his brains out.

Before me, Bastian's fingertips twitch.

"If you have a weak stomach, you shouldn't have asked to watch!" The words snap out of me, more bitter than I intend as I think of every pair of eyes that watched me in horror and disgust.

This work may be messy, but this is what it takes to use my

magic, and that's all there is to it. Last night, I made a mistake and let myself get overwhelmed—by Kaven, by Aunt Kalea, and by the terrified faces of hundreds of Visidians. But I am not a servant to my magic. It's mine to command, and I want others to see that.

As Bastian blinks clarity to his vision, he keeps his attention far from the dissected limb. I cover it with the burlap.

On one hand, I understand his reaction. The first time Father showed me how to dissect something, we started with a foot, which are full of messy, sticky tendons that goop around your fingers and are nearly impossible to work around. I'd been upset about staining the dress I'd worn that day, but having magic not only means learning how to live with it, but also how to accept it as part of you. When I first began practicing soul magic, death felt like a tragic, sickly thing. But as the protector of Visidia, that was a hurdle I was forced to cross long ago. If Bastian wants to use me and my magic, he should understand what he's using.

"I never took you as the type to faint." I can't contain the bitterness that drips into my words.

He rubs his neck. "Sorry." Though his words are clipped with annoyance, they're genuine. "It's just so . . ."

"Impressive?" I try to ignore how his reaction stings. My magic *is* strange. But why can't people see that it's also amazing? "I took on this magic to serve Visidia and protect my people. *Impressive* is the word you're looking for."

His brows are knitted like he's contemplating something, and I don't like the look of it.

"Maybe you should check on Ferrick." It's not necessarily a suggestion, but Bastian takes it as one. I eye him warily as he rubs his hands over his face.

"No, no. I'm sorry. It's not the blood that bothers me. I've just never been quite so *thorough* with someone's body before.

Should I start to feel ill again, I'll leave. I promise. But this is something I want to see. You're right, it's . . . impressive."

I press my lips together as I slowly pull back the burlap to reveal the hand. Bastian struggles to keep his face frozen and shoulders steady. He's barely breathing, knuckles pressed into his lap to steady himself, but it's clear he wants to stay.

And because I want someone to understand my magic, I let him.

CHAPTER TEN

We finish washing and drying the bones several hours later, just as Ikae's terraced mountains begin to loom over us. My mouth is dry as I stare up at their extravagance, gripping the ledge of the ship to steady myself.

The terraces look like dozens of giant steps have been carved into the stark white mountainside, each of them filled with lakes of pink water and surrounded by dazzling houses all in a variety of colors and styles. Some are enchanted so that purple smoke billows out of tall chimneys and into the setting sun, while other homes look as though they're made of shimmering sea glass. Rows upon rows of vineyards stretch far up into the mountain peaks, where the sunlight shines the brightest. Mornute's primary source of income has always been from exporting alcohol. Just thinking of all the wine they're making up there has my mouth watering.

The azure bay is swirled with soft green foam, though

when I peer over *Keel Haul* and into the water, I can still see the boastful coral reef that rests below. The thunderous cheers that fill the air have driven the fish into hiding, but the bay itself thrives with life.

I hear the people of Ikae before I see the anchored ship they pile onto, cheering as they wave soft pink flags into the air.

"Two gold pieces on Romer!" someone yells, met with a smattering of cheers and applause.

"Three gold pieces and a pearl on Keanu!"

I lean over the ledge of *Keel Haul* to get a better look, and am sucked in by the frivolous figures parading around the ship. It's only been a day, and yet feathers no longer appear to be the current style. Despite the fierce humidity, women wear heavy gowns of pastel fish scales that catch the light of the sun and sting my eyes.

The men are just as extravagant. The majority wear luminous trousers and simple pastel tops with giant scaled shoulder pads. Others have attached the scales directly to the skin of the neck and beneath their eyes, and have adorned their trousers with bubbles or shifting fabric that mimics an ocean's wave.

On the plank, two men stand side by side in only their undergarments. Their oil-slicked bodies are lean and cut with muscle.

"What is this?" I ask Bastian. The pirate leans beside me after twisting the helm and steering us to the far right of the bay, out of the other ship's path.

"Cannon Rushing," he answers. "Also known as the most ridiculous sport known to man. Ahoy!" He yells the last word, loud enough to draw the attention of those on a neighboring ship. Several people wave in acknowledgment.

"Good spot?" Bastian yells.

We're met with a mix of raised flute glasses and rueful

hoots before the people on the opposite ship return to whatever they're up to.

A lady with beautiful obsidian skin and lilac hair waltzes her way around the deck, holding a shimmering fish-scale pouch. She extends it to anyone who shouts out a price, and they drop their money into it without hesitation.

"I've never seen anything like this."

Bastian snorts. "And you won't anywhere else."

The men on the plank lower themselves to a crouch. They grip on to the plank as a sun-flushed woman behind them raises a pink flag into the air. She holds it there, taunting, then swoops it down with a high-pitched laugh.

The ocean trembles and I jump back from the ledge of the shaking *Keel Haul*. The neighboring ship spits out a cannonball, which hurtles past the cleared-out bay. My ringing ears burn, but I can't look away. I throw myself back against the ledge and watch as the two men from the plank dive into the clear water.

They've already swum a yard by the time they resurface, throwing their arms in front of them and rushing toward the sinking cannonball.

They're racing.

"You've got to be kidding."

One of them dives for the cannonball and comes up short. The other is still behind, flailing his arms as he tries to catch up. Meanwhile, the ship's passengers cheer and wave their flags as they sip from flasks and fancy flute glasses.

"They're wasting blasting powder," Ferrick says.

"They're wasting *money*," I correct him, pressing my fingertips against *Keel Haul*'s wood. One of the men surfaces with the cannonball and the onlookers go wild. They yell for him to hurry back so they can move on to the next group.

"Of course they are," Bastian muses. "What else do you do

with a limitless supply of gold, besides spend it all on games simpletons could never afford?"

I know he's being sarcastic, but I'm sharply reminded of what I've heard of Kerost's suffering. I can think of a few ways to put their spare change and extra time to use.

I pull my focus from the cheering crowd as Bastian docks the ship.

The difference between Arida and Mornute does not stop at the games we play. The buildings here are lavish and enchanted—glossy white exteriors and pristine glass windows for one shop, and lilac spires that sweep impossibly far into the sky on the next. Everything is made to capture the eye, including the peachy pink sand across the shore.

The bay is stuffed full with merchant bilander ships and an occasional traveling caravel. With every ship blending into the next, hopefully *Keel Haul*'s white wood and small frame won't stand out too fiercely. Though she's certainly a difficult ship to miss.

It's strange to have a steady surface beneath my feet. Within minutes of disembarking, I already miss the back-and-forth lull of the waves, though Ferrick couldn't be happier. After he spends the first few minutes emptying his stomach on a pile of rocks, he pats his hand on the ground and groans happily.

"I'd almost forgotten what it's like to have a body that stays in one place," he sighs.

"Don't get too comfortable. Once we get our intel, we're out of here." Bastian shifts around us to take the lead.

The docks connect directly to the heart of the city, and wood gives way to sleek streets that appear to be made from stained glass. The sunlight makes them wink with dazzling pastel shades. They're almost too beautiful to step on, but I realize they're nothing more than another enchantment when they easily hold my weight.

The town around us roars with life, fragrant with the perfume of baked sweets and buzzing with gossip.

"SHRIMP!"

I nearly stumble as a man passes by, yelling at the top of his lungs.

"Two pearls for shrimp, four for snapper! SHRIMP HERE!"

"Four pearls for snapper?" I echo. "There's no way anyone would pay him that."

As soon as the words leave my mouth, two women approach the merchant with their twin boys trailing behind. The boys are rowdy, slugging each other in the arms and dodging the other's counter with a mix of laughter and jeering. They draw our attention at once, and the light in Bastian's eyes turns shadowy. He observes the boys with a set jaw and an indiscernible expression. When his eyes flicker across the faces of the parents, he stuffs his hands deep into the pockets of his coat and turns the opposite way. The parents are all smiles as they fish a gold piece and several pearls from a small emerald pouch and place them into the merchant's hand. The Suntosan couple doesn't even think to barter as they make off with two snappers and some shrimp.

"I hope that's the greatest shrimp to ever grace their tongue," I say.

Bastian just grunts and ushers us through the street. There's no way to keep track of everything happening around us. I'm overwhelmed by the persistent yells and beckoning of merchants selling everything from chiffon gowns to lychee juice. They crowd the streets with their sharp perfumes and baked goods, as dolled-up tourists and Ikaeans with heavy pockets enjoy their wares.

Unlike Arida, this place does not have natural beauty. It's eccentric and bustling, and I love every inch of it. Though there's no denying how frivolous the town is with its wealth.

"It's so different," Ferrick says, eyeing the shimmery yellow tile of a hat shop.

"You've never traveled, either?" Bastian asks.

Ferrick shakes his head. "Only to Suntosu. My father is an affluential healer, trusted by the Montaras. He was favored by the queen—he even delivered Amora. It got to the point where we were visiting so frequently, my father decided to move us to Arida when I was seven. He returned to Suntosu when he retired last year, and I visit on occasional holiday. But sailing isn't exactly my favorite hobby."

"Well, all the islands are vastly different," Bastian notes. "Mornute has the highest tourism rate. It's easy to get to from most islands, and pretty enough to want to visit. It's a town made for the wealthy."

The sparkle of a faint aquamarine gemstone catches my eye, tempting me from behind the glass of a jewelry shop.

I want to explore every one of the shops, yet the lights behind the glass windows dim as the marketplace slowly begins to close down. Men and women bundle themselves in embroidered coats and shimmering fish-scale capes as the nighttime breeze rolls in from the coast.

Farther down the street, at the edge of the cobblestone, voices grow louder as taverns begin to fill.

Bastian follows my gaze.

"Fancy a drink?" he asks, and at first I can't tell whether he's serious. But then goose bumps trail up my arm and neck as he presses a gentle hand to the small of my back and ushers us toward one. Through the window, I see it's fully occupied by beautiful men in perfectly fitted suits and vibrant makeup, and by striking women in shimmering scale gowns and eccentric headpieces of pastel fish heads. One woman even has what appears to be a real starfish stuck to the left side of her face.

I should tell Bastian no. That we need to hurry and keep

going, as he said earlier. But instead, my words betray me and I find my feet are already moving me forward. "You're sure we have time?"

"Trust me, this is exactly where we need to be." His fingers wind around the door's handle as his wicked grin widens. "We need to lie low until the nightlife has died down, and besides, there's someone here I need to see."

I bite back my grin as the door swings open. Inside, the air is wild with gossip and music.

A hearth with green flames sits in the back corner of the tavern, radiating the heat of burning hawthorn. It lures me forward, into the happy chatter and uninhibited laughter. I relax despite the thick crowd, coaxed by the gentle lullaby of an accordion dancing in the air. I do a double take when I notice it rests alone on a stool, playing entirely of its own accord. There's no musician in sight, yet patrons liberally toss gold coins and colored pearls into a tin cup set before the stool.

Bastian hunts down a table near the back and motions for us to sit. While Ferrick moves slowly, trying to keep his regrowing hand tucked beneath the ruby cape he's borrowed, I make my way swiftly through the crowd and take my seat. With Curmanans able to spread news so quickly, people will no doubt be looking for me. But they can share only words, not images, and not everyone knows my face.

In the thick of the crowd, the noise augments in the wine-dense air. Though the patrons in this tavern are extravagantly dressed, no one bothers to sneer their distaste at Ferrick and me. Too many people must pass through here for Ikaeans to concern themselves with our off-trend fashion choices.

Patrons slosh their drinks as they fall back into their chairs, feasting on pastel petit cakes and laughing over silly jokes and conversation. All they want is to have a good time. No one's remotely suspicious of us.

Bastian smiles at a woman with a tray in her hands, dressed more simply than the others in a plain gown of soft lilac. She nods and says she'll be with us shortly.

When Ferrick takes his seat, he immediately points to the two exits. "This isn't a good idea. Amora is *royalty*. She shouldn't be subjected to something as filthy as a tavern. What if someone recognizes her?"

"Why don't you try saying the R-word a little louder, if you're worried about someone recognizing her?" Bastian growls.

"This 'filthy' tavern has some of the most extravagant people I've ever seen." I shoot Ferrick a look, and he doesn't disagree. Still, his face contorts into a mask of annoyance, brows sinking low into his forehead to create deep lines. He'll wrinkle himself prematurely if he keeps this up.

"And we won't be here long," Bastian adds. "For now, try to blend in."

The barmaid arrives at our table. Her face and chest sheen with a thin veil of sweat, and her pale cheeks are flushed from her bustling. Still, she's polite when she approaches.

"What can I get you?" She looks each of us over, likely taking in our strange clothing. Her eyes rest on me a moment longer than the others, and something in my gut sinks.

She can't recognize me. Not yet. Not when I've only just left Arida.

The woman doesn't flinch. The hand she's placed on her jutted hip tells me I'm being paranoid and should stop wasting her time. She's probably thinking about the other hundred things she has to do after taking our order.

"We'll take some of those cakes, two glasses of ale . . ." Bastian's voice draws off as he eyes me.

"Mead," I answer.

"And a glass of mead," he echoes with a hint of surprise. "We'll also take the freshest catch of barracuda if you have it."

My stomach curls at the idea of fish with mead and cakes, but there's something in Bastian's eyes that tells me he's not asking for a meal.

"We don't serve that here," the woman says dismissively, though her eyes darken as they assess Bastian. He tips his head back to flash her one of his toothy grins, as if that will charm her. But the woman only stares on, unimpressed.

"Well, where might I find some?" He stretches a hand onto the table. From between his two middle fingers there's a flash of a small gold coin.

The woman sets her hand on the table, and Bastian slips her the coin so quickly that, had I blinked, I would have missed it.

"I hear you can find it near Maribel's, sometimes. It's the shop with the pink bubbles. Trust me, you'll know it when you see it." She drops the coin down her top. "Barracudas are easier to catch late into the evening, but they disappear quickly. You'll want to get one before sunrise."

"Thanks for the tip," Bastian says. "I'll be sure to do that."

The woman smiles as she steps away from the table. "I'll be back with those drinks."

Only when she's out of earshot does Ferrick lean forward. "Was that something . . . illicit?" Quiet horror laces his words.

Never has anyone rolled their eyes with as much dramatic flair as Bastian does now. "If you don't lighten up, mate, others will smell your fear. You reek of it. And take off that bloody hood already, would you? You're drawing more attention to yourself."

Ferrick balls his only hand into a fist in his lap. "Aren't either of you worried? Technically, Amora, everyone considers you a fugitive. With as many Curmanan mind speakers as your family has staffed, surely the other islands will have been alerted by now."

A drink slaps down on the table. We all still as the woman unloads the other two, then a platter of petit cakes that makes my mouth water at once. They look incredible—tiny and decorated with slick pink-and-lilac fondant, or with tiny sugar flowers dusted with glitter. The woman leaves without another word, carrying her half-full tray to another table, and I pop a cake into my mouth immediately.

Bastian reaches for the ale and takes a long swig before sighing into the golden liquid. "Haven't you any sense of adventure?" He eyes Ferrick from over the mug. "Any at all? Or was it all hiding in the tip of the pinkie finger I chopped off?"

Ferrick bristles. I set one hand on his good arm as I reach for my mead with the other. It's bright gold and crisp. When I lift it to my nose I'm nearly knocked back. The sweetness barely masks the intensity of the alcohol.

"Ferrick's right to be concerned," I say. "You said we were here for information; to figure out a way to reach Zudoh. So why all these riddles?"

Bastian runs a finger around the rim of his ale before taking another sip. "We *are* here to find a way to reach Zudoh. I've friends who can give us the information we need, but let's just say they're highly sought after, and not huge fans of staying in the same place for long. The riddles are for their benefit, not yours." He lifts the ale to his lips again, but this time his eyes flicker up to look at me from above the rim. "I'm on your side, Princess. I've no magic, remember? I'm perfectly aware that you could kill me in a second flat if you chose to, and I quite like myself alive. All I want is Kaven gone."

"You've mentioned that," I say. "But what I don't understand is why the leader of a rebellion against Visidia would steal *your* magic. How are you involved in all of this?"

Bastian sets his mug down but keeps one hand cupped

around it. His lips are a tight line. "If you're implying that I'm part of the rebellion . . ."

Ferrick tenses beside me, but I shake my head. "If the rebellion wants to end the monarchy, they also want me dead. You'd have tried to kill me last night, or back in the prison when I was weaponless. And you never would have told me you were Zudian."

Ferrick looks as ill as he did back on *Keel Haul*. It's clear he's mentally processing the news as his forehead scrunches. "I've never met a Zudian before."

"And I've never met someone who could regrow a severed limb," Bastian muses. "Alas, we both exist."

I lean back to take another petit cake, easing the tension. "I thought Zudians hated Visidians? My father told me they took issue with the way the Montaras ruled."

Bastian shakes his head. "Zudoh was banished because of *Kaven*. Because he wanted the throne to burn even back then. Most of my people have nothing to do with this; they're only afraid of what Kaven will do to them if they bow to the crown."

"More afraid than of what my father will do to them if they don't?" I ask, and a shadow passes over Bastian's face.

"King Audric is a vague threat—someone we only hear about, but rarely see. Kaven is the one who holds power over Zudoh. His magic is as strong as it is dangerous; he doesn't focus on using it protectively, like the rest of us. Instead, he wields his magic like a weapon. I escaped from Zudoh when I saw the chance, but it wasn't until after he stole my magic and took control of my home. Kaven's the one people see, so he's the one they fear. Not your father. The two can't even be compared."

The cake is metal as I swallow it down, jagged and painful.

"So . . . Zudoh doesn't hate Visidia?" Ferrick leans back in his chair, arms folding across his chest.

Bastian leans back as well, and lifts the ale to his lips. "If they do, it's only because Visidia didn't step in to stop Kaven earlier. Without him, Zudoh would be thriving. But he's the reason we've been cut off from trade. From travel."

They have every right to their anger. A person's magic is part of their being. If Father truly knew there was a man out there who had somehow learned to steal it, wouldn't he have stopped them? Why would he ignore it?

"We'll put a stop to him swiftly," I affirm, taking a long sip of my mead. "Before his reach stretches any further in my kingdom."

Bastian's quiet for a moment, then eventually lifts his drink to mine. "I'll drink to that." He nods expectantly to the ale before Ferrick, as well.

Ferrick sighs and relents to it. I've never seen him drink, but he downs half the mug in two gulps before setting it back on the table. "I'm not okay with this," he points out, "but I'll do what I can to help."

"Good." Bastian fishes a pink pearl from his pocket and tosses it into the cup before the accordion. The instrument dips as if bowing, not missing a note. "Then drink up, everyone. We've at least another hour to kill, and then it's time to catch some barracudas."

CHAPTER ELEVEN

By the time we're done with the tavern, I've polished off my mead and five petit cakes. Bastian never showed hesitation in ordering for me, though it's unclear if he can actually afford my meal, as well as the six pints he and Ferrick polished off.

Bastian excused himself to the bathroom minutes ago, and upon his return I notice a small leather pouch newly tied to his belt. It jingles as he walks.

"Time to go." He places three silver coins on the table. Though he feigns a level of easiness, his skin shines with sweat and his fingers twitch at his sides, too jittery. This money doesn't belong to him.

Ferrick's laugh fills the room. It's a boisterous, drunken sound that reaches the ceiling and causes several people to look our way. He's always flushed easily, but right now his entire face is so red it rivals his flame-colored locks. His glossy green eyes are bloodshot and filled with amused tears, though no jokes have been told.

"One more!" He tries to tug the pirate back down into his chair, but Bastian swats his hand away. Ferrick looks at his swatted hand with a deep frown

"One more and I'll have to roll you out of here." Bastian's eyes nearly twitch to the back of his skull. "And we don't want to overstay our welcome." He peers down to his pouch.

Ferrick takes one look at it and gasps. "You *stole* that?" he asks, too loudly.

If looks could kill, Ferrick would long be gone. The room quiets, and I'm certain Bastian feels the attention of the other patrons as well as I do.

My skin crawls with the presence of their roaming eyes and spiked curiosity. Bastian's shoulders shake as he struggles to maintain composure, eventually settling for placing a firm hand on Ferrick's arm.

"We need to go." Both the intensity of Bastian's voice and the prickle of attention from patrons makes that obvious. I clear my throat and gather my things before I slide from the table.

The ache that stirs from the idea of leaving surprises me. I wish there were enough time for me to sink into a barrel of mead and fill my body with a hundred more lavish petit cakes. To chat with Ikacans about silly things like fashion and trends.

I clench my fists tight and remind myself that one day I'll have that opportunity. But only if we keep moving.

The tavern's warm air has turned hot from breath and bodies as everyone eyes us. I keep my head low, not giving them the chance to glimpse my face. Ferrick begrudgingly follows, stumbling every few steps. His ruddy face twists into a scowl at Bastian, as if challenging the pirate. Bastian's brow arches, but he says nothing as we weave through the crowd and make our way out of the tavern.

The cool breeze and the ocean's mist are quick to greet us. It sinks through my remaining warmth, making me wish I had a heavier coat.

The streets are a whisper of what they were only hours before, and it's clear now why Bastian wanted us to wait. This late in the evening, everyone is either at home or in one of the taverns, enjoying Ikae's nightlife. The stores lining the streets are dark and empty; no one's around to see us sneak inside. Bastian leads us around the back of Maribel's, which, sure enough, we know is our store the moment we see it.

The shop looks as though it's made from thousands of pink bubbles that shimmer, pop, and redevelop as we approach. It creates a quiet little symphony that reminds me of the *pop pop pop* of sparkling wine.

Though it looks fragile, the shop is sturdy as Bastian tries the handle. It gives easily beneath his grip.

My fingertips itch with desire as the door opens into an expansive shop with gorgeous clothing lining every wall. No longer is it formed by bubbles, but the floors and walls are a rich marble.

"You'll need supplies for the journey," Bastian says, "so take what you need while I search."

"Search?" I echo. "For what?"

"Have you ever seen a barracuda? If you see a symbol with one on it, let me know." Bastian crouches low at the threshold. He leans against it, as if using the frame for support as he draws a shaky breath. If I didn't know any better, I'd think the pirate was nervous.

Slowly he peels himself away, shifting through the clothes.

I leave him be, my heart thumping in my throat, heavy with desire.

The inside of the shop is breathtaking. Every article of clothing imaginable lines the wall, from fish-scale coats to chic, fitted dresses. In Arida, I'd had all my clothing personally tailored or imported. Being able to walk into a store and pick something out is unheard of.

I'm more in love with this place by the second.

Somewhere beside me, Ferrick hiccups. "You want me to *steal*?" he asks in horror, his flushed face pinching. "I should . . . I should call the authorities on you, you pirate!"

I take a coat from its hanger and toss it into Ferrick's arms. He flinches, then about three seconds later, stumbles back in surprise.

"We're not stealing," I tell him sweetly, draping another shirt in his arms. He crinkles his nose distastefully. "I bought this store for you as an engagement gift. I want you to take whatever you'd like."

His face smooths, eyes brightening with drunken delight. "You're so wonderful. That is"—he hiccups—"so nice."

"Yes, Ferrick, it's incredibly nice." I press a gentle hand to his shoulder and guide him forward. "Now go pick out some outfits."

For a moment he simply stands there, looking at the spot where I pressed his shoulder with a tiny smile. I roll my eyes and get back to work.

A fitted navy shirt made of linen catches my eye. I snatch it up and drape it over my arm, letting myself pretend for a moment that I'm out shopping with friends. That we came all this way not to end a rebellion, but simply to travel and be merry.

My evening in the tavern with Ferrick and Bastian has spoiled me. In there, it was almost easy to believe that none of this was happening. That my demonstration of magic was excellent, and I'd finally proven myself strong enough to end my training and sail the kingdom.

But the tavern was a beautiful lie.

I focus instead on the task at hand. I don't need gowns, but clothing loose enough for me to move around; just not so loose that they snag on *Keel Haul*'s rigging.

Since I've always been fitted for clothes, the pants are a mystery to me. I hold them to my waist and use my imagination to determine whether they'll fit. I drape a few pairs, all in a variety of pastel Ikaean colors, over my arm for good measure. The coats are next. I make a grab for a scarlet one that's similar to the one I'm borrowing from Bastian when my heart stops cold.

On the hanger beside it, there's a coat as iridescent as opal. *Zudoh.*

I jerk my hand back like it's poison, and hear a sharp intake of breath behind me. Bastian's gaze is hard on the coat.

Though Kaven may be making a stir, Zudoh's been banished from the kingdom for years. So why does this shop have Zudian clothing?

This only confirms Bastian's been telling the truth— Kaven's reach is spreading. We have to move quicker.

When I turn back to the pirate, his expression darkens. But he doesn't seem surprised. "Let's get going," is all he says before reaching behind the coat to check the wall.

Ferrick stumbles across the room, laughing quietly to himself as he grabs hold of whatever he sees, careless of whether it will fit. I sigh and add a few things for him to my pile. My arms grow weak from the weight of all the fabric, but still I grab two thick capes—one for me, another for Ferrick—and a wide-brimmed hat because I like the way it looks. Though I already have one pair of boots, I snatch another for good measure.

I'm confident I cannot hold anything else, no matter how small, when my eye catches sight of a sparkling morganite necklace. I go to take a step toward it when the ground rattles with what feels like a dozen pounding footsteps.

"Quiet!" Bastian demands from somewhere behind me. He drops to a crouch as the shadows of several figures pass the window. I press myself flat against the wall and peer through, squinting to see the colors they wear—capes in an intense sapphire blue. Silver trim and a shining royal emblem catch the light of the oil lamps as they pass.

Visidian soldiers.

"No one gets off this island. Search the ships!" one of them yells, waving the rest of his group forward while four soldiers remain on the docks.

I try to flatten myself further, but I can only suck myself in so much. "They'll know we're here the moment they search *Keel Haul*." I think of the gown and sapphire jewels that sit in my cabin. Surely no one else in Visidia would own such items. Bastian's eyes narrow, skimming briefly over my satchel. I shift the clothes in my arms to cover it. "We're not fighting my soldiers."

"Then we have to hide." Bastian flicks a look at the back wall, and I wonder what it is he's searching for back there. But there's no time to ask as Ferrick, very drunk and very confused, starts waddling toward a display headpiece. Bastian grabs at his foot with a hiss, and Ferrick gasps.

Though nerves urge me to clamp my eyes shut, I force myself to watch so that I can prepare to run.

Someone steps toward the glass. His sharp face is lit by the glow of the lamp as he peers into the shop.

It's Casem. I swallow a gasp as he catches my eye. My guard's face tightens, and if I didn't know better, I'd think he was more afraid than surprised.

When he starts to open his mouth, I shake my head quickly, willing silence into him. Neither Bastian nor Ferrick can see him, and I want it to remain that way.

Don't say anything, Casem. One word, and I'm as good as dead.

"Please." I mouth the word, and something in Casem's expression cracks. He runs a tongue over his lips, and again I shake my head. His hesitation is obvious in the worrisome way his hands twitch against the glass.

"Anyone in there?" another soldier calls from outside. I suck in a breath and shut my eyes, awaiting my fate.

This is the end of my journey, and I've nothing to show for it. Visidia will be left without a fit animancer. Aunt Kalea will take my place, and with her dual magics, the kingdom will fall.

"No," Casem answers. My eyes flutter open as he steps away, giving me one last look before turning his head. "It's empty."

"Hurry up, then!" yells a voice I don't recognize. "We need to find the princess quickly, before anyone else does."

I start to smile, but Casem turns to follow the other soldiers down the street as they search every shop and tavern. He doesn't look back.

When we can no longer hear the sound of their boots against the cobblestone, Bastian exhales in relief. He pushes back a rack of trousers, and there on the wall is a tiny symbol, almost invisible—crossbones of two fish skeletons.

"Found it! Everyone, this way!"

I drag the clothes back into my arms, and from the corner of my eye I spot the necklace once more. It's not in a case. Nothing is protecting it. It simply sits there, shimmering and beckoning me with its spectacular glory, and I find myself completely enamored by it. Most of the jewels I have back home are sapphires. I've never seen anything in this soft, handsome shade of pink.

I can't help myself when I reach out.

But I must be drunk, because as I wrap my fingers around the stone, the world swims. I can't sense where my feet are or how to move them. They're heavy as lead and refuse to budge, holding

110

me upright. The clothes drop from my hands as thousands of ants run across my arms and nestle into my hair. My ears.

I want to scream but don't dare open my mouth because they're on my lips too, threatening to enter. The necklace remains wound around my fingertips and I clutch it tighter, my body seizing up.

"Princess?"

I can't shut my eyes. Shadows fill the corners as the ants stretch and morph into thick purple beetles whose wings buzz angrily against my neck. I want to swat them away, but my hands are too heavy. Have they been stung? Eaten away?

"Stars!" Bastian rushes forward. His face is panicked as thick beads of sweat roll down his neck, though he sheens too heavily for it to only be nerves. I stare at him, hoping he can see the panic in my eyes.

In all of our conversations, Yuriel has never mentioned something like this. Enchantment magic is meant to be fun—a drop of shimmer upon reality. But as the beetles crawl up my nose and drop into my clogging lungs, my chest constricts so tightly I can hardly breathe.

When Ferrick reaches out to try to tug away the necklace, Bastian shoves him away. "Don't touch it!"

"What's wrong?" Ferrick asks briskly, sobering some. "What's happening to her?"

Bastian ignores him, jaw clenched as he eyes the necklace. He takes hold of both my shoulders. The beetles crawl up his hands, but he doesn't seem to notice. "Listen to me, Princess. Whatever you're seeing is all in your head; this magic is triggered by touch. All you need to do is drop the necklace and it will stop."

"Just take it from her!" Ferrick argues, ripping a dress off its hanger in a drunken attempt to wrap it around his hand. But Bastian throws out an arm to keep him back.

"No. Let her feel this," he says. "She needs to see what it's like to fight this kind of magic."

I try to open my fingers, but the insects buzz angrily and morph yet again into spiders of a hundred varieties—crawling, burying into my flesh, working at my lips to try to get into my mouth before giving up and using my ears, instead.

My knees buckle, but ultimately I remain in place. I don't *want* to feel this. I want him to hurry up and pry this blasted necklace from my hands.

"Amora." Bastian dips his head to mine so that our foreheads touch and he's all I can see. "Focus. You're stronger than this magic. Open your hands and drop that necklace."

My breaths are ragged from the spiders inside me, but I shift my focus entirely onto those breaths and on clamping my eyes shut. I've no idea how long it takes for my visions of spiders to disappear, but eventually I fall into the comfort of the darkness behind my eyelids.

Within me, the spiders still.

"Good." Bastian's voice sounds like a faraway dream that I fight desperately to reach. "Now drop it . . ."

My hands may still be lead, but I can at least focus on them now that my eyes are shut. My hand jerks and rattles as I move it, but slowly I pry my fingers from the necklace, one at a time.

It clatters to the floor after what feels like hours, and instantly I'm flooded with warmth. I suck in a gasp as the sensation of my body returns. The weight of the lead has disappeared, and I'm light and floaty once more, swaying on my feet as I readjust. The insects are gone, and my lungs are clear.

"You okay?" Ferrick places a hand on my back in an attempt to steady me, though he's the one that sways.

"I'd no idea enchantment magic was like that." I'm breathless as I shake myself off, still convinced something's inside my ear.

"It's not." Bastian's voice is quiet as he eyes the fallen necklace. "But Zudoh's magic can be. Congratulations, Princess. I believe you've had your first experience with curse magic."

My chest constricts. First the coat, and now this?

"Kaven's influence might be spreading quicker than we thought." His voice is cold, though it's not me his frustration is aimed at. "It's a wonder you were able to break out of the curse so quickly. I thought I was going to have to try to pry that thing out of your hands."

"That was *quick*?" I rasp. "By the gods, I thought I was going to be suffocated by a thousand spiders."

I jump as, outside, someone begins yelling. The voice sounds distant, but it's clear we've worn out our welcome. With palace guards and the royal Visidian soldiers on the island, we need to hurry and get out of here.

With the edge of his boot, Bastian scoots the necklace off to the side. "Let's keep moving."

Ferrick nods and follows him to the back wall. I glance over my shoulder, ensuring they're not paying attention as I wrap my hand in one of my shirts to hide my exposed skin. I scoop the necklace back up and tuck it safely into the stolen boots.

The chance to study Zudoh's magic has been handed to me, and I don't intend to pass it up.

I follow the boys to the back wall of the shop. The wall looks no different from the others, except for the tiny markings of crossbones. Bastian knocks on them once. Then twice, and suddenly the wall splits clearly down the middle and opens like a door.

CHAPTER TWELVE

Ferrick and I stumble back in shock as an alarmingly tall man knocks the hangers back and peeks out from behind them. He wears a rich lavender suit that looks as though he's pulled it straight from the constellations. A shooting star flies across his legs and onto his vest, shimmering through the sky that winks with his every step.

"Evening!" he says pleasantly, as though there's nothing strange about standing in the middle of what was a solid wall only seconds before. Then he squints at Bastian, and his lips curve into a grin. "Well, now! I didn't think we'd see you any time soon." He stretches a long arm out to push the wall open wider, as if opening a door. On either side of him, trousers tilt askew on their hangers. "Welcome, welcome. Come on in."

The wall continues to stretch until it reveals a room of a dozen colors, enchanted lights swirling behind him. When the man steps back, those colors reflect off his cool umber skin in shades of pink, orange, and then a vibrant, sharp red.

My body tenses with uncertainty, but there's no denying the echo of soldiers somewhere nearby. I force myself to follow behind Bastian as he steps into the strange lights, and with a nervous glance, Ferrick does the same.

The wall slams shut behind us.

The air is hazy with pungent cigar smoke and raucous laughter I somehow couldn't hear only a moment ago. My eyes widen as I take in the enchanted interior. The marble floor shimmers an iridescent turquoise that darkens and stretches like the ocean before it shifts to a deep violet. The farther in we venture, the louder the music of piano and horns becomes.

Aside from the man in the star suit, the only ones inside this strange place are women who do not don the typical Ikaean style I've grown accustomed to. While the colors remain shades of soft pastels, the dresses are shorter. Tighter and simpler. Two women with pink hair cropped to their chins and matching satin dresses kick their feet and dance with the quick rhythm of the music, sipping from tall flutes of effervescent or deep goblets of wine. Others spend their time smoking cigars that puff sweet violet smoke and chatting, while more fill the back booths, sitting with their bodies pressed too closely to only be having friendly conversation. A few of them wear attractive suits tailored to fit their bodies perfectly, something I've yet to see any woman in Ikae wear.

Across the floor, behind the piano, a glass wall overlooks Ikae's bay. And though we can see people as they pass by, no one seems to be able to see us.

"This is impossible," I whisper, breathless. "How did we not see this place before?"

"Because it wasn't there before." The man in the star suit laughs. "It was covered by an enchantment. When you find the entrance to our club, that's when we lift the veil. And we never use the same entrance twice. Now, let me help you with those."

He rests his hand atop my pile of clothing, and the trousers at the top lift in the air. I choke on my breath as the other pieces follow, folding themselves into the trousers and shrinking. Shrinking, shrinking, shrinking, until the entire stack is no larger than my pinkie. He draws a small teal ribbon from his pocket and swiftly ties it around the miniature trousers before handing them to me.

I promptly tuck them into my satchel. Beside me, Ferrick rubs his eyes in disbelief.

"Just untie it when you want them," the man says, only smiling at the strange expression I'm surely making. "What's your name, lovely?"

"We're not here to chat, Liam," Bastian interrupts. "We're here to talk to Shanty about a job."

"Shanty, huh?" Liam sets his hand atop Ferrick's pile of clothing and repeats the enchantment. "Let me guess, this has something to do with all those guards running around outside? I suppose they must be looking for Princess Amora, don't you think? I heard her ceremony was one for the books; it's a shame I missed it." His silver eyes flash to mine, and the smile on his glittering lips stretches.

Magic clenches my gut as I instinctively set a hand upon the dagger beneath my cloak.

Liam gently shakes his head. "There's no need for that. We make no judgments here at Barracuda Lounge. This is a place of . . . opportunity."

"Barracuda Lounge?" My skin crawls as I think back to Bastian's conversation with the woman at the tavern. "Just what is this place, exactly?" Liam is no longer the only one paying attention to us. Behind him, dozens of women examine us with keen interest.

"This is where you come when you need the type of help or information you can't find anywhere else." It's a girl who answers—a beautiful blond with generous curves. She wears a slinky red satin dress that clings to her body and leaves little to the imagination. Her eyes are the same color, as are her lips, which pucker sourly as she glances at Bastian.

"You owe me money," she growls at once, arms folding. "If you think I'm helping you again, you're more of a fool than I thought."

Liam's face never falters from its grin. "Your assistance is precisely what he requested, Shanty."

The girl rolls her eyes. "Of course it is. Then pay up, pirate. You know we don't work for free."

Though I'm well aware of the freshly stolen pouch of coins hidden beneath his cloak, Bastian's face contorts into a convincing grimace. "You know I'd pay you if I could. But I've been trying my hand at more honest work, lately. Only taking what I need, you know? I'm afraid keeping my hands clean doesn't make for too much coin."

Shanty waves a dismissive hand and turns to go. "Then I'm not interested in what you have to say. Get out of my club."

"Wait a second—" Bastian reaches out to grab Shanty's wrist, and all at once there are a dozen barracudas behind her with weapons at the ready—knives, spiked whips, and other rather creative tools I've never before seen. I swallow hard and set my hand upon my satchel as their lips twist into vicious sneers that force Bastian to quickly release his grip.

There's no question as to whether Barracuda Lounge was aptly named. No one sits at the piano or holds the swaying saxophone, but somehow the swanky rhythm knows to quiet as the tension rises.

Shanty turns her focus to me, eyes roaming over my body in a way that forces heat to my cheeks. "The princess may stay, of course. My barracudas and I will assure that she remains safe."

Though I suspected Liam had already guessed who I am, I falter when Shanty confidently announces my title, as though she recognized me from the moment I stepped into this strange place.

"How'd you know?" I ask, earning a quirk of her brow.

"Please." She snorts, blond hair shifting to baby-pink waves that she bats over her shoulder. "You may be cooped up on your island, but that doesn't mean the rest of us are. It's my business to know faces."

Something about the way she says that forces shivers down my spine.

"The pirate and I have something to take care of," I tell her after licking my dry lips, squirming under her scrutiny. "I'm afraid I'm stuck with him for the time being."

Shanty casts a dramatic sigh toward Bastian. "*Fine*. Out with it, then. Tell me why I should further help someone who's already in my debt."

"Because you'll be offering your assistance to the future High Animancer of Visidia," I say for him, ignoring the way my stomach clenches again, cramping up. I set a hand upon it, trying to steady my nerves. "And I have to think that's a good person to have on your side."

"Funny, because I heard your performance didn't quite go as expected." She cocks a brow.

"By the season's end, that won't matter." I put every ounce of conviction into my words as I can muster. "I've a plan to earn my title."

"But we need your help," Bastian finishes.

This earns her attention. She pauses, head cocking as a thoughtful grin eats its way across her face. "So you're saying that the future of Visidia's throne is up to me?" She licks her lips. "What a position to be in. But you know, it's interesting. I received a counteroffer to this very same issue a few weeks ago."

My body numbs as Bastian tenses beside me. "What are you saying?"

"My barracudas and I have quite a bounty on our heads, you know. And we were offered an interesting proposition to help take care of that . . . assuming we help eradicate Visidia's monarchy."

My magic thrums to life, warming my core and stretching into my forearms. I want to sink into its protection, but hesitate.

I heard your performance didn't quite go as expected.

The memory of Aran's bloodied, mangled body eats through my brain. Rather than reach for my satchel, I tighten my grip around my dagger's hilt.

I can't risk letting my magic loose in a crowd this large. Not until I know for sure I'll have to fight.

Not until I know that I'll have to kill.

Bastian mirrors me, moving for his sword. But a girl with soft blue hair presses a dagger to his throat before he can even get the blade out.

"Stars," he growls. "You women really love these things."

Ferrick throws his hands in the air as one of the barracudas points a long, thin knife at him. Though he may be able to regenerate, even the most powerful Suntosans can't mend a fatal wound.

I stiffen expectantly, waiting for a knife to my own throat. But surprisingly, the barracudas leave me alone.

Shanty looks Bastian over and arches a fine pink brow. And then she laughs, a soft but dark sound. "Oh relax, pirate. I'd never accept a deal with Zudoh. Even with Kerost, they don't have the numbers to take on Visidia. I know a losing battle when I see it."

"It may be a losing battle now, but Kaven's influence is spreading." I don't sheathe my blade as Shanty's attention flickers to me. She tilts her head, catlike. "Stores here carry Zudian clothing. I found a necklace possessed with Zudian curse magic, as well—"

"Oh, I bet that was a fun time," she teases.

I side-eye Bastian, who swallows against the blade on his throat, then say, "Should Kaven win over another island, there's no saying how bad things might get for Visidia. I need to put an end to his rebellion before it spreads any further."

She nods her head side to side, as if considering this. "Aye, but I don't see where I fit into this problem. As I've said already, there's a price on my head. Why should I help the kingdom that put it there?"

"Because I can get rid of it," I say firmly, watching the interest lift in Shanty's eyes. "And because if Kaven gains control, there's no telling what might happen to this lounge of yours, especially since you refused to help him. Kaven can steal magic."

Though a grin had been previously curling at her lips, it straightens away at once. "Can he, now? Well, that's a problem." She waves her hands, and the barracudas relax their weapons. "I'd like to help you, Princess, but let's confirm one thing: Are you telling me that, should I lend my services, you'll lift the bounty on me and every one of my barracudas?"

"Consider it done." Though I may not know what put that bounty on their heads in the first place, it's not as important as protecting Visidia. Not to mention that if the rebellion's already tried to team up with the barracudas once, there's nothing to say they won't try again.

And something in my gut tells me Shanty isn't someone I want to make my enemy.

Ferrick's face retracts. "This doesn't sound like a good

plan—" His words cut off as I give him a swift nudge with my elbow.

"Very well, then. What can I help you with?" A wicked gleam crosses Shanty's ruby eyes. The music kicks back up, and once again the club is thick with smoke and chatter as everyone slinks away to resume their business.

"We need a way to Zudoh," Bastian says, rubbing tenderly at his throat.

Her attention bounces to him and she nods, waving us over to two leather booths in the far corner of the club. Taking a seat on the opposite side, she swings one leg over the other and leans back comfortably. She pays no mind to the generous slit of her dress, or the way it exposes a smooth, round thigh.

"The water surrounding Zudoh's been cursed," she announces easily. "Unless you're invited in, it's nearly impossible to get there without triggering it. Fully manned ships have sunk in those waters. I've heard too many stories of curious sailors who have tried to visit, but never made it back. If the curse itself doesn't kill you for getting too close, it's said the smell of a thousand dead and rotting fish might do the trick."

Bastian works at his jaw, the gears in his head visibly shifting. "Surely there's a way to get around the curse?"

"Around?" She laughs. It's a soft sound, warm and inviting, but laced with an edge that sends shivers up my neck. "No. But there might be a way to navigate *through* it. You'll just need some assistance."

"Yours?" he asks. "Amora has jewels. We can pay—"

"And you have a pouch full of stolen coin!" I argue, shooting him a glare. He at least has the decency to look mildly embarrassed, and turns his face away.

Shanty's eyes roam over Bastian curiously, likely looking for the well-hidden pouch. "I would never dream of stepping foot on that ship of yours. And it's not my assistance you'll need, regardless. If you want to get to Zudoh, you're going to need to find yourself a mermaid."

My blood runs hot. "Absolutely not. Anti-poaching laws were put into effect for a reason; their population is dying out."

Shanty tilts her chin up proudly. "Ah, but there's a flaw in that law. It's only considered poaching if you disturb them while they're still in the sea. The law says nothing about a mermaid on land."

My blood boils. "So what, you want us to kidnap one? Just how will a mermaid help us, exactly?" Mermaids are no easy target. They're rumored to have powerful magic that comes in the form of songs. One that can control the tides at will or summon creatures from the depths of the sea, and another meant to seduce anyone susceptible to a woman's charm into the water and lure them to their deaths. In exchange for their protection, they're no longer allowed to use their siren magic against us. But that doesn't mean they *won't*.

"Mermaids can sense magic," she explains. "Namely ones that make things different than they normally are—like Zudoh's curse magic and Mornute's enchantment magic. A mermaid would be able to sense the curse barricading Zudoh, and show you how to navigate a path."

"And how are we meant to find one?" I press my lips together and settle back in my seat.

"It's been rumored that there's one somewhere on Kerost." Shanty inspects her fingernails as she speaks, watching the color change from a dangerous red to a deep plum. "If you can't tell a mermaid by her face, you'll be able to tell by her scars. Once they trade their fins for legs, it's said mermaids have giant scars running down either side of their thighs—scars on their neck, too, where their gills should be."

There's a moment where I almost consider it—because if this is what it takes to save my kingdom, can I really say no?—

but I shake the temptation away. There's no way I'm kidnapping a mermaid.

"Either she comes with us of her own free will, or not at all," I tell them, leaving no room for rebuttal. "If we have to, we'll find another way to reach Kaven."

"No one said we have to kidnap her," Bastian says. "Let's just focus on finding one, and then we'll go from there."

Ferrick frowns deeply as he tilts his head back against the leather. But he doesn't argue. He looks like he just wants to take a nap that's long enough to sleep off his ale.

"It sounds like you're all in for quite the adventure." Shanty's eyes slit like a cat who's spotted its prey. "But first, let me tend to those faces of yours. We'll have to get you past those guards if you're to get back to your ship."

She closes the space between us and my skin buzzes with the thrum of unfamiliar magic as she brushes a soft thumb over my cheeks and brows, turning my face every which way to scrutinize me. She does the same with Ferrick, whose neck retracts so far that he's formed two chins, both of them equally appalled.

"My face," he says between grimaces, "is *mine*."

"Yes, love, and it will still be yours." Her fingertips are hot against my skin. "The enchantment I can offer is only temporary, but it will give you plenty of time to get back to that ship of yours."

The most I've ever experienced Ikae's magic was when Yuriel made my fingernails different colors when we were children, and I've no memory of how long that lasted. Curiosity warms my nervous stomach.

"Does it hurt?"

Shanty's quick to shake her head. "It's only a glamour. You won't feel a thing."

"Then do whatever you need to."

Ferrick grumbles as though I've cursed us to some miserable fate, but he'll get over it.

When she presses her fingers against my temples this time, it's like my skin is melting. I gasp, flinching away on instinct, but Shanty's grip is tight and expectant.

The enchantment doesn't hurt, necessarily. It's a strange, foreign feeling. Alarming at first, like my skin's the wax of a burning candle. But then, as I accept the changes happening, the warmth spreads pleasantly throughout my body. It's like I'm being pampered.

One of the barracudas must sense my curiosity, for she brings me an ornate hand mirror. I try not to wonder how often they must do this for them to have one lying around, and hold it up. I watch with awe as my dark brown curls lighten into a soft shade of lavender and shrink, shorter and shorter, until my hair stops above my ears. Worry catches in my throat, and I reach to touch my hair in a panic, expecting it to be gone. And yet my fingers brush through my curls as they always do.

"Like I said," Shanty says, amusement in her words, "it's only a glamour. Try not to touch your hair; to everyone else, it will look as though you're stroking the air."

Shanty's fingers roam my jaw next. I draw a sharp breath as she widens the structure and sharpens the bones. She spends several minutes altering the color of my eyes, and then thickens my brows into two perfect powder-pink arches. I have to resist scratching at the stubble that glamours my cheeks, trying to remind myself that my skin will still be smooth to the touch.

"Wear a coat to cover yourself," she says simply, waving to my chest. "No one should recognize you like this."

I barely manage a nod, unable to pull my hands away from my cheeks. "I'd no idea enchantment magic could do this."

Shanty's lips stretch into a smug grin as she moves on to Ferrick, cropping his red waves and strengthening his jaw.

"Most people can only do parlor tricks; simple things like changing hair or eye color, or altering the fabric of their clothing. I'm one of the few full face-shifters." She enlarges Ferrick's eyes and softens them into a pastel blue to match his new hair. "But I'm training to be a full body-shifter. When I'm trying to play the part of someone else, I can't tell you how many times *these* have gotten in the way of a disguise." She motions to her own chest and drags her hand over her thick waist and down the generous curve of her hips for emphasis. "But yes, enchantment magic can do more than most people give it credit for, or that most take the time to uncover. All barracudas have found ways to expand the use of our allegedly frivolous magic, but few deal with faces."

Though it should reassure me that Shanty's one of the few who can perform this magic, my eyes wander, counting the women in the lounge. There are at least twenty barracudas, all with strangely unique enchantment magic.

"I can't make any two people look perfectly identical," Shanty murmurs, as if sensing my unease. "And I can't alter height or size like Liam can, nor can I replicate someone else's facial features perfectly. It's more about working with the features someone already has, and adjusting them. Like a temporary game of dress-up. Enchantment magic is no different from any other—everyone uses it a little differently, and is more comfortable using it in certain ways."

Shanty beams as she pulls away from Ferrick with dramatic flair, proudly showing off her work. He looks different enough not to be recognizable at first glance, but when I'm up close, squinting at the perpetual worry in his eyes and the thin bridge of his nose, he's still very much himself.

Shanty's magic is not a miracle by any means, but if I look as altered as Ferrick, we're different enough to get away with this.

"What in the gods' names have you done to my face?" He gasps as he touches it, pastel-blue brows furrowing. "I'll never be able to trust another face for as long as I live."

Even drunk, he's right; if face-shifters exist, then who might I have passed in my life, thinking they were someone different than they were? Even if Shanty is one of the few, the existence of this magic is far from reassuring.

"You both look quite handsome." Amusement glints in Bastian's eyes, but there's something off about them. They're weighed down tiredly, and his skin has grown ashen, covered by a thin veil of sweat.

I shoo him away as I stand, and am promptly ushered away by Shanty. She says something to one of the other barracudas, and they disappear for a moment before returning with a handful of Ikaean clothing—white trousers, a soft pink frock and vest, and a coat heavier than the weather calls for to mask the shape of my body. I change into them swiftly, and my insides roil as I examine my widened jaw and growing stubble in the full-length mirror and decide there's no way anyone would recognize me.

My face isn't my own.

Ferrick has changed into an outfit similar to mine, and as Shanty examines us for a final time, she beams proudly at her work.

"Don't forget to keep your end of the deal," she purrs, teeth gleaming with terrific pride. "Otherwise I might have to pay the kingdom a little visit myself. And you won't even see me coming."

My breath hitches, but I force my nerves away. "I wouldn't dream of it."

Shanty nods her approval and waves for Liam to join her. He's there within seconds, silver eyes skimming over Ferrick and me with pleased amusement. His expression never shifts; it's like he knows something no one else in the room does.

"Please see that our guests are escorted out," she says, and the man nods swiftly before stretching an arm around Bastian's shoulders, ushering him back the way we came—to an empty black wall with a tiny knob handle.

He twists the knob and pulls the door open. "Please stop by again, should you ever require our assistance." The words may be light and friendly, but he gives us no time to respond before steering us out onto stained-glass streets, somehow in a completely different area of town than where we entered. His face once again shines from pink to red as the lights flicker against his skin, half visible in the shadows of the wall's crack. Without warning, it slams shut.

I watched Liam open that door, and yet, on this side, the stone wall is smooth. There's no handle or button, just a single stone with a tiny etching of skeletal fish crossbones, in a random alleyway we've been dumped off in.

For a long moment, the three of us stare at the solid stone slab, trying to process everything that just happened and the strange place we've emerged from.

Eventually, Ferrick huffs a quiet, disbelieving laugh. "I can't tell if I'm drunk, or if that's the weirdest magic I've ever seen."

"Both," I answer, and he doesn't disagree.

My blood pulses as I stare, enthralled such a place could even exist. Gently I run my finger over the light gray stone, but it feels no different from the others.

This is the magic of Visidia's people, but used in strange ways I've never before seen. Ways I never would have known existed if not for seeing it with my own eyes.

What a strange, wonderful place.

"We're not in the clear yet," Bastian says, drawing my attention back to the situation at hand.

I've a rebellion to stop; there's no way a few soldiers or an impending execution will keep me from that.

"Do you have an idea in mind?" I ask.

Bastian's jaw quirks slightly, the sheen of sweat on his skin even heavier than it was inside the warm lounge. "All we have to do is get on the ship." His words are slow, breath so labored it sounds as though he's winded enough for the three of us. He must not have wanted us to know how much the alcohol affected him; I can only hope the cool sea breeze does him some good.

"And then what?" Ferrick asks. Though he seems to be sobering up some, he wears the perpetual glare of someone nursing a headache after one too many drinks.

"And then we take advantage of the fact *Keel Haul*'s magical and faster than anything else on the water." Bastian smiles tightly, and out of habit I run a finger over the lip of my satchel. Though I don't plan to use my magic on the soldiers, I find comfort in the action.

I square my shoulders and draw a breath to steady myself. "Let's get going."

CHAPTER THIRTEEN

Unlike Arida, whose nights are brightly lit by torch and starlight, nights in Ikae exist in a multicolored haze. The glow of enchanted oil lamps blankets the busier streets, but the alleyways are left forgotten. We stumble through them half-blind, following the echoes of bellowing soldiers who scout the docks.

Most of them scour the city. We've carefully avoided several small groups already, but there's no getting around them this time. Fortunately, only a few are posted on the docks, while others search the ships anchored there. They don't seem to have reached *Keel Haul*, yet.

I run a hand over my jawline, hoping the sharpened bones and stubble are still there to disguise me.

"Act natural," I tell Ferrick, biting the inside of my cheek as his shoulders tense and his face pinches together with the attempt.

Perfectly natural, indeed.

We file out into the streets, and Bastian immediately begins boisterously talking about this morning's rousing game of Cannon Rushing. I almost fake a laugh in response, but sharply halt the noise almost as quickly as it starts.

I may look different to others, but my voice is still my own.

We earn the immediate attention of two soldiers who flank the entrance of the docks, and I tense with recognition—it's a seasoned guard named Antoni, and a newer soldier, Karin. I don't remember either of their magics, and because they wear the same sapphire uniforms of palace guards instead of the color that represents their home island, it's impossible to know what they practice. I keep my eyes far from them, not wanting to find out.

"Stop there!" Antoni yells, his voice low and guttural. "The docks are closed for the night."

Bastian falters, pretending to be thrown off guard. "Closed?" he echoes, as if testing the taste of the word. And then he frowns, deciding he doesn't like it. "Why did no one mention this earlier? How long do you intend to keep them shut?" His voice begins to rise, sounding half flustered and half ridiculously insulted. It's truly quite impressive.

The guard's brows furrow. "Emergency shutdown. I'm afraid you'll have to leave."

Beside me, Ferrick is stiff as stone. I say a silent prayer he keeps his mouth shut.

"You don't understand," Bastian argues, "my brother's getting married in the morning, and our outfits are on that ship." He points to *Keel Haul* and inhales a sharp, angry breath. "He's marrying Mornute's baroness, and if I don't make sure her fiancé has his outfit—"

"As well as her ring," I add, trying to keep my voice a low baritone.

"—his outfit and her ring, yes. If I don't have those, she'll have my head."

The guard frowns, forehead creasing with annoyance. Likely not wanting to deal with the amount of protest he senses we're willing to offer, he looks toward Karin, who sighs knowingly.

"I'll escort you up," the woman grumbles. "But make sure you're quick about it."

"Of course," I say, and Ferrick nods in what I think is an attempt to be enthusiastically thankful. The soldier gives him an odd look, but only rolls her eyes. She assumes we're nothing more than a trio of silly young men.

She's no knowledge of the weapons at our hips, or the lies of our faces.

We travel swiftly through the docks, the presence of *Keel Haul* so close that victory pounds in my heart's anxious beating.

But it's short-lived; Casem and his group have returned from searching the town.

"Someone claims to have seen her," a soldier in his group announces. "She was with two men—we can presume the princess and her fiancé both fled and are seeking sanctuary with someone."

I keep my head tucked down and my legs moving. Ferrick's the first to ascend the ladder up *Keel Haul*, trying desperately to hide that a partially missing hand is what's slowing him down. Bastian quickly follows, and I'm only a few steps away.

I silently pray they don't look toward me. But tonight, the gods must be laughing at my poor favor.

"What do you think you're doing?" I recognize the voice as Casem's.

Karin hesitates as Casem closes the gap between us. Nerves eat my stomach raw, cramping it so fiercely I grimace.

"Don't worry, sir," Karin says. "There's no crew on board their ship. I was escorting them up to fetch their outfits for the baroness's wedding tomorrow."

Casem's eyes narrow sharply. "The baroness is still in Arida for Princess Amora's birthday," he says, and I nearly stumble on my own feet.

Karin spins to face me. But when she does, her eyes don't reach my face. They hesitate on my white trousers, noticing first what I don't feel until a moment too late.

Blood.

It's seeped through to stain the crotch and upper thighs of my trousers, and I understand now it wasn't worry that's been cramping my stomach for the past hour.

Casem follows Karin's focus, and his cheeks flush pink. "My apologies, sir. If your clothes are aboard that ship, please allow Karin to escort you to—" His words stall as he stares down at my pants, and hesitation knits his brows as though he's seen something off. When I peer down to see what's caught his attention, my entire body numbs.

My satchel.

When Casem throws his attention to my face, his eyes spark with immediate recognition. "Amora?"

I don't think, or wait to figure out whether this woman has magic. I grab Karin by her shoulders and use every ounce of strength and adrenaline to shove her off the dock and into the water.

"Time to go!" Bastian yanks himself up the ropes of *Keel Haul.* "Hurry and grab on!"

The docks ignite with life and fury. Bastian's a far quicker climber than I am; his years of experience have paid off. Though I manage to grip the ladder, Casem does the same.

"Amora!" He grabs my left ankle. I twist and kick my foot from his grip, ready to demand he release me. But when I glance down, it's not determination in his eyes. It's panic.

"Push me into the water," he whispers sharply. "Tell me where you're going, and then kick me down."

"Why would I—"

"Then I'll tell them you're going to Valuka! I'm going to grab you, but you need to push me into the water."

And he does just that. Casem stretches to grab at my leg once more, but his grip looks stronger than it truly is. I snarl and twist out of it easily, slamming my boot down into his face. He yelps and loses his grip, slipping from the rope and into the water below. But I feel a rush of his Valukan magic before he falls, discreetly pushing higher and hastening my climb. I wince and send him a silent thanks for his help.

Above me, Bastian and Ferrick lean over the railing to pull me up. One soldier forms a ball of fire in his hands, preparing to toss it at the ropes. But several other soldiers lunge and get in his way as they dive for the ladder that Bastian's quick to swing up and over the ledge.

They don't rush to their ship, likely thinking we've no crew and no means of escape. But that's their biggest mistake.

The moment I'm on deck, the sails bloat with the crisp night air, allowing the sharp breeze to wrench it from the docks. Bastian runs to reel in the anchors and I follow, ignoring the sticky blood coating my thighs as I help him.

"Get back to the ship!" Casem yells from below, choking and spitting up water. "The princess is escaping to Valuka!"

Even if they had a Valukan with an affinity for air or water aboard, I doubt they'd reach us in time. *Keel Haul* zips from the docks and plunges into the open sea, faster than any Visidian ship I've ever known.

I risk a look back as the soldiers flock to their ship, but already they're specks in the distance.

I slump onto the deck as my adrenaline slows, attempting to calm my breaths. "We need to be more careful moving forward."

Ferrick groans. "We should find another ship. Now that

they've seen this one, there's no chance they won't send every-one looking for the only white ship sailing the kingdom."

The stars flicker and dim in Bastian's eyes. They become dangerous things, sharp as the sword he has sheathed onto his belt. "We can't abandon *Keel Haul*." His sharp chin juts toward the quiet waves. "Besides, leaving this ship would mean we'd not only have to find another vessel, but also a crew. Who knows how long that might take? As Amora said, we'll just have to be more careful from here on out."

Though Ferrick frowns, the logic is enough that he doesn't protest.

Mist rolls onto the deck, bringing the cold with it. I miss the cloak that waits, magicked and miniature within my satchel.

"How far to Kerost?" I ask, only then noticing how pur-posefully the boys are looking away from me. I don't think it's the cold that flushes Ferrick's cheeks.

"Don't you want to change?" he asks awkwardly, clearing his throat.

I peer down at the mess of my white trousers, soaked with salt water and stained with blood. It's unexpected, as my bleed-ing is often irregular, happening perhaps once a season. Every time it comes, my lap looks as though it's the sacrificial altar of a small animal. The ridiculousness of it's enough to make me laugh, which causes both Bastian and Ferrick to grimace uncomfortably.

"You should eat something with iron tonight," Bastian offers, trying hard to look me in the eye so he can feign com-fort. "I hear that's good for those who are . . . indisposed."

Ferrick nods in vehement agreement. "I hear salmon helps with that. Perhaps tuna would work the same? I can catch some for you, if you'd like." His jaw sets into a determined line, and I laugh even harder.

"You two are acting like you've never known someone to bleed before." I draw myself to my feet and pull the miniature clothing from my satchel, waving it at them. "Come on, then. If you want me to change so badly, help me organize. Do you think you can handle a little blood, Bastian?" I cast a rueful smile as I undo the ribbon Liam secured on the clothes, letting them fly out and spill into his lap. "I wouldn't want you to faint, again."

CHAPTER FOURTEEN

I refuse to acknowledge the skinned tuna that's laid out for me as I join the boys on the deck early the next morning. Bastian eyes me as I feast instead on hardening ginnada and stale honey cakes.

"Don't worry," I tell him. "The blood's taken care of."

Bastian's nose wrinkles when I smile at him between bites.

Ferrick's severed arm has grown back in its entirety, and though his glamour has mostly worn off, his red hair still holds the smallest tint of blue. He sits across from me with his legs tucked against his chest, staring at the horizon as Bastian taught him. He's adapting so slowly I doubt he'll ever find his sea legs.

I pity him. Mornute and Kerost are on opposite sides on the kingdom; it's at least a five-day journey for the average ship. We may be able to make it there in four with *Keel Haul*'s speed, but since we're heading far to the southwest edge of Visidia, the sea will be colder. And that means the tides will be rougher, too.

"We should be careful," Bastian says as he carves through the tuna. "It's been a while since I've been to Kerost, so I can't say what their current state is, or how much of their population Kaven's recruited. I think it's best if we lie low while we're there." My stomach growls when he takes a bite of the meaty fish, but since the boys only caught it because they think my bleeding makes me weak, I refuse to take any.

"I shouldn't have to hide from my people," I tell him between angry bites of another honey cake. "I should be able to talk to them as I am."

Bastian slurps up another bite of the raw fish before shaking his head. "Well, that sounds like a lovely plan, assuming you're looking to solidify your execution and completely lose the possibility of outmaneuvering Kaven." He slices a few more pieces and slides them over to Ferrick, who groans and looks away as his skin sheens greener. "One step at a time, Princess. Right now, we need a mermaid so we can hurry and get to Kaven. *Then* you can help Kerost. So wear a heavy cape and pants, and keep your head low so no one recognizes you. Depending on how far Kaven's reach has spread, we could be severely outnumbered."

Every time Bastian mentions Kaven, he spits the name. I can practically feel the rage he fights to quell, and can't help but wonder again—how did Bastian get his magic stolen in the first place? What was he doing with Kaven?

I want to press the issue, but for now it's better to keep my guard up and continue to let him lead. After all, he knows this island far better than Ferrick or I do, and we need him if we're going to reach Kaven.

"I'll wear a cape," I tell him eventually.

Appeased, Bastian nods. "Now, do either of you have questions?" He sits straight, posture oddly perfect. He's far too well-mannered, and every day his outfit is something exquisitely tailored and overall marvelous. Still, there's no denying he's a pirate. The easy way Bastian moves around *Keel Haul* only comes from years of practice, as does the way his eyes scan the ocean, always seeing and knowing something no one else can.

I'm convinced Bastian is the strangest man I will ever meet. My curiosity about him grows every day.

"When can I learn to sail *Keel Haul*?"

Bastian bites the inside of his cheek. "Do you have any questions about *Kerost*?" he specifies with the arch of one finely manicured brow. I can only imagine how long he must spend before a mirror, grooming himself.

I shake my head. "Keep my head low, don't let anyone see me, and stab anyone who tries to hurt me. I get it."

"I never said to stab—"

"Bastian." I press my hands to the deck and lean toward him. "I'm kidding. I can handle myself. But we have several days until we'll reach Kerost. This is the perfect time to teach me to sail."

He doesn't move, only stares back at me, expressionless. "You know *Keel Haul* is partially run on magic. She doesn't require much maneuvering."

"But you'd know how to sail her even if her magic broke, wouldn't you?" I press, not about to let him back out of our deal.

His nose scrunches distastefully, but he relents. "Fine, but no sailing, yet. First, let's get you more familiar with the ship. You can climb the rigging."

My blood's like harsh ocean waves as it pounds its excitement in my ears.

"You're fine here?" I ask Ferrick, who mumbles something

incoherent and waves me away to follow Bastian toward *Keel Haul*'s rigging. Though the ropes sway on the breeze, they seem stable. If I don't lose my footing, I should be fine.

"Have you ever climbed before?" Bastian squints from the bright sunlight. The winds carry the sharp coolness of the water, but the sky is bright and my body is warm from the morning rays. There's no better type of day to be on the sea, and certainly no better day to practice scaling the rigging of a ship.

I wipe my palms on my pants. "Never. My father would sooner die than allow that. He thinks ships are too dangerous for me." I snort, recalling the eighteen years of work it took before he even let me touch the helm.

Just thinking about him makes my throat thick with emotion. If only he could see me now.

"There's nothing to catch you if you fall," Bastian says. "You should be fine, just be careful. It's your first time, so go slow. There's no one to impress."

I scan the space above, searching for any potential mishaps. But *Keel Haul* keeps steady and the rigging is stable to my touch. It's practically inviting me.

I grind my feet into my boots, ensuring a snug fit as I wind my fingers around the ropes. I barely lift one foot before I look down. My racing heart's a trickster, telling me I'm already high up on the rigging. In reality, it'd only take a single step to hop down.

Ferrick watches cautiously from the deck, his eyes narrowed and anxious.

"You sure you want to do this?" Bastian's words lighten with amusement as he pulls himself onto the rigging beside me, sporting a silly grin. It makes me want to push him off the ropes as much as it makes my stomach flutter in a way I'd rather not think about. A pirate has no right to look so handsome.

I peer up once more, skin hot with nerves, and tentatively grab on to another groove in the rope. I try to tell myself that my body was built for this. That the lean muscles that thicken my arms and curve my thighs—built from years spent with Casem and his father, training with blades—were made for this moment. They won't let me fall.

The rigging sways beneath me as I draw it toward my chest and ease onto the next step, one at a time. Bastian's beside me, slow and patient as I cautiously ascend *Keel Haul*. We're halfway up when my foot misses its mark and I falter, digging my hands into the rope and gasping for breath as I hang there.

Bastian has his body protectively around mine within a second. His warm chest presses against my back, steadying me, then he slowly eases his foot beneath mine and guides it back into position. My face goes hot as his hand sets on my hip, making sure I've caught my balance.

"Relax." His words are a mere whisper; they buzz pleasantly against my neck as the wind knocks wispy curls into my eyes. "We're climbing up the windward shroud, the weather is mild, and you have a handsome and experienced pirate to look out for you. You can do this."

My eyes shut as I summon the courage to keep climbing.

Step by step, not looking down or any farther up than I need to, we continue our climb.

My hands are raw from the ragged ropes. Forming a fist around them hurts, but mentally every step becomes easier than the last. I hardly notice when Bastian stops. His eyes rest on mine, gleaming wickedly against the sunlight. He wraps one arm through the ropes, then flips himself to face the sea. He winds his other arm similarly, protecting himself from falling, and winks.

"You want to see Visidia, don't you? Take a look at your kingdom."

Sweat beads on my forehead. I can't will my limbs to move.

Bastian's words are gentle when he speaks again. "It's worth it. Trust me. Just wrap your right arm in the rope and turn."

Easier said than done. My heart beats so fiercely I fear it will break my ribs. There's only one way to settle it.

I don't look as I wind my arm through the rope, as I watched Bastian do. It holds my weight easily, and though I know it won't drop me, it's another moment before I'm able to release my free hand, trust the ship, and spin my body around.

When I open my eyes, I'm not sure I've ever seen anything so beautiful.

"Amora! Are you all right?" Ferrick calls from below.

I laugh.

I'm fine.

Perfect.

The ocean below twinkles as if dusted with millions of crystal shards. Bastian and I are side by side with the seagulls, so close I could reach out and snatch a fish from one of their beaks. They squawk at us, either welcoming us or offended by our presence. A laugh rattles me when Bastian squawks right back at them.

By Cato's blood, this must be what it feels like to be free. I never realized how nice it would be.

I turn toward the pirate. His eyes are mirrors of the twinkling ocean as he stares far into the horizon. His chest is still and his breathing easy, relaxed.

I understand why he's made the ocean his home. It's marvelous and uninhibited. Tangled in the ship's rigging and overlooking the sea like its figurehead, a small part of me can't help but wonder what it must be like to live like this. To go wherever you wish, day after day.

"Look," the pirate whispers. I don't understand his quietness until I see where he nods.

Dolphins. There's an entire pod of them below the surface,

painting the water as pink as their skin. One pops up, then another, as my heart swells. It's like we're on top of the world.

"Beautiful." Bastian's face has gone soft and gentle. He doesn't look anything like one of the dangerous, pillaging pirates I've heard stories of. "It's beautiful, isn't it?"

"It's the most amazing thing I've ever seen," I admit. "You're lucky. You get to see things like this every day."

His smile softens and his gaze grows distant, as if he's seeing something an ocean away. Dolphins dip and bob in the water. They shrill happily, flocking around *Keel Haul* like it's their plaything.

Bastian leans back. He's turned the ropes into part of his body, trusting them fully as he reclines. "How long have you wanted to travel?" he asks quietly. When I turn to question him, he only laughs. "I can see it in your eyes. A kingdom is too small for you, Princess. You should be ruler of the entire sea. Not everyone adapts to life on water as quickly as you have. I mean . . ." He nods down to Ferrick, who sits on the deck squinting up at us.

I can't deny it. "Ever since I was a child. When I was ten, I wanted to sail to Valuka to hunt down the fire serpent that's said to live in their volcanoes. I tried to form my own crew, but no one would spare me a second glance."

"I'm not sure how I would feel about a child as my captain, either," Bastian says with a laugh.

I shake my head at him. "It was never about my age. My parents were only able to have one child, who would be one of only two heirs to the throne. My father has always been protective. He commanded that I stay on Arida, and no one was ever willing to go against him. I tried to stow away a few times after that, but I was always caught. Now they do a full sweep of every ship before they leave the docks." Though I laugh softly at that last fact, it's more to cover the discomfort of the memories. They're not my fondest ones.

"My father's always had a thousand tales of his adventures," I continue. "There were stories of how he scaled the mountains of Valuka on the back of a wild kelpie, and of the night he had too much wine in Curmana before he went deep-sea fishing and reeled in one head of a hydra."

Despite how much the memories make me ache, recalling those stories also makes me smile. When I was a child, I loved listening to them every night before bed. But as I grew older, that stopped being enough. I no longer wanted to listen to them; I wanted to live them.

I've always wanted to travel through Visidia with Father. Together, I dreamed that we might one day face the Lusca, or possibly even team up to find that fire serpent.

But now, I wonder if those dreams can ever be our reality.

"He never brought you along?" Bastian asks. "Not even once?"

The words spur a strange discomfort within me. The expression on Bastian's face is enough for me to know he's looking for more of an answer than what he's asking for.

"Never. It was always one excuse after the other with him."

"And you never stopped to think that maybe there was more to it?" He lifts his chin sharply. "That he could be hiding something? I can understand not letting you go on your own, but it seems odd to me that he wouldn't even take you with him."

I turn to look west, toward Kerost, and think back to the necklace buried beneath a protective stocking in my boot—magic from an allegedly banished kingdom, that had somehow found its way onto Mornute. The threat of a Zudian named Kaven, who is forming a rebellion against Visidia for a goal that could end in the kingdom's ruin—the ability to learn multiple magics. The very same goal that nearly destroyed the kingdom in the past, and that I've been fighting so hard to protect.

Only days ago, I was to claim my title as heir to the throne, and yet I knew none of this. There must be more to it that I'm not seeing. Father wouldn't keep something this important hidden from me . . . would he?

I shut my eyes against the sea, letting the wind press me back against the rigging. It's a long moment of silence before my skin itches, and I peek one eye open to see Bastian watching me. His eyes are narrowed, lips turned down in a frown that matches the lines of his forehead.

"Why not run away?" he asks, so quietly that I almost believe I'm hearing things. "One mistake, and your people turned on you. Your *parents* turned on you. So why protect any of them? You clearly love sailing, so why not find yourself a crew, and save yourself?"

The thought hadn't even occurred to me.

"From the moment I was old enough to recognize what I was, I knew I was made to one day lead Visidia." I look out at the waters of my kingdom, feeling the truth of those words in my bones. "I know I've still so much to learn, but I love my kingdom more than I will ever love anything else, myself included. I want to make Visidia as strong as possible, and ensure my people are safe and happy. My blood and my heart belong to Visidia, and they always will."

It's a long moment before Bastian twists himself in the ropes, flipping his body back around. His smile is nothing like the cocky one he usually sports. It's soft. Gentle. A little sad.

"Let's keep going, then," he says. "I've a mast to teach you about."

My stomach flutters as I grip the ropes with one hand and match his movements. It's easier, this time. *Keel Haul* yields to me as I follow Bastian with an ease I never knew I could manage.

I'm no longer afraid.

CHAPTER FIFTEEN

The remains of tattered wood buildings shudder in the sharp wind, threatening to crumble should the wrong breeze strike.

The air is brisk and heavy from the rain that threatens Kerost's gray skies. I pull a ruby cloak around me like armor, disguised beneath the full hood. It hides my curves while I tuck my hair away for good measure.

Bastian's shoulders twitch as we claw our way up the bleak shore. Damp pebbles grip my boots, fighting to pull them down as I struggle with my steps. I have to be careful. Beneath my stockings, buried at the toe of my left boot, the enchanted necklace I stole from Mornute waits to be used, should I need it. I curl my toes around the chain, ensuring it's there.

Unlike in Mornute, the streets of west Kerost don't bustle. There are no merchants; no laughing in the desolate streets.

There's only hammering.

A small group is dispersed across uneven gray and black cobblestone. They threaten us with dangerous glares, wiping sweat from their foreheads and chests before returning to their work.

Men, women, and children alike bend over uprooted buildings and structures, some of them hammering at planks of wood while others pass out the mass of supplies around them. Their faces are worn and their lips press into flat lines. They work in silence, and they work *fast*. Impossibly fast, a whirlwind of flying hands and hammers.

It's time magic; I never imagined seeing it used by so many would look this strange. Though they don't have the power to alter time itself, they can either speed or slow their movements down, influencing how bodies interact within it. Those before me warp time to hasten their movements, hands moving in a blur that's nearly impossible to follow as they work quicker than any human can sustain.

I can only imagine how taxing it is on their bodies.

This is not the simple fix I'd hoped for. This island is on the verge of collapsing. All of Visidia should be here helping, not wasting their money on silly water sports or lavish birthday celebrations. Valukans with an affinity to earth should be here repaving and cleaning up the destroyed buildings. They should be erecting new buildings while Curmanans with levitation clear rubble. Stars, we could even get those from Mornute to help them design once the rebuilding was done. And yet there's no one here but the Kers. The Valukan aides who can manipulate water never should have been taken from this place—it's fallen to ruin.

Father could have given an order to clean this island up within days. So why didn't he? The Kers seemed to have supplies for rebuilding, but is that truly all he offered?

"This is a full season after the storm." Bastian weaves

through the streets with feigned confidence. "It hit the island early spring." He wears a cloak as well, as do the majority of the villagers. Ours are nothing glamorous, but with theirs torn and faded gray from soot and overuse, we look entirely out of place.

I keep my ruby cloak snug against me and close the space between myself and the Kers hard at work.

Bastian hisses a breath. "What are you doing? I doubt we'll find a mermaid *here*, we need to keep moving."

I ignore him and crouch between a child no older than eight and a woman too old to be his mother, and reach out my palm for his hammer. "You should take a break. Let me help."

The child peers up with cheeks full of dirty smudges, scrutinizing first my face, then my new clothes. My gut sinks at the way he eyes them with desire.

The woman is the one who gestures for him to hand over a hammer, her hands twitching in and out of vision. Her face flickers too, moving so quickly it's as if she's snapping in and out of time.

"It's not every day we see a new face around these parts." Her voice is like sliding gravel, coarse and grating. "A couple of storms, and suddenly people no longer believe you're worth their time."

Leaning over, the hood of my cloak looms over me, obscuring my vision. Somewhere behind me, Bastian groans as I push it back.

"Did you get these supplies from King Audric?" I ask.

Her hands slow as time adjusts around her, back to what I can keep up with. Her eyes are a bitter green that lift to inspect me before she barks a harsh laugh. "We have no king. Blarthe gives us these supplies."

The hammer in my hand is so heavy I barely have the sense to lift it. My chest is tight, constricted, but I don't look back at the others even as they loom behind me.

"They're not from Kaven, then?" Ferrick keeps his voice quiet as he peers around at all the workers. Too many of them are children.

The woman's jaw works as though she's clenching something between her teeth. "Better not to speak that name around here. You never know who might be listening."

"Then what about Blarthe?" Bastian presses. He crouches next to the woman, whose face is stern as she shoves a hammer hard into his chest. He grunts, and the young boy sniggers quietly. His hands have slowed to a stop, and sweat coats his peeling, sunburnt forehead.

"Why are your hands empty?" the woman huffs. "They look plenty capable to me. Perhaps if you use them, I might feel more inclined to answer your questions."

Bastian scowls but drops to his knees all the same, and Ferrick eventually follows.

This woman and child are not the only ones interested in us. We've earned the attention of all those working to restore this building—a small shop, by the look of it. I grip the hammer, the anger between their brows and the tightness of their lips all the encouragement I need. Against Bastian's advice, I shed my cloak and dig my knees into the ground for support.

I may not have the speed of the Kers, but angry determination constricts my throat and weighs my hands every time I pound the wooden planks, over and over again, until my skin is slick with sweat and my breath comes in pants.

Each strike of the hammer echoes my shame and anger. This is worse than anything I imagined. How could Father let this happen? Our people should be *here*, not dancing beneath torchlight and drums, or trading pearls for overpriced snapper as part of our kingdom suffers. How could he not even send them supplies?

Though the young boy doesn't complain, his face is tight with pain as he hammers. His hands are chapped, the angry red flesh raised. I spy Ferrick watching him work.

"Hey," Ferrick says gently, drawing the boy's attention. "What's your name?"

The boy hesitates, turning to seek permission from the woman who appears to be looking over him. When she says nothing, he turns back to Ferrick and says, "My name's Armin."

"Those hands look like they could use a break, Armin." Ferrick shifts so that he's closer to the boy, crouching before him. "Why don't you let me help heal them for you? It'll only take a minute."

Again, Armin looks toward the woman. Her small nod is enough for him to drop his hammer and shove his hands into Ferrick's chest with a grin.

Armin scrunches his nose as Ferrick works, making a face through the strange feelings that come with healing—always a quick flare of pain, and then an almost unsettling warmth.

Ferrick tries not to let on how exhausting his work is, but it's in the tension between his brows and the tight line of his lips. It's in the stiffness of his hands, which cast a faint orange glow onto the boy's skin as he mends Armin's hands.

"This is amazing!" The boy stares at his hands in awe when Ferrick falls back and wipes the sweat from his forehead. They look like the hands of a child—soft and no longer cracked or peeling.

People begin to cast looks at Ferrick and Armin from over their shoulders as they work, their interests piqued.

"I'm glad it feels better." Ferrick smiles as he turns to the woman next to Armin. He extends a hand. "I can help yours, too," he offers, but she bats his hand away with a huff.

"I'm in pain for a reason," she grumbles. "And I always

want to remember what that reason is. Help them, instead."
She points behind Ferrick, to a small group of people who have
congregated.

"I have this catch in my shoulder," one says at the same
time another asks if he can get any relief for his aching neck.

Ferrick's mouth slackens as he stares up at the hopeful
faces. But he doesn't hesitate. He ushers everyone to form a
line and pats the ground in front of him. The first Ker sits and
offers Ferrick his left ankle, and the healer promptly gets to
work.

My attention is drawn away only when the woman beside
us presses a hand against my back, and my body lurches. I don't
realize how quickly I've begun to move until my hands become
a blur. Though the rest of the world is the same, I'm faster than
ever, sped up so fiercely that my breaths come in sharp gasps
as I try to adjust. The wall I work on goes up quickly, nail after
nail, panel after panel, but with so few of us, it still takes too
much time.

Bastian works silently beside me, hammering, lifting,
grunting, with movements almost too quick to make out. I've
no idea how long we've been going, but none of us try to stop
the other. We work in a wordless understanding that, for now,
this is the least we can do.

After everyone's healed and the shop we've been hammering away at stands proud, the woman whisks sweat from her
brow and leans back to take in a series of long, tired breaths. I
try not to look at her, so wrinkled and aged beyond her years.
She presses a hand to my shoulders again, and it's as though
all my energy is sapped out of me.

I gasp, choking for the breath that tries to escape, and
drop my hammer to the dirt as my hands slow. While working,
I hadn't noticed this tiredness; it catches up to me at once,
nearly knocking me back. My hands are stiff and calloused, as

though I've spent a full week working. I press my palms to the ground, trying to steady myself as time catches back up to me.

This magic is a strange, dangerous thing.

"You've the same hardness to your face as your father." Her voice is cool as the breeze when she speaks.

I whip my head up to look as strands of her red hair pale into a stark white. Her voice is quiet enough that, at first, I believe I'm hearing things. She keeps her attention ahead and on her work.

"Except your eyes are different. His tell lies with their smile, bright enough to make you believe them. But you?" Those bitter green eyes flick to me for the briefest moment before her hands start up again, hammering away. "You glare. Like something's wrong, and you're the only one who can fix it."

My tongue is dry and my mind numb. I'm not certain if her words are praise or further condemnation, but the woman doesn't clarify. She simply finds another plank of wood and gets back to work while others set bricks around the structure. Shakily I pick my hammer back up and do the same, slower this time. The woman watches me from the corner of her eye.

"Kaven showed up after the storm," she says after a moment, chilling my blood so fiercely my wrist seizes before its next strike. "After your father took away the Valukans who'd been helping us tame the tides. We needed the help; we wanted safety and comfort for our families. Kaven preyed on that. He offered us a chance to help him end the king, so that we could learn to protect ourselves and our home with Valukan magic. Many accepted his offer, for they had no better choice. But you won't find those people here. Kaven's set them up in Enuda, on the southern edge of the island, and no one who's gone has made it back." She turns her face away, voice dropping. She doesn't need to say what she's thinking aloud; we all know the danger of multiple magics. How they consume you slowly, and then all at once.

"Blarthe rolled in after Kaven to prey on the stragglers, bringing three ships stocked with food and supplies," she continues after a moment. "He's in charge, now."

My hands shake so fiercely I have to squeeze them tight to grip the hammer and strike again. "Why didn't you take his offer?" I ask, because it's the last bit of hope I have. If all these people refused Kaven because they still believe in Visidia—and in the Montara monarchy—then there's time to turn this around.

The woman grinds her teeth together as though I've slapped her. "No one's going to take me from my home." Each word is fierce as a cannon strike. "Blarthe is no saint. Some might say he's even a worse option. But for those of us who want to remain living in the place we call home, he's our only choice. So thank you for your assistance," she whispers eventually, though the words are anything but soft praise. They bite. "But if you truly care to help, then the next time you come here, it better be with an entire fleet. And it better be soon."

I dip my head and lift the hood of my cape back over it so that no one can see how deeply her words sting, or the shame on my face.

Behind me, Ferrick's crowd has dispersed. His skin is ashen and sweat dampens his shirt. But still, he sets a hand on my shoulder, silently offering to heal my hands.

Like the woman, I push him away.

"Let me feel it," I tell him. "I want to remember the reason for this pain, too."

From then on, nothing but hammers sound until daybreak.

———

There are no long goodbyes when we continue our journey hours later. We leave only with leaden, guilty consciences, throbbing hands and shoulders, and instructions on where to find a man named Blarthe—as the one who runs this town, he has the best chance of knowing where we can find a mermaid.

We dodge bent and rotting oak trees as we travel through cracked cobblestone streets, footsteps painfully slow as our work takes its toll. Even the grass here is sad. It's dying in most places, brown and ready to snap.

Here, the people we run into are few and far between. Those we do see pass us, lugging building supplies up the winding streets, to where others hammer away at rapid speed. From what I can see, much of Kerost's landscape is flat. There aren't mountains so much as there are hills with yellowing, overwatered grass. More Kers climb those mountains, building homes on the highest peaks—but they're not high enough to hide from hungry tides.

This island is fragile, leeching onto life. Its pulses of willful survival strike my core like a heartbeat.

This isn't the kingdom I imagined ruling, and I'm sharply, painfully aware that my father's choice is the reason why. No birds roam the sky and the air is quiet even of insects. The land is gray and covered in upturned rocks and dark soot. My hands throb again, confirming Kerost needs more than a handful of people with time magic to help restore the island. They need the backing of our kingdom.

We take another series of turns before arriving at a small cluster of buildings, all of which are built from dull gray pebble stones. Some are chipped and punctured with empty holes.

Voices filter from behind one stone slab door, beneath a deceptively elegant sign that says VICE. I immediately adjust my cloak around me, skin crawling from nerves I can't quite explain. There's something off about this place.

Ferrick squints at the sign. "Even if he does know where

we could find a mermaid, how do you intend to get him to tell you?"

Bastian pats the side of his cloak and the pouch he stole from Mornute jingles, heavy with coin. "Everyone has a price."

There's a makeshift handle built into the stone slab. Bastian doesn't wait another moment to use it.

I'm nearly knocked back by a pungent odor as warm air greets us. Ferrick chokes on it, but quickly stops himself when Bastian elbows him in the side.

The smell is a mix of vomit, oily bodies, and what seems like iron. I know better, though. I'm familiar enough with the smell to know it's blood. Yet the lustrous panels of dark wood are spotless.

I peer up enough to see the store itself doesn't quite match its nauseating stench. The walls are painted a handsome amethyst with thick whorls of silver and gold that swoop from the crystal chandelier on the ceiling and thin as they near the floor. There's a bar in the corner constructed from ivory—sleek, polished, and impossibly different from everything outside.

Dozens of Kers sit on heavy bar stools, a giant spinning wheel between them. A tiny ball whirls around the middle, floating over a series of squares and numbers as the wheel spins and spins.

"Care to try your hand at a game of roulette?" a raven-haired woman asks Ferrick, her eyes gleaming with mischief. "Just last week, a friend of mine won *five years*. What do you say, handsome? Come give it a try."

The entirety of Ferrick's face floods a deep crimson. Beside him, Bastian scoffs.

"We've no interest in your rigged games," he says. The woman pouts her full pink lips, but I pay little attention.

It's as though I've been struck. My knees buckle as I suck in a sharp breath, eyeing the handful of Kers who sit around the roulette wheel, gambling away not money, but years off their lives. They're time trading—a rare and banned practice where only the most skilled Kers are able to transfer time from one person to another.

And they've no shame in their actions. They do it openly, not trying to hide their crimes.

Kerost truly has been abandoned.

Someone slams into my shoulder, forcing me to bite back bitter words as I stumble. But the man who knocked into me doesn't look back. He drunkenly sways past the wheel and toward the back of the strange store, where another line is forming.

Everything about this place feels wrong. But the longer I'm here, the more the smell of iron fades beneath the sweet scent of warm vanilla and heavy spices of cinnamon and nutmeg. The aroma twists around me, attempting to calm me and mask the stench of blood.

Women in a variety of silks are lined up in the back. Some hold their jaws high with determination while others look shy and bashful. All their eyes, however, are cool and lethal as they slice through the crowd.

A young man stands before them. His hair's blond as sand, and the smoothness of his milky-white skin matches the ensnaring grin he flashes at the crowd. We catch him in the middle of a spiel he speaks fluently, undoubtedly well practiced.

"—so let's forget all our struggles then, shall we? It's worth it, after all! One night, after all our hard work, to finally be treated as a man should!"

There are grunts of agreement from the crowd, full of men who hungrily eye the women before them. My anger swells; it takes everything in me to keep my mouth clamped tight.

I assume this man must be Blarthe, though he seems too young to run this place. He has to be somewhere in his late twenties or early thirties, though it's hard to tell when his skin is spared from even the slightest wrinkle. He's bright where the other men are barely standing, exhaustion weighing them. I highly doubt he's the one who's been doing any of this "hard work."

He waves the first woman over, a Ker with smooth pale skin and spiraling waves of red hair. Though Blarthe opens his mouth to speak, she interrupts him.

"I want five weeks," she says haughtily, earning a roll of the eyes from several of the girls behind her.

Blarthe's grin wavers with annoyance, but he catches himself before it breaks his placid face. "She means two weeks," he offers instead, teeth gleaming.

Someone in the small crowd raises their hand, and the girl steps down to take it with a grin. The man who's bought a night with her gives a wave to the crowd as he and the woman disappear to a private room in the back.

A stunning Ker with russet skin and silky black hair steps forward next, smirking at the hungry crowd she's drawn.

The pattern continues, girl after girl. I search their faces for any sign of discomfort, but the higher the amount of time they earn, the more their eyes glint.

Only when the auction is complete does the crowd disperse. Blarthe grins as he pats the backs of several men, ushering them toward the roulette wheels, or to tables filled with patrons playing cards. His hearty laugh doesn't fit his young face.

Others line up near the entrance opposite us, their faces worn and hands outstretched. When they reach the front of the line, they prick their finger with a pin and press their bleeding thumb against a sheet of paper.

"One week," says a young girl once she's done offering her blood. The worker in charge of the area nods, makes a note, and then hands her several stacks of wood and a bucket of nails and supplies.

When the girl turns back out the door, her face is ashen and eyes hollow.

Only when Blarthe makes his way behind the polished ivory bar do I force my attention away and steel myself. We step forward, taking three seats near the end.

Blarthe's quick to eye us, and roughly slides over three mugs of ale. Some of the amber liquid and its froth spills out over the edge and falls onto my cape.

I bite my tongue. It's going to be next to impossible to get the smell out of the fabric.

"It's not often I get new faces," he muses. "Where are you kids traveling from?" The words are spoken too loudly. Too brightly.

"We're Valukans," I answer, not missing a beat. "We're on our way to Enuda, just passing through." I eye the ale in front of me. It'll be suspicious if I don't drink it, but the smell that wafts from the mug is a peculiar one. It reminds me of a rotten apple—strangely sweet with a foul undercurrent. I take the pint in one hand and slowly lift it to press my lips to the glass. I fake the smallest swig.

When my face lifts, Blarthe's eyes are all over me. There's a scar through his left eyebrow, and another at the side of his lip, but aside from that his skin is flawless. Yet his sharp green eyes are too aged for the rest of his uncomfortably youthful appearance.

Magic pulses within me, warning of danger. I want to latch onto the pulsating, ravenous thrumming in my blood and keep it close. My fingers brush against my satchel, seeking its comfort but finding only nerves in its place.

There are too many people here. So many that, should something go wrong with my magic again, it'd be a bloodbath.

Never before has my magic been a source of anxiety. But for now I have to stuff it back down, nerves prickling at my skin. I only allow myself to reach for the harmless part of my magic—soul reading.

This is the first skill I learned, and by far the easiest. It's gentle and peaceful where the rest of soul magic is vicious, and I don't hesitate to wrap it around me like a second cloak and wait for my and Blarthe's eyes to meet.

His soul is like algae. Slimy and sticky, as if constantly attempting to ensnare others. It's rotted and peeling at the edges, similar to Aran's, the prisoner I executed back in Arida. Though his face is smooth and inviting, I understand within seconds how dangerous and vicious a man he is.

The beast gnaws within me, wanting to devour this soul it senses me considering.

Annoyance stirs in my chest. At the execution, I lost my focus and paid the price. But the journey I'm on is to prove myself as the ruler Visidia deserves. And the queen of a kingdom should not fear her own magic—she should relish it.

So that's exactly what I do. The mistakes I made in the past do not make me weak; instead, I'll use them to become stronger. I'm done being afraid of my own power.

I swathe myself in the full strength of my magic. It flares like fire within my chest, searing my fingertips and easing the tension in my shoulders. I relax into it, because this time, I will not lose control.

Beside me, the boys are tense, but Blarthe's focus eventually drops as he wipes out a crystal mug with a plush amethyst rag. Only when he relaxes does all of Vice seem to take a breath. Several men at the bar had been hanging on to his every word, likely more than just patrons.

Behind us, the ball of a roulette wheel clacks quietly. A woman playing it hisses at her loss.

"Why have you come here?" Though Blarthe keeps his voice low, its sharpness cuts me like a knife.

Bastian leans forward, fingers dancing along the mug but refusing to drink what's inside. There's a sword under his cape, and a dagger plus a satchel full of teeth and bones beneath mine. If we need to use them, the last thing we need is ale clouding our judgment.

"We're looking for a mermaid," Bastian says, wasting no time.

A crooked grin parts Blarthe's lips. He chuckles, too dark and low for his body. "Every man is looking for a mermaid, mate. I don't blame you."

While Ferrick flushes, the comment isn't enough to dissuade Bastian. "Three gold pieces for any information you have." Bastian guides Blarthe's curiosity toward his hand, where he produces a single gold coin from between two of his fingers. He rolls it into his palm, but the shopkeeper's face remains impassive.

"You seek me out, needing my help, and yet you think it wise to insult me?" he asks, harsh eyes slicing into us. I flinch back, nerves feasting on my bones. "I don't barter with something as simple as coin, kid."

"I'm not asking you to hand her to me. I'm only asking for information." Bastian rolls the coin between his fingers and up his sleeve.

"If I told you where a beached mermaid was, it'd be as good as giving her to you," Blarthe says. "And there isn't enough coin in the world to make that a worthwhile trade."

Ferrick begins to push himself from the bar. "Perhaps we should look somewhere else," he suggests, a nervous bite to his words.

Bastian ignores him, tensing his jaw. "How much do you want?"

"I already told you, I don't barter with coin." Blarthe sets down his mug, and the room snaps into silence as several of the patrons cling to his words. "I barter with time. Six years for information about mermaids."

I lean back, noticing those playing roulette have now stilled. At the card tables, all heads turn to face us. It's clear these are no ordinary patrons; they hang on Blarthe's words, waiting for his command.

"Okay, now I *really* think we should go," Ferrick urges under his breath. This time, I agree.

Beads of sweat dot Bastian's brow, but he's yet to reach for his sword. I catch another metallic whiff of blood beneath the false, soft spices, and pray it's not the smell of our future.

The roulette wheels cease their clacking and go silent.

"I'm afraid I've no time to trade," Bastian says, keeping his voice firm. "And it seems as though I've wasted yours."

Blarthe snorts. It's a deep, guttural sound that's strange on his rosy lips. The lips of a man who has stolen his youth. Then his scarred face contorts, and I anticipate the first sign of danger.

"Perhaps you don't have any time," he says, "but the princess might."

I unsheathe my dagger. Magic flares within me, white-hot and ready.

"Stars, Princess," Bastian grumbles under his breath. "Does *everyone* in this blasted kingdom know your face?"

Several patrons rise to their feet as Blarthe chokes on a throaty laugh. From beneath the bar, he draws two wrinkled posters, one with Ferrick's illustrated face and the other with mine. WANTED ALIVE is written in thick letters across the top of each. And though Ferrick gulps, my lips tighten as I look at the image of me—they've drawn me too thin, and my nose too sharp. And I certainly don't scowl as deeply as the depiction staring back at me.

"Arida's High Animancer sent an entire fleet this morning,"

Blarthe says. "They scoured the whole town, looking for a little lost princess and her fiancé. Said they were fugitives. They're probably in Enuda by now." He motions to the several men who surround us. No longer needing to be concealed, I toss back the hood of my cape to look directly into the eyes of the man whose soul my magic craves.

"How much does this say they're offering for information on the princess?" Blarthe peers down at the poster. "Ah, yes. Twenty gold pieces, just for information." His attention turns to the men who now surround him. "Give it a season, and the price will triple. And I'm sure we can find a way for the princess to earn her keep in the meantime."

I spit at Blarthe's feet.

"Run, Amora." Ferrick's hand is on my back. "We'll hold them off."

But I won't flee. Bastian's scanning the room, most likely in search of a clever way out of this mess, and the increasing layer of sweat on his face and neck tells me he's drawn the same conclusion I have. We're going to have to fight.

And if there's one thing I learned in my years of training with Casem and his father, it's to never let your opponent strike first.

I tighten my grip around my dagger's hilt and throw myself onto the counter.

The quiet whooshing of hastily drawn blades rings in my ears, following the clashing of metal as Bastian parries a quick blow. Most patrons bolt at the first sign of violence, leaving only a handful of men inside.

"Anyone who brings me the girl can consider their debt paid!" Blarthe's yell bleeds into the walls and fills the room.

I ram my blade into his shoulder and he snarls. He manages to snag a fistful of my hair and drag me down; if I weren't so vain, I might consider slicing it away. Instead, I dig my fingernails into his forearm hard enough to draw his blood. I free one hand, grip my dagger, then wrench the blade from his shoulder as uncleanly as I can manage. Blood pools through his shirt, and my blade bathes in it.

"Damned whore!" Blarthe lashes out at my face, and I barely dodge the blow. He rears back to kick my stomach so hard that I slam into the stone counter, the breath stolen from my lungs. For a moment, I see stars. Magic is what draws me back into reality, lulling me with sweet promises.

It's as though it whispers to me: *We can get out of here. All we have to do is kill him. Aren't you hungry, Amora?*

And gods, I'm starving.

Ferrick's on the other side of the counter. He leans in and offers me his left hand. Because I don't have time to dig through my satchel to find the bones I need, I wipe my blade on the back of my hand, saving Blarthe's blood, and quickly reach over and slice off two of Ferrick's fingers. He barely winces before I snarl at him to go help Bastian, who's in the middle of sparring with three men at once.

There's a small fire in the back of the shop, and now I have all the supplies I need.

I sheathe my blade and dive over the countertop. Blarthe catches my foot at the last second and yanks me back. My face hits the stone and my mouth fills with blood. I can't choke on it or spit it up; I can't mix my blood with Blarthe's. So instead, I swallow it back down.

Mindful of Ferrick's severed fingers, I grip the opposite edge of the counter and pull myself forward to kick Blarthe's face. My heel catches his nose and I tumble to the floor, stirring up dust around me.

"Whatever you're doing, do you mind doing it a little quicker?" Bastian lifts his sword in front of him in time to knock another one back. One man lies bleeding and choking beside him while Ferrick stands on top of a fallen roulette wheel, dealing with two more. He wields his rapier with skill, though it's nothing compared to the sharp swords and daggers the others use with murderous intent.

One of us will die if I don't move quickly.

I'm faster on my feet than Blarthe, who struggles to pull himself over the counter. Magic rattles my bones and pulses through my veins. It fills every inch of me with shadows that whisper sweet promises, telling me I can do anything I dream.

I wrap the whispers around me and smear the fingers along the drops of Blarthe's blood on my hand. It's not enough blood to kill him, but it's enough to bind his soul to the finger I toss into the flames.

Halfway to me, Blarthe stumbles and roars with pain. He twists and clutches his left hand. One of his fingers has fallen off, the price of my magic's equivalent exchange. It lies on the dirty floor, a pile of scattered cards around it. The blood that spills from the severed limb eases the tension of my magic. Now *that's* enough to kill him, should I have to.

"Call off your men!" I slip a tooth from my satchel and drop to a crouch to wave it over the hungry flames. They singe my fingers, eager for something to devour. "Otherwise I'll destroy that pretty grin of yours."

I imagine the strange sensation he's feeling—a tingling, burning numbness in his mouth. With his blood puddling onto the floor, I can do anything I want to him. If I could just get to it.

What he doesn't know is that I need more blood to kill him, and I won't let on. I hold the control in this fight, and I grin as fear flashes in Blarthe's glare.

"Call off your men," I repeat, enunciating each word.

This time he listens. The clashing steel silences after another sharp smack.

There are too many bodies for Vice to be silent—someone chokes in the corner, spitting up thick wads of crimson blood. One man has just managed to corner Bastian against a broken table, and leans into him with a blade. He looks the most annoyed with the sudden stall.

Bastian pushes the man away with a growl.

"I am Amora Montara, Princess of Visidia and future High Animancer." I ignore a loud hiss from one of the men. "You've harmed me and my men. By law, I can kill every one of you. If you think I'm incapable, I dare you. Try me." I form a fist around the tooth and squeeze it tight. Blarthe winces.

I keep my expression neutral as I stare at the men, one by one, memorizing their faces. The mood in the room shifts as they watch the blood dripping from Blarthe's hand and into thick puddles on the floor. To them, I'm the gatekeeper of their damnation. And though I don't want to hurt these men—most of whom I'm certain have no choice but to work with Blarthe—I need them to believe that.

Neither Bastian nor Ferrick has moved into a safer position. Like the rest of the men, they're struck by surprise. Bastian at least manages to look properly impressed.

"We're looking for a mermaid," I tell the crowd. "And we're not leaving here until we find one."

CHAPTER SIXTEEN

The only mermaid in town is a young woman named Vataea, and when pressed, the men admit Blarthe has imprisoned her. Vice doubles as Blarthe's home, and he's hidden Vataea in one of the back rooms, only to be brought out for "special" occasions.

I grit my teeth firmly, not wanting to imagine what those occasions might be.

I send Ferrick back to get her. There's no way I'm abandoning my position by the hearth, and Bastian is better help with a sword should the men lash out.

"He's taking too long." Bastian moves to stand beside me, dipping his blade into the puddle of Blarthe's blood that covers the scattered playing cards. He then holds his sword out for me, making the blood readily available.

Blarthe's face is flushed an angry red, but he plants his feet into the ground and keeps still. Sweat isn't just a sheen on his face; it drips off him in beads and sours the shop's already dank air. One wrong move and he knows I'll toss this tooth into the fire. I'll do it over and over again, until he can't even think about standing back up.

Ferrick really is taking a while. I sent him back almost fifteen minutes ago.

The shop is eerily silent, so much so I consider sending Bastian to check on him until the air shifts. The men in the shop turn their heads toward the back hall as footsteps approach. I follow their eyes, and while I *see* Ferrick, it's like I can't even look at him. The woman standing beside him demands every ounce of my attention.

She's young in appearance, physically near my age, though something in her golden eyes hints she's much older. Her velvety skin is lightly tanned and brushed with a golden sheen, unblemished by even the tiniest freckle. Her black hair glides to her hips like perfect silk, and while she's thin and delicate-looking, there's a fierceness in her tensed jaw as she approaches. She juts her chin high in defiance, and jerks her body away from Ferrick as he tries to lead her.

This poor girl is dressed in dirty rags that hardly conceal her body. They leave clear the soft skin of her stomach and end just below her hips. I stare at the entirety of her smooth thighs. Like Shanty promised, they're marked with thick flesh-colored scars that run all the way from her inner thighs down to her bare feet.

The mermaid is breathtaking. If Bastian wasn't looking before, he certainly is now. Even Ferrick's cheeks are flushed pink as he walks beside her, forehead pinched like he's trying not to stare.

"What do you want with me?" Her voice is jarringly powerful, though there's enough honey in her words to tell me not all the myths are false. Six words, yet she wields them like a weapon; it's said a mermaid can sing one sweet song to lure sailors into the sea, and another to summon the ocean and all its creatures. This girl might not look it, but she's dangerous. I feel it in my bones.

"If you touch me again," she says, "I will tear the hands from your body and rip your throat out with only my *teeth*."

Bastian goes to speak, but I stop him. I imagine Vataea has had enough of men for a lifetime.

"We want to get you out of here," I say.

Her steely eyes—previously glued to Blarthe—whip toward me. There are heavy, tired shadows beneath them. She's smart enough to piece the puzzle together, probably because of his sweaty skin and the blood crusting around his lips. Though she smiles thinly, her words are cold. "And take me where? To another island, only for me to be imprisoned and used again?"

"We don't intend to kidnap you." I make sure to hold her stare, though the way she watches me is like a constant challenge. My lips dry, unsettled. "We need your help."

Vataea's head falls back, and she laughs. It's a delicious sound, sweeter than honey cake. It sends a warmth through my body that spreads through my cheeks and settles into my belly.

"My *help*?" she echoes. "I've never heard it called that before."

I open my mouth, but Bastian pushes forward. "We need to borrow your magic. I have a ship. In exchange for your assistance, we'll get you out of here and will release you once your help is no longer needed."

"So you want to take me and use my powers?" Again, she smiles, thin and lethal. "How does that make you any different than Blarthe?"

She has no reason to trust us, and I don't blame her. Whatever Vataea's been through has made her cold and harsh. And yet I can see the smallest shimmer of hope light her face. She *wants* this to be a better option, and to get as far from Kerost as possible.

Her question causes Bastian to falter, but I want Vataea to trust us. "You'll be well compensated for your time. Lend us your magic—and nothing more—for no longer than half a season. After that, we'll drop you off wherever you wish, and you'll be free to do as you please. As the Princess of Visidia, I give you my word."

She leans back, assessing me. "You're the daughter of the High Animancer?"

"I am."

Blarthe responds before she does. "The mermaid belongs to me." His once crisp voice goes hoarse, thick with rage and bile. "You want her, you buy her."

I reach into my satchel to retrieve a handful of bones and skim them along the blood that sits on the tip of Bastian's sword. I smile back at Blarthe. "And you belong to me. Consider yourself lucky if the only payment you receive is a spared life."

Blarthe's damp skin turns ruddier by the moment, fists clenching at his sides as he looks between me and the mermaid. Wrinkles begin to wither the smooth skin of his forehead while the surrounding men look on, no doubt wondering whether there will be another fight.

Bastian readies his sword while I lean closer to the fire, holding two bloodied finger bones.

Blarthe looks away, shoulders sagging with defeat.

Vataea's grin could only be wider if Blarthe was on the floor struggling for his last breath—or maybe if this entire town was burning to the ground. I've no idea what she's gone through, but my imagination tells me she has every right to want this man dead. I motion for Ferrick to bring her closer and she comes willingly.

She's taller than I am by an inch or two, and I can practically feel the challenge roiling off her as she approaches.

Up close, Vataea is even more gorgeous. My throat closes and my palms sweat as she sizes me up.

"What do you say?" I have to choke the words out. "Do we have a deal?"

I stretch my hand forward, and the mermaid snatches it up. Her skin is smooth, hands so soft they make mine seem overworked.

"Your father was good to my people. He protected them when I could not," she says. "I will agree to those terms. Half a season." Her words are a song I could listen to all day, yet I force myself to clear my throat and turn my attention back to the situation before me. We got what we came here for, so it's time to get off the island and back to *Keel Haul*. Preferably without dying.

I turn to Blarthe's men. "Walk down the hall and wait there until we say you can move."

The moment I step away from the fire, we'll lose our leverage. Because of this, I have Bastian fetch me a rag from the bar, and douse the material with a bottle of rum. I wrap it around a poker that leans against the hearth, feed it to the flames, and watch my torch ignite. If they come after me, I've the fire I need to not go down without a fight.

I turn to Vataea and the others. "You three, start toward the door. And keep her safe, she doesn't have a weapon." I point to the exit. Both boys stare at me as though I'm a hydra's third head.

"Bastian can take her, and I'll stay with you. We'll go together," Ferrick argues.

He means well, but I fix him with a dangerous look until he caves and starts for the door. Slowly, holding the makeshift torch in front of me, I inch my way after them.

The men behind me stir against the walls, restless. They whisper their plans, and I try not to listen because the last thing I need is fear slowing me down. I take a swig of the rum, but don't swallow.

"Get me back that mermaid, and I'll return all the years you've ever lost," Blarthe tells his men, too loud to ignore. "Don't let them get away!"

The moment I'm at the door, Blarthe and the others lunge. I take a sharp breath through my nose, then spit the rum into the fire of my torch, breathing it like a dragon onto his skin. Around him, the other men stumble back and scatter.

I may not kill Blarthe tonight, but that doesn't mean he shouldn't suffer for his crimes until I return for him.

When his skin chars and distressed screams fill the night, I drop the torch and run.

CHAPTER SEVENTEEN

Pain stabs my calves as my feet slap against the cracking pavement. When my boots catch a stray rock and I roll my ankle, I bite through the searing pain, catch my balance, and push myself at full speed after the other three.

Vataea is surprisingly nimble on her feet. She and Ferrick lead the way through the winding alleys and mud. Bastian's a few steps behind. He keeps looking over his shoulder at me, then past me. His grimace is enough to tell me I need to run faster.

Bastian reaches his hand back and I lurch forward to take it. He yanks me beside him with a grunt. The pain in my ankle swells deeper. Every step feels like a thousand needles stabbing into my flesh, but the bruises along Vataea's back and the rags she wears assure me there's no option but to run.

Bastian must sense something's wrong because his grip

tightens on my hand. "Don't worry, I won't let them touch you."

I believe him. There's something in his voice that fills the words with truth. Something in the way his touch sends shock waves through my body. I wrap my fingers tight around his hand and keep running.

Something *swooshes* through the air and nicks my ear. I gasp, the pain hot and searing. Three men close in behind us.

One of them sneers, chucking another rock toward me. I duck just in time, but the next one hits Bastian on the shoulder. His muscles seize and he grunts, but there's nothing we can do. If we turn and fight, more men will join these three within minutes.

The ground softens beneath my feet as we reach the wet pebble shore, each step more slippery and more painful than the last. The stench of brine and seaweed fills the moist air.

Ferrick is already helping Vataea onto a dinghy. She looks back at us with a grimace and yells something indecipherable at Ferrick, pointing to the ties securing our boat to the land. He undoes them but stands with one foot on the pebbles and the other in the boat, holding it in place.

Bastian shoves me forward and I nearly fall face-first into Ferrick, who pulls me onto the dinghy. He gives it a firm kick into the water before falling into place beside me.

Bastian's still running. One stone hits our boat while another smacks him in the head. He sways, and the men behind him draw their swords.

"Bastian, run!" I scream. He pushes forward as best he can. The ocean is to his knees by the time he reaches the dinghy and drags himself onto the cramped space. The dinghy rocks, threatening to tip us over, but I silently beg the ocean for its help.

Just this once, it listens.

Ferrick and I are quick to grab the two oars, but the men have followed us into the water. There's still enough time for them to grab on to the dinghy and yank us back.

I spin to Vataea, who snarls at the approaching men. Her breaths are quick and feral.

"Do something!" I growl, pounding the oar into the water. I use every bit of strength left in me to propel us forward, away from the approaching men. Ferrick does the same, but the water is so shallow it's hard to gain headway. The men lurch forward, trying to grab the edge of the dinghy. "You've a song that can control the sea, don't you? Give us a wave or something!"

She jerks her focus to me, though her eyes slip to the water. They fill with longing as her breaths steady.

She's going to leave us.

I want to reach for the cursed necklace in my boot to use on one of our pursuers, but I can't tear myself away from rowing long enough to grab it. It's useless in this fight.

A thin man with a scar over his eye dives forward and grabs on to the edge. He's got a solid grip, but I whack the oar down on his hand with all my strength. The man draws it back with a hiss of breath.

"Please," I beg Vataea through gritted teeth. "This kingdom needs us so much more than you know. Please, help us."

She squares her shoulders and furrows her brows, never turning away from the ocean. My heart drops when she throws herself over the dinghy.

The moment she hits the water, the sea flashes an iridescent gold. The men following us curse. All but one throw themselves from our boat and bolt to the shore.

I catch a flash of tail fin beneath murky green water as the gold fades. Her fin is a startling rose gold; the tips shimmer bright as jewels, like a shining trinket I'm tempted to reach into the water and take. If not for the need to defend myself from the remaining pursuer, I might have followed after that fin.

"She's leaving?" Ferrick asks breathily. "I thought we had a deal!"

While I fend off the men and their storm of rocks and hungry hands, he's still rowing the other oar with everything in him. The water is less shallow by the second. It's looking like we're about to escape free and clear when the thin man throws himself at us again. I whack his hand once more, but this time he only grunts.

He reaches for my cape, latching onto it and trying to tip us into the water. I grab the dagger at my side, but Bastian has already drawn his blade. Ferrick, sickly and green, digs his oar through the waves and does his best to steady us.

"Get away from this boat now and we'll spare your life," Bastian says. His words slur, and I wonder how hard that stone hit his head.

"Give me the princess and I'll spare yours," the man replies. His eyes light with excitement as he tries to lunge past Bastian. He truly thinks he has us cornered, and he might be right. Bastian's eyes keep crossing. The man reaches for me again and I claw my fingernails into his skin, trying to throw him off balance. We need to get him off the boat. We need—

Someone is singing. It's a language I don't understand, and a voice unlike any I've heard.

Forget honey, this is unparalleled sweetness and silk. Everyone stills, attention shifting to the mermaid who is only a few short feet away. She watches us with golden eyes that rest above the sea. Water clings to her smooth black hair, which floats around her like a dusky halo. Her lips are beneath the surface, but still her precious song calls to us.

Vataea's eyes flicker briefly to my side. A signal. I force myself to break away and look at Ferrick and Bastian. Their faces are slack. They stare unblinking at the mermaid, lost in the trance of her song. Ferrick tries to stand, but I push him back down onto the dinghy's small wooden bench. When Bastian moves to stand as well, I sigh and collapse into his lap while draping my feet over Ferrick's thighs, locking him in place.

The mermaid's spell is working *too* well. It's everything I can do to keep them from chasing after her.

She lifts her lips out of the water. I try not to stare at how soft and full they are as she parts them, singing another verse.

The dinghy rocks as the skinny man throws himself away from the boat and swims toward the mermaid. Both Bastian and Ferrick try to do the same, but I grind my boots into the bench and stiffen my legs to keep Ferrick down. As for Bastian, I pinch his cheeks in my hands, trying to get him to look at me. He struggles, but I don't let him turn away. His breath is warm on my lips. It takes me by surprise, softening my body enough for Bastian to knock me down as he stands. I rush to my feet, swaying the dinghy, and throw myself back on top of him and Ferrick.

"Kiss them," the mermaid whispers, her words wrapping around me. The scrawny man has already reached her. She smiles as she holds his shoulders, body pressed close to his. "This song is one for anyone who can be seduced by a woman's charm. So a kiss from a woman is the quickest way to break the spell. Here, I'll show you." She draws the entranced man forward and presses her lips against his. His fingers dig into her bare shoulders, pulling her against his body. It takes only a second longer before his eyes snap open in realization.

It's already too late.

He tries to scream but the mermaid's fingers sink into his skin as she drags his body beneath the water.

I've heard stories of what mermaids do with those they

entrance. Some say they devour their hearts to prevent themselves from aging. Some say they drag sailors down to their home beneath the water and imprison them. And then there are some who say a mermaid doesn't need a reason to drown anyone. They'll tell you that mermaids do it for fun.

As Vataea disappears, I'm left with two men who are about to throw themselves after the mermaid if I don't do something quickly.

I sigh, staring at Ferrick's lips. I was always going to have to kiss them one day, but the time has come far too soon.

Ferrick doesn't budge as I lean in and press my lips against his. He tastes like the sour ale he sipped on at Vice, lips soft and fuller than I gave him credit for. His hands twitch at my sides and settle on my hips, attempting to draw me in. He pulls my bottom lip between his teeth and bites it gently. It's something that would normally elicit a heat in my belly, but while Ferrick's a fine kisser, I feel nothing.

When I draw back he gasps for a breath, flushed from his forehead to his neck. He looks at me, but the expression is so surprised I'm not sure he recognizes what's happening. I shift my attention to the pirate whose lap I'm sitting on.

Bastian's skin is smooth as I cup his face in my palm, trying to draw his attention to me once more. He's eyeing the water with an animalistic hunger that sets nerves crawling along my skin. I try to ignore why this makes me so anxious as I lean in and press my lips to his.

Bastian's quicker to respond than Ferrick. His hand slides from my thigh to my waist, and then to my shoulder. He grips it tightly, crushing me to him. My entire body swells with warmth and I find myself kissing him back with the same urgency. Bastian's other hand rests on my back and beneath my shirt, caressing my skin. His tongue brushes mine, tasting me, and chills pulse through my body like electricity.

This is how a kiss is meant to make me feel.

I have to force myself to pull away, sucking in a breath.

Bastian's eyes are open, staring. His chest moves in quick, heavy breaths. When he realizes where his hands are, he clears his throat and draws them back to his sides. "I'm sorry," he whispers breathlessly. I'm about to tell him it's fine when his eyes move toward the water once more. "I thought you were . . ."

"Vataea," I finish for him. The words hit me like a tidal wave. "You thought I was the mermaid."

He ducks his head and opens his mouth to speak, but I don't let him. I push myself from his lap and grab the oar, thankful for an excuse to look away. Painting a smile onto my lips, I begin to row. "She told me it was the quickest way to break the spell. The only thing you have to be sorry for is being so susceptible to a woman's charm. The same goes for you, Ferrick."

I turn to Ferrick, whose sharp face is turned from me as he rows. His shoulders are slumped as though an anchor is pulling him to the sea. My smile falters.

"The two of you were about to drown yourselves chasing after a mermaid," I tell them, sharper and more defensive than I mean to be. "I had to kiss *both* of you, Ferrick."

He balls his hands into fists and stuffs them against his sides. "Both of us. Right."

I'm spared having to say more by the shifting water on my side of the dinghy. I lean over to spot the mermaid, who peers up at me with large, enchanting golden eyes. Crimson blood stains her lips.

"Did it work?" she asks.

I nearly laugh, but the sound catches in my throat. "It worked."

"Good. Then help me up." She stretches her hand up, and my body tenses as I try not to stare. Somewhere in the ocean she's lost her rags. I hand Bastian my oar and make both him and Ferrick turn away before I pull Vataea into the dinghy and offer her my cloak. The scales of her fin shed away and separate into two bare, scarred legs.

"That," she says, "is the most fun I've had in years."

CHAPTER EIGHTEEN

I've never been happier to see *Keel Haul*. I drag myself aboard and collapse onto the deck. I'm a suffocating fish, wet and quivering as I struggle to regain my breath. Every muscle in my body aches or throbs. My ankle is red and swollen while my biceps and hands burn. I'd ignored the searing pain in my arms to help row the dinghy, but now that I'm safe and aboard, I feel *everything*.

Ferrick is quick to crouch beside me, warm hands wrapping tight around my ankle. I brace myself as the injury flares, just for a second, then fades, leaving my skin warm and tingling.

"Thank you," I tell him, but he turns away without looking me in the eye.

Though Bastian staggers as he walks, he hurries to draw up *Keel Haul*'s anchor and get the ship moving. "While I'm glad we're alive, I'm pretty sure that could have gone a lot smoother." He peels off his coat, grimacing at the splattered blood it's painted with. Some of it's his own, though Ferrick makes no move to heal him. His voice is still a bit thick, but ultimately Bastian appears to be stabilizing.

I clamp my jaw and turn to look at the mermaid, still wrapped tightly in my cape. Her eyes dance with delight as they dart around the ship. She reaches toward a ledge and smiles at the wood beneath her fingertips.

Bastian follows my gaze, and his expression darkens into one I can't decipher. He clears his throat and the mermaid turns to him. Her smile is unwavering.

"Welcome aboard *Keel Haul*," he says. "Would you mind sharing a bit about yourself? Age? Where you're from? Why you didn't change the tides so we could get away from Kerost without having to kill a man?"

"Back off," I growl, dragging myself to sit up. "There's a difference between murdering for fun and protecting yourself or others, and you don't get to talk to her like that. The only reason we got off that beach alive is because of her."

Bastian's lips press together in a grimace. It's clear he's still angry as he pushes up his sleeves and jerks the sails free from their binds, letting the wind bloat them. In his gut, however, I hope he knows he's wrong. I don't want to be thought of as a soulless killer, and I doubt Vataea does either, despite her words when she got out of the water. The mermaid wraps my cape around herself tightly, not shrinking back as she stares at Bastian.

"Mermaids are supposed to have an arsenal of songs," Bastian argues. "She could have made the ocean protect us, or altered the tides to move us quicker. Or, I don't know, summoned a giant whale to knock everyone away! The point is that we could have been long gone by now."

"Perhaps you should have used *your* magic," I snort. "Oh, wait, you don't have any."

Vataea breaks her glare only when Ferrick walks out of the

cabin and offers her a small armful of clothing. He's been so quiet I hadn't noticed he left.

Vataea takes the pile with a grateful nod and shimmies into a pair of oversize pants beneath the cape. I make a mental note to gather some of my clothes for her, too. She's taller and slimmer than I am, but they'll fit better.

"The sea is a fickle beast," Vataea announces as she buttons the pants. "Anyone can enchant a man who does not think with his head. Calling upon the sea, however, is a skill that few can master. Besides, I was hungry."

I nearly snort again, but now isn't the time. Bastian slams his fist against the edge of *Keel Haul* and the ship groans in protest. Only then does he look partially apologetic.

"Great," he growls. "We came all this way for a mermaid, just to get one that's defective. We don't have the time for this."

Vataea's eyes narrow to dangerous slits, but she's not the one who acts first. It's Ferrick who steps forward, thrusting an open palm into Bastian's shoulder. The pirate blinks down at where Ferrick hit him. It takes a moment longer for his anger to set in with a sneer.

"What's your problem?"

"What's *your* problem?" Ferrick snarls. "Last I checked, you can't do anything on your own. You're a useless pirate who has to borrow magic because, somehow, you were stupid enough to lose your own."

Bastian's hand flies to the pommel of his sword. "Say that again."

Ferrick laughs. It's a dark sound, unnatural for him. "We're useless without these girls. Vataea's magic *saved* us. You don't get to call her defective after she's been made a prisoner for gods knows how long. Apologize."

Vataea looks at Ferrick as if seeing him for the first time.

I understand, because it's the same for me. I've never seen him so riled up.

Bastian has no immediate response. The tense muscles of his arms flex as he loosens his grip on his pommel but doesn't release it. He won't draw his blade; I can tell by the way he holds himself. Back in Vice he stood like a coiled snake, ready to spring with a moment's notice. Now, his body is awkward, looking for something to do. He opens his mouth to speak, clamps it shut, then furrows his brows and tries again.

"I'm sorry I called you defective." The words are tight in his throat. "I didn't mean it. I'm just stressed; we can't afford to make a mistake right now. We need someone who can sense Zudian magic. If we try to charge ahead only to discover you're unable to do the job we need done, the three of us are as good as dead."

"My connection to the sea may be weak, but that doesn't make *me* weak," Vataea says. For the most part her features are relaxed and unbothered, but I think back to the blood on her lips and wonder how long this girl can hold a grudge. "I'm able to sense your silly curses, pirate. In fact, I can sense one right now." She lifts her chin, and Bastian practically withers beneath her glare. His fists clench tight at his sides.

"There's a curse nearby?" I ask. Vataea dips her attention to me with a vicious grin.

"Yes, but it won't affect us." She turns back to Bastian. "I could have left, you know. I could've kept my fins and continued swimming. But I struck a deal with you, and mermaids are honorable. We pay our debts and keep our deals. That is, unless you no longer want my help?"

Bastian draws in his bottom lip and bites down on it with a sigh.

"Ferrick's right," he admits. "I have no magic, but the three of you do. It was foolish of me to imply that you were somehow weak when you're the one we all need the most. I've no intention of backing out of our deal, Vataea."

I let the apology sit for a moment, digesting it. Vataea needs far less time. Her lips curl into a coy smirk.

"Then I'll stay. Though rest assured, it's not for you." Only when her eyes catch Ferrick's do they brighten. She places a hand on his chest. "Though you don't seem quite so bad. Perhaps you'll be spared."

"What do you mean by that?" Ferrick asks, a tinge of worry in his voice.

"I've a collection of men who I intend to repay for how generous they were to me." Vataea's smile gleams wicked. "Dismemberment for anyone who ever tried to touch me. The tongue flayed from those with wicked mouths. And the hearts eaten from any man who's ever told me to smile."

Ferrick goes deathly still. The only noise on the ship is that of the fluttering sails, and the lapping of the waves that grow fiercer as we shift our direction to the southeast. After what feels like one incredibly long and awkward moment, Ferrick gently takes hold of Vataea's hand and eases it away from him. "I'm flattered, but I'm afraid I'm already spoken for. Or so I thought."

The words grind into me like a rusted knife. That's not fair; I never asked to be engaged to Ferrick.

"It was only a kiss," I say. "The two of you were going to drown if I didn't do something. That was the only way to pull you both from the trance."

"It was the *quickest* way," Vataea corrects me.

"Only a kiss." Ferrick's face twists as he sneers. "Right. When you kissed both of us, it was *only* a kiss. We're engaged, Amora! I didn't ask for this, either. But by the gods, the least you can do is try to act like I don't physically repulse you."

I draw a step back.

"I used to think you were too good for me," Ferrick whispers, shaking his head. "But you're the most naive, materialistic person I've ever known. You think you're so clever. Born to be the greatest animancer there ever was, or whatever. But maybe you're not what the kingdom needs at all, and perhaps you never will be. Get over yourself."

My chest constricts, though I've no idea whether it's from anger or hurt. Who does he think he is? He doesn't know the truth—that I'm the *only* one. That without me convincing my people to grant me another chance, Visidia will eventually fall.

Aunt Kalea can't accept soul magic. It will kill her. And then what? Who else is there to take on the Montara magic, and keep the beast within us at bay? Father won't live forever, and someone needs to be ready to take his place.

"We did what had to be done, end of story." Bastian steps between Ferrick and me. "If you want to throw yourself a pity party, do it somewhere else. We've more important things to take care of."

"No, *you* have more important things to take care of." Ferrick closes the space between himself and the pirate. "The only reason I came here is to help Amora, my *fiancée*. But if you want to take that task over then be my—"

The tension in my chest snaps. I step in front of Ferrick and shove him away from Bastian.

"Enough," I say. My words are fierce, but controlled. "I've had enough. Think whatever you want of me, Ferrick. You're angry because you think I owe you something, but I don't. I've had too many people controlling my life to add someone new to the picture."

I don't stop when his spine straightens and his chin dips, brows furrowing into a glare. Instead, I push forward. "When our parents arranged for us to be married, it wasn't by my choice. You're possessive! You act like you own me, yet we're only connected by politics and magic. And don't forget that

I outrank you, so don't you dare talk to me like I'm some foolish child. Believe me, I know Visidia deserves the best, and I'm trying my hardest to be that for them." I jab my hand into his chest again, and Ferrick stumbles back.

"I'll never love you." The words are harsh, but he needs to hear them. "Not like that. Not in the way you want. Stop acting like this is something that will change, or that I owe you a chance. I owe you nothing."

I don't need words to understand what's in Ferrick's eyes. Anger, hurt, betrayal. It's all there.

"Do you really think I want to spend the rest of my life with someone I know will never love me?" he asks quietly. "I never asked for this; I deserve happiness as much as you do. But this is what's happening, and unlike you, I'm at least trying to make the most of it."

The fluttering of the sails all but stops, betraying me with its silence.

I force myself to look away and try to fend off the guilt that sinks its teeth into me, devouring my pride.

Ferrick brushes past me, heading straight into the cabins.

I storm the opposite direction with a hiss of curses beneath my breath, clenching the starboard ledge. Bastian follows, quietly watching as I try to steady my anger.

No matter how hard I try to push away Ferrick's words, they sink into my gut. *Maybe you're not what the kingdom needs.* But what does he know, anyway? Once we get to Zudoh, I'll stop Kaven and find a way to introduce Zudoh back into the kingdom, and enlist all the islands to help Kerost. Our economy will thrive. More ships will be produced with Zudian wood. More homes. Trade between them and their closest neighboring island will boost Kerost's economy significantly.

I was led here on this journey for a reason, and Ferrick's words won't stop me from believing that.

But even so, knowing what I must do, I can't help but think of the stories whispered at night about Zudoh, or the way we were hushed for even saying the island's name.

"How long has it been since you were in Zudoh, Bastian?" I ask, my voice tightening.

"I've been living on *Keel Haul* since I was ten." He clips his words short and bounces on antsy feet.

"And you've never thought to go back before?"

His eyes are on the sea, knuckles white as he grips the edge of *Keel Haul*. Though there's a slight breeze, the ship moves slowly in the still water, probably as hesitant to move forward with this mission as the rest of us. After a long moment of silence, he pushes away from the ledge and walks past us, stopping only when he's at the stairs that lead down to his quarters.

"It's been a long day, and we're all tired," he murmurs, voice hardly louder than the wind. I want to argue, but the look on his face stops me. I recognize the pain he wears; it's enough to dry my throat into silence. "Try to have a good night." Bastian descends the steps and leaves Vataea and me on deck. When I make no motion to follow, Vataea turns to me, head tilted.

"You said you sensed a curse when you stepped aboard this ship," I whisper. "What exactly were you referring to?"

"I sensed three, actually, if you want to count the one in your boot." She smiles, teeth pearly white. I only notice how sharp they are when they catch the glow of the moon. "But they're nothing to worry about right now." She takes my hand and gently draws me toward the cabins. "Now show me where I'm to sleep, will you?"

She doesn't seem to notice how numb my body is or how quick my breaths come.

Bastian's magic's somehow been cursed away; that one's a given. Then there's the cursed necklace I've stuffed into my boot.

But as I stumble into the cabins behind Vataea, I can't help but wonder—what's the third curse?

CHAPTER NINETEEN

My head hits the pillow, but every time I shut my eyes, I can't help thinking that *Keel Haul* is too still.

She pushes forward with the same anxiousness that eats at my nerves. And if she's afraid of our destination, then perhaps I should be, too. There may be people looking for me on every island, but Zudoh has been banished from Visidia for eleven years, left to wither and rot in its own time. No one will ever think to look there for a lost princess. If something happens to me, my people will never know my fate.

But I have to wonder, did Father truly keep me from these other islands because he worried for my safety? Did he keep me on Arida so I'd have more time to learn how to control my magic, and keep myself out of the very mess I'm now in? Or is it possible that there's more to it?

What could Father be hiding?

I'm tired of scraping for answers. Anxiety crawls at my skin, and the cabin is suddenly small and suffocating. Gods, I need air.

I push myself from the hammock and tug on my boots and cloak before climbing the stairs to the deck. The air's no longer warm with summer heat; there's a bite to it. It's one that sinks into my core and casts shivers down my spine.

One that promises summer won't last much longer, and reminds me of Aunt Kalea and her enchanted eyes. The fate of Visidia depends on these next few days.

We can't stop moving.

The sky is thick with starlight. It blankets the sea and casts a silver glow along the deck of *Keel Haul*, painting the ship bright. The main sail acts as its own moon, full and luminous as it pushes forward into the black sea.

There's a quiet rustle of clothing flapping in the wind, and I turn to find I'm not alone. Vataea sits cross-legged near *Keel Haul*'s barnacle-covered, serpentine figurehead, tempting her fate by how dangerously close she sits to the water. Her body is still as I approach, but I know she's aware of my presence because she doesn't flinch when I take a seat behind her, closer to the railing.

"Do you mind if I join you?"

Vataea shakes her head. "Please do. It's been ages since I've had another woman to talk to."

I cross my legs as well, wishing I were daring enough to move closer to her. She has a perfect view of the water, but one strong wave and she'll be in the sea.

"I've missed the ocean," Vataea offers without prompting. She leans forward and draws a long breath of briny air. "It's good to be back."

I'm not sure what I'm supposed to do. I'm used to giving commands, not support. I know what it's like to have things bottled up inside and feel the need to share them with someone, but I've usually only complained to Mira, or kept problems to myself. It's foreign to be on this side of things. Hesitantly, I set my hand upon Vataea's shoulder and squeeze it gently, just once, as Father does. It's all I know to offer.

"How long were you kept in Kerost?"

Vataea's laugh is as soft as the ship's quietness calls for, but it's spine-chilling. "About two seasons. And before that, a year on Curmana. Blarthe is a traveler; he goes wherever he has the most to gain. For nearly two years he's kept me with him, far from water. He used me as a way to lure customers into whatever temporary shop he opened up. One man even tried to pay for a night with me, once—fifty years. But when I tore out his eyes and bit off his cheek, Blarthe started keeping me tucked away. I was his trophy after that—something to show off when he needed the boost. A prize he felt he'd won by capturing me."

My chest seizes. Two years is a long time to be trapped anywhere—let alone with that monstrous man. I can't begin to imagine the things she must have suffered through. I wonder, what might someone's soul look like after that sort of experience?

Soul reading is the innocent part of my magic, effortless and always eager to be put to use without repercussion. And though me sneaking a peek would go unnoticed by her, the idea of looking into Vataea's soul curdles my stomach. She's only just escaped Blarthe; the least I can do is give her the privacy I doubt she's had in some time.

"Do you intend to return to the sea, then?" I ask, unable to imagine wanting to go anywhere other than home if I were in her position. And yet Vataea shakes her head.

"I've no intention to return there any time soon," she answers. "For centuries my kind have been hunted, and now hardly any of us remain. No matter what we may want for ourselves, there's a pressure to repopulate." Her forehead scrunches ever so slightly as she says this, as if recalling memories.

"I understand the need for children," she admits. "We need to ensure mermaids continue to exist for centuries to come. But that's not the life I want for myself. What I want is to see what it might be like to live on land. Mermaids are able to have legs, so why shouldn't I use them?" Though Vataea playfully wriggles her toes, the small smile on her lips is a sad one.

"After your father passed laws to help protect my kind, there was a push for many of us to go ashore and conceive a child before we returned to the water," she continues. "But when I left, I had no immediate plans to return. I've wanted to see what you humans are like for ages. I want to spend time on your islands, trying your food and seeing everything that land has to offer. I'd like to feel the sun on my skin for more than a few minutes at a time. Explore my new body. I enjoy being with women, but I've also wondered what it might be like to be with a man." She brushes a hand over her thigh, as if still fascinated by the skin there, and then sighs. "Unfortunately, I lasted no more than a week before I was taken, so there's still so much out there for me to see. I'd like to experience it all."

Vataea's spirit is one of adventure. She wants to explore the world. To see all it has to offer her. If there's anything I understand, it's this desire that she and I share.

Shame weighs my shoulders, though she deserves better than me shrinking back from her truth. Was my kingdom truly so damaged that Vataea couldn't travel for longer than a week before being poached? Even despite the laws Father has put in place?

"I'm so sorry you went through this," I tell her. "You should be free to travel wherever you'd like without worry. If you'd like to see more of the kingdom, Bastian and I will get you wherever you want to go once this is all over. I could even escort you back to Arida myself, if you'd like? It's beautiful there—waterfalls, red sand, and almost all the plants glow at night. The gardens there are one of the most beautiful places you'll ever see . . ." My words trail off as my mind starts to linger on Arida and all that's happening back home.

I always wanted to sail, and I love it even more than I thought I would. But gods, I miss my family.

Are my parents worried about me? How is Yuriel dealing with everything? And what do my people think of me now—am I not only a monster to them, but also a traitor for fleeing?

Vataea leans back on her hands, sporting a soft smile. "You're not the first to tell me of its beauty. So long as you can promise that it will come with plenty of royal perks, I suppose I wouldn't mind a trip to Arida. It must be quite the place, if you miss it so much. You'll have to promise to show me around."

"I'd be happy to," I tell her, trying to ignore the weight of her words as they fight to burrow into my skin. All my life I've wanted to journey from Arida. And as much as I love the ocean, I can't help but miss my parents. My home. Gods, even my bed.

"Arida is an amazing place," I admit, swallowing down my longing. "But I can't go back there, yet. Kaven isn't the only threat to Visidia. If I can't figure out a way to earn back the trust of my people, Visidia will be in danger."

"So you made a deal with a pirate for help?" she snorts. "He might be charming, but you don't strike me as someone so easily lured."

"He was the best option I had," I argue, quietly, "Do you really think Bastian's charming?"

"Of course he is!" Vataea's laugh throws me off guard. I sink into the sound, chest warming. I can't remember the last time I was able to just sit and chat with another girl. Growing up in Arida, my closest friends were Casem and Mira. While I care deeply for them both, the fact that everyone who lives on that island is employed by my family isn't lost on me.

I never knew how much I wanted this—how much I was missing it—until now.

"You must think he's charming as well," Vataea teases. "Otherwise you would have drowned the poor boy."

I've no control over the strange face I make at her. "What are you talking about?"

"You think a mermaid's enchantment can really be broken so easily?" Vataea angles herself toward me, laughing. "The kiss only works if the enchanted one has romantic feelings toward the person who kisses them. I figured you'd snap one of them out of it if you were lucky. You are far luckier than I thought."

I lean back on my hands. After our kiss, Bastian said he'd been thinking of Vataea, not me. But I broke his enchantment all the same.

The pirate is a dirty liar.

"It was a gamble," I say. "You expected one of them to follow you."

Though Vataea presses her lips together, the expression she wears is smug. I was right to think she's dangerous.

"I would've brought him back to the boat once I was finished," she says coyly. "Or tried to. Call it a calculated risk." She's as confident in her actions as I am lucky.

It's so easy to like Vataea, but if legends are true, she's the most dangerous one on this ship. I'll have to remember this the next time I decide to blindly follow her instructions.

"I want you to know that I truly appreciate you helping us," I tell her, because I see the longing in her as she stares out at the sea, raw and palpable. Vataea doesn't need a ship to travel; she could swim to any of the islands in half the time it would take *Keel Haul*. And yet here she remains, agreeing to help the same people who have destroyed her home and family. "I'll pay you however much you need for your travels, of course, but know that we would have helped free you from Blarthe regardless of your decision to help us."

A thin smile crosses her lips. "My kind have been hunted since long before I was born. My mother was killed by poachers, and many of my sisters suffered a similar fate, stolen for our scales or for our bodies. This is no new problem, but your father was the first to recognize us as members of Visidia. He gave us his protection when no one else seemed to care." She brushes her fingers along one of the figurehead's barnacles, chest heaving with a sigh. "It's not about the money; you are his daughter, and you need help only I can provide. I know what that's like. A mermaid remembers those she's indebted to, and she always repays."

My chest warms, disregarding the cool air on my skin. I'm glad to know that, at the very least, Father has done well by these people. That there's at least one person who still loves their king.

"That said," Vataea continues, her lips stretching into a wicked grin, "I'll certainly be taking the money. I've places to go and plenty of food to try, after all."

I laugh, about to ask more about her home and the place she most wants to visit when a squelching noise pierces the silence and something in the water causes the ship to jerk violently to the side. I grab on to the rail to steady myself, but Vataea has nothing but the figurehead to cling to. She gasps, trying to dig her nails into the rough barnacles as the ship rocks again. *Keel Haul* groans through its masts as it fights against a sea that was perfectly fine only moments before.

One look at the horizon shows the waters are tame everywhere but beneath *Keel Haul*. The noise grows louder; it's like the base of a waterfall, vicious and thrashing. But there's no waterfall in sight.

"Hang on!" I yell as Vataea grips the figurehead as tightly

as possible, struggling not to slip. I stretch over the bow, reaching until my arms ache, but there's too much space between us. Without risking a fall, I can't grab her.

But I do see the source of the noise. Directly below, a whirlpool eats away at *Keel Haul*, hungrily chomping into the wood and attempting to devour it whole. It rattles the entire ship as *Keel Haul* tries to fight its way free, knocking Vataea further off balance. Water splashes onto the deck and her fingers glisten with dampness, more slippery by the second.

A door slams behind me and I look to see Ferrick hurrying out, wide-eyed and searching. When he spots me at the bow, he rushes forward, likely ready to drag me away until he spots Vataea struggling to hang on.

"Get back!" He nudges me aside and leans his longer body over the ledge, but it's no use. Vataea's hold slips as *Keel Haul* teeters and thrashes in the water. I lunge for her again, but her fingers brush through mine as her head smacks against the figurehead. I feel her phantom touch on my skin as her body hits the waves with a splash that sounds as terrible as the screeching behind us.

I stumble back, shaking, to find Bastian frozen behind me. There's another screech—more like a garbled wail—and I follow his terrified stare.

I will my heart to stop. If it stops now, then I won't have to know what happens next.

I thought Zudoh would be the scariest part of my travels, but I was wrong.

The Lusca is far, far worse.

CHAPTER TWENTY

The beast that bursts from the water is the color of ink and moonlight. The stars catch its scales, turning them silver as it roars. I double over, covering my ears from the shriek of what sounds like metal grating against metal. Even in the worst of my nightmares, I'd never be able to imagine such a wretched sound.

The Lusca. The legends of this beast have traveled through word of mouth, told to scare disobedient children. But no one has ever been able to prove its existence.

Probably because no one has survived to tell the tale.

The creature has eight inky tentacles with sharp, jagged hooks. Its body is that of a leech, giant and round, with a permanently open mouth it whines from. Several rows of bloodstained teeth fill that mouth, with bits of fish and squid dangling from them. I imagine our bodies will be the ones dangling there, soon.

"Where are the others?" Bastian gasps. The question hitches in his throat.

"Vataea fell into the water." My voice shakes as I remember the horrible crack of her head hitting the figurehead. But given her gills, it's not her drowning that I'm worried about. "We need to get her out of there before the Lusca sees her! Ferrick and I tried to—" I make a motion toward Ferrick, but he's no longer in my periphery. My heartbeat triples as I spin around, but he's gone. Only when I lean over the bow do I spot his red hair in the sea below as he struggles to break out of the shrinking whirlpool.

"You idiot," I hiss at the water.

Bastian presses a hand to his chest as he watches the beast. He's shaky, body swaying as *Keel Haul* makes a final push to break from the water imprisoning her. Only when she steadies does Bastian suck in a relieved breath and draw his sword. It looks useless against this giant beast. Laughable.

"You want to *fight* it?"

"What else are we supposed to do?" he rasps. "*Keel Haul's* fast, but there's no way we're going to outrun this . . . thing."

"The Lusca," I say. I know in my bones this is the creature of the legends.

Bastian's face hardens, but he doesn't disagree. Everyone knows the stories.

"Ferrick jumped in?" he asks.

I nod, chest tightening when I hear the words aloud. Ferrick's a selfless fool for jumping after Vataea, and he's a selfish fool if he thinks he can die when our last words to each other were so cruel.

But I won't let him die. Not tonight.

"If we can't run, we need to drop anchor so they can get back up." The ship rocks too fiercely, jerking as though it's stuck in the eye of a storm. We need to steady it.

"Drop it, then," Bastian says. "I'll keep the beast busy."

Without a second glance, I dash to the cathead. There's no time to drop the two bower anchors, and they'll take too long to haul up if we need to make a quick escape. Instead, I unfasten the stopper and let the main anchor drop. I toss the ladder for them to climb, but neither Ferrick nor Vataea is in sight

The Lusca screeches until every hair on my body stands. Ten red, spider-like eyes stare at us from around its oversize mouth. It could easily swallow ten dinghies at once, but *Keel Haul* is thankfully barely too large to swallow whole.

The monster spots Bastian as the pirate's sword catches the glow of the moon. He holds it in front of him, as though the thin blade will be able to do anything against a sea monster.

The Lusca lashes out with one of its hooked tentacles. Bastian dives out of the way, raising his sword just in time to counter. He gets in one solid gash before the monster snarls and withdraws its massive tentacle. The sound rattles the ship and forces me to cover my ears again. They burn as though they're about to bleed.

As the Lusca draws back, its tentacle knocks into *Keel Haul*'s helm and scrapes against the wood. It must hit Bastian too, because he stumbles back as if struck. He tucks his left hand around his stomach and struggles for breath.

I rush to his side and put my arms on his shoulders to steady him. "Are you all right?" His chest rises and falls as he regains his breath.

"I'm fine," he grunts. "Find Ferrick and Vataea. Get them back on the shi—"

The Lusca's no longer looking at us. One at a time it blinks its beady red eyes toward the left, and I run to the bow to see what it's spotted.

There's no hiding Ferrick's red hair in the silver water. He's a flame in the middle of the sea, and Vataea's shimmering rose-gold fin isn't helping.

The mermaid's head is down, limp. Ferrick has her over his left shoulder. There might not be a whirlpool anymore, but the waves crash angrily against *Keel Haul*, strong enough to sway the heavy ship. They slow Ferrick. His head bobs in and out of the water as he struggles to swim forward, dragging Vataea with him.

"I dropped the ladder!" I yell. "Hurry!"

But the Lusca's already seen him. Its throat opens and its teeth wriggle excitedly, each like a dead squid with a pointed tip that drips black poison.

When it lashes its tentacles toward Ferrick, I scream for Bastian. "We need to do something!" Though I've no idea what that could be.

Ferrick hugs Vataea close and ducks beneath the water before the tentacles strike. The Lusca roars and draws back for another shot.

Bastian sprints toward the edge of the ship closest to the Lusca. He raises his sword above his head and waves it in the air, trying to draw the beast's attention.

It works. All ten eyes are drawn to the shiny sword before they sink down to the man holding it. Bastian's stone-faced and ready to go again.

"I assure you, I taste better than the guppies in the water." There's an edge in his voice. "Come and get a taste."

The monster lurches forward and Bastian stabs at it again. The tentacles are thick and goopy; they catch the blade, but are too thick to slice through. Its inky blood pours from the tentacle and stains Bastian's cheeks and hands. He rips his sword back with a grunt, dissatisfied he's done nothing.

Except, he hasn't done nothing. He's given me an idea.

I need the Lusca's blood. Or, better yet, its tentacle.

"What are you doing?" Bastian yells as I throw myself from the bow and run toward the Lusca. "You're going to get yourself killed!"

"Distract it!" I grip the rigging and hoist myself onto the slippery ropes, beginning to climb aloft toward the mast. The Lusca's attention is still fixed on Bastian. It lifts three tentacles into the air and slams them down into *Keel Haul*.

Bastian's sent flying, his head smacking against the ship. *Keel Haul* roars as the Lusca sinks its tentacles into the ship, dragging it forward.

I wrap my wrist in the rope and swing myself so I face the beast. I unsheathe my dagger and hold it close as the ship tilts and the rigging hovers above the Lusca.

This creature is extraordinary; something of legends. If I want to beat it, then I'm going to need to be extraordinary, too.

I ready my dagger, send a quick prayer to the gods, and throw myself from the rigging. I hit the monster's thick skin with a smack that knocks the air from my lungs. Bastian yells something behind me, but I can no longer make out his words.

The beast is slippery, with skin like a whale. There are notches and grooves in its back from where other creatures have torn chunks from its skin, and I dig my heel into one of those grooves to steady myself. The Lusca roars.

None of its ten eyes can move upward. They're fixed in a circle around its mouth, unable to see me. Even so, it lashes one of its tentacles at me and roars when it instead strikes its own back.

I dig my heel farther into the beast's back and fall to all fours as it thrashes. My nails scramble for purchase in any groove they can find, and I struggle to work my way out of my left boot. From the corner of my eye I catch a flash of red. Ferrick's making his way around the ship, toward the ropes.

Bastian turns to help him, but the Lusca seizes up and throws two of its slimy tentacles in the air. They hammer onto *Keel Haul*, hooks tearing at the wood. When I squint through the haze of the mist I see Bastian grab at his chest. His strangled choking fills the air.

When the Lusca raises another tentacle, I drive my dagger into its back and finally kick my foot out of its boot. I scramble back to my feet, but without the traction from my soles, the Lusca's skin is even more slick and slippery as it flails.

I dig my toes into what I can, desperate for what's inside that boot.

Beneath my stockings and wedged beneath a thin layer of canvas lies the cursed necklace I stole from Mornute. I've been careful to keep it from touching my skin, saving it for a time where it might come in handy.

One brush of my skin against the necklace and we're done for. But if I can slip this onto the Lusca . . .

One of its tentacles finally finds me. It knocks me off balance; I start to slip off its back, but grind my blade into the flesh on its side and hang on to the hilt. The Lusca's wails are deafening.

Bastian leans over the opposite side of the ship, helping Ferrick and Vataea up the ladder. His back is turned away from the Lusca, trusting me to handle this beast alone. I can't let these three down.

I lift my free boot and bite down on the lip of it, clenching the leather between my teeth so I can use both hands to drag myself back up onto the Lusca's back, thankful for its massive size only this once. I keep on all fours and clench the hilt of my dagger until I catch my balance against the Lusca's slimy skin. The beast struggles against my movements, tentacles thrashing. One of its hooked barbs finds my back and pierces through my skin. I scream against the searing burn as thousands of black dots fight to steal my vision.

But I don't let them take it from me. I jerk my blade from the beast's flesh as it readies another tentacle. Pulling myself up, I drop my boot back into my hands and shakily attempt to brace myself.

My chest is tight; every breath fills my lungs with fire.

Poison. The Lusca's barbed tentacles seep with poison.

My hands are no longer my own. They're ghostly and foreign. I see them move as I hold my boot, but the spreading poison makes it feel like they belong to someone else.

Water rains down on me, and through my haze, I slowly look up. The Lusca has every tentacle lifted, curved and ready to strike down on its own back. On me.

My hands are unsteady, but I grip my boot tightly, and though the world blurs and darkens around me, I shake the fog from my vision and wait. There's only one chance to get this right.

I wait until the Lusca roars, confident enough to strike down with its full force.

I wait until one tentacle strikes my back again, and until another nearly slams into my face, going for the kill. The moment before it hits, I grit through the pain and throw my hands up, capturing its tentacle in my boot.

The Lusca has no time to draw back. The moment it connects to the necklace, the beast freezes. Its tentacles form a cavern above my head, and I stumble back as water rains onto my face from its lifted, unmoving limbs.

Shivers rip through me with such force they nearly bring me to my knees. I claw at any remaining strength I have and latch onto it, forcing one foot in front of the other. Step by excruciating step, I make my way across the beast's still back and toward the tip of one of the tentacles.

The necklace has completely frozen the beast. The Lusca cannot scream as I slice through its tentacle, but I relish in knowing it can feel every inch of my blade. Its flesh is thick, and requires far more energy to cut through it than I have to offer.

But I've no other choice. I dig the nails of one hand into the tentacle to hold my body up as I sear through its flesh. My breaths come in constricted gasps as the poison tears through me; I don't have much longer. I rip the tentacle the rest of the way off and its inky blood coats my hands as I hold it.

There's power in the Lusca's blood. Pulsating, fierce, wondrous power. It's strong in a mythical way I've never known. I've stopped the Lusca, but I can't just let it sit here for someone to discover, or for something to remove the necklace before it starves out. I need to get this tentacle back on the ship and light it on fire. I need to *kill* it with my magic.

I need to get back on *Keel Haul*.

I need—

Balance is a distant thing I can no longer maintain. My foot slips on the back of the frozen beast and I grip the severed tentacle as though it might somehow rescue me. Ten red, unblinking eyes watch as I trip and tumble off its back.

My body refuses to listen as I try to reach for my dagger, wanting to use the Lusca's body to slow my descent again. But my arms won't unwind from around the tentacle.

I shut my eyes as the ocean swallows me whole. Water floods my lungs, and I choke on the one thing I love the most.

The sea. The waters of my kingdom. They'll be the death of me.

CHAPTER TWENTY-ONE

I wake in a room flooded with warmth. Moonlight spills from behind open velvet curtains, and a dimmed oil lamp burns on the mahogany table beside me.

A soft mattress draws my body in, lulling me back to sleep. I didn't mind sleeping in a hammock, but now that I'm reminded of what I was missing, I want to wrap myself between the lavish navy blankets and never come out. Exhaustion urges me to sleep for a solid week.

Maps and atlases cover the floors and walls. In the dim light, I make out one wall where clothing hangs, pristine and sorted by type and color. Coats on one side, linen shirts on the other. More men's shoes than I've ever seen in one place form a line on the floor.

Bastian's sitting in a chair, hunched over his desk. He wears only a thin black linen shirt and loose trousers, more casual than I've ever seen him. The definition of his arms and shoulders catches my eye as he examines something that sits on the table. His back is to me, broader and more muscular than I realized. With how quickly he can scale the rigging and drag in *Keel Haul*'s anchors, I should have expected he'd be strong.

What I don't expect is how much I enjoy the way the black shirt looks against his warm brown skin. I also don't expect the thought of how his back and shoulders might feel beneath my hands, powerful and firm.

Bastian pushes away from his desk with a sigh. The Lusca's tentacle rests before him. I remember wanting to bring it onto the ship with me, but I never made it that far. How did both the tentacle and I get here?

He startles when he turns and catches me staring. "You're awake." He searches my face carefully. "How do you feel? I'm sorry about your clothes. Vataea changed you; Ferrick needed to see how deep your wound is."

I know the Lusca hit me, but I don't remember the wound being deep, nor do I remember any blood. All I remember is flashes of tentacles, water, and eventually complete numbness.

I look down at myself for the first time, finally noticing the stiffness of my body as I try to move.

"Careful!" Bastian moves to the edge of the bed. "Ferrick was able to stabilize you, but we had to drain a lot of your blood to get the poison out. Even a Suntosan healer can't return lost blood." His body is tense as the skin between his brows wrinkles into lines that age him ten years. Looking at them, my head spins. I try to speak, but the words burn.

Flashes of dark, blood-tainted water slosh behind my eyes as I recall the memory of drowning. Of gagging on the sea as I fought to resurface. My throat scorches as though I've swallowed gallons of straight rum. I take my time until I'm able to speak through the pain.

"How bad was it?" I rasp. "How long have I been out?"

Bastian smooths a loose curl from my neck and tucks it back into place. His touch is gentle, as if too much pressure might shatter me. "Two days." He raises his hand when I begin to sit up in protest. "Relax. This far south, the waters start to get rocky from the cold. Even with *Keel Haul*'s speed, the trip to Zudoh will take three. You need to rest." He says the last part with a long, drawn-out sigh. "You must have a death wish, you know that? Jumping into the water with a sea monster? You were nearly killed."

"But I wasn't." I try to grin, but my lips are chapped from sea salt and I grimace as they split open. Even bone tired and barely able to move, the adrenaline surging through me is undeniable. It boils in my blood and speeds my heart in a way I've never known.

Is this how Father felt, after his adventures? After he tamed a kelpie and chased the leviathan?

Until now, no one has been able to document proof of the Lusca's existence.

No more getting out of bed, Father once told me. *The Lusca will snatch you, if you do! It'll grab your ankles and gobble you whole! He makes his favorite meal from the bones of disobedient children, you know . . .*

In some stories, the monster was rumored to have a shark's head. In others, it had three heads and poisonous tentacles. In my nighttime paranoia, it was an oversize beast with long, slimy tentacles made for snatching ankles, and dagger-long teeth for chomping through the bones of children. But compared to the real thing, my imagined Lusca was a puppy.

I can't wait to tell Father that I not only faced the beast, but that I bested it. I only wish he'd been there to see.

"How did I get back on the ship?" I try to wet my cracked lips, but my mouth is too dry.

"I jumped in after you." Bastian says it so simply, like the answer is obvious. "It took me a while to figure out how you did it, but freezing the Lusca was genius, I admit. Though you shouldn't have risked yourself like that."

I tip my head back on the pillow, clamping my eyes shut in protest against the dizziness. "It's what had to be done."

For a moment there's only silence. No words. No footsteps. Perhaps not even any breathing aside from my own. When Bastian does speak again, his words may be quiet, but they're sharp as a blade.

"You really will do anything for your people, won't you?"

I want to open my eyes and remind him I've already given my answer, but when I do, Bastian doesn't look smug or angry. His face is shadowed by the oil lamp, jaw strong in his profile. He shakes his head just barely, as if to himself. "You're a Montara; your father banished my island from the kingdom. He destroyed my home. I tried not to be a hypocrite, because who am I to judge someone by the family they come from? But still, I wanted to hate you." His fists clench and unclench at his sides, eyes pinched at the ground like he's struggling with some sort of internal war.

"And do you?" I ask.

He shakes his head. "No, Amora. I haven't been able to hate you since the moment we first spoke."

I can hardly tell if the wooziness I feel is from my injuries, or because of Bastian's words. My skin is hot, but I can't get myself to look at him. Slowly, carefully, I reach up to take his hand. He tenses at first, but his shoulders slowly relax as I motion for him to sit at the edge of the bed.

Warmth spreads through my chest as I let a small portion of my magic work its way through me, using it to search his soul and confirm the suspicion that knots in my stomach.

On the first night I met Bastian, I thought my magic was too tired to see the entirety of his soul. But as I look at it now, it's still the misty light gray it was before, with the edges fading into wispy smoke that refuses to show me the rest. I see only half of him.

"I saw you during the fight, Bastian," I say. "I heard you scream."

He stills, but doesn't pull away.

"The first time the Lusca struck, I never saw you get hit," I press. "It struck *Keel Haul*, and yet *you* reacted. As if you were the one in pain."

His eyes catch the moonlight, and for a moment they're silver and doused with stars. He leans his weight onto one arm. "What are you getting at?"

The words are a challenge I can't back away from. Though he's tense, it almost feels as though Bastian *wants* me to know. I can feel it in the way his hand closes halfway around mine, his thumb brushing my wrist, practically begging me to say the answer out loud and free him from his secret. I wonder how long he's been holding on to it.

"You said before that *Keel Haul* was a magical ship." I lift my chin, holding his attention. "And Vataea said she sensed curse magic the moment she stepped aboard *Keel Haul*. Now that I've seen that magic in action, I think I might understand what one of those curses is. Every time you were hit by the Lusca, the ship reacted. Every time the ship was hit, you felt the pain. You and *Keel Haul* are connected by this magic, aren't you?"

His hand forms a fist in the sheets. He flexes his jaw and looks out the window, at the dark sea. "What if we are? Would it change the way you think of me?"

"No. I'd want to understand."

He grinds his teeth together, hesitant, but the words come quickly. As though he desperately wants to share them. "It's Zudian magic, as you guessed."

"How?" I ask. "Curse magic stays contained, doesn't it? When I let go of the necklace, the curse followed it, not me. I wasn't cursed permanently."

His sigh tells me it's more complicated than that. "Zudoh used to be the most popular island in the kingdom. It was often visited by curious tourists and people who sought potions and protective cursed charms to bring back to their own islands. About thirteen years ago, this started to change.

"Part of Zudoh wanted to separate from the kingdom," he continues. "They wanted to expand their reach, their power, and do more than make trinkets for rich tourists. They saw a way for their magic to grow. But to achieve that, they needed a way to create curses that could last forever—by binding them to a person's soul."

"They learned *soul* magic?" My palms are clammy with sweat as I inhale a sharp breath. King Cato restricted it to the Montara bloodline, to protect our people from the beast he fought off centuries ago. "But it's not meant to be learned by others. It's the Montaras' burden to carry."

"And it can only be the Montaras' burden," he says. "That's why Kaven had to create something new. It's essentially *cursed* soul magic. You can't *destroy* someone's soul like you can with Aridian magic, but you can *curse* one."

The room's temperature drops ten degrees. Even with the warmth of Bastian's hand against my skin, I shudder. "How are they still alive?" Multiple magics break down a person's body and soul until they eventually cease entirely. Protecting people from that is how my magic even came to exist.

"I don't know," he admits, "but it's the truth. Those who practice this magic can steal and curse half a soul."

How would a cursed person even continue to exist, with half of them missing? I'd call Bastian a liar if I hadn't seen his soul myself. "How does it work?"

Bastian's face darkens. "First they use soul magic to access someone's soul. And then, using their victim's blood, they can curse part of their soul into anything. Take my relationship with *Keel Haul*, for example. Kaven cursed me to this ship; that's why I'm forced to stay on it, and why I get sicker the longer I'm away from it. A person can't live comfortably with only half their soul."

I think back to his clammy skin and sharp breaths during our time in Ikae. We'd only been off the ship for a few hours. "What would happen if *Keel Haul* were destroyed? Would you die?"

Bastian shakes his head. "I'd survive, but it wouldn't be a life worth living. I'd become a shell of a person, empty and void. I'd desire nothing but my broken soul."

My head spins as I try to process this. "And what would happen to *Keel Haul* if you died?"

"As much as I love her, this ship is nothing more than a ship. *Keel Haul* holds part of my soul, not the other way around. Should I die, she'd go back to being a normal ship, no longer bound to anyone. I feel what she feels, as my soul is within her. It doesn't work the other way around; nothing of her is within me. I can use our connection to help sail her, but that's the extent of my power over *Keel Haul*."

My skin cools with sweat. "Can everyone in Zudoh do this?" Because if they can, how does he expect us to win this fight? One drop of blood, and our souls would be as good as gone.

Bastian shakes his head, voice taking a defensive edge. "The last I heard, only a few practiced this magic. It started off as a small group, brought to life by the son of the island's leading ambassador—Kaven.

"What you need to understand is that our magic isn't meant to be like this," he continues. "It's meant to be protective. To put wards on your house so that you can sleep easy at night, or dissuade children from touching things that may be too dangerous for them. Things like that. But Kaven broke away from this style of curse magic and formed something dark and new, and if you're not with him, you're against him." When Bastian speaks of his home island, his words are passionate. Yet cool sweat licks my throat, my body sick to its core. Kaven isn't a simple opponent. He's a wielder of an unheard of new magic, which makes him dangerous.

"Why wouldn't my family do anything about this?" I ask. "My father wouldn't stand for such a twisted magic."

"Your father was the one who declared Zudoh's banishment from the kingdom, when their intention to learn soul magic became clear. He took Suntosan healers off our island, and cut us off from trading. He probably thought they'd never manage to learn it—that this mess would sort itself and they'd come back begging to be a part of the kingdom again. But he was wrong. This magic has divided Zudoh, and the island is in a crisis. The Montaras are the reason my people are struggling." His grip relaxes on the sheets as he peels himself away.

The ship stirs with the same discomfort that claws at me, swaying uneasily against even the smallest waves. It is not the confident, magical ship I'm used to.

"How long has half your soul been cursed to *Keel Haul*?"

Bastian tries to smile, but it withers as the weight of the truth hits him. "Since I was a child. Zudoh's a small island, so there was no hiding from Kaven. I was young when he tried to recruit me, promising kids he'd teach us magic like it was a shiny new toy. My parents wouldn't let him have me, so he had them killed and took me away—as he did with every child he could get his hands on—to study cursed soul magic. I never learned it, though."

I shiver. I never imagined this level of evil. Murder and stolen children? Cursed soul magic? This is what Father turned his back on?

Why? All this time cooped up on Arida, practicing our magic—was it because he's that afraid of starting a war?

"Before he was killed, Father had been teaching me to sail, and after a year of being forced to study under Kaven day and night, I knew his ship was the only way for me to escape. For a week I snuck food and supplies aboard, and then one night, when I thought everyone was asleep, a few friends and I made our escape. Only, Kaven must have been hiding there, waiting. He killed the others, and to show everyone what he was capable of should they disobey him, cursed me, and ripped away my magic. The moment I touched the helm, my soul ripped in two and bonded to *Keel Haul*. But he made a mistake, and didn't think through cursing me to a ship. I commandeered it and escaped before he could stop me."

Energy and anger simmer off his body. I reach out to put my hand on his shoulder, and Bastian stiffens.

"Surely there's a way to break the curse?"

His teeth grind together, sharpening his jawline. "As I've said, to make a permanent curse on someone's soul, their blood is needed. And the more Kaven takes, the stronger he becomes. But this magic has a weakness—to keep control of their magic, its creator must always keep some blood of the cursed person." Bastian leans forward. "Kaven is a vain, prideful man. He collects leather bracelets smeared with the blood of those he's cursed. He wears his favorites like a trophy, and keeps others close to him on Zudoh. To ensure his charms remain intact, he treats these bracelets as you treat your satchel, rarely leaving Zudoh so that he never has to stray too far from them. But if we can destroy those bracelets, every curse he's ever made will break, and he'll be weakened."

"Do you think yours is one he keeps on him?" I ask. "One of his trophies?"

Bastian snorts. "I know it is."

I can't decipher the expression Bastian wears as the oil lamp flickers and dims, struggling for life. It casts the bed in a hazy burnt-orange glow. Shadows dance in the hollowness of his cheekbones and curve along his neck, down into his shirt.

Years of traveling on the sea, moving freely from one island to the next without constraints, should have filled him with wisdom and life. I've always been jealous of those who travel. Jealous of adventures and experiences I could only imagine.

But I have family and friends who are likely worried and awaiting my return. Bastian, I sense, doesn't have this. His family is gone, and his soul has been cursed to a life of solitude. The stars in his eyes aren't only crafted by adventure. They've been formed by years of loneliness. Of looking up into a sky full of dreams and never being quite able to reach it.

He looks so, so lonely.

"Why didn't you tell me this, earlier?" My blood is hot, skin clammy. "This is far worse than just defeating a rebellion, Bastian. I don't know that I can handle this on my own."

His face and shoulders fall with shame. "I never wanted to go back to Zudoh. I meant to live out the rest of my life like this, bound to this blasted ship and as far away from Kaven as I could get. I lived in fear of him for years—knowing my island was in trouble, but too afraid to do anything about it. But the more I tried to avoid thinking about the people who must still be suffering, the more it started to eat me alive. I couldn't focus. Couldn't sleep. Then I heard Arida was throwing a celebration for their princess."

This isn't the Bastian I'm familiar with. This person is raw. Angry and vicious.

"I was visiting Valuka when I heard your performance was coming up," Bastian says. "Aridian magic is what Kaven always wanted, and I knew then that it was the only thing strong enough to stop him. I figured I could at least try to convince your father of the dangers he was ignoring. I wanted him to know that Kaven was a true threat, though it was naive of me to think he'd do anything after so many years of ignorance. But then I saw you." His fingers hover over my knuckles, hesitant. It takes a long moment before he can press them against my skin, encompassing my hand fully. I think to pull them away, but I can't find the power to.

"I swear it was as if the skies opened and showed me my chance. There you were, confronting your father about the very person I came to warn him about. When you needed a way to escape Arida and redeem yourself, I truly believed that the gods led me to you for a reason."

My head swims as a wave of nausea settles in. Whether it's from the poison or the secrets being spilled one after another, I can't be sure.

"Please understand I've spent years running," he whispers. "I'm tired. Every moment I'm away from *Keel Haul*, I grow sicker. I want my freedom back." He wears a ghost of a smile before shaking his head. "But the people of Zudoh are imprisoned, too, and I've neglected them too long. You asked me before why I didn't go back sooner, and it's because I was a coward. When I escaped, I could have tried to find a way to help them, and I didn't. Now, Kaven's trying to destroy the rest of the kingdom, just as he destroyed my home. I'm ready for it to end, before he hurts anyone else. And I truly believe, after all of this, that we're meant to do this together."

He feels as though he has a duty to the people of his island; there's nothing I understand more. His hand is rough but warm as I tighten my grip.

"No more secrets." I hold Bastian's scrutiny until he relaxes with a heavy exhale, realizing I mean my words. "I understand your reasons, but this changes things, Bastian. There can't be any more secrets."

It takes a moment before he responds, his words quiet. "No more secrets. I swear it on my honor as a pirate."

"I thought you preferred the term *sailor*?" I try to tease, but the words are weak as my dizzying vision forces my head back to the pillow. My fight with the Lusca is catching up to me.

Bastian laughs softly. It's unnerving how much I like that sound.

"Let's not fuss over semantics." He squeezes my hand once, then stands and dims the oil lamp until it's barely a flicker. "Try to get some rest. We've one more day before we get to Zudoh. We'll need to be ready."

And I'll need to prepare.

Through the dim light, I focus on the Lusca's severed tentacle and the thick barbed hook that curls at the tip. I shudder at the memory of how quickly its poison ate away at me. How it robbed my vision and made me a victim of the sea's wrath.

What a brilliant weapon that hook could make.

CHAPTER
TWENTY-TWO

The room's empty when I wake the next morning. I ease myself onto shaky feet, stretch my stiff bones, and snag one of Bastian's coats to wear over my thin linen shirt. The moment I open the door, Ferrick's there waiting. He jumps to his feet, and I'm surprised to see his coloring is normal and his movements quick. He's finally adapted to traveling on *Keel Haul*.

"Amora!" He nearly knocks me back when he throws his arms around me. "By the gods, I'm so sorry. How are you feeling? You were already in the water by the time I realized what you were doing. The Lusca, Amora! Can you even believe it? We faced the *Lusca*." He's wide-eyed and shaking with a strange mix of relief and excitement.

The last time Ferrick and I spoke, the conversation didn't exactly go well. But when he dived into the water after Vataea, panic filled me every time I couldn't see his red hair bobbing in the water.

I wrap my arms around Ferrick's waist and pull myself into his chest, hugging him as tightly as I can—still weak from the blood loss, it's not much. Unlike Bastian, whose touch was tender and careful, Ferrick nearly crushes me to his body. His warm breath sighs relief into my neck as the tension in his body softens.

When I draw back, Ferrick looks at me with a gentle smile.

I will never love Ferrick in the way he wants, but he's one of the most caring men I've ever met. Nothing he's done since joining me on this journey has been for himself, and it's time I acknowledge that. I can't hate him for a decision my parents made.

"I'm glad you're safe," I say. "And I'm sorry about before; you didn't deserve how cruel I was." Gods, I can't remember the last time I apologized for anything. But Ferrick was right; he asked for this marriage no more than I did. "It was incredibly brave of you to jump in after Vataea. How is she?"

Ferrick swallows, regaining his composure. "She smacked her head when she fell and was knocked out cold by the time she hit the water. But she's fine now, no injuries. And I'm fine, too. A little tired, but I'll live." He smiles with his eyes, squinting the corners of them.

I squeeze his shoulders. "Thank you, Ferrick. I know my injuries were deep. And I know it had to be exhausting to heal them, especially after getting Vataea safe and finishing off the Lusca."

Ferrick's brows lower against his eyes and he looks away. "About the Lusca . . . We cut a few more of its tentacles off to be safe, but it's a legendary beast, and Bastian and I didn't feel right about killing it. The necklace will fall from it soon enough. Hopefully it'll return to the sea, and we'll never see it again."

I press my lips together. Their decision seems noble, but it's not the one I would have made. The Lusca is a legend, yes, but it's also a threat. If I hadn't lost control of myself, I would've ensured its death.

But with a defeat that grand, I doubt the beast will attack another ship any time soon.

Only when I step fully onto the deck do I recognize how grim the sky is. We're east of Kerost, heading to the southernmost point in all of Visidia and into a frigid, thick gray haze that sinks into my skin. The waters on the horizon are bleak—green rather than the crystal blue I'm used to. They churn angrily. *Keel Haul* has regained her confidence as she plunges onward, but that doesn't stop the tides from beating against her, urging the ship to turn back.

No dolphins flank our ship. There are no seagulls to fill the sky, because despite the stories I've heard about the endless schools of rare fish in these waters, the sea here looks dark and diseased. I fear that if I dip my hand into the water, my flesh will dissolve in the murky green tides.

There's no life here. Everything is still and silent.

I catch sight of Bastian on the rigging. He's high up near the sails, mending a patch destroyed by the Lusca. When he catches me staring, he cocks his head, as if waiting for me to ask a question I don't have. I turn away quickly.

"Look who's finally awake!" Vataea emerges from the cabin and waves at me, a delighted crinkle in her eyes. She's dressed in my new clothing, and though it fits her well, it almost looks wrong on her body. She looks strangled by fabric.

Guilt swells inside me. I should have tried harder to prevent her from falling from *Keel Haul*. I should have saved her.

"I hear you were the star of the show," Vataea says. I've forgotten how smooth and welcoming her voice is, as beautiful as music. She steps forward and presses a kiss to my cheek.

My throat numbs and I struggle to remember how to

breathe. I thought breathing was supposed to be a natural instinct, but apparently that's not the case when you're kissed by a mermaid.

Beside me, Ferrick's fair skin has betrayed him yet again. He blushes a fervent, fiery red.

"Ferrick's the one who really saved you," I say, watching as the mermaid's playful expression splits into one of surprise. She turns to him. No one's told her.

Ferrick's blush grows deeper.

"Is this true?" Vataea asks.

Ferrick lifts his hands and tries to dismiss the question with a wave of his arms. "It's no big deal," he manages to stammer. "I just wanted to make sure you were all right since . . . since you're part of the crew, now." He clears his throat only to choke as Vataea presses onto her toes and kisses his cheek, as well.

Ferrick looks as though he needs medical attention by the time she pulls away. When he casts a guilty glance my way, I only smile.

When Bastian joins us, his skin sheens with sweat from a full morning's work, and his dark hair is wild, ruffled by the wind. I quickly look away, my cheeks heating.

"Glad to see everyone's in fine spirits," he says, skimming over Ferrick, "but it's time we discuss Zudoh."

"What's left to discuss?" Vataea inspects her nails. "We already made our plan. Get in, kill the man, get out."

Bastian's jaw twitches. "We never talked about what's going to happen once we arrive. There are parts of the island that are dangerous. Your siren magic only works if you're in water, right? You're not always going to have water around to protect you."

She peers up from her nails and her eyes narrow into dangerous slits.

"I want to talk about *weapons*," Bastian says before Vataea can cut off his tongue. "I have my sword, and Amora has her dagger. Ferrick, you still have your rapier, right?"

Ferrick nods.

"Good," Bastian continues. "Then all that's left to take care of is finding a weapon for you, Vataea. Have you ever used one before?"

"Bits of coral, here and there."

From the way he grimaces, it's clear that's not what Bastian had in mind. Before he can say anything, though, I draw my dagger from my belt and offer it to Vataea. She looks down at it, then at me.

"Take it." I press it into her hesitant palm. "Just to borrow, until we get off Zudoh."

Bastian stretches his lungs with a dramatic sigh. "How does this solve our problem? Now you're the one with no weapon, Amora."

"I have an idea," I say simply. "Take me back into your quarters and I'll show you."

He lifts a brow. "Now, now, Princess. There's no need to be so forthcoming. If you want to accompany me into the captain's quarters, you need only suggest it."

Ferrick turns away with a shake of his head.

I ignore it, jabbing Bastian's shoulder and rolling my eyes. "Just follow me."

This time, as Bastian laughs, I don't suppress the shudder that passes through my body and settles into my core. He bows at the waist and extends an arm forward.

"Lead the way."

———

When I show Bastian what I intend to do with the Lusca's poisoned hook, he claims to have knowledge about building weapons. But as he hovers over me, feasting on my creation with curious delight and not one word of helpful advice, I realize that's a lie. He's only here for the show.

Under normal circumstances, I prefer to work in private. There's something richly satisfying in giving all of yourself up to an act of creation. It's like magic. It demands your focus and requires a small piece of your soul to complete.

Yet this is the second time now that Bastian's tricked me into allowing him to watch me work, and the only reason I let him stay is because I like the way his presence causes my skin to prickle with anticipation and awareness. That, and I appreciate the satisfied noises he makes in the back of his throat whenever I do something particularly clever.

Until I can find the supplies to make a proper hilt, the weapon I've created is crude. The giant hook is large and sharp, similar to a blade. I've spent the past five or six hours meticulously shaping it into a dagger with scattered atlases and the corner of Bastian's bed—anything heavy enough to work the thick hook. Now it's firm, pointed and curved at the tip with a sharp, hooked edge. Its danger lies in its jagged edges and the poison lurking inside it. There's no way to test it, but the poison should latch onto anyone whose blood it draws.

For now, I've fastened rope tightly around the bottom as a hilt. It doesn't look like the strongest weapon, and its range is limited, but I've bashed it against enough things to know it's durable and powerful.

I imagine it will cut through skin slick as gelatin.

"You certainly have a creative mind, I'll give you that much." Bastian leans around me to eye the desk. He's close enough that his chest presses against my back as he breathes, and the warmth of those breaths tickles my cheek. "Where'd you learn so much about weapons, anyway?"

"I had a guard back on Arida named Casem," I say as I run

my finger across my new weapon, careful not to break skin. "His father was a weapons master, in charge of instructing our soldiers. He's also one of my father's closest friends; Casem and I trained under him when we were children, and sometimes he would bring us into the forge so we could watch the weapons being made."

"And you think this blade will truly work?"

I nod. The wound the Lusca gave me was small but deep, and still it was enough to knock me out cold. If I attack someone with this, I don't intend to make a small wound. I intend to kill.

"Of course it will." I hold it to the window, into whatever light has managed to sneak through the thick haze outside. It's a rich navy hue, with iridescent specks of turquoise and silver floating inside the material. From the right angle, it looks as though there are things moving from within the weapon, like microscopic leeches waiting for blood.

I wouldn't doubt that possibility. This weapon is part of the Lusca, after all.

"I've made a legendary weapon. I'm sure it will work better than I can imagine." I set it beside my sheath on the table. I'll have to be far more careful with this weapon than my normal dagger.

"If it's a legendary weapon," Bastian says, "it deserves a legendary name."

It's like he's taunting me with how close he stands. My heartbeat races as Bastian inches his way closer.

He's right, but I've never named a blade before. The weapon I've scrounged up is truly one of a kind. A magical thing. "Do you have a suggestion?"

Bastian laughs, shaking his head. "It doesn't work that way, Princess. The one who creates the weapon is the one who gets to name it. But I imagine it deserves something dangerous."

"I'll think on it." I press my lips together, trying to ignore how he has one arm draped around my chair while he moves beside me, maintaining our tight space. There's an entire room around us, and yet he's nearly pressed against me.

He smells of sea and sunlight. Of adventure. It clings to his shirt and makes its home in his hair. I find myself wanting to let my fingers roam through it, to shake out the tiny grains of sand trapped there.

There's a split second where the air shifts. I turn to catch him looking at me, and when I think he might turn away, he doesn't. His grip tightens on the chair, and I think of the way those hands felt as they held my hips tightly to him. The way his lips felt against mine when we kissed, and how I didn't want it to end.

Perhaps he and I want the same thing.

I run my tongue over my lips, tasting the nervous words before I speak them. "Do you remember when I freed you from Vataea's trance?"

He draws his head back. I can't tell whether he's bemused or taken back, but he obliges all the same. "Of course."

His words taste like challenge. I take the bait. "Well, she told me something funny about it."

His right hand is on the desk. I trail my fingers toward it, slowly, brushing one gently across the back of his palm. He draws his bottom lip in, but otherwise doesn't budge. "What did she tell you?"

"As it turns out," I say softly, "it's impossible to break any-one out of the trance unless they have feelings for you."

"Feelings?" he echoes, shifting his right hand so his fingers weave between mine. "You mean like this?"

He kisses me, drawing his body firmly around mine. His lips aren't soft. They're rough and imploring, continuing where we left off. He tastes of salt. I drink him in, winding my arms

222

around his neck, through his hair, over his shoulders. He shifts so he can wrap his arm around my back and pulls me from my chair with a quiet grunt. Seconds later, I'm against the wall, his hand wrapped in my hair and his lips roving my neck. My body is so warm I fear I might melt right here, pressed against Bastian's chest.

I catch his jaw and bring it back to my lips, tasting the salt, the sunlight, all of it. All of *him*. I've kissed many boys before, but none of them felt like this. None of them made me fear my heart might burst through my rib cage and combust from working so hard.

I don't want him to pull away. I want to bury myself in the warmth of his body and explore this feeling.

He ends it too soon. When he draws away, I'm not only breathless—I'm *hungry*. I want more.

There's a matching hunger in his eyes as they roam my body, his chest rising and falling quickly from shaky breaths. Desire pulses within his stare when his eyes reach mine, but he forces it back and plasters a grin onto his face.

"Is that an honest enough answer for you?" His voice is filled with a huskiness that only makes my hunger grow.

"I'm not sure." I reach for his hand, pulling him back to me. "Show me again?"

This time, we don't stop.

CHAPTER TWENTY-THREE

The taste of salt remains on my lips even when Bastian and I eventually make our way back to the deck. The memory of his hands on my waist, fingers curling against me, still burns my skin.

I feel as though I've gotten away with something as I step outside, surprised when I'm met by icy, frigid air.

I hug my arms around myself, contemplating sneaking back down for my coat.

"We're close," Bastian says, scanning the horizon. His muscles tense.

Ferrick and Vataea have made themselves comfortable on the deck. They've a small pile of food between their too-close bodies, and there's a confident spark in the mermaid's eyes. It doesn't look like Bastian and I were the only ones getting a little friendlier.

Ferrick clears his throat and stands as Bastian and I

approach, as if to distance himself from Vataea. "So how do we do this?"

"We need to keep a low profile," Bastian responds immediately. "We don't want to tip them off. I'll anchor *Keel Haul* farther from the island and we'll take the dinghy. I'm hoping the fog can keep us covered. Vataea?"

"Yes, Captain?" she asks, voice playful.

"You'll have to go ahead of us, to show us a safe path. If you can, stick to the southern edge of the island; we'll be safer there."

This far south, the water is surely too cold for the average human, but Vataea doesn't hesitate. It's clear she's missed the ocean by how quickly she moves to the edge and throws herself into the sea. I imagine it has to hurt, but when I look overboard, the shimmering rose-gold tip of her tail fin disappears beneath the surface. All that's left is a small pool of iridescent gold that mixes with the murky water and eventually disappears.

Behind me, Bastian clears his throat. "You know, I rather like being called 'Captain.' I think I should make it my mandatory title. Like how we call Amora 'Princess.'"

Ferrick's brows arch as a bemused grin sets upon his lips. "Good luck getting that to catch on." He clasps Bastian on the shoulder as he passes, moving to join me on the edge of the starboard side. His eyes rove the dark water, looking for any sign of Vataea. But she's nowhere in sight. He taps an obsessive rhythm against the wood. His fingers still as the water moves.

Vataea appears as if out of nowhere, nearly gagging in the middle of the sea.

"This water is *disgusting*!" she snarls, glaring down at the sea with distaste. "It's all dead fish and algae, and I keep getting fish scales on my lips!"

"Can you feel the curse?" Bastian presses, which makes Vataea huff in annoyance.

"It's still ahead. But the farther I go, the worse it's getting." Her lips sour into a grimace. "You owe me for this, pirate." Begrudgingly, she lowers herself back into the dark green tides. It's difficult to keep track of her, but every so often she lifts her fin from the water and gently slaps it down, creating a path for *Keel Haul.*

The ship no longer moves hesitantly. It's lithe and eager, readily altering its course toward the south. There's little wind in the stagnant air, but still it presses forward as quickly as possible.

Bastian moves to stand at the foremost point of the ship. He grips the ledge so tightly the muscles in his arm bulge and contract. It's him who's spurring the ship forward. There's a readiness in his set jaw and determined grip.

He looks like a man eager to take on the world.

Vataea leads us to a small cavern formed by jagged, weather-worn rocks. The area's shrouded by the same thick fog that makes it difficult to see any more than three hundred feet before us. It should hide *Keel Haul* perfectly.

I step toward the helm as we ready to drop anchor. It's smooth against my palms.

Being here reminds me of the last time I sailed *The Duchess* with Father, and the memory fills me with longing.

I miss him. I miss Father, Mother, and all of Arida. I wonder what happened after I left. I imagine Yuriel already mourning his loss, while Aunt Kalea packs her bags to move to Arida. I imagine my parents yelling at the Visidian soldiers to hurry and find me. Father's forehead would be creased, like it is when he's worried. Mother would be sunk in her chair, picking at the skin of her nails while he paces around her.

The thoughts bring an unexpected rush of anger. Before I see them again, I have to fix Father's mistakes.

I cannot fail in Zudoh.

Worry plagues my lungs, constricting each breath until it's as though I'm back in the sea with the Lusca, choking on water. I press my hand to my new blade, then to my satchel, and steel myself.

A gentle hand rests on my shoulder. At first my memory fools me, tricking me into believing it's Father. But when I turn, Bastian stands in his place.

He stands close, taking my hands in his and repositioning them on the helm.

"What are you doing?" I ask, running my nails over the smooth wood. I want it to feel rougher. Worn in. He only uses it for show.

But even so, desire warms my palms and spreads welcome heat up into my chest. The plummeting temperature is now nothing more than an annoyance.

"You're going to sail us into that cavern." He points ahead. The rocks look bigger than they did earlier—looming and vicious, with jagged points threatening to tear into the wood of a poorly steered ship.

"Perhaps we should try in an area that's more open?" I start to pull away, but Bastian blocks me.

"I trust you." His words burn my skin with tiny prickles of heat. "You know what this ship means to me, and I trust you to sail it. Perhaps you should trust yourself, too." He's challenging. Confident. "I'm going to let *Keel Haul* out of my control, just for now. If anything starts to go wrong, I'll jump back in. There's no better ship for you to practice sailing on, Princess."

He removes his hands from mine and steps back, putting enough distance between us that it doesn't feel like he's hovering.

I lift my eyes to the horizon. The rocks feel both impossibly close and strangely far. My breath hitches in my throat, but when I look back at Bastian, he's smiling. Even Ferrick's watching, a small grin on his lips.

"Tighten your grip, but never doubt your gut instinct," Bastian whispers, nodding for me to turn back around. "The key to being a good captain is to always trust yourself."

I stretch my lungs with fog and breathe as my grip tightens on the helm. I turn it to the left, ever so slightly, and *Keel Haul* obeys. It's not pulling the other way, or struggling against me. The ship doesn't laugh at my commands. It searches for a leader and listens, respectful.

I press my fingertips against the wood, falling into the moment. The world is black in my periphery. All I see is the crest-shaped cavern, the impending danger, and *Keel Haul*.

The world moves quicker. I twist my grip on the helm to redirect the ship. It obeys with a satisfying groan; the sails catch the whisper of a breeze and bend to my whim. My heart races as we approach, and under my breath I repeat a steady stream of prayers that lasts until the ship rattles, slowing as we sail along the middle of the cavern's pass.

Breathless, I spin to Bastian, whose ridiculous smile mirrors my own. He's already stopped the ship, but he steadies its place by dropping anchor.

My hands shake against the helm as I stare at the cavern. Pride has made a home for itself in my swelling chest. It snatches my breath and flusters my already quick heart. The rocks no longer look jagged; they're smoothed by the sea. Perhaps I've been played by a trick of the light? Or was I so worried, I imagined the threat was greater than it was?

"So what do you think of sailing?" Bastian asks smugly.

I smack him lightly on the shoulder, then fall in to hug him tight, laughing because I can't find my breath and words don't satiate me. Nothing I say will do justice to the overwhelming pleasure swirling inside me. There are no words for the satisfaction of the sea's salt on my face and the brine in my lungs.

Bastian knows. He doesn't need words, because he knows the feeling well. I recognize it in his lopsided smile.

We've shared an experience only a few people will understand, and it's marked our souls. The sea is a beast more fearsome than even the Lusca.

But we don't need to rule it. We need only for it to trust us. Work with us. Be partners.

I've finally been accepted.

But the moment doesn't last long.

"Don't go any closer!" Vataea bolts out of the water with a gasp, grabbing hold of the cavern rocks to steady herself. Her entire body quivers, eyes glazed over as if sick. I rush to the ledge, ready to toss the ladder down for her.

"What happened?" Ferrick asks as he rushes to my side. "What's wrong?"

It takes Vataea a moment to catch her breath, and though she manages to steady herself, the shaking never quite stops. "This isn't a *curse*. Beyond this cavern is a plague." She clings to the rocks as though they're the only thing that can save her. I glance back at Bastian, whose jaw tightens as he glares out at the water.

Our moment of reprieve is already a distant memory.

"Can we navigate through it?" I ask, receiving a sharp snort from Vataea in response.

"Not a chance. This is stronger than anything I've felt before."

The wind and excitement that filled me only moments ago is knocked swiftly away. We've no time to turn around and reassess our options. It's now or never.

Zudoh's a smudge in the distance as I sink into the railing, mind reeling. There's no way we can give up now. Not when we've come this far. The air here is cold, clinging to the start of

229

autumn. Any day now, Aunt Kalea will be asked to accept soul magic. If she admits the truth, she'll be executed for the treason of learning enchantment magic. But if she lies to protect herself, she'll die from dual magics, and the beast will let loose its vengeance on all of Visidia. I have to make it back to Arida before either of those things happens.

Vataea's managed to steady herself, and with her mouth set in a firm line of determination, she sinks fully back into the water. I straighten as she disappears, and the boys tense as if they're worried she'll vanish completely.

But I know better. I don't worry when she's gone for a full minute, nor five.

There's a flash of her fin the moment before she emerges back at the cavern rocks, her eyes slit. Fierce.

"We can't get through the barrier." She sinks her nails into the rocks like claws. When she peers up at us, her grin is bright and sharp. "But we can go under it."

CHAPTER TWENTY-FOUR

"**A**re you sure this will work?" I linger at the end of *Keel Haul*'s rope, waiting to drop into the water with the others. We've hidden the ship behind the crest of the cavern, shrouded by the thick layer of gray fog that looks every bit as ominous as our situation feels.

Ferrick wears a deep frown of unease. "To think that this is truly how I'm living my life." He sighs, brushing a wet hand through his waves and flattening the hair down to his scalp.

"Most men would die for this opportunity." Vataea lifts a defiant chin into the air.

Ferrick's snort is mixed with a sharp, nervous laugh. "Most men *do* die for this opportunity."

Vataea's lips pucker thoughtfully, but my breathing shallows when she doesn't disagree. She dismisses our concerns with a flourish of her hand. "It will work if we hurry. Mermaids have been bringing humans into the water with us for centuries."

"Aye, to kill them," Bastian mutters, though Vataea pretends not to hear.

Though allowing Vataea to use magic on us is more than a little disconcerting, we're out of options.

I push off the ropes, hot with adrenaline that promptly freezes as I sink into water cold as ice. I nearly choke on it as I fight the urge not to bolt back onto the ship, gasping for breath. Both Bastian and Ferrick reach out to help drag me closer to them as they cling on to the slick rocks of the cavern to stay afloat.

If the surface is already this cold, then by Cato's blood, I can only imagine what it'll be like to dive.

"How deep do we have to go?" I ask between chattering teeth, clamping down on the inside of my cheek to steady them.

"Deep," Vataea admits. "The border of the curse is close, and it runs deep. We need to make sure we get a safe enough distance under it, so stick close to me. There should be a break in the curse at the start of the shore, where it was probably cast. But we won't have much time to reach it."

Bastian grimaces, no doubt thinking the same thing I am— even swimming as fast as we can, there's no guarantee we'll reach the shore in time.

"There's truly no other option? No other sea magic you could try?" I ask, to which Vataea only shakes her head.

"Nothing I'm strong enough to currently use. If at any point I sense a break, I'll take you up and give you more air. But otherwise we'll have to keep moving."

Ferrick wrinkles his nose. "And what happens if we have to surface before we reach the shore?"

It's Bastian who responds, squinting down at the murky tides. "You'll be caught in the curse, and I can't imagine any of us will be able to save you."

Memories of my prior experience with curse magic bring a

232

fresh round of shivers. The bugs swarming all over me hadn't felt imagined. If Bastian hadn't been there to talk me out of it, I've no idea how long I would have stood there, limbs numb and mind paralyzed by fear.

Bastian's words are nothing but a kind way to say that, should that happen to us in the middle of the ocean, we'll drown.

"Then that's that." I force my body to steady so I can look at least moderately confident with our plan. "There's no reason to stay here debating it. We should keep moving."

"We should," Vataea echoes. "All you have to do is remember to hold your breath to sink. When we're at a safe level, start breathing normally and you'll stabilize. Is everyone ready?" She goes to take hold of my shoulder, but Ferrick moves between us.

"I'll go first," he says, leaving no room for challenge. "Just to make sure it's safe."

Though Vataea rolls her eyes, she doesn't hesitate. She grips Ferrick tightly by the shoulder and presses her lips to his. She breathes air into his lungs as they kiss, dipping lower and lower into the water, dragging him below the surface.

My stomach cinches when Vataea resurfaces alone.

"If he comes back up, we'll have to start over," she says.

I catch a flash of red beneath the surface. The water is too murky to see Ferrick fully, but I gasp and slap his hand away when he pokes my hip to prove he's there.

"It works," I huff, shooing Ferrick away. Bastian exhales a quiet sigh of relief.

"Good. He'll start sinking soon," she says. "Time's against us, we need to hurry."

Bastian tries to appear calm when he looks at me, but he's fighting chattering teeth and worry that creases the corners of his eyes.

233

"Guess I'll see you on the other side," he says, drawing a breath. "And if not . . . well, it was a pleasure sailing with you all, and Vataea, try to keep *Keel Haul* cleaner than your cabin." He offers himself to the mermaid, nerves tensing his jaw. She peeks at me from over his shoulder, hesitating for a moment, but I offer a gentle nod.

Even so, I'm alarmed by the sharp pang that rattles me when her lips press against Bastian's. It's a vicious thing, surprising me so fiercely I turn away. The jealousy that eats at me is far stronger than I ever expected. Their kiss isn't one of pleasure; it's necessity. I know this.

But gods, I never anticipated how much I would hate it.

Fortunately, Vataea is quick about it. When she resurfaces before me, she takes hold of both my shoulders and eases me from the safety of the cavern. I draw a sharp breath at the coolness of her fingers on my neck.

"Relax," she urges, loosening her grip. "The more relaxed your breaths, the longer you'll last down there."

I nod, and she doesn't give me even a second longer to prepare before her lips are on mine. They're sea soaked and a little gritty from the salt, but somehow still impossibly soft. I'm dizzy as she keeps them pressed against mine, submerging us beneath the water before I can gather my senses.

No longer is my body cold; it floods with warmth, like she's somehow breathed life into me.

I hold my breath, keeping my eyes clamped shut as we sink deeper and deeper into the water. Only when her hands lift from my shoulders do I breathe, steadying myself. And though it stings a little, I open my eyes to find the murky water is much clearer than it should be. Alarmingly so. Vataea didn't just give us breath—she gave us a glimpse of what it's like to live in her world.

It's unlike anything I've seen before. Far below me, fluorescent green eels conceal themselves between jagged rocks, waiting to strike. Small schools of strange flat fish swim in the distance, traveling east of us. Something monstrous in size lurks in the shadows deep within the darkest depths of the sea, and I know in my gut not to venture anywhere near it. The Lusca isn't the only monster in these waters.

Though the colors of these creatures are sharper and their outlines clearer, I don't only see them—I *feel* them, as though I were the ocean itself.

I whirl to Vataea, who stretches her hand out to me. A knowing smile plays on her lips, like she understands exactly the awe I'm feeling. I have to wonder if this is what she felt when she stepped onto land for the first time—a sense of otherworldliness. A sudden understanding that there's so much more out there than we ever could have realized.

I take her hand as she pulls me along, knowing there's no time to be distracted, but wishing we had all the time in the world to simply explore.

Vataea is three times as fast as the rest of us. I swim as quickly as I can, following behind her, but by the furrow of her brows and the twitchy annoyance of her fin, it's clear we're not moving as fast as she would like. With every smack of her fin against the water, she spurs at least four feet ahead while the rest of us struggle with each foot.

Though I've always thought myself a strong swimmer, wading around in Arida has little comparison to deep-sea diving. While Vataea sports only her fins, the rest of us are fully dressed and armed, and we're slower for it.

I've no idea how far below we are, but the pounding in my ears and skull tell me it's probably best not to think about it.

Surprisingly, Ferrick is the quickest of us three. Even with the weight of the extra clothing he's tied around his belt for Vataea, it's clear he's slowing his movements in an attempt to keep closer to me. And though I would have thought Bastian to be quicker than he is, he clearly spends more time atop the ocean than within it. He's struggling as plainly as I am, biceps straining as he forces himself to swim faster.

Though exhaustion's already setting in, I do the same, trying to use my legs more than my arms. But as a shadow passes and cold water grazes my back, I throw myself against Bastian and make a grab for my new weapon. He grabs my waist in surprise, steadying me, and we both glance up.

Above us swims a fever of giant zapa rays. And if I wasn't already holding my breath, I would've surely lost it at the sight of them.

They move with a grace impossible to replicate, their fins like delicate wings that fan through the water, making their bodies glide. Each one is at least triple my size, massive and beautiful, with bodies outlined in a vibrant blue that sparks as they swim. It makes them look as though they've got electricity coursing through them, though in reality they're one of the sea's most peaceful creatures.

Ahead of us Vataea waits, worry wrinkling her brows. We need to move faster, but there's no way Bastian and I are going to be quick enough. At least not as we are.

I grab hold of Bastian's wrist, yanking him up. His forehead crinkles, head shaking in protest, but there's no time to argue. I yank on him again, this time until he begrudgingly follows.

No matter how hard I kick, my two feet will never have the strength of a fin. If we're going to get through this, we're going to need to borrow some.

The zapa rays have no fear as I approach. Rather, some of them swim a little closer, tilting and circling us curiously. I press my hands gently against one's back, flattening my fingers against its rubbery skin.

Still, it doesn't pull away, fearless.

When Bastian catches on to what I'm doing, his eyes light with surprise. He slows to move to the one behind me, lowering himself down upon the ray until he can get a gentle grip on it. Slick as their bodies are, it takes a moment to find a way to safely latch on.

I sink myself onto my ray, smoothing my fingers against its skin.

Still below us, Vataea's lips curl into a grin. She pushes Ferrick up, goading him to join us before she swims ahead of the zapa rays. She spins to face them, eyes a molten gold as she parts her lips.

The song she sings this time is a soft one, light and gentle. The zapa rays swish their fins slowly in response to it. She motions to the right, moving slowly at first, and they follow her.

They may not be the fastest beast in the sea, but as we're weighed down by too much clothing and heavy weapons, they're faster than we could ever be. And by Cato's blade, they're glorious.

All the years stuck in Arida, and this is what I've been missing.

It doesn't feel like we're swimming; we're flying. Gliding through the water as if it were light as air. Every yard we travel brings a new wave of colors. The sense of new creatures somewhere nearby. A rush of adventure that I cling to.

Vataea leads the fever, navigating the waters with a finesse I can't help but envy. As large as these creatures are, and traveling at twice the speed I could manage, we cover the distance swiftly. It's clear we're approaching Zudoh when the water darkens to murky navy, and bundles of seaweed smack me in the face and attempt to wind around my wrists and ankles. We hit what looks like a wall of dead fish—some of them float to the top while others are still sunken in the water, their skin peeling from their bodies. Only then does Vataea stop singing. The zapa rays halt, all of them twisting away like a synchronized dance. I push myself off the ray's back and stroke a hand along its smooth underside as a silent thank-you. One of its massive fins grazes my cheek, and then they're gone, heading east toward Suntosu.

My eyes burn in this filthy water, and I can barely make out the others. I feel one of their hands close around mine, large and calloused—Bastian.

Lead sinks into my stomach, making my body colder and the need for breath sharper. I clench Bastian's hand tightly, knowing that if I'm already feeling the need to breathe, it must be even stronger for him.

Our time's nearly up.

Bastian pushes me ahead, freeing our hands. It's impossible to tell how close we are; dread constricts my throat and makes each movement frantic. Desperate.

I swim as quickly as I can, kicking until my legs sear from pain. Pushing my arms so hard until they act purely on instinct, entirely numb. My throat burns as my senses dull, the water darkening in my periphery. Algae licks my heels and seaweed constricts my limbs, fighting to slow them.

I've no idea if Bastian's still behind me, or where Ferrick and Vataea are, but I don't stop. I push, because now my lungs are screaming for air as I fight to surface. But just as sand scrapes my knees and the end is in sight, Vataea grabs my hand. She drags me back, her mouth agape and eyes wide with panic.

Ferrick's behind her, his own eyes fluttering as his breath wanes. Bastian takes hold of my hand and tries to free it from Vataea, but she shakes her head fiercely and points above us to the shore.

My heart plunges when understanding dawns—there's no break in the barrier. They've attached it to their shore; something we didn't expect, as it means Zudians must also suffer from this curse. They must not even be able to access their own sea.

If we surface now, even right at the shore, we'll be trapped in a curse.

Vataea whips her head around, searching with terrified golden eyes. Shakily she lifts her hands and parts her lips with what at first sounds like a song, but quickly darkens into something sharp and vicious. She's chanting by the time a thin bead of water swirls within her palm as she tries to call upon the sea. But it doesn't listen.

When Ferrick's lips part, air bubbling out of his mouth, dread sinks its teeth into me and rips all hope. My throat tightens.

Tightens.

Tightens.

The ocean tried to claim me once already and I escaped it. This time, I won't be as lucky. Specks of darkness sink into my vision as the water floods up my nose and down my throat. I open my mouth on instinct, gagging on it.

The last thing I see is the horror on Vataea's face and the water swirling in her hands. Her chanting gets louder, until it's like she's yelling at the sea itself, but the water swallows and garbles the sound as I try to focus on it.

There's water in my eyes. My nose. My throat and lungs.

But then it's just . . . gone.

I choke on the air that surrounds me, desperate for it, and I'm not the only one. Gagging up water, I squint my eyes open to see Ferrick and Bastian doing the same. They clutch their chests and raw throats, squinting and blinking bloodshot eyes.

I want to settle myself upon the sand to dry my freezing body, but we're still in the water, a bubble of air formed around us. I shake the seaweed tangled in my hair and around my arms away as Vataea pushes us forward, chanting dagger-sharp words under her breath.

Blood flows freely from her nose, but she doesn't stop pushing until the sand is beneath us and we break through the surface, protected by the strange pocket of the ocean she's formed around us.

We fall to the sand as the barrier snaps. I hit knees-first and a sharp jolt spirals up my spine. I bite back a yelp, sinking my fists into the sand. Vataea's across from me, her fin gone in favor of legs. Ferrick shakily untangles her sopping tunic from his belt and tosses it her way.

Ferrick pants prayers under his breath while Bastian dry heaves into the sand.

"I thought your sea magic was rusty," the pirate grits out between ragged breaths, his body shaking.

"It is." Vataea's palms are shaky as she wipes the drying blood from her nose and examines it with a grimace.

I feel a rush of gratitude toward Vataea. It would have been so much easier for her to leave us in the water. Without her help, we'd certainly be dead. But after the fight with the Lusca, something between the four of us changed. I trust them, and I get the sense that they're all starting to trust one another, too.

It's like we're becoming a real crew.

"When we get to Arida," I tell her as I fall to my back, sucking in air like I might never have it again, "I'm throwing a banquet in your honor. You can have all the gold and all the food you want. Thank you."

Grunts of agreement echo my words, and I sneak a glance at Vataea, who dips her face toward the gray sky and exhales a sigh of relief. The tiniest hint of a genuine smile plays at her lips.

Once again, I can't help but be thankful she's on our side.

CHAPTER TWENTY-FIVE

While Ikae's streets are stained glass and Kerost is made from cracking cement and cobblestone, Zudoh greets us with towering gray peaks and limestone caverns that stretch through the beach and deep into the land. Thankfully this area appears to have been long deserted, so no one's around to see our arrival. There's not even a bird in the sky to crow a greeting.

I hug my arms tightly around myself as we travel along the shore, having paused long enough to catch our breath. Frosty air bites my skin, still damp from soaked clothes and wet hair, and I shiver. Several yards ahead looms a giant building with reflective glass that winks at me in the sunlight that's slowly beginning to peek through the thinning gray fog. I squint back at my reflection. The building is bigger than any I've seen before—sleek and white, with strange panels atop the roof.

It must have been beautiful once, but now the white beams are covered by a light gray film and scorch marks. Several of the windows are broken, revealing nothing but empty darkness within. On the roof, nearly all the panels sit twisted and ready to fall, while the charred front door tilts on frosted hinges.

"What is that place?" I ask, breath fogging in the air. By Cato's blood, it's cold as late winter here.

Bastian stares first at the building, then at the endless sand surrounding us. His brows sink, creasing his forehead in a series of thick, worried lines.

"It was a workshop," he says, though his voice is barely a whisper, cracking at the edges. "We made medicine and protective charms, and engineered new materials, like the wood of our trees—" He moves as if to point, but his words cut off swiftly. There are hardly any trees, and the ones that exist are half-charred.

Bastian jerks his head to the other side, toward shipless docks. Planks of wood that haven't been burned away are rotted through, many of them crumpling into the water. With each passing breeze, the wood groans with despair that Bastian echoes.

"This isn't how it's supposed to be."

Zudoh's sand is not white or tan, but gray. The closer it gets to the water, the darker it becomes. The water has formed a thick tar-like ring near the low tide as rotten algae clings to the shoreline. It's green and crusty like dried blood, and I grimace knowing that's what we swam through, and what clings to my curls and my clothes, slicking them down.

I try not to look at the pile of bones scattered on the ground, too large to belong to any animal I can imagine. There's no trace of skin or muscles; the bones have long since been cleaned by maggots and scavengers. Small, frayed pieces of rope and chips of wood dot the bones.

"What did it look like before?" I ask, keeping my voice low. It's quiet here, but that doesn't mean it's safe.

"It was beautiful," he says. "Bright white sand. As bustling as Ikae. The people were happy. There were trees everywhere, even here on the sand."

I squint at the gray ground and realize it's not just sand we're stepping on. It's ash.

This part of Zudoh's been burned to a crisp.

Bastian crouches upon the sand. He scoops up a handful, examines it, makes a fist around it. I don't follow him, because I understand what he's feeling. He was born here, and though he's been gone for many years, Zudoh's still his home. If something happened to Arida while I was gone, I'd never forgive myself.

Even the ocean is silent, nothing more than a whisper licking my ear. For once, it doesn't put me at ease. It chills my bones and raises the hairs along the back of my neck, plaguing me with paranoia.

Where are the people? The animals? The *life*?

"There were hardly any fish left alive in the water," Vataea says. I shiver, remember the feeling of slimy scales and decaying fish we swam through. "That's probably why the Lusca attacked. The legends always said it liked to roam the cold waters near Zudoh, but if there's no fish for it to eat here . . ."

"Then it has to start looking elsewhere." Bastian sighs. "There's no way my people can live this way forever. We have to fix this."

"And we will," I say, not needing to touch the earth to know its struggles. "You said there were trees here, before?"

"Hundreds of them," Bastian says. "They've all just . . . burned away."

"Not all of them." Ferrick steps forward and points toward the south side of the island. I follow his focus, blinking a few times to ensure I'm not seeing things. About a mile ahead, a thicket of startling white birch trees stretches across the island like a wall.

"It's dangerous that way," Vataea says. "I sense more Zudian curses."

"Then that's our way to Kaven." Bastian straightens, determination hardening his stare. "We should get going."

Something within those woods causes the magic within me to stir, curious. It urges me forward, lulling me toward the trees. But Vataea doesn't move. She turns her stony face toward craggy limestone mountains across from us instead, where a sea-slick cavern is formed at the edge of the beach.

She nods her head to the side, silently willing me to follow her as she starts toward it. Her eyes are sharp as daggers as she scans the space, but it's nothing more than a few boulders nestled at the edge of a mountain.

I glance behind me. Though the sun has finally made an appearance, it's already late afternoon. We've no idea where Kaven is or how long the journey through Zudoh will take us, and the last thing we need is to have to travel through unfamiliar territory at night. Especially when we're wet, freezing, and with a pirate who gets sicker the longer he's away from his ship.

"We should keep going." Gently, I take Vataea's arm.

She hesitates for only a moment, still glaring at the cave, but eventually relents. The moment we go to turn and walk away, a strange squawking sound pierces the air behind us. I reel, weapon in hand, but there's nothing but gravel and giant stones looking back at us.

"Is someone here?" I ask, trying to peek behind the stones and into the mountain.

After the Barracuda Lounge, nothing would surprise me anymore.

Zudoh answers with unsettling silence, as though holding its breath and waiting for us to leave. The discomfort wraps around me, flooding my arms with goose bumps.

When the sound doesn't come again, I hesitantly turn back

to start toward the woods, certain it must be nothing more than a strange bird. But I keep my dagger ready all the same.

When we take a step away from the area, the squawk sounds again. Only, it's not actually a squawk, but strange, garbled words.

"Don't go in there!" someone manages, though the words are immediately muffled once more.

"Shut up, you birdbrain!" The voice behind the snarl is decidedly feminine.

The voices draw my attention to the corner of the cavern, where thin pillars of jagged limestone form the back wall. Tucked in the far corner behind them, almost unnoticeable between a formation of boulders and the stalagmites, a young boy's face peeks out from around the stone. He's there for only a second before a pale hand yanks his head down.

"I've already seen you," I say, though I'm met by only silence once more.

Beside me, Vataea rolls her eyes. She wastes no time closing the space between us and the kids, crawling over damp stones and splaying across them on her stomach to peer between the stalagmites.

"Where is your village?" she demands.

Now discovered, the girl hiding behind the boulders rises to her feet to glare at Vataea face-to-face. Though young, likely around thirteen or so, her pale, freckled face is hardened and her eyes vicious.

"Why do you want to know?" Her words are spitfire, sharp and unforgiving. "So you can burn it down?"

Vataea's face contorts as she twists herself off the rocks. Somehow, she manages to look elegant while doing so. "Fire's not exactly my preferred method of destroying villages. But if you'd like to hear a song . . ."

The girl's hands are balled into shaking fists at her sides.

Beside her, an even smaller boy rises to his feet. His hair is so light that it's nearly white, and it's beautiful against his olive skin. He hunches his shoulders a bit as he eyes the girl beside him, hesitating before he speaks.

"I don't think they're here to hurt us, Raya . . ."

The girl whips her head and her lips curl back into a sneer, but the boy doesn't back down.

"There's only four of them," he presses. "If they wanted to hurt us, they'd have brought a fleet. And they're definitely not Kaven's."

Raya's lips pinch together as if to weigh the truth of his statement. Though it does little to placate her, her fists relax and the hostility in her voice eases. Her eyes flicker from Vataea, then to me, assessing.

"Who are you," she asks, "and why are you here?"

The island is no longer quiet. Footsteps kick up sand behind me as Bastian and Ferrick draw forward, caution in their eyes, their hands clenched around their weapons, ready.

The kids draw a tiny step back as they approach, and Raya pushes the small boy behind her. Both of them gape up at Bastian with too-large eyes, as though he's somehow threatened them. Bastian's face contorts. He takes a quick step back and drops his hand from his blade.

"We're not here to fight you," I tell her. "I'm Amora Montara, the Princess of Visidia."

Though the girl's skin pales, she makes no motion to relax or give away her thoughts. The young boy, however, has no such hesitation. He covers his mouth with a gasp and nudges the girl in the side. She swats his hand away, ignoring him.

"You didn't say why you're here." Raya barely breathes as she fights to hold her chest proud and feign calmness. But her eyes are unblinking and her chest quivers.

I return my weapon to its sheath and close the space so only the rocks are between us.

"We've come to help," I tell her. "To stop Kaven."

The boy drops his hands from his mouth and begins to turn.

"Ari—" Raya growls in protest, still side-eyeing Bastian with deep scrutiny. Ari shoves her hand from his shoulder and crouches.

"It's not safe for you here," he says. "Not even to talk. Kaven's eyes are everywhere; he probably already knows you're here. You shouldn't have been able to get past the barrier." The boy waves us forward, as if expecting us to climb over even more rocks and weave between the stalagmites to follow him into the small crevice of space he shares with Raya.

"Don't touch this one." He nods precisely to the stone he presses his small hands to. "Zale cursed it to make sure no one would be able to find the entrance. If you don't know where to touch, you'll get trapped in the curse until you forget what you were doing."

He slips his fingers into a tiny crevice and pushes the stone to the side, revealing a small hole he waves us toward.

"We'll take you to our camp," he says, quiet and urgent. "You can speak with Zale."

Ferrick shoots me a look, waiting for me to make the call. Bastian's fingers dance on his thigh, tapping anxious, tense beats. But I don't share either of their blatant hesitations. Though it's true we could be walking into a trap, I trust the urgent tone in the boy's words and the way Raya scowls as she waits for me to step forward, not liking what's happening but accepting it needs to be done.

Her angry caution is enough to win my trust. I climb over the stones and drop to my hands and knees, crawling through the darkness.

The air is damp and stagnant, nearly suffocating in the tight space. My lungs are heavy and the ground's chill bites at my palms and knees as I crawl forward. The others are directly behind me.

"Is everyone doing all right?" I ask.

Bastian responds with a breathy laugh. "Couldn't be better. I've got a nice view."

Though he can't see it, my eyes practically roll straight out of my skull to compensate for the heat that warms my cheeks. If this space were any larger, I would have turned and punched him on the shoulder.

"Enjoy it while you can, pirate."

Fortunately, it doesn't take more than a few minutes for the walls to stretch around us and the world to brighten as we ascend into the depths of a cavern, able to stand tall. Stalactites dangle precariously from the ceiling.

Beneath the surface, luminous jellyfish-like creatures skirt over the water. They shine through the murky tide, a green light that brightens the stone walls.

"What is this place?" I'm breathless as I stare down at the small creatures. At my feet, a tiny salamander with long gills poking from its neck flees from its hiding place and dives away from us, toward the opposite corner of the cavern.

I sneak a careful look at Bastian, whose chest rises and falls shakily. His lips are pressed together as he scans the cavern, eyes brimming. Zudoh's shore is a desolate, burnt wasteland, but this cavern is the picture of undisturbed beauty. It's a small glimpse into the island I imagine he remembers as his home.

"It's beautiful," I tell him.

His eyes flicker briefly toward me, throat bobbing as he nods.

"I thought I knew every inch of this island," he whispers, voice stolen by the cavern. "But thank the gods I was wrong."

I clasp a hand to his shoulder and squeeze, just once, certain we see the same sign—Zudoh may be suffering, but this island isn't gone yet. If a place like this still exists, then there's hope.

But even with that hope, Bastian's shoulders slump a little more with each step he takes. As the others walk ahead, I set my hand upon his shoulder. "This is what you wanted, isn't it? We're finally here."

He meets my eyes for no more than a fleeting second and offers a small, tense nod. "It's just been a while. I'm . . . not sure if anyone will recognize me. Or if there's even anyone left for *me* to recognize. I was so young."

"All we can worry about right now is making the most of our time here." I smile, expecting Bastian to mirror it, but his jaw is tense and his shoulders rigid.

"Amora, there's something you should—"

"This way!" Ari yells as he dashes ahead of us, making both Bastian and me flinch in surprise. I turn back to the pirate to let him finish, but he screws his mouth shut and nods ahead.

"We should keep moving." And before I can stop him, he turns to catch up with the others.

I want to press, but decide to give him the time he needs to process whatever it is he wants to tell me. Back home for the first time in years, I can't imagine the emotions he's going through.

"Our village was destroyed," Ari tells me as I catch up to them, trying to ignore the way Bastian purposely avoids looking at me. "But some of us were able to start a new camp. It's secret, and we're not supposed to leave, but . . ."

"But Ari and I sneak out sometimes, to scout," Raya says when his voice fades shyly away. She nods to Ari's side, and he lifts his coat to reveal a tiny silver telescope. "We saw your ship. Zudoh's the only place with wood like that. If it belonged to Kaven, we wanted to be able to warn our families. But then we watched you anchor your ship so far out; the last thing we expected was Visidians to wash up on shore."

Her eyes squint angrily; whenever she looks at me, it's as though she's scrutinizing my soul and doesn't favor what she finds. Her face isn't soft, but taut with a sharpened jaw. Though she's young, the world has hardened her.

This should never have happened to her.

"Is Zale the one in charge?" I ask, keeping my voice quiet. This place feels almost holy, a peaceful haven meant to remain untroubled.

Ari's lips twist, forehead scrunching into a dozen wrinkles as he considers this. Finally, he sighs. "Over here, she is. But the other side belongs to Kaven. Like I said, we're not supposed to go there."

From the corner of my eye I see Bastian's hands balling into fists. They're shaking.

"You have to tell Zale you're going to help us," Ari says urgently. "Hurry! She'll be so excited, come on!"

He bounds ahead, to where sunlight signals the cavern's exit. All I can see is a glimpse of water feeding into banks of emerald-green grass and, when I squint, a haze of shifting figures.

"Don't let your guard down," Ferrick offers, though I sense no danger. My nerves are settled but I check that my satchel is secured tightly at my hip.

A dozen faces jerk toward me as we exit the cave. Unlike me, they don't hesitate to grab their weapons.

CHAPTER TWENTY-SIX

It takes everything in me not to grab my new dagger. Sweat licks my brow as I look into dozens of frightened but determined faces.

The villagers before me hold weapons I'm unfamiliar with—dual axes linked by a black chain, sleek white staffs, and even some strange smoking tubes that look like something better left not inhaled.

Ari and Raya step in front of me.

At the sight of the children, a woman's eyes flash with angry concern.

"What were you thinking, bringing people here?" she growls. The corners of her eyes crease as she looks us over, focus lingering on the weapons at our hip. She doesn't look worried by what she sees.

Though the woman looks maybe only a decade older than I am, her skin is pallid and withered. She wears her black hair fastened into a long braid that curls over her shoulder and sits in heavy plaits below her chest. Her hooded amber eyes narrow with scrutiny.

The axes she wields do not tremble in her firm grip.

"They're going to help us," Ari urges, waving for the others to set down their weapons. They ignore him.

"We're not here to hurt anyone," I say as Vataea, Bastian, and Ferrick fan out around me. Everyone here whispers when they talk, so I'm careful to follow their lead, not wanting to further upset them. "Like your weapons, ours are for our protection. We'll only draw them if forced, though I sincerely hope it doesn't come to that."

The woman's eyes narrow further and she looks Ferrick and Vataea over. The two of them stand closely, hands lifted before them in a display of truce. She looks to Bastian next, eyes sparking with surprise. She flinches, and Bastian mirrors the movement, shoulders hunching as though he intends to wilt into himself.

"I recognize you," she whispers. "Don't I? By the gods, you look just like—"

"I used to live here," Bastian says, cutting her off swiftly. "But it was a long time ago." Again his hands tremble in his lap as he tilts his head to me in a small nod, quick to take the focus off himself. "We're all here to try to help. This is the Princess of Visidia, Amora Montara. She had no idea what condition Zudoh was in until now."

Disbelief paints her features. "How would the princess not know about Zudoh?"

"I ask myself the same thing," I tell her. "My parents have managed to keep Zudoh's fate hidden from everyone, not just me. If you put down your weapons, I'll tell you everything. We want to help." I'm careful to not seem commanding, knowing that angering anyone with a weapon pointed at my face might not be the wisest move. "We're here to discuss restoring Zudoh to the kingdom."

"We found them on the shore," Raya quietly offers, ignoring the dark-haired woman's glare. "They were about to head into the woods."

"How exactly did you get into Zudoh in the first place?" Zale challenges. "No one gets in unless Kaven invites them."

I point to my hair, slick with algae and sea muck. "If we were invited, I assure you we'd look a little more presentable. Please look at my hair. My clothing. We swam through a wall of dead fish to get here."

Zale hesitates for a moment, though the tension in her shoulders eases some as she watches me pick a fish eye from my matted hair. Her nose curls, and she waves for those behind her to relax.

As the weapons lower, Ferrick exhales a breath so heavy with relief that it seems to relax the woman at least marginally. She stretches her hand out to me.

I take it swiftly. Her hands are worn and rough, making me immediately aware of how soft mine are in comparison.

"You can call me Zale," she offers as she nods me forward, leading us toward the camp. Though Ari attempts to stray several paces behind, Zale's eyes find him regardless, searing into him so fiercely that the boy winces.

"I don't care if you find one of the gods wandering lost on that shore," she scolds. "Don't you dare bring anyone else back here again."

Ari peeks at me and I flash him an apologetic shrug.

The camp is larger than I expected, and decidedly more thriving. On this side of the cavern, it's as if the Zudoh we saw upon our arrival was a cruel lie.

Here, Zudoh is bright white sand, healthy green grass, and rows upon rows of tall trees. They're similar to birch in color, but significantly thicker, with massive roots that weave in and out of the earth like overstuffed worms. In every direction, a ridge of rocky mountains stretches endlessly into the sky, shielding the camp. It's a clever hiding place.

Their homes are made from the same white wood of the trees, small but sturdy. Like the building back on the shore, strange metallic panels coat their rooftops, though these are significantly smaller and less sleek.

"They help us harness energy from the sun, to keep our homes warm," Zale explains when she catches me looking. "They store heat during the day, and release it at night."

We pass a group of Zudians seated around a strange formation of rocks—a taller one in the back, smaller stones around the middle, and nothing in the front. Between the stones is a tunnel of sorts, and in the middle, a raging fire.

But its smoke doesn't rise into the air. Instead, it filters out through rocks and into the tunnel, leading toward the cavern where a few more people are gathered. They hold canteens in their laps, fill them with water, and then bring them back to the fire, where someone waits with a variety of containers. The water goes into the containers murky, and emerges clear.

They work in a routine—fetching the water, filtering the water through the strange containers, boiling it, filling canteens, and then setting them aside to cool.

Realizing how much I've taken our spring water for granted, I try not to stare as we pass, mesmerized by how efficiently they work.

"That makes it safe to drink?" I ask, and Zale nods with a smile curling on her lips.

"Not one person has gotten sick from the water," she says with an air of pride. "And, even if they ever did, it wouldn't be a problem."

I follow her finger as she points to one of the buildings we pass. It's larger than the others, and through the open door I see two kids sitting in chairs—one boy who looks like he's about to vomit, and a girl who offers up a scraped knee. Two Zudians stand before them, dressed in long tunics that must have once been a bright opal, but have since dirtied into a murky gray. One places a hand on the girl's knee, and the other on the boy's stomach. At the hazy orange glow around their palms, I nearly choke. Ferrick echoes the sound.

"That's restoration magic," Ferrick says. "They're using Suntosan magic."

But it's more than that; they're using *multiple* magics.

I stumble as bile rises to my throat, making the camp spin. Practicing multiple magics is the threat the Montaras have spent their lives protecting the kingdom against.

I don't bother to reel back my surprise, and Zale's been waiting for it.

"Remember that we don't live under the laws of Visidia," she says quietly, her voice a fierce whisper. "Your father took the healers away from our island when he banished us. He left our people to suffer. What else were we supposed to do?"

"But it's not just about Visidia!" My throat's so dry that the words are almost painful. "Having too much magic is deadly. Using multiple magic is—"

"Necessary," she finishes for me. "And look around you; do we look sickly? We've been practicing multiple magics for years, ever since we were banished. Despite the kingdom's claim, nothing has happened to those of us who chose to wield more than one type of magic. If we wanted to survive, this was necessary."

I tear at the skin around my nails as my vision bounces from face to face, taking in all the magic I failed to notice before.

The hands that manipulate water and build structures into the earth. That heat the flames and heal the sick.

There's no way this could just be *fine*; this has been our law for centuries. If the danger of multiple magics was a lie, then how could the Montaras come to have our soul magic? How would King Cato have first established Visidia?

I don't want to believe it, but as the young girl jumps from her chair with a healed knee and the boy's color returns to his skin, there's no denying what Zale says.

They can wield multiple magics. And their smiles certainly don't look corrupted as they send the children on their way. They're not suffering, or struggling from their bodies carrying too much magic. Their souls aren't disappearing.

They're fine.

Dozens of eyes settle on us as we cross through the site, most of them curious, but others protective. They try to catch Zale's eye, and she ushers them away with a gentle shake of her head.

"I'll be fine," she tells them, and a tiny flame flickers in her palm when she says it, showing she's willing to fight with a magic she shouldn't even have.

I try not to focus on the multiple magics any longer, because if I do, I'm going to be sick.

Instead, I focus on the camp. Though there's no absence of people here, there's certainly an absence of noise. Even as groups of Zudians free-climb a cliffside with foot and hand holes carved out by Valukan magic, their movements and chatting are no louder than a gently sung lullaby. Not even the children scream as they run through the camp, chasing one another.

"They're going over the mountain in search of food," Zale says before anyone can ask, seeming to take pride in our awed faces. "We cursed the land to misdirect others—it's the only safe area we have, but it's a trek." Something lingers in her words and the squint of her eyes, but she leaves it unsaid.

"Why's everyone whispering?" Vataea's thin brows sink low into her forehead. I'm glad I'm not the only one unnerved by it. Zale's sharp eyes flit to her. "Because if Kaven finds our camp, we're done for."

Vataea's fingers press against her sides, nails scratching uncomfortably at her trousers. "How have you survived here so long? If there aren't even fish in the water, surely your food supply can't be doing well?" she asks as Zale waves us forward and into what I assume must be her home. There's not much to the place—just a small table, a hanging bed made from ropes, and a few knickknacks—but it hides the bite of cool air from outside and settles my nerves. She motions for us to take a seat on the floor, soft and padded with smoothed white birch. Vataea sinks back on her hands, but Bastian is rigid. His focus is pinched tight.

"It's been hard. We've a lake that's beginning to run dry, so we've been trying to engineer new crops on the other side of the mountain," Zale says as she lowers herself to join us on the floor. "But the land isn't taking to it well. I'll admit it's been a struggle, but if we venture any farther out, we risk capture." She looks toward the door, shoulders slumping. "My mother was one of Zudoh's best scientists. She studied plants, and tried to find ways to make them larger, or even grow quicker. She's the one who founded this camp, and did most of her experiments here.

"Kaven killed her years ago, when she was trying to sneak others into our camp," she continues after a moment's pause. "But the trees she engineered are in abundance, here. Their wood is light and pliable, and the trees grow back to full size within months of being cut. Her dream was to use them to create newer, faster ships. And we've been trying to do the same."

Thinking of *Keel Haul*, I sneak a glance at Bastian, but he keeps his attention firmly focused ahead. Despite the coolness of the air, sweat slicks his skin.

"Trying?" I ask, prying my focus from his trembling hands and returning it to Zale. There's tension in her jaw as her eyes bore into me.

"The king burned our ships," she says in a voice that's pure gravel. It slices straight through me slick as steel, catching my breath in my throat. "For years he cut us off from traveling; only recently has Zudoh produced enough wood to manufacture ships again, which is how Kaven's been able to grow his army in recent years. But it's been slower for us, since we have so few people to help build." Her words ring heavy with pain and exhaustion.

I think back to everything I knew about Zudoh. That they were banished. That they turned against Father in a fight, and that he was wounded.

But they weren't just *banished*. They were imprisoned, their ships burned as they were left here with Kaven. All of this—all the suffering and fear that's happening upon Zudoh's soil—is because of him.

Nothing I say will be enough, but still I tell her I'm sorry through a throat that's thick with cotton.

Part of me wants to believe that, if this is the truth, then Father surely must have had a good reason. But what possible reason is there that would warrant landlocking an island?

"We'll be finished with one in another season or two," Zale continues. "It's been years in the making, as there aren't many of us to work on it between all our other tasks. But it's almost finished."

"You don't sound as pleased about this as I would expect," Vataea says.

"Would you be pleased if you had to choose between your family and freedom?" Though Zale's never struck me as anything but powerful, I notice for the first time how small her hands are as she balls them into fists on her lap. "We build the ship over the mountain, so we can get it to the water when we're stocked and ready to try to break the barrier. Though we've created tools to make the climb possible, I'm afraid not all our people are fit for that journey. If we're to leave, we'd have to leave some of them behind."

"What about using Curmanan magic?" I press, though even suggesting they use another magic feels wrong on my lips.

Zale smiles sadly. "Our camp is small. We've a few who've tried to practice it, but levitation is a high-level skill. None of us have been able to master it, and we've no time to keep trying. It would take years we don't have. We even thought about using Valukan earth magic to build a path through the mountain, but it would take too long to do it slowly, and would be too loud to do it quickly. Once we get over the mountain, we need to be quick to collectively try to break Kaven's curse. He'll notice the moment it's down, so we won't have time to linger. Climbing is our only option."

My nod is slow as the words sink in. I can't let this happen.

"Why does he have such a hold on this island?" Ferrick asks. My palms are slick with sweat I wipe over my pants, trying to relax enough to focus on Zale's answers.

"Kaven believes everyone should learn whatever magic they want," Zale tells us. "And he thinks that Montara magic—your soul magic—should be something we practice widely. But what he *refuses* to believe is that some are perfectly content with only having their one magic. That not all of us wish to spend our lives mastering every form of magic out there."

"How big has his following grown?" Bastian asks so quietly his words are barely audible.

Zale narrows her eyes and inspects him again. Her cheeks hollow as though she's biting the inside of them, assessing him like a puzzle.

Bastian tries not to look her directly in the eye.

"Not as large as it could be, since he's trying to force

people to learn a magic many of them can't handle," she eventually answers, ceasing her scrutiny. "But probably half of both Zudoh and Kerost follow him. I don't think he has much of a hold on the other islands; maybe small numbers if anything. It's not practicing multiple magics that makes people sick you know. It's only when they try to learn Aridian magic."

Ferrick looks vaguely ill. "What do you mean, Aridian magic? There's no way anyone else can learn that." He turns to me to see if I share his surprise, and I sink into myself. "Did you know about this?"

"I didn't want to believe it either," I offer him quietly. "Not until I saw it."

Understandably, this answer doesn't please him. He sits back on his hands, shaking his head as Zale explains. Beside him, Vataea listens intently.

"It's far from proper Aridian magic," Zale clarifies. "But somehow Kaven's created a version that's not quite right. He used to kidnap people and force them to learn it. Now that he has a following though, he shares it with them. But most who try to learn this magic suffer and die immediately. Those who survive become warped. Corrupted, like him. That magic is likely what made him so awful in the first place."

Even though I already knew this, hearing it again makes me shiver. Bastian's head dips to the floor, while Ferrick chews anxiously at his bottom lip. Vataea's forehead creases as she watches Zale, waiting for the woman to say more.

"Everyone should be able to practice whatever magic they wish," Zale says fearlessly. "I don't disagree with Kaven on that. But where the king keeps magic from us, Kaven forces it on us. He's destroyed Zudoh, and now he's set his sights on the other islands. Soon he'll be knocking on the palace doors." Her eyes narrow as she waits for my reaction, but I feel no anger toward her. Only confusion.

All my life, the ban on multiple magics has been Visidia's most primary law. Father always said it was to protect us, and I believed him without question. It's why I accepted my magic. Why I pressed my blade into the arm of that first prisoner, and why I've taken so many lives since.

I drop my head into my palms. Was *everything* a lie?

"If we promised to take care of Kaven and restore this island, would you consider rejoining Visidia?"

Her face tilts up, eyes brimming. She doesn't hesitate when she nods and says, "Absolutely," like that one word is the only truth she knows. Like it's the prayer she whispers every night. "We care little about kings or politics; all we want is the chance to live comfortably again, whether it's on this island or another. To exist without worrying whether someone will kidnap our children or force us to learn a magic we want nothing to do with." Her lips curl, and heat burns fiercely within my chest, igniting my speeding heart.

"You're not leaving anyone behind." I'm quick to my feet and Bastian and Vataea follow suit without question. Ferrick, however, is slower to rise. His eyes squint ahead at Zale, expression tight. "Where do we find Kaven?"

Zale stiffens, shoulders pulling back as her spine straightens. She looks us over, lips pressed into a fine line. Her eyes linger on Bastian longer than any of us, and for a moment I worry she'll refuse our help. That she'll call the others to help eliminate us. But then she stands as well and says, "He's through the woods. But Zudoh's nights are cold and dangerous. You'll freeze in those clothes. Our healing ward is empty; the four of you should stay there for the night. We may not have much to offer, but if you're going to help us, then let us help you."

Though Ferrick looks wary and Bastian can't seem to look Zale in the eye, my clothes are still soaked and my hair slick with algae that won't dry. Getting lost in the dark or freezing in the woods won't get us anywhere.

And so I accept Zale's offer, and she guides us toward the door as she stands.

Outside the hut, a few dozen Zudians wait for us, not bothering to hide their eavesdropping. Though their eyes never stray from us as we journey back to the small building where we watched the children being healed, they dip their heads ever so slightly as we pass, offering hesitant thanks.

It's only a small amount of trust, but it's trust from my people nevertheless. Pride heats my cheeks and hastens my footsteps. I bow my head back to them before Vataea and I are escorted into one building, and Ferrick and Bastian the other.

It might not seem like much to the others, but I'll use their trust as my armor, and the fate of my kingdom as my strength.

Come tomorrow, Kaven will no longer be a threat, and I'll restore this kingdom.

CHAPTER TWENTY-SEVEN

I'd hoped a bath would make me feel cleaner. But as my wet hair drips onto the hands I hold before me, all I can see is the blood that has forever stained them.

I've been practicing soul magic since I was a child; nights in the prison with Father form some of my earliest memories. Back then, I believed what he told me: we do what we do to protect the kingdom. The overall well-being of Visidia is more important than eliminating a single corrupted soul.

Once again, I think of the first time I helped with an execution. It's been years since I've thought of it, yet it's been heavy on my mind ever since my failed performance. When I close my eyes, I see my five-year-old self standing in the prison cell next to my father. I recall the woman's blood pouring over my fingers as I pressed a blade into her arm, and the way magic latched onto me in that moment—a shadowy beast that clung immediately to my soul. I suffered for weeks after that as I fought the magic down, forcing it to bond to my soul without overtaking it.

I thought what I was doing was right. I gritted through the pain so that my kingdom wouldn't have to.

But it was a lie. Everything Father ever told me about this magic and our duties was a *lie*. And I believed it because I trusted him more than anything. He wasn't just my father; he was my inspiration. The type of ruler I aspired to be like, loved and respected by our people.

But my view on the world was skewed and limited, aiding the lies he fed me with a silver spoon.

My chest heaves with sharp breaths as tears roll freely down my cheeks. I don't bother trying to hold them back.

Outside this wall are Zudians who practice more than their own magic. Their souls are whole. Their bodies aren't exhausted. They're perfectly fine.

I wipe a tear away and it rolls down my fingers, but I don't see it for what it is. Instead I see the blood of the first woman I ever executed, trailing down my finger like a serpent.

If not to protect Visidia, then what was her death for?

At the sound of my door creaking open, I quickly wipe my eyes and dry my hands on my pants. Though I expect a freshly bathed Vataea, it's Bastian who staggers in without knocking, a flask in his hand. He takes one look at me, and his face drops. "Are you crying?" he asks in a voice lightly slurred.

I jerk my head away so he can't see my bloodshot eyes, and press my trembling hands into my cot. "Gods, what are you doing? Get out! This isn't the time to be screwing around."

"I'm not screwing around." When I point to the flask in his hands, his face nearly melts off by how impossibly deep his frown stretches. "This? This is courage. Here, I brought you some."

Though I turn to yell at him again, my mouth turns dry as

I notice for the first time that his bloodshot eyes mirror mine. I know at once it's not from the alcohol.

Slowly, I take the offered flask and pop off the lid, greeted by the sharp sweetness of rum.

"Where'd you find this?" I ask, my mouth burning as I take a swig and pass it back to Bastian.

"I'm a pirate," he answers, though the edges of the words are bitter. He nearly spits them. "Every pirate has a flask."

He takes a drink, and then it's my turn again. This time I'm more liberal with my sips.

"If you came here hoping to continue what we started back on *Keel Haul*, you've picked the wrong night."

Bastian's nose crinkles. "I didn't come here to fool around. There's something—" His words cut off with a sharp hiss of air. He presses a hand to his forehead, squinting his eyes shut against the pain. Sweat licks his cheeks and the space above his lips as he crumples over, trying to steal deep breaths between his teeth.

I toss the flask onto the cot to grab his shoulders, steadying him. "Bastian? Hey, breathe! What's happening?"

He tenses beneath my grip and remains like that for a long moment until his breathing steadies and his muscles begin to relax. When he lifts his head again there are tears in his eyes and a crack in his voice. "What's happening is that I shouldn't be here. I should have never returned."

I help him straighten, wordless as I offer him the flask. He downs it and draws another from the inside pocket of his coat.

"Courage," he says again, "and a remedy for straying too far from my curse."

Though I pity him for the pain he must be in, I don't let him take a drink from the second flask. I press it down when he lifts it to his lips.

"We need you sharp tomorrow." I keep my voice stern. "I'm

sorry you're in pain, I truly am. But you have to fight it, just for this last night."

Rather than argue, his face cracks and he drops the flask into my hands with a shaky breath. For a long moment he's silent, staring straight ahead at the door as though he's trying to burn it with his eyes. But then his shoulders crumple.

"Did you see the way Zale looked at me?" He practically chokes the words, shoving his face into his palms and breathing deeply into them. "Stars, she looked at me like I was *him*. Like I'm the one who did this to them. That's how they're all going to look at me, Amora. And I deserve it. I deserve the pain. I deserve this entire blasted curse. Look at me! I walked in on you crying, and didn't even ask you what was wrong." Looking down at his hands, he sighs and adds quietly, "I hate seeing you hurt."

I desperately want to open the second flask and take another swig. I want to feel it burn all the way down, numbing my pain with each sip. But it's as I told Bastian—one more day. We have to be sharp for one more day. "I'm crying because I've realized the truth," I tell him quietly, letting the words ring with the full force of the conviction I feel. "I'm just as bad as Kaven. I've taken as many lives as he has, if not more."

"Don't say that." Bastian's snarl is so vicious that I flinch. "Kaven's taken lives for no reason. He's trapped Zale and her people here on this tiny stretch of land, and forced them to find a way to survive. He's forced them to take a magic they don't want, just so he can gain power. You've taken lives, Amora, but it was never like that."

My focus wanders to my hands, tightly clenched and resting on my thigh. "It doesn't matter. I still killed them. I still made that choice."

"You thought you were protecting Visidia." Bastian takes one of my hands and moves it slowly into his lap. "It's not your fault you were told a lie."

266

But I don't want to believe those words. Because it's like Zale said—I'm Visidia's princess. How could I not know the truth?

"And it's not your fault you were cursed," I say, but Bastian's as unwilling to accept kindness as I am.

Again he runs his hands over his face. Threads his fingers through his hair. He shifts and sighs until the distractions no longer work. "There's something I have to tell you."

I still. His chest stops its trembling as he looks straight at me, his words firm and determined. I'm not prepared for the next words he speaks.

"I haven't been honest with you, and I'm sorry for that. I'm sorry I didn't tell you this earlier, but I didn't know how." He pauses to run a tongue over his lips, and presses his free hand into his thigh, as if to brace himself for the words he's trying to get out. "You need to know that Kaven's not just some man on the island I happened to know of. You always wanted to know more about him, but I could never get myself to talk about him.

"It's because he's my brother, Amora." His words waver. "It's because as much as I know I have to face him, I'm terrified. He was my responsibility. My blood. I should have stopped him years ago, but instead I ran."

The tension in my chest is suffocating. I drop my hand from his shoulder. "Did you know the truth about practicing multiple magics? Did you know it was all a lie?"

He shakes his head fiercely. "I promise I didn't. Kaven's nearly ten years older than me; I was a child when he started to teach everyone cursed soul magic. He said multiple magics weren't dangerous, but I refused to learn. I . . . I thought he was lying. Too many people died when they tried to learn it. But now I realize that it only ever happened when they tried to learn Aridian magic."

I press my head into my palms. "Why didn't you tell me sooner? You had a chance to come clean about everything before, when you told me the truth about you and *Keel Haul*."

He practically wilts into his own body. "I'm a pirate," he says quietly, as though the words are a dangerous curse. "All my life I've had to play that role just to survive, and the more I played, the more the lines got blurred of who *I* really was. I've never had someone else in my life that I've cared for the way I care about you, and I guess . . . I'm still getting used to that. If I told you the truth, I thought you might hate me. Because look at what Kaven's done." He gestures around the room. Around the camp, as though it's enough of an answer.

"These people are too afraid to even talk at normal volume," he says. "The children can't even yell and play freely. They're terrified of being killed by my *brother*. I couldn't risk you finding out, because . . ."

"Because you needed me," I finish for him, drawing my hand from his. "You were using me."

He looks away, but doesn't deny it. "Only at first. I needed you for your magic, yes, but I was telling you the truth on *Keel Haul*, Amora. I wanted you to stay. I don't have anyone else I care about in my life, not really. But I found myself wanting you in it. I didn't want to risk losing you by telling you about Kaven. Looking back, I know that was selfish of me, and I'm sorry." He runs his fingers through his hair. "I wanted to tell you the truth now, so that you still had time to make a choice."

"What choice?" I echo, unable to conceal my hurt in the way my words bite.

"If you want to leave, I understand." He squeezes his hands shut. "I can fight Kaven on my own, as I should have done ages ago."

I bristle, because who does he think he is? No matter what lies I've spent my life believing, there's always been a single

268

truth I've known without a doubt—I was made to protect Visidia.

I think of the look in Zale's eyes when I swore to help her. I remember the warmth in my chest as the Zudians bowed their heads to offer me their thanks.

And I realize now it doesn't matter if my magic was a lie, because I can still fulfill what I believed its purpose to be. With everything in my power, I will protect and restore Visidia.

"I would never step down from this fight," I tell Bastian, pouring into the words every ounce of conviction I feel. "But he's your *brother*. Did you come here with the intent to kill him or not? Because if he refuses to step down, there won't be time for hesitation."

"The man we're to face tomorrow is no longer my brother." Bastian's eyes hollow with sadness. "He's ruined the lives of too many. I can face him; it's facing everyone else that worries me."

Those words break something in me, because as I look at Bastian now, slumped and broken and barely managing to hold on, I understand him better than I ever have. Gently, I take hold of his chin, tipping it so that our eyes meet. His scruff is rough against my fingers. "Believe me when I say that I understand, and that I'm afraid, too. Look at how Visidia's withered under my father's reign. I understand being embarrassed by what your family has done, but you are not your brother, as I am not my father. Do you understand that?" And as I say the words aloud, it's as though a weight falls from my shoulders.

It's not too late for us; we are not the mistakes of our family. We have the opportunity to change Visidia for the better.

"But you didn't know," Bastian whispers. "The king kept you shut away on Arida. I spent years knowing about Kaven's plans, and I didn't do a thing about it."

"But we're here, now. *You're* here, now. Those people out there?" I point to the door, but never let my attention waver from his. "They're counting on us. Don't you dare say you or I shouldn't be here; this is exactly where we need to be."

"I should have told you the truth earlier." When he shuts his eyes, I release his chin.

"You should have." My insides prickle with heat as I try to process everything. Bastian *should* have told me; we promised each other there would be no more secrets. But I can understand why he held on to this. Seeing the state of Zudoh, I can understand his desperation and fear. In his situation, would I have acted any differently? Even now, staring the truth dead in the eye, I still want to believe that Father would never be capable of sitting idly by and letting this happen to our kingdom. That all those years he kept me locked on Arida truly were to protect me, and not to hide his mistakes. I want to believe that he would do better than this; that he'll swoop in any minute to save Visidia, and prove it was all one big misunderstanding.

Bastian, likely, wanted the same. These people we both have to face are the people capable of hurting us the most—they're our blood. When Bastian ran, I've no doubt he had every hope that his brother would stop. That, eventually, they'd come to a peaceful understanding.

But even our idols—even those we want to love and trust more than anything—can let us down. It's time we accept it and face the reality they left us with.

"I forgive you," I tell Bastian, letting the words sit on my tongue for a moment to truly ensure I mean them. "But only if you fight with me tomorrow. I'll stand by you as you face Kaven, and you by me as we face the king. Fear is part of life; all that matters is what we do with it. So think of the people who are counting on us. We have a chance to fix this."

I can tell he's mentally processing the gravity of those words as his lips press together and his head dips. Quietly, he says, "I'll stand by you."

"Then tomorrow morning we're going to march through those woods and find Kaven. We're more than our blood, both of us. Doing what we can now is all that matters." The words give me courage I cling to tightly, using it to wipe away the despair I was drowning in mere moments before.

"I don't deserve your forgiveness," he says. "I don't deserve anyone's."

"Yes, you do." The pain in his eyes is the same that I feel. "If I can't forgive you for one mistake, then how can I expect Visidia to forgive the Montaras for a lifetime of lies? Take the forgiveness, and know that from this point on, we're truly in this together. I understand the choice you made, Bastian. I understand it better than anyone."

I press my lips to his, and at first the kiss is tender. But as tears begin to wet his cheeks, that tenderness gives way to something raw and passionate. Something almost desperate.

When Bastian knots his fingers into the back of my curls, his touch is electricity. I shiver each time his thumb strokes the back of my neck.

Falling back in the cot, I make fists in his shirt and pull his body on top of mine. His lips are rum sweet as I drink him in, nodding permission when his fingers hesitate at the edge of my tunic. When his hazel eyes catch mine, my body ignites.

Bastian's hands are warm and rough as they slip beneath my tunic, roaming the skin of my stomach. Exploring the curves of my hips.

My eyes flutter shut as his lips find my neck. He alternates between peppering soft kisses and gentle bites. I hold him to me, one hand wrapped around his back and the other curled tight in his chestnut waves.

I want this.

I want *him*.

There's a heat in my belly that pushes me forward, guiding

my fingers to the buttons of his shirt. He makes no complaint as I fumble to undo them. The moment it's off, he slides down so that his lips are on my hip bone and I have to grip the cot to steady myself as they rove lower and lower, until he's kissing the skin of my thighs.

His fingers slide beneath the band of my pants and I tense, not realizing I've hardly been breathing this whole time.

Bastian pauses immediately, warm eyes flickering to mine as he draws back up and plants a tender kiss to my lips. It's the taste of rum on them that spurs me back into reality. I pull back quickly, drawing heavy breaths. My body is too aware of him; every inch of me that he's touched burns with desire.

"Are you okay?" Bastian asks urgently, tucking a loose curl behind my ear. "We don't have to do anything, Amora. We can stop."

"I don't want to stop." I catch his hand in mine and draw it to my lips, kissing his palm. His fingers. Knuckles. "But we need to. You're drunk, Bastian."

"It was only a few drinks," he protests, peeling his grip away to kiss my neck once more. "I'm fine."

Despite how much I might want it, I press my hands to his chest and ease him back. "We'll have other chances," I tell him calmly. "Hopefully many more. But tonight isn't one of them."

He opens his mouth as if to say something, but closes it with a quiet sigh. Gently, he eases himself off me, sitting on his knees at the edge of the cot. My body aches with the missing weight of him. I feel too light. Too cold.

Slowly I set my hand on his thigh. He takes it with a smile.

"I couldn't do any of this without you, you know." He squeezes my hand gently. "I want you to know that I'm incredibly thankful for you, and I'll see you in the morning."

"You're a pirate, Bastian Bargas." I smile when his lips crack at the name. "You would have found a way."

He slips his fingers free and pulls me into a gentle hug. It lasts for only a moment before he eases away. He doesn't look back at me until his hand is on the door. "It's Altair, by the way. Bastian Altair." And then he laughs, a soft and quiet sound. "Stars, I haven't said that name in ages. It . . . feels good."

In my cot, I smile as the door shuts behind him.

CHAPTER TWENTY-EIGHT

Only Zale sees us off as we sneak away early the next morning, and we make our way deep into the woods as the sun rises. For the past hour, these woods have tried only to devour us.

The white birch trees are dampened with the early morning mist that's rolled in from the shore. The farther into it we plunge, the more they consume. Overgrown roots grab at me, bruising and cutting my ankles, attempting to wrench me into the earth. Below us, the ground is covered with soot that coats my boots black.

My weapon can't help us here. Its poison is too powerful to waste on naughty trees. A breeze shifts through the branches and they rustle, as if laughing at me.

"I'm trying to *help* you," I growl at the island, tripping over dead bramble and broken twigs. The trees here are the same white birch as the ones from Zale's camp, but they're thinner. Weaker, and normal.

Vataea trails carefully behind me, mimicking my movements to avoid injury while Ferrick grimaces and grunts beside me, smacking away sharp branches.

"Ferrick, Amora, wait—"

I trip on soot when I turn toward Vataea's voice, barely able to catch myself on a stump.

In front of me, a small black fox pokes its head out from behind one of the trees. It's the first sign of life I've seen on this side of the island since we arrived in the woods probably an hour ago. I still, watching as the creature slowly eases out from behind the thin tree, its curious golden eyes never wavering from mine. Shadows fan out around its feet and wrap around the beast. I draw a step back when I see them, breath catching in my throat.

"Bastian?" I ask, daring to look away long enough to check over my shoulders. "Vataea?"

But no one's there.

I stumble back as the space around me stretches farther into darkness, dragging me with it. The trees are at least a mile away, now. Figures weave in and out of them, calling my name.

But the voices are a warped echo that alert the hairs on my neck and force my breaths to come in gasps.

"Amoraaa . . ." they call, both a whisper and a shout. "Amoraaa?"

I twist so I'm on my knees and try to drag my shaking body back to a stand. But the moment I'm back on my feet, I wish the earth would have swallowed me whole just as it did the trees.

The fox looms over me, massive on its hind legs. Its face is sharp and pointed, black ears poking out from the hood of a sapphire cape. Its golden eyes rove my body, and when they settle on my face again, a jagged row of teeth gleams at me.

"Are you lost?" the fox asks, its breath foul as it heats my cheeks. "Why don't I help you find your way?"

It leaps into the air, and though every part of me knows I should move, I only watch as the fox twists its body. Its mouth stretches. Stretches. Stretches.

And it swallows me whole.

The darkness morphs into blinding white light as I jerk to my feet, gasping desperately for air.

No longer am I surrounded by trees; there's nothing but the beautiful red sand of Arida, and a figure waiting for me on the beach.

Though his back is turned to me, I recognize Father by his crown—the skull of a legendary Valuna eel, with rows of sharp teeth stretching above his forehead and around his jaw, while a spine of jewel-encrusted bones glides down his back.

"Father?" I try to say, but the words burn my throat as sand fills it, choking me. It comes out my nose. My eyes. I fall to my knees, silently begging Father to turn to me.

Look at me. Please. You have to help me.

My vision swims. I grab on to my tongue, thinking perhaps I can dig the sand out myself. But I can't control my hand. It blips in my vision, first by my side, then at my throat. On my tongue again.

I try to scream, and though no sound comes out, Father turns to me slowly.

Only Father doesn't have golden eyes or rows of bloodied teeth.

The fox wears his crown. His cape. And it smiles at me, eyes glinting as it draws forward, growing twice its size with every step.

It freezes only as something strikes my face. The fox whips its head to the side and growls.

I see nothing that could have struck me, yet I'm knocked back a step. The fox whimpers and shrinks to half its size.

Amora!

The sand no longer burns my eyes. It drains from my throat, and I can breathe again.

The fox snaps its giant eyes to me. "I can't help you unless you let me," it whispers, trying to crawl closer. But I finally find my legs again, and kick myself back against the sand.

Focus, Amora! You need to focus!

I squint my eyes shut, and see a glimpse of Bastian and Ferrick standing over me.

When I open my eyes again, it's the fox, the heat of its gaping mouth on my face.

Focus!

I dig my fists into the sand, suck in a breath, and slam my eyes shut as the fox lunges for me again.

The world spins and warps back into focus as thousands of birch trees sprout around me. I suck in desperate breaths, body shaking as I try to find my focus. The trees stretch impossibly high, covering the sky with their thin but bountiful branches. They're all I see, but gentle hands smooth over my forehead.

"Is she okay?" I recognize the desperate voice as Ferrick's. He's somewhere beside me.

"She will be," Bastian answers, closer. "Stars, Princess. It's almost as though you *like* being cursed."

I swallow, heartbeat slowing thanks to the gentle fingers that comb soothingly through my hair. When I manage to focus and dip my head back, Vataea frowns down at me.

"Sorry," she says. "This place is riddled with tricks. I stopped Ferrick, but I couldn't get to you in time." She helps me ease onto my feet, both Bastian and Ferrick in front of me with their hands out, ready to help.

"I hate these woods," I growl, and though my words are bitter, they seem to put everyone at ease. The lines of worry in Ferrick's forehead smooth themselves, and though Bastian drips with sweat, he seems to stand a little steadier.

"Did it get you, too?" I ask as he wipes the sweat from his forehead. "You look like you're about to fall over."

"No, I'm just tired." He doesn't need to elaborate that it's because of how far we're traveling from *Keel Haul*. Bastian tugs his shirt away from his chest, fanning himself. And even now, when danger breathes down our necks, heat stirs within me and I struggle to take my eyes off him, remembering the way his skin felt beneath my fingertips last night. "What did you see?"

I think back to the fox that stood looming over me in Father's crown and cape, and shiver. "A fox," is all I say, not wanting to remember the details.

The tension in Bastian's jaw loosens as he nods. "Foxes are tricksters. Sounds like it's an advanced curse, one that's made to take advantage of the victim's biggest fears. Honestly, I'm surprised you escaped the curse at all. Let alone so quickly . . ." His voice trails off as he side-eyes me.

Unlike him, I'm less concerned with how I got out of the curse than I am about what the curse showed me: Father, a monster in disguise. I swallow hard.

As we journey deeper into the woods, a smattering of homes spreads out before us, tiny cabins surrounded by dead trees. Though the place looks desolate, smoke lifts from a fire pit that sits between cabins. The fire itself has been snuffed out, but the coals still burn hot.

It's clear this land was once beautiful; it sits at the base of a mountain, with the roar of a nearby waterfall offering a peaceful ambience. The buildings are similar to the one on the main shore—white and sleek, with large glass windows.

Half of them have been burned away, while the others are in shambles with broken windows and peeling, rotting wood. I step toward one of them, and there's a flash of movement in my periphery.

"Did any of you see that?" I ask, lowering my voice.

Though no one answers, they don't question me. As Bastian shifts his gaze across the terrain I start to doubt myself, thinking maybe I'm still hallucinating from my curse when another flash of movement crosses the trees.

Bastian flinches; this time, he's seen it. He grabs hold of my shirt and tugs me against him as something hot and sharp whizzes by my ear. It hisses as it passes, smacking into one of the houses behind us and striking the wood.

It's a knife. Gooey, thick sap oozes from it and drips down the wood.

Poison.

Vataea readies her steel dagger with deft fingers, and I mirror the action by drawing my newest blade—Rukan. A name inspired by the jellyfish whose poison is said to cause the worst pain a person could ever experience.

I force every distraction away as five figures emerge, some of them jumping from the roofs while others encircle us from the sides. Their eyes gleam with calculation, bodies coiled with muscle. They wield strong weapons—knives, swords, and a dagger that looks to be made of bone.

I hold my poisonous blade tightly, ready.

One of the girls, a lithe blond who carries the bone dagger, rakes her hungry eyes over me.

I lift my blade to her in warning, and her eyes shift to examine its strange blue hue. If I were her, I'd be nervous to see such a strange weapon. If she's smart, she'll back away.

But she doesn't.

I glance at Ferrick as the group surrounds us. He and

Vataea stand back to back, him with his rapier and her with the dagger.

"We're here to talk to Kaven," Vataea says. "Let us through." Her words are greeted with immediate scorn as those surrounding us laugh. Vataea's out of her element with a blade as her weapon instead of her voice, and she looks it.

"Let you through?" One of the men laughs. He's hardly twenty and yet his voice is heavy with a rasp. "After what Visidia's king did to our island? I don't think so."

"We want to help reconnect Zudoh to the kingdom," I say, never looking away from the girl who clutches her blade before me. "But to do that, you have to work with us."

The girl before me twitches her hands. I swathe my magic around me and immediately see the vengeance her soul craves with its entire being. Sensing danger, she coils tight and readies herself to spring.

"We don't want your help," she growls decidedly. Around her, the others hold their chins high in agreement.

"Drop your weapons and walk. We'll see if Kaven has time for a chat." She's lying. I sense the very moment the girl decides to kill me because her soul turns a deep, muddy red—the color of congealed blood. The corners of it crack, threatening to peel.

In my mind, I see the blood of my first kill sliding down my fingertips. I remember the monster within me thrashing to life for the first time. And for a moment, I hesitate.

Perhaps I was a monster to kill her. Perhaps I was a monster to kill all of them.

But everything I've done, I've done with the goal of protecting Visidia. And I won't be sorry for it any longer.

Perhaps a monster is exactly what this kingdom needs.

This girl has made her decision, and I'm not about to wait and let her strike first.

Clutching Rukan tight, I lunge forward and plunge my

blade deep into her stomach. Her eyes go wide and she sways, the blood swelling out of her and painting her shirt red. It's a fatal wound, poison or not. Her green eyes go glassy. Blood dribbles from her lips down to her chin before she staggers and chokes on it. She falls a moment later, spasming on the ground.

The other four watch, stunned. I take her dropped bone dagger and clean it on my pants. This isn't how I wanted it, but the faces of the Zudians from earlier sit at the forefront of my mind. I made a promise to protect them, and I intend to deliver.

One of the younger boys runs to my victim and falls to his knees. His body caves in, as though his entire spirit has been knocked from him. Blood covers his tan hands as he presses them to her chest, trying to stop the bleeding.

I wish it didn't have to be like this, but they've made it clear they'll never be on our side. I shove down my sympathy; if defeating them brings me one step closer to restoring balance in Visidia, then they've brought on a fight I've no intention of losing.

He slams his hands against her, shaking. But it's pointless; she's already dead.

"Amora," Bastian growls under his breath, trying to back away. "We need to leave."

Impossible. The other two boys and remaining woman ready their blades and charge.

With a weapon in each of my hands and their death in my satchel, I'm ready.

I strike out with Rukan again, finding resistance at the tip of my dagger as it snags and catches on skin. A male voice cries out, gruff and angry. He stumbles in my periphery, clutching his arm. I should focus on the others, yet I'm stuck staring as tiny blue lines crisscross and weave their way across the man's skin.

The poison's working.

Years of fencing are serving Ferrick well as he lifts his rapier to parry the incoming blow. Though his opponent's sword is heavier and more threatening, Ferrick is at an advantage with his speed. He yanks his rapier back and jabs the blade hard into his opponent's chest. The man falls back, clutching at the blood soiling his shirt. It's not a deadly wound, but it's enough to sting.

My own opponent is all lines and angles, sharp with rage. His sword hand quivers as his other bleeds onto the dirt. He doesn't know any better. My magic practically screams to be used, and I won't ignore it or tamp it down any longer. One drop of that gushing blood is all I need.

The coals in the nearby fire pit are cooling, but hopefully still hot enough to burn.

I surprise my opponent as I drop to a quick crouch and sweep the bone dagger across his growing pool of blood. His movements are slow and off balance; if he wants to survive, he needs to hurry and wrap his arm. Yet, he doesn't move. His eyes dip to the bone blade, then to the ground where the dead girl it belonged to lies. He lunges at me with a snarl.

I smack hard against the ground. My shoulder digs into a jagged rock and sharp pain seizes me. I hate that I scream, but the pain takes me by surprise.

"Amora! Get up!" Vataea yells, then gasps. Her opponent strikes her across the cheek with the hilt of her weapon. Vataea doesn't cry out, but snarls. I'm pinned on the ground beneath this man, but she can't help me. No one can.

"You killed her!" The man's breath is sour and he reeks of blood. His skin grows more ashen by the second. While he struggles to sit up and keep his eyes open, his grip no longer wavers on his dagger. He lifts it over his head and points its tip to my chest.

He's twice my size and too heavy to knock down, but losing isn't an option.

It's him or me, and I refuse to die on this island.

I jerk my hips up with all the power I have, trying to throw him even more off balance. He tilts to the left and I use the momentum to reach forward and stab both my blades into his thighs.

He doesn't scream. Instead, he chokes on a sob and the sound flusters me. The blade falls from his hands as I claw my way to a stand.

My magic flutters and festers as the sound of his pain sears itself into my memories. It'll be there later, I'm sure, waiting for me when I close my eyes tonight. But if there's one thing I learned from my performance in Arida, it's that I can't allow myself to be distracted while using my magic.

The poison and blood loss have rendered my attacker useless, and Ferrick, Bastian, and Vataea are holding the others back. I sprint to Bastian first. His shoulder and chest are cut, but neither wound is deep. He presses something into my palm as I pass—it's nearly an entire handful of hair. I make a fist around it, welcoming the magic that thrums to life, warming me.

The man Bastian's fighting watches me cautiously as I make my way to the fire pit. Bastian uses his distraction to knock him to the ground and throw himself on top.

"Last chance to save yourself. Where's Kaven?" Bastian presses the tip of his blade against the boy's thick neck.

He spits a wad of blood to the side. "You really think that will scare me?"

Bastian presses his blade deeper. "Probably not, but she should." He points to me. I stand several feet away, at the edge of the fire pit.

The thick-necked man stares at me, then at the hair in

my hands. Realization widens his eyes. "It can't be. There's no way."

"Oh, there's a way." I open my satchel and draw several teeth from inside. I wrap the hair around it, and then hold the bundle directly over the still-hot coals. Sweat beads over the boy's brows.

The others have slowed, probably wanting to figure out what this boy's outburst is about.

Ferrick seizes the opportunity and stabs his rapier into his opponent's leg, knocking him to the ground while Vataea rushes the girl and wraps her hands around her opponent's dark hair. She brings the dagger down, chopping half the hair from one side. Quickly, Vataea draws back toward me and offers it with a wicked sneer. I take the hair, but I won't use it yet.

"I am Amora Montara," I tell them as the coals begin to sear the back of my hand. "I hail from Arida. I am the kingdom of Visidia's princess, the future High Animancer. And whether you choose to stand in my way or not, I will restore this island to the kingdom."

I don't think of the dead girl on the ground or the way the blond boy cried out when I struck the final blow. I don't think at all. I'm in full control as I open my palm and let the man's hair and a handful of teeth fall into the flickering embers.

The man beneath Bastian tosses his head back and yowls in pain. He doubles over and grabs at his face, clawing at his mouth in an effort to rip out his scorching teeth. The coals still burn, but since the fire isn't raging, they sear slowly rather than burn all at once.

"*This* is soul magic," I say as the man beneath Bastian shakes and sputters violently. His mouth bleeds from how desperately he claws at it. It's more than enough blood for me to end his life, but he's too distracted by the teeth that slowly burn his gums to still be a threat.

Now, there's only one opponent left—the girl whose hair I hold. She watches the man screaming before her with round, fearful eyes.

"This is a very, *very* small taste of the things I can do," I warn her. "I can melt your bones, destroy your fingers—one by one—rot your teeth, your eyes, your tongue. I am a monster, and if you stand in my way, I will destroy you." I mean every word that passes through my lips, and this girl knows it.

"I'm only going to ask you this once," I say. "Where is Kaven?"

She opens her mouth to speak, but never has the chance to give an answer. There's a rustle in the trees, and the quiet snapping of twigs beneath boots.

Bastian's grip tightens on his sword. His shoulders stiffen as the figure emerges, and breath flees my lungs. Somewhere off to the side, both Vataea and Ferrick inhale a sharp, surprised breath.

It's clear to all of us who this man is, because he looks just like an older version of his brother. But where Bastian carries the kiss of the sun on his skin, Kaven has been raised and fed by moonlight.

He's exactly what I expected, and yet somehow entirely different. While he looks similar to Bastian in the face, he's taller, and lithe where Bastian is broad. He doesn't look like an adventurer, or have the same coiled muscles that give Bastian his strength in a sword fight. His chin is lifted high and proud; if I didn't know better, I'd say he almost looks like a noble. Everything about him feels intimidating.

Strands of gray travel from his roots and dust his inky black hair, and his cheekbones are striking on his gaunt face, sharp enough to cut glass. But it's not until his eyes find mine that I buckle, the intimidation settling into my bones from the coolness of his gaze. I can practically see the calculation behind his steel-gray eyes, and I understand at once that Kaven doesn't rely on blades to win his battles. His mind is his weapon.

He combs long, bony fingers through his hair, and on his wrist are dozens of thick leather bracelets, smeared with maroon stains. I remember Bastian's story—this is where he keeps the blood of those he's cursed, like a trophy. It's where he holds not only his power, but also Bastian's curse.

The chance to break Bastian's connection with *Keel Haul* and restore his magic is right there within reach. Taunting us.

My fingertips numb as a rush of coolness floods through me.

"Four intruders," Kaven says, voice surprisingly calm, "and you couldn't take care of them?"

Kaven's frigid presence is enough for the man beneath Bastian to stop screaming, and for the dark-haired girl to drop to her knees in a bow despite the imminent danger. In her distraction, Bastian takes his chance to shove the pommel of his sword into the back of her head. The girl chokes on a gasp as she stumbles forward onto her face, eyes rolling back as she passes out.

Bastian wastes no time. He ducks around me, chest heaving as he arcs his blade and brings it to the skin of Kaven's throat. Rage is in his jaw. His shoulders. His breaths. Bastian reaches to Kaven's belt and disarms the dagger sheathed there, tossing it to the dirt.

If he's bothered at all by the blade at his throat, Kaven doesn't show it. His smile is slow and mocking. "Welcome home, brother. I never suspected you'd show your face here again, especially with the princess in tow." Kaven's voice is predatory, but Bastian doesn't waver.

"Brother?" Ferrick echoes quietly, anger in his eyes. "You never told me Kaven was his—"

"I just found out," I whisper to him. "And now's not the time. It wasn't my secret to share."

Bastian nicks Kaven's throat in warning. None of us move to strike, giving Bastian this moment with his brother to see what might happen.

"Zudoh hasn't been my home for a long time. You made sure of that." There's a quiver in Bastian's voice. "Look what you've done to our island. To our people. This needs to stop; break my curse and step down, or I'll end you here."

Kaven lifts his chin higher, and Bastian's blade cuts deeper. Every movement he makes feels precise and calculated, as though his mind is constantly working three steps ahead of his words. "You want your magic back? After all these years, you wouldn't even know what to do with it. It would eat you alive."

"Maybe so," Bastian says as he eyes the dozens of thick leather bands woven around Kaven's wrists with hunger. "But it's time I take back what belongs to me."

The right corner of Kaven's lips twitches upward ever so slightly. I've seen Bastian make the same expression, and while it's charming on him, it makes Kaven look dangerous. "And how do you intend to do that?"

"Zudoh will be returned to Visidia." I hold my jaw high, fiercer than I feel. "Give Bastian his magic, break his curse, and step down from your position as Zudoh's leader. This island is dying. If you don't let us step in now, it's going to be too late."

Kaven scoffs. It's a soft sound, but it sends dangerous chills up my spine. "I'm more of an animancer than you'll ever be. You Montaras claim to be masters of souls, and yet you don't even understand your own magic. Don't you wonder why it challenges you, constantly? Why it tries to consume you?"

"I know why," I snort. "I know all about the beast that King Cato bested."

Kaven's next words are spoken casually. So confident and self-assured that they freeze me. "Are you sure?" he asks, eyes narrowing as he searches my face. Slowly, as to not scare Bastian into using his blade, Kaven points behind him and toward a towering waterfall I can barely see in the distance. "Everything you need to know about your family—the truth behind your magic, the knowledge of what they've done to this island and to Visidia—is there."

Bastian shakes his head in warning, but the magic within me pulses with hunger as Kaven gestures.

"That's what you came for, isn't it?" he presses. "Answers? Let me show you the truth; there's no need to make me your villain. Bring your weapons if you'd like; only the five of us will go. The rest of you . . ." He peers at the others, most of them bleeding on the ground or already dead, and huffs a tired breath. Blood trails from his throat where Bastian's blade still quivers. "You're no use to me."

His soul is a swirling mass of shadows and deep, peeling purples. Parts have begun chipping and fading, and I know not to trust him even remotely. But he's right about one thing: I'm tired of scraping for answers. I set out on this journey to prove to my people that I'm the future ruler they need. But if I don't know the truth of Visidia and its magic, then that will never be possible.

I approach Bastian and take hold of his forearm. "Drop your weapon," I tell him. "I need to see this for myself."

When he hesitates, I pull his arm back again until he lowers his weapon to his side. "Don't do this, Amora," he grits out as Kaven wipes his neck and draws back a safe distance. "You're walking straight into the belly of the beast."

"That's fine," I tell him, thinking of the shadowy one coiled within me, waiting to strike. "I know how to handle beasts."

Kaven smiles at his brother. "Follow me, then."

With so much of the land burned away, it doesn't take long for us to cross the flat, wooded terrain. Cool air bites at my skin, and Bastian shivers. Though his sickness is getting worse, he stays at my side as we approach the waterfall, movements rigid and stiff. His hand never strays from the pommel of his sword.

There's a small cavern tucked behind the roaring water, hidden to anyone not specifically looking for it.

Ferrick hesitates as he squints at it. The rocks barely gap open; there's no telling how small the space may be, or what might await us inside.

"We may have opposing views, but I'm not an uncompromising man," Kaven says. "If it's answers you want, you need only to enter. And maybe when you emerge, you'll understand what it is that I want for this kingdom. But there's room only for one, Princess. You'll have to trust that the others will be safe out here."

I practically snort. *Safe* is not something I'd ever associate with this man.

"How do we know it's not a trap?" Bastian asks. "That no one's waiting for her, inside?"

Kaven waves a hand at me, arching a knowing brow.

"I don't sense any other souls," I answer his wordless question with a shake of my head. "It's only us."

But is it, truly? The magic within me is fully awake, writhing and anxious, goading me toward the cave with a force I've never before known it to possess. Within it is something my magic wants more than anything else.

"Be careful," Vataea says. "There's something dark inside that cave." She strokes the hilt of her dagger and glares at Kaven all the while. He arches a thin brow, but she refuses to look away. Kaven's alone; against the four of us, taking him out should be easy. Yet he doesn't appear worried. He stands with his arms crossed and his stance leisurely.

"Will you be okay?" I ask Bastian, reading the anxiety creased into the wrinkles on his forehead.

"I'll be fine," he says fiercely. "It's you I'm worried about."

"I'll be okay." I draw a breath and lift my chin. Though the others don't look convinced, I pull my attention away from them and move forward. "If anything happens, yell for me."

Kaven's laugh is nothing more than a quiet huff of air. "Nothing will happen until you get back, you have my word."

At the lip of the cavern, I turn over my shoulder to steal one more look at them all. "As I said, yell for me."

CHAPTER
TWENTY-NINE

The cavern's darkness is blinding. A musty stench penetrates the air, thick enough to make me choke as I step inside.

Though the entrance is hardly large enough to fit one person, it widens the farther in I venture, expanding into a circular space just large enough to stretch my arms out. The only sound is the soft pattering of water droplets as they splash to the floor, and the only light is from strange translucent blue insects that hide in the far corners of the cavern's jagged ceiling. A fog of light emits from each one, brightening the back space enough for me to get a glimpse.

Slabs of withered wood cover a small portion of the floor. Blankets of fur are tossed in heaps beside it, glistening with the fresh droplets of water. As I step closer, I notice that's where the musty smell is coming from and scrunch my nose. But I don't turn away.

Instead, I crouch to inspect the strange items littered across the insect-rotted wood. Sharpened metal scraps and makeshift knives are coated in thick layers of dirt.

I narrow my eyes on one knife in particular, rusted by blood and time, and the beastly magic within me pulses with longing. I try to ignore the magic that gnaws at my fingertips, luring me closer and closer. I know what it is without question.

This blade is one of legend and lore. One that saved Visidia; one that created it.

I have sworn on this blade and its owner time and time again—Cato's skinning knife.

I forget how to breathe. How to stand. I sink to my knees, and set my hand atop it.

"I can't do it!" the man snaps.

I've never seen the first king, not even in pictures.

King Cato ruled centuries ago, and though all we have to remember him by are the stories that have been passed down since he established the monarchy, I know without a doubt it's him before me.

His complexion is a light olive and his build much slimmer than the grand figure I imagined. He sits cross-legged in front of me, only my body isn't mine. This body has skin that's several shades lighter than my own, similar to Cato's, and her frame is petite. I know myself as Amora, but I'm also this young woman, living through her thoughts and memories. I have an abundance of dark curls plaited into an elegant braid, though a few of them have escaped, coiled tight behind my ears or hugging my forehead and cheeks.

I let myself sink deeper and deeper into this woman's mind, until her thoughts are my own.

"You must relax," I tell him. The words that escape my lips are soothing, though I've no control over them. "Curse magic isn't as hard as you think it is, I promise. Just give me your hand."

Cato nods as he gives it to me, but lines of worry embed themselves deep between his brows.

I draw his hand into my lap. "Think of what you want others to see. Think about it deeply, as if it's a memory you're recalling." I press a needle into his finger. A small bead of blood bubbles to the surface, and I turn Cato's hand to press his finger against a pebble laid before us on the stone floor. I dab the blood onto it.

Cato's eyes squint shut as he focuses, only peeling his hand away after a hesitant moment.

"How did that feel?" I ask, and Cato's lips twist into a small frown.

"It didn't." He warily eyes the pebble. "Did it work?"

I touch the pebble, waiting to see if a curse envelops me. When nothing happens, I fill my face with warmth and keep a small smile on my lips even as my shoulders slump, knowing this will upset him.

I don't need to say anything for Cato to understand. He groans, fingers running through his chestnut hair and over his face as he pushes himself onto his feet.

"It's nothing to get upset over!" I insist. "Plenty of people wield only one magic, don't be frustrated." But the truth is that his frustrations are something I'll never understand.

When I was young, I discovered I had the ability to see souls, a magic no one else had yet discovered. And I learned that I had an affinity for other magics, too, like curse magic and the ability to heal.

For weeks I've been trying to teach Cato curse magic, but the only magic he's been able to learn is the one I taught him when we were children—soul magic. Back then we kept the magic between the two of us, a bond shared between best friends. He used to love the idea of a magic only the two of us practiced, and begged me to never teach anyone else. But in recent months, our magic has stopped being enough for him. Now he craves more.

I try to set my hands atop Cato's arm, but he jerks it away with a grunt.

"Says someone with an abundance of magic," Cato scoffs. "If a woman can master more than one magic, it makes no sense why I can't."

I reel back as if struck, confusion twisting my face.

"You say *woman* like it's a dirty word," I tell him sharply. "Remember that I'm the one who taught you soul magic, Cato. I'm the one who discovered it."

Cato takes one look at me and his shoulders sag. He steps forward, cups my face in his palms, and kisses my forehead. My skin warms from the softness of his lips, and I relax into him.

"I'm sorry, Sira." His voice softens several degrees as he drops his forehead against mine. "You know I didn't mean it like that. I just want things to be better for us."

"We're fine as we are. We don't need an abundance of magic to have a good life," I whisper gently.

And though I mean every word, his jaw tenses. "Magic is power, Sira. It's respect. How good of a life can I give you without that?"

I lift my hands to Cato's cheek, gently stroking my thumb across his stubble. "You worry too much, my love." I offer him a gentle kiss before easing away toward a door, knowing he needs time alone to work through his frustration. "We're fine now, and together we will only grow. There's no use dwelling on the things we've no control over."

I mean it kindly, but Cato doesn't know I can still hear him when I step outside.

"No control," he grumbles under his breath. "We'll see about that."

The shores are flooded with people—some of them fishing and others climbing up giant trees, laughing all the while. My heart leaps into my throat as a young boy clambers up one of the tallest trees only to dive straight off it. But before he's anywhere near the ground, he blows a gust of breath down at the sand and the air seems to thicken beneath him like a pad. It rushes to meet him, bouncing him back up a few more feet. But when he bounces back up, he slows his body with time magic. He laughs, flipping in the air, moving so slowly it's as though he floats.

His skin glistens with sweat as the sun beats down on him. When he finally lands back on the ground, he scrambles for the tree once more. Beneath him, a tiny blond child tries to copy him, breathing air at her feet. She doesn't get any higher than a foot off the ground.

I weave pretty stones and shells around thin pieces of leather as the children play. I prick my finger with a needle, smooth the blood across the leather as I attach a curse, and let it dry. I'm making cursed necklaces for the local girls, to keep them safe from anyone with foul intentions. As I'm bent over my work, three children flock around me, one redheaded boy and two twin girls with russet skin and tightly coiled curls—Lani's girls and Markus's son. They've given themselves brightly colored eyes—pink, purple, and gold—and giggle as they coat my hair with a lovely shade of lilac. I don't mind letting them have their fun, laughing as they banter over what shade to try next. One of their parents can fix the color for me, later.

On the grass across from me, Cato skins a fish whose scales still glisten from the sea. He's been in a mood today, so I try not to pay him too much attention as he continually flicks his focus to me, his movements becoming progressively angrier until I'm too distracted to do anything but give him my attention.

When I do, he glowers. "Are you trying to make me feel bad about myself?"

I still, as do the children behind me. Gently, I press one of the girl's shoulders and nudge them away with the promise of playing with them later.

"Of course not." I look at him firmly. "Why would you even think that?"

Cato wipes away the sweat that's pooled onto his neck. "Because you can sell your little cursed charms and protections, while all I have is the ability to fish. I already know you're able to provide more than I can, so why do you insist on rubbing it in?"

I press my lips together and exhale a gentle sigh. "It's not a competition. They're just little protection charms. You're the one feeding us, and your fish make more money, too. Hardly anyone is interested in my silly cursed charms."

My stomach churns at the sight of the half-finished necklaces and bracelets in front of me. The shells that litter the ground are beautiful, just waiting to be cursed. I'd planned on making dozens of them, but now I can hardly bring myself to look at them, knowing how much they upset him.

Cato doesn't say anything. He only glares for another moment before returning to his work. I continue with my curses, running a finger over the leather as I contemplate my words.

"Has something happened?" I make my voice tender, the way he likes it. "Have I done something? I don't mean to pry, but you've seemed on edge lately, and when I happened to see a glimpse of your soul—"

Cato freezes. His head whips up, green eyes vicious daggers. I flinch back.

"We agreed to never soul-read each other." Every word is enunciated, seeping with vicious poison.

A pale, sunburnt woman using magic to float a net over

her head and into the water stills, turning to eye Cato. I don't recognize her, though I do recognize one of the men who takes notice and steps forward.

"Everything all right here, Sira?" His voice is a soothing baritone, thick with fatherly concern. Wrinkles crease around warm amber eyes that melt into his dark brown skin as Basil assesses the situation, and my skin heats with embarrassment.

"Everything's fine, Basil," Cato growls. "Don't you have babies to heal?"

I ball my hands into fists, hating that he speaks to someone I care about so cruelly.

Basil ignores the snide comment by looking at me expectantly.

"It's okay," I murmur quickly, because I don't want to risk Cato getting any more upset. "Cato's just been a little stressed."

Basil doesn't appear convinced, but he nods all the same. "Glad to hear it. How about we let him work off some of that stress, then? If you're still thinking of trying your hand at healing, Sira, you could come sit in with us for the day."

Cato's lips twist into a sneer, but he doesn't look away from his fish. I gather up my things with a swift nod. "I doubt I'll be any good, but I suppose it's worth the try."

Those words are only for Cato's benefit, so he doesn't feel worse about his inability to learn other magics. But the truth is that Basil's words ignite a sharp desire within me.

All my life, magic of all varieties has called to me, opening up for my exploration. Though I was able to teach Cato soul magic, he's no idea the extent of the magic I know, or the others I intend to learn.

And because I love him, I'll never tell him.

Basil smiles and guides me forward, down the path leading up to Arida's main town.

"You know you don't have to put up with that man," he

whispers after a long while of silence, keeping his voice low. "You deserve better."

"I'm fine," I assure him, as if saying it over and over will somehow make it come true. "Really. Cato's just going through a tough time. Ever since we began talking about marriage, all he seems to think about is how to pave a better future for us. He feels people will respect him if he has more magic. He still thinks his soul magic is too weak. I'm worried that perhaps I've put too much pressure on him."

Basil purses his bottom lip in surprise. "There's no shame in being able to soul-read. You were the first to discover this magic, Sira. You should be proud of it."

I bow my head with a small nod. "I am, I promise. Cato's just been obsessed with learning something new, but nothing's working. It's been ruining him, making him draw away from me. I've been worried about him for weeks now, so the other night I took a look at his soul . . ."

Basil stills. "Did you see something?"

I wind my arms tightly around myself, wishing I didn't have to recall the images. A thin veil of sweat coats my skin as chills rush up my spine.

"It's rotting," I say, barely managing even a whisper. The words sink my stomach, making it burn. "And it's getting worse every day. Pieces of it are falling away, as if it's disappearing. I've never seen anything like it."

Basil stretches a soft, wrinkled hand forward to take hold of mine.

"You be careful with that one," he warns. "I fear no good will come from him."

———

Late one evening, I wake to find that Cato is not asleep next to me, and the door to our spare room has been left ajar. I toe at it, trying to silently widen the gap before crouching to peek inside.

The space before me is dark, free from even the smallest oil lamp or an open window to allow in the glow of the moon.

As my eyes adjust, I make out Cato's wide-shouldered figure seated on the floor. His back is turned to me, and as I silently ease the door open a fraction more, the small creature in front of him becomes clear—a rabbit.

It shakes fiercely within its cage, cowering in the corner as Cato reaches inside. In his hand is the same small blade he was using before to skin fish, and the rabbit's squeals are deafening as Cato flicks it across the creature's leg, drawing blood. He plucks a strand of fur from the creature.

I cover my mouth, whether to prevent myself from screaming or throwing up, I can't be certain.

Cato coats the plucked rabbit fur with the blood on his knife, holds it between his fingers, and then dunks it into a small water bowl beside him.

I've never before heard a sound like the rabbit makes. The gurgled choking of a creature struggling to breathe, trying to figure out why it's drowning when nothing but air surrounds it. It makes a desperate, almost childlike scream that sets my hands shaking.

I toss the door open and kick the water bowl across the room, and Cato jumps to his feet in surprise. The rabbit takes a desperate breath, coughing and trembling as I run for the cage and scoop it into my arms.

"The gods don't give us these creatures so we can torture them!" My breaths are sharp and quick, and I'm unable to stop my trembling. "What were you thinking?" I draw a step back toward the door, fear and rage warring in my chest.

Cato grins. It's one of the most gleeful expressions I've ever seen, and it looks wrong on his face. Until now, I hadn't noticed how much life has been drained from him; his skin is pale and dull, and his body has withered, making his face gaunt and sharp. Just how many nights has he been sneaking off to this room, locking himself away in the dark?

"It's magic," Cato says, almost giddy. I draw a few more steps toward the door. The poor rabbit is still shaking within its cage.

"What magic?" Though every instinct wills me to run, the love for this man I've known since I was a child locks me in place.

I have to at least hear his explanation.

"Soul magic," Cato whispers. "My magic. I decided if I couldn't learn more magic, then I'd just have to change what I already had."

I draw my own soul magic around me, comforted by its warmth. Its lightness. It welcomes me into it, flooding me with heat as Cato's soul opens up to me, revealing stark whiteness. The sight of it steals my breath, as there's hardly any color left; hardly a single trace that a soul was ever even there.

"What happened to you?" My voice cracks. I clench the cage closer to my chest, as though it will somehow keep me standing.

When Cato closes the space between us, I do everything to keep my legs from buckling. "I did this for us," he says. "For you, so you didn't have to be embarrassed by me. So that we could have a better life, together."

I shake my head, a few loose curls shaking free from my thick braid. "I was never embarrassed, not even a little bit. Cato, your soul—"

"Trust me." His voice is sharp and surprisingly earnest. He tries to reach out, as if to take my hand, but the rabbit squeals in horror as he approaches. I flinch back, throat constricting.

"What have you done to your soul magic?"

Cato waves the question away with a flourish of his hands. "This magic has always been inside of us; I'm simply choosing to look at it in a different way. Sira, you've told me before that you love me. If you weren't lying about that, then you should trust me. Trust that I'm going to pave a new way of life for us."

I try to ignore my fear. This is Cato, after all. Cato, who was red-faced and shy as we shared our first kiss on the shores of Arida years ago. The boy I snuck out to visit while growing up, just so that we could hold each other and gossip beneath the moonlight. He was the same man I shared my bed with each night, and who woke me up with a shower of kisses each morning.

But he's no longer that person, and hasn't been for some time.

I say, "I trust you," though it's the biggest lie I've ever told.

"Good." Cato reaches out to stroke his thumb across my cheek, and I try not to cringe beneath his touch. "For now, you and I are the only ones who need to know about this."

———

Basil's the fourth to die this week.

If it weren't for the blood coating his lips and chin, he'd look peaceful here on the sand; almost like he's sleeping. Almost like he'll wake up at any second and tease me for staring.

Behind me, Cato makes a show of my friend's corpse, parading it about and telling anyone who will listen, "This is what happens to those with multiple magics; the gods are punishing us for our greed!"

Twelve have died so far, and because the island's afraid, people eat his words up.

But I know the truth. The gods are not the ones behind these deaths—Cato is.

I remember the night I confronted him. How I'd looked

into his eyes and realized there was no longer even a small spark of the boy I once loved left in this wicked, callous man.

"Dead because his magic lashed out? You really expect me to believe that?" I'd shouted.

His response had been to snatch my face in his hands and dig his fingers into my skin. My eyes had pooled from the pain as his nails clawed into me, but not hard enough to leave a mark. Never enough to leave a mark.

"You will keep your mouth shut," he'd said. "Or I swear to you that I will destroy every soul on Arida."

That was the day the first body had been found, a week after I'd caught him with the rabbit. I wish with everything in me that I'd done more to stop him then, but no matter how hard I search, I can't seem to find any fight left within me. He's taken all of me.

"We have to stop this!" I've no idea who speaks, because I don't turn to look. I keep staring at Basil, waiting for him to open his eyes. Waiting for him to take a breath. I don't even hear Cato approach, though I jerk my hand from his when he tries to take it.

"I have an idea." He takes my hand again, fingers pinching forcefully into my skin so that I can't rip away. "Sira can take your magic away!"

"What in the gods' blood are you talking about?" I don't care that my words are harsh. "No, I can't."

Though Cato's face doesn't twist in surprise, it does sour. He politely excuses himself from the others by digging his nails into my palms, forcing me to follow him until we're far enough from the others that he can speak freely.

"You've always wanted to help people." He says it like an accusation. "Now you have that chance. Those with multiple magics need to free themselves from danger. You can take all but one of their magics, Sira."

"I will not."

He wraps his arms around me as if in an embrace, though one hand bends my arms at a painful angle. The other holds my mouth to his chest, so that it muffles the sound when I cry out. "You will take their magic." His snarl comes with a smile. If anyone were to turn to us, they might think he's being sweet. "I don't care which, let them choose. But you will take it, or gods help you, I will make you watch as I destroy every last one of their souls. Now put on a smile, my love, and keep your mouth shut."

With tears in my eyes, I listen. Because what else can I do?

"Be careful with it," I tell the frightened girl in front of me, just as I've told each of them before her, "for that charm will forever hold part of your soul. Break it, and you'll live, but you'll never be the same."

But I'm not the same, either.

For weeks I've obeyed Cato, using a mix of soul magic and curse magic to steal magic away from others. It disgusts me that it's not even hard; I do it by diving into their souls and ripping half from it. Then I curse that half into a charm for them to wear.

When I finish, the girl's mother pulls me into a tight embrace that sets my body on fire. "Bless you, Sira," she says, as though I've saved her daughter by stealing her restoration magic. Rigid, I'm barely able to offer a nod. But she's too relieved to notice, and together they hurry out the door.

As it shuts behind them, I add another bracelet to my wrist.

That girl was the last of them. Now, everyone has only a single magic; the whole island has been purged.

Day by day the number of leather bracelets on my wrists has grown—marked with the blood of those whose charms I control. The power over so many souls has turned my gentle magic into a seething, hungry beast.

Part of me wants to peel the bracelets from my skin and hide them out of my sight, but I can't risk Cato finding them. I won't risk him gaining control of these people, or the power that comes with their blood.

My heart has become more calloused with every magic I steal, sickened by the praise of those who thank me for being selfless enough to take care of them first, instead of worrying about my own multiple magics. They love me for doing this, and praise Cato for having this idea and saving them all from their demise. He's a king in their eyes, guiding them to safety. And because the island is still in shambles—because our people are still fearful and looking for guidance on how to navigate living with only one type of magic—they make his title real. And they make me their queen.

Stars, if only they knew. If only they could tell why I've stopped being able to look into their eyes. If only they could feel the guilt that plagues me, turning my hair gray and withering my skin.

If only they knew how I hate myself as much as I hate Cato.

He finds me later that night by the shore, staring out at the ocean and silently begging it to claim me.

"It's your turn," he says flatly. "It's time to get rid of everything but your soul magic."

My eyes flash to meet his, icy and sharp; I always expected this moment to come.

"And what if I refuse?"

"Then I'll kill you," he says. "Though I hope it doesn't come to that. We were always meant for this, Sira. You were always meant to be behind me as I ruled."

His words are so ridiculous that I laugh. It's a fierce, bitter sound that feels far too natural on my lips. I scratch at the leather bands around my wrist.

"You cannot kill someone who is already dead," I say as his eyes go cold. He grabs my hand and presses the handle of his skinning knife into my palm. I glide my thumb over its cool steel, settled by the blade.

"I did this for you," he growls, "so that we could have a better life. You should appreciate the work it took for me to get here. I didn't just get us a home, I got us a kingdom."

I nearly laugh again at the word *kingdom*. It bubbles in my chest, threatening to burst, but I swallow it down like lead. There's no rationalizing with a man who craves nothing but power.

"You'll give up your magic," he demands. "Now."

If I tear half my soul away and curse it into a charm, I've no doubt he'll take that charm to assure I can't ever break my curse, or anyone else's.

But Cato's controlled me for long enough.

"Why can't I keep curse magic, instead?" I ask him flatly, flicking the skinning knife open.

"Because then you'd have to live on a different island." Though he drops this news casually, the words grind into me. "We're expanding the kingdom. I'll keep a small group here on Arida; twenty advisers for each of the magics, to help build my kingdom. The others will spread out to the island that uses the magic they chose. As the only two with soul magic, you and I will reign."

My blood boils so fiercely I can't seem to catch my breath. "What about the families? If a child practices a different magic than their father, would you really split them up?"

He holds his jaw high. "The family can remain together. But should they practice a magic other than that of the island they live on, we'll have to imprison them."

305

"You've already taken so much from these people," I say. "Are you so afraid of being viewed as weak, that you'll take choice from them, too?"

"It's not about being weak." He practically spits the words at me. "It's about being fair. Never again will anyone feel like they're not good enough. There will be no competition. Everyone will work together, learning the same magic of their island."

My hands shake. "And what of soul magic? It's hardly fair to keep it for ourselves. This magic is powerful, Cato. I never shared it with others because I was always trying to make you feel important. You wanted it to be our own special practice, and I agreed so that you could feel like you have something no one else has. But if you're so worried about fairness, shouldn't we be sharing this magic with anyone who wants to learn? We can make it the magic of Arida."

Shadows fill his cheekbones and sharpen his face. "Soul magic is too powerful. In the wrong hands, it would be dangerous. Other than the two of us, no one else can ever know this magic."

The response that sparks within me is sharp bewilderment. I throw my head back with a vicious sneer. *Dangerous*, he says, as if it wasn't him who wrecked the lives of hundreds and destroyed their peaceful home. *Fair*, he says, as though that's ever been what he's concerned with. As if he wasn't ever just jealous of me and everyone else with more magic than him. As if he doesn't love that everyone now praises him, and has made him a king.

I rise to my feet, but it's no longer in resignation. I drag the skinning knife across my palm and close my fist around it, coating it in my blood.

I'll separate my magic, fine. But it won't be so he can control me. I'm done with Cato. This man is nothing more than a coward trying to justify his need to feel important. To feel powerful. And it's time someone put this small man in his place.

I tear into my own soul, ripped and bruised and shredded. It's so simple, as easy as breathing. But it's not curse magic I rip from it; it's soul magic.

Cato stretches his hand out expectantly, but rather than give him the cursed knife, I shove it deep into his palm.

He reels back, his face so astonished that it's clear he never expected I might do something to harm him. But as he's no longer the boy I used to know, I am no longer that girl.

The blood coating my palm mixes with his, and I slap it across his forehead.

I hardly know what I'm doing. My body is three steps ahead of my mind, acting on the angry impulse writhing within me. Acting on the power and the heat of the charms around my wrist.

"You will forget my name," I snarl, pinning him to the ground. Cato buckles and attempts to throw me off, but somehow I manage to keep him down. My body convulses. With rage, perhaps. Or maybe with fear.

"You will forget my face, and that anyone ever loved you. May this magic be every bit the beast you are; may it curse your bloodline for all of eternity, almighty *king*." I spit the word. "The moment you harm another creature, may this magic eat you from the inside out. May it spend its existence trying to accomplish nothing but the eradication of your soul. Should you let your guard down for even one moment, may it consume you entirely. Cato Montara, I hope it destroys you."

I slam Cato's head against the ground, and his eyes glaze over. By the time my mind and body catch up with each other, I practically fall off him, shaking so fiercely I can't even scramble to my feet. My breaths come in sharp, desperate gasps, icicles shooting up my spine and through my veins. They're all-consuming, but I can only laugh.

Never did I think it possible to curse a person directly, but with this vicious power I've gathered from the cursed bands around my wrists, I've done just that.

I laugh and laugh as Cato's eyes go white, his body convulsing as the curse tears into him, settling into his blood.

He's nothing more than an angry little boy who's ruined countless lives with his own jealousy. And now, finally, I'll make him pay for it.

When he jerks his head to me, his eyes are wide with fear, but I only smile as my heart collapses.

It turns out cursing another person's life directly takes a substantial payment I hadn't quite expected, but I don't mind giving my life in exchange.

"The people of Arida will forget what I did to them." Shaking, I smear my blood over the grass, then into the dirt, trying to bury it as deeply into the soil as I can get it. "Everyone on this island will forget what they have lost."

It's the last bit of kindness I know to offer. Choking, gagging, unable to find air, I curl the skinning knife tightly in my palm and make my final curse.

I give it my memories. I fill the knife with the story of this past year, and drop it onto the shore for the waves to bury. I want my friends to live in peace; I want them to forget the pain of all they've lost.

But perhaps one day, when the kingdom is ready, they'll find this knife and learn the truth of who King Cato truly was. Perhaps one day they'll know what I've done.

A wave grazes my fingertips, the water pushing the knife deeper and deeper into the sand until the blade's been devoured whole.

All air flees from my lungs as my body stills, slackening into something both so heavy and entirely weightless at the same time.

Arida fades from my vision, and I draw my final breath.

I stagger back, and Cato's skinning knife clatters to the ground.

There's a lump in my throat I bitterly swallow down as I stare at my trembling hands—no longer Sira's, but my own. In my mind's eye, I once again see the blood of my first prisoner gliding down my fingers.

As Sira, I understood curse magic perfectly—you decide what you want people to see, and curse an object with that image or story by connecting it with your blood. There's a chance someone could have made this whole thing up, but this curse was nothing like the one with the fox; it was far too real. Every breath Sira took was my own; I felt every emotion. Every ounce of pain and fear. It was curse magic at a level that will never be rivaled.

And it showed me that the magic within me isn't meant to be vicious.

Sira's soul magic was never a beast that waited to consume her the moment she let down her guard. It was gentle and inviting. Comfortable.

Her curse on Cato is what makes my soul magic behave the way it does. And the cursed soul magic she used to get rid of everyone's magic—the one she hated herself for even possessing—is exactly the kind of magic Kaven uses, now.

Everything I grew up believing—about my blood, my magic, my lineage—none of it was real. This isn't the way it's meant to be.

All this time, has Father known the truth?

I don't know how long I sit in the cavern, letting the truth sink in. I only stand because I know I have to, and my head spins with the toll of this knowledge as I make my way back out.

Bastian's the first one I see, his sword drawn. He may not have it pointed at Kaven—whose stance is unbothered and face expressionless—but venom masks the pain in his eyes, and I know he won't hesitate to use it if he has to. Vataea mirrors his protective stance while Ferrick crouches at the lip of the cavern, impatiently waiting.

When Ferrick sees me, his shoulders sag in visible relief and he steps forward to grab me in a swift embrace. "By the gods, you were in there forever."

Though I want to sink into the warmth of a familiar body and relax until the fog of my brain clears, I force myself to ease away from him.

"I'm fine," I say shakily, turning my attention to Kaven.

He watches with keen eyes, brows furrowed. "Do you believe what you saw?"

I nod to let Kaven know the truth. "I do."

He doesn't smile or gloat like I thought he might. He only says, "My grandfather found that knife buried in Arida's sand years ago. He brought it back to Zudoh with him, but was too much of a coward to do anything with it. My father inherited it on Grandfather's deathbed; King Audric had just taken the throne, and Grandfather wanted his son to share the truth with the king and the kingdom. But my father was weak and cowardly, just like him. I found the knife in his study years ago."

Bastian practically roars. "You don't get to talk about our father, Kaven. You *killed* him!"

"He was a coward," Kaven spits. "He wanted to keep this a secret from the world."

"He kept it a secret so Visidia didn't end up like it is now." Bastian holds his sword tight while Kaven folds his arms across his chest, a deep viciousness in his eyes.

"What King Cato did was wrong," I say as I move between them. "But this is not the way to fix his mistakes, or my father's." I dig my nails into my palms until my hands steady.

Should one of the brothers make a move, I can't be dwelling on Sira's curse. I need to be ready to fight.

"The king has known the truth for years, *Princess*," Kaven says, and the words stab sharp as daggers between my ribs. "I showed him the blade, willing to compromise if he told everyone the truth. But the king is yet another coward, just like Cato and my father. In his fear, he had half of our population destroyed in an attempt to stop us from asking the wrong questions or forming the wrong ideas. I assume you saw the ash on our sand? It's from the trees your father had burned by Valukan soldiers. The bones on the shore? They were casualties of a war started by him. All to silence us."

I think back to the ash on the shore. The bones. The ring of algae so thick it looked like tar. All of it was caused by Father.

If he truly knew about our magic, then the man I thought I knew so well has turned out to be a perfect stranger. Father was a coward to leave so many people here to suffer in Zudoh, just so he didn't have to face the truth of our history.

My hands curl into hard fists as I press them against my sides.

No one back home seems to know the truth about Cato. The stories about him are always so proud—he's thought to be a powerful animancer who was able to establish a kingdom and revive our population while we were on the brink of destruction. He had each island represent only one magic, to help the kingdom repopulate without temptation or greed.

But in reality, he was nothing short of a coldhearted murderer who sought to weaken others for his own glory. And if there's truth in Kaven's words, Father's following in his steps.

He didn't keep me on Arida to protect me. He kept me there so that I'd never learn the truth: he destroyed Zudoh to keep them from rising up. And he didn't want me to ever find out.

My chest is so tight I can hardly breathe. Every revelation is another blow that fights to knock me back, but for now, I must remain standing. This is no time to drop my guard.

"What makes you think you're any different than Cato?" I ask Kaven. "You're destroying lives for the sake of your own beliefs, just as he did."

Kaven only shakes his head. "I want to fix the damage he's created, and lead this kingdom on a new path." Every word he speaks becomes sharper than the last, more forceful. "If a few lives must be sacrificed for that, then so be it. Aridian magic doesn't have to be a vicious weapon. You've seen the reasons it lashes out. But I can help you. We can fix your magic, and restore this kingdom to what it was meant to be."

Bastian bristles beside me.

"With you as Visidia's king, I assume?" I keep my eyes firm on Kaven's, whose words cause my chest to knot. Restoring Visidia is what I've wanted all along, but Kaven doesn't seek restoration, he seeks vengeance. My family may be responsible for originally destroying this kingdom, but that in no way makes him its salvation.

"Yes, if that's what they want to call me." He says it so simply. "I will be their leader into a better future. And it starts with the Montara blood—it starts with your father. If you care about the future of Visidia as you claim, you will help me."

"You're right that the curse needs to be broken," I admit. "But I'll find another way. So long as there's air in my lungs, Kaven, you will never rule Visidia."

"You should rethink your position while you still have the chance." Kaven's voice rises as he takes a step closer. "The Montaras aren't meant to rule. Cato was a liar and a cheat who separated the kingdom for his own gain, and your father is a coward who burned our ships and exiled us here. You can be better than them, Princess. Step down, stand by my side, and we can restore soul magic to what it should be."

I grind my heels into the dirt, fearful my knees may give out with all the turmoil roiling within me. Because on one hand, nothing Kaven says is *wrong*. The Montaras were never the brave leaders I believed they were. They were never meant to rule.

But that doesn't mean that I have to be like them. And I'm sure as stars not going to stand by Kaven's side while he enacts his vengeance.

"How would you do it?" I ask, keeping my voice soft. Making it waver. Because Kaven's hungry for blood, and if he thinks I can help him get it, then he'll tell me what I need to know.

"Your curse is in your blood," he says, and there's a furor in his eyes. "The knife was coated with it. And when your father visited us eleven years ago, I stabbed him and mixed his blood with our spring water so that Zudians would have traces of that magic within them. They need only to accept and practice it. That's what I've been training them to do. If the curse isn't contained to only one person—if all of Visidia has it—it's possible we can break it. The curse would become too big to sustain itself. And once it's broken, we can restore soul magic to what it should be."

I think of Sira's magic—so open and free—and I crave that feeling, again. I never knew magic could be like that.

"But we don't have enough of the curse within us," Kaven continues. "We need more of it. If we had more of your father's blood, we could—"

"No." I've heard enough of his plan. "There's got to be a way that doesn't involve hurting my family or spreading the curse to more people."

Kaven's face falls, hardening into something monstrous.

"There isn't." The flat tone of his voice sends shudders down my spine. "What's one life in exchange for helping your entire kingdom get the magic they deserve?"

The words are a strike to my chest. They're the words I've believed in all my life—*one life does not mean more than the safety of my kingdom*. That's what I always told myself when I was deep in Arida's prisons, taking the lives I thought I had to.

And even now, knowing how wrong I was, I would not claim that Kaven's statement is untrue. One life is not worth the lives of the kingdom, but there has to be another way.

I think of Bastian, a boy cursed at the age of ten after watching his parents killed. Of Zale, fighting for her people with everything she has. Of the countless others that Kaven has killed in his pursuit of soul magic.

My kingdom does deserve magic, just as I deserve to have mine feel the way it did in Sira's curse. But Kaven's methods will not be how we achieve that. I will find my own way.

"The future of Visidia isn't yours to decide," I snarl. "No harm will come to Visidia or my family."

Ferrick's hand is on my shoulder within a second, stilling me. "We know what he wants," he whispers. "We know he's still building an army. If we leave now, we have time to tell your parents and devise a plan."

Kaven doesn't miss his words. "You really should have taken my offer, Princess." Each word hits like the strike of a blade. "Because I'm afraid that's where you're wrong. I'm not *building* an army; I have one. And you're out of time."

CHAPTER THIRTY

I look past Ferrick and Vataea, fighting to steady my trembling hands as dozens of figures emerge from the woods. Only when they get closer do I see that some wear vests and worn boots of deep amethyst—Kerost. Others wear magnificent sapphire blazers and the matching capes I'd recognize anywhere. The silver emblems of their capes shine through the rolling fog, winking at me mockingly.

My own royal soldiers.

I step back on trembling legs, not wanting to believe what I'm seeing. "What's going on?" I ask, though deep down I already know. I don't recognize any of the Kers, but familiar faces are among my own people.

Like Casem's.

My guard's eyes widen when he sees Ferrick and me. He stands at the edge of the woods beside Olin, his father—the man who taught us both how to wield a blade and protect ourselves. The man who stands at Father's side daily, acting as Arida's top adviser.

Though Olin's never been the warmest man, his crystal eyes were never half as frigid, nor a quarter as dangerous as they are now. And never before has he sneered at me with such raw hatred.

"Zudoh isn't the only island that's tired of your father's reign." Kaven steps through the soldiers to stand before me, his chin proud. "Your father brought only the soldiers he trusted most when he came to destroy this island—his top advisers. But what he miscalculated is that not all of them agreed with him. He didn't think to consider that some might *like* the idea of our magic being open for all, especially after they saw the power of our multiple magics in battle, and how the king could take down twenty people at once, just with strands of their hair or drops of their blood. Like myself, they want to be able to practice soul magic."

He nods to Olin, and my heart drops. "Did you truly think everyone would stay content with the monarchy keeping that magic entirely for themselves? With robbing people of their freedom, and telling them which island they must live on just because of the magic they choose to practice? It's time for things to change. The day my island burned was the day others realized that, too."

I try to catch Casem's stare, remembering the last night we were together on Arida, and how passive the palace guards were during the puppet show. How they let people openly disrespect their king. I'd sensed something was wrong, but Casem waved my concern away. He's been part of this all along.

Why then, in Ikae, had he protected me?

Sweat beads at my temple as I step back, the bramble of dead roots and leaves crunching beneath my feet. It's certainly not all Aridian soldiers who have turned on us—only about fifteen or so—but I've no doubt that if they're here, others who feel the same way are waiting back home.

Kaven steps forward. "The Montaras restrict us. Your little runaway was the perfect excuse we needed to get everyone away and consolidate our army. For that, I must thank you. Your High Animancer will never see this coming." Someone presses a dagger into his palm, and he curls his long fingers around the hilt.

My own daggers feel heavier than normal as I lift them. They weigh my trembling hands.

As Kaven approaches, I do my best to tighten my grip on them and keep them ready. My palms won't stop sweating.

Visidia deserves better than what they've gotten, and it definitely deserves more than this man. He's nearly as far gone as Cato, but I won't make the same mistake Sira did by waiting. I still my shaking wrists, and lunge.

The woods erupt into chaos.

Bastian weaves swiftly around the birch trees, using them as shields to dodge his opponents, and as tools to outmaneuver them. He feints a left around one before banking right, ducking the blow of an opponent. His counterattack sends them face-first into the bramble, bleeding.

I force myself not to look at the face. Not to see if it's anyone I recognize.

"Don't let them get your blood!" I yell, wrapping the full force of my magic around me, letting myself sink into its darkness. Its ferocity. "We don't know which of them might practice Kaven's magic."

Ferrick remains close behind me, using his speed to best his attackers and ensure that I only have to deal with Kaven. Vataea's nowhere in sight; I've no idea when she snuck away, but I hope she's somewhere safe in these woods.

Kaven fights with only one dagger, but he's skilled and

quick as he rushes me. He weaves around my movements and strikes at my waist. I barely dodge in time.

Kaven uses the same technique as Sira used to curse all of Arida; I can't let him steal even a drop of my blood.

I slice my bone dagger through the air. Kaven ducks to avoid it, countering with a swift kick to my stomach that sends me flying into Ferrick's back. He tumbles, but is the first to right himself and pull me up by my arms.

"Let me help," he says urgently. But without fire, there's nothing I can do with his offered limbs.

I push off Ferrick and swing at Kaven again, just as he's about to bring his dagger down. He moves like a soldier, every motion precise and calculated. He dodges my blow, ducks around me, and grabs hold of my hair as Ferrick lunges at him. I try to yank myself free, hardly noticing the yells and the stench of smoke and fire plaguing the air.

Kaven curses and tosses me to the ground. He swats at his tunic; the fabric has caught fire.

Vataea stands behind him, holding several blazing branches like torches. She feeds the flames into the dehydrated bramble beneath us, which hungrily sponges them in and ignites the woods.

I look at her through the veil of smoke beginning to form, and she smiles.

I force myself from the ground and Ferrick is ready. He barely flinches as I toss the bone dagger and scramble to grab a fallen sword from the ground, using it to make a clean cut through his left arm, at his elbow.

Kaven's struck by surprise and shifts his focus onto Ferrick. Wrong move. I take hold of the severed arm in one hand and thrust my blade deep into Kaven's stomach with the other.

My world grows cold the instant blood soaks his shirt

and stains my hands. The farther his blood trails down my skin, the further the cool burn spreads, like a monster devouring my flesh.

"Aridian magic isn't the strongest, little princess," Kaven seethes through his teeth. "Mine is. Let me show you."

Pain freezes me. Kaven's cursed his own blood as a means of protection, and I'm lost to the magic he's formed around me. It's one full of vicious shadows that plague the corners of my vision and snarl at me, snapping dagger-like teeth. I can't do anything but scream as the cool steel of his blade slips beneath my skin. It's like a thousand stingrays stab their barbs through me one by one as Kaven tears through my arm. I scream, my grip on the dagger slackening.

It's just a curse, I remind myself as the shadows tangle around my ankles, dragging me into the earth.

I make my mind blank, letting the shadows do whatever they'd like. Because no matter how much they snarl or constrict around me, they're not real—Kaven is.

I will my body to focus on what it's doing outside this curse. To wrap my fingers around the dagger, and *push*.

Though I don't see my weapon, I feel the invisible weight of it in my palms. The shadows rise, stretching as if forming a gaping mouth, preparing to devour me. But I look through them.

Bastian said it surprised him how quickly I could escape a curse, and now I know why—I've spent my entire life fighting Sira's curse on the Montara bloodline. Compared to her magic, this is nothing.

I drive Rukan forward with everything in me.

There's a scream. This time, it's not my own.

As the shadows of the curse fade, a world that smells of smoke and iron takes its place. My fingers twist around Rukan's woven hilt, and I rip my weapon from Kaven's stomach.

My shoulder's numb, hot with my own blood from where Kaven cut me. High on adrenaline, the pain hasn't fully set in.

Kaven clutches his stomach as blood soaks through his shirt. "How?" is all he can ask.

"You're not as strong as you think." My body trembles as I slide the edge of my blade over Ferrick's severed arm, coating it with Kaven's blood. Then I feed it to the fire as the smoke rises, shrouding us.

Kaven digs his hands deep into the bramble and screams. Blood leaks from an invisible line on his skin as it begins to tear around the elbow. The skin beneath it bubbles up, sizzling to match what's happening with Ferrick's in the flames.

His arm begins to melt away from him, bones and all, and the leather bracelets on his wrist burn with it.

Somewhere behind me, I hear Bastian's quiet gasp as the bloodied bracelets burn, but I don't stop. I strike, fully intent on delivering the final blow, when something slices through the air beside me.

I whirl with just enough time to avoid the blow of an Aridian soldier, and his sword clatters into the earth. Behind him, at least five others are approaching, their weapons raised.

There are too many of them for us to win. And not just them, but Kaven, too. Though injured, he still fights.

There's something in his hand I can't quite see, and with a dawning horror, I watch as he slides it over his blade.

His blade that drips with my blood.

My insides twist as his curse on me takes hold. My body singes like a fresh wound doused with alcohol, every breath full of fire.

I go to lunge for the dagger in Kaven's hand, to stop him, but Bastian grabs hold of my wrist.

"I'm sorry," he rasps. His eyes flash sharp and silver as he pulls me into him. "It's too late. I'm so sorry."

"Don't let them leave!" Kaven's yell sounds like an echo somewhere in the distance. I clutch my chest as a vicious cold blossoms within me, hazing my vision.

Bastian grabs hold of my hand and forces me to run. White-hot pain shoots through my arm, nearly bringing me to the ground. Ferrick bounces on his feet behind Vataea, who uses her makeshift torch to ignite the bramble beneath us. Several soldiers stumble back as the flames roar to life, quickly moving to find a different path. But a few of the Kers manage to speed themselves up in time to make it through the flames.

A man in amethyst lunges for us, movements so fast they blur. He slams his blade into Ferrick's shoulder, and the healer falls back with a grunt. The man arcs his weapon in preparation for another attack, but something sharp and silver gleams from the trees and hits him square in the eyes before he can manage to swing. The man falls back, and my head whirls.

Casem pants, a bow in his shaking hands. I stare at him and his lip quivers, face dripping with sweat.

"Amora," he whispers, "I'm so sorry. I only wanted to find you. I thought this was . . . I mean, my father insisted I come, but I had no idea that . . . By the gods, I'm so sorry, I—"

"There's no time!" Ferrick grabs Casem by the collar of his blazer, his shoulder already knitting itself back together. He pushes him toward us, and Casem stumbles, trying to keep up.

"Talk later," Bastian says, "run now."

I can barely follow that command. Bastian's the only reason I'm still standing, bearing the majority of my weight as he hauls me through the forest. Every step jars my shoulder, causing the pain to build into something so exponential I can no longer tolerate it. My vision blurs and I try to decipher what's happening around us; all I'm able to make out is a hundred distorted colors, and blurred outlines. There's screaming, and I think it's Vataea who whirls around with a snarl.

At some point my vision fades entirely. I've no idea how much time has passed before I see Vataea again. This time, she's covered in blood and our surrounding landscape has shifted. Footsteps are harder.

Sand.

More blood. How long have we been running?

I think I fall at some point because I taste sand and salt, but I'm lost to whatever's happening inside my body. My gaze flickers between real life to blinding white, and when I try to summon my legs, I can't even feel that they're there. They buckle as someone continues to haul me forward, dragging my limp body through the sand.

"Vataea!" I don't know who yells her name. "Now would be a really great time to show off more of that sea magic of yours!"

I hear the quiet snap of a bow. Wet sand sloshes around my boots, but I don't see or feel it as much as I hear it. It mixes with the garbled sounds of voices and clanking steel as everyone fights. Everyone except for me.

But my eyes won't focus enough for me to be able to help. My body's hot and paralyzed, dead weight to whoever carries me.

It's not Vataea. I catch her face in a passing blur; she's bleeding from the nose as she raises the tides over her head, chanting a vicious song. It looks like the ocean stretches around us, the water parting. But I can't focus. I can't watch. All I see are flashes of blood. Sand. A wall of dead fish around us.

"It's going to be okay." I only know the voice belongs to Bastian when his calloused hand cups the side of my face. It cools my feverish skin instantly.

"Kaven's down," he whispers. "Vataea's taking care of us. Stars, I wish you could see her out there, Amora. She was incredible. But we're getting out of here, okay? You're going to be fine."

But his words are a beautiful lie, for when I close my eyes against his cool, wet palm, shapeless magic no longer waits to greet me in the darkness.

My magic is gone.

CHAPTER THIRTY-ONE

I am nothing.

I sink into the sheets of Bastian's bed and pray they'll devour me. Five days. It's been five days since we made it out of Zudoh. Five days that I've been down here, broken and bleeding, hiding from the sun.

I am nothing.

My armor, my magic, my soul, all stolen from me.

Dully, I consider for the hundredth time what Kaven could have cursed it to. I never saw a charm, like the ones Sira used. Nor do I feel ill, as Bastian is when he spends too long away from *Keel Haul*.

Could my magic be cursed to the blade Kaven stabbed me with? If so, would it take a while for the initial illness to set in? Or is it somewhere around me, like in *Keel Haul*?

I scratch my nails along the back wall of the cabin, but feel nothing. If I were cursed to the ship, wouldn't I feel something?

Gods, I was a fool to let Kaven have my blood.

White-hot anger boils within me and seeps through my pores until I can't take it anymore. I claw at the healing wounds along my palm until they pool with fresh blood, tired of this cruel guessing game.

I am nothing. Nothing. Nothing. Nothing.

My magic wasn't even *real*. It's an abomination of Sira's soul magic. Not a beastly thing like I was made to believe, but a curse meant to destroy the Montaras. To plague us for generations.

My magic was never meant to be the way that it is. And yet I ache now that it's been stolen from me, empty without my magic.

Perhaps it wasn't right, but it was mine. And with everything in me, I believed I was using it to protect my people and become the best ruler for them that I could be.

Pain consumes me in the form of the scream I take out on the nearest pillow. When I pull back from it, scarlet blood has marred the pillow's pristine white surface. I press my palm against the fabric and smear the blood even further.

My magic has to be somewhere close. But where?

"Amora?"

I flinch. Sunlight floods through the crack in the door and covers the floor like a rug. I glare at it, eyes burning.

"Get out." The last I saw the others was to tell them the truth of the Montara curse. I remember the horror on their faces. Their pity. Even thinking of it now is more than I can handle.

The door shuts, but someone continues to watch me. With a snarl ready on my lips, I twist around, ready to let them feel the extent of my anger. But when I see the satchel Bastian's holding in his hands, I can't maintain it. A sob threatens to rattle my core, but I slam it away behind the barriers of my empty heart.

"Get that away from me." I want to snatch the satchel from his hands and throw it against the wall over and over until every bone and tooth inside has shattered. Instead, I wind my arms around my waist and dip my head.

That's not my magic he's holding. It's only a sad reminder of my failure.

Ferrick stands beside Bastian. His shadow grabs the dim light of the oil lamp and shifts from foot to foot in an uncomfortable dance.

Bastian's shadow is less anxious. It's steady and confident as it makes its way to my side. A firm hand sets atop my shoulder.

"We need to talk." His words hold no room for disagreement. He forces my chin up until I'm left glaring at him, needing him to leave.

I've failed the Zudians I made a promise to.

I couldn't help the Kers. Even my soldiers have turned on me.

Visidia deserves better than me, so why can't he leave me alone?

"Have you noticed how slowly *Keel Haul* sails?" Bastian asks quietly.

My palms throb with pain as I ignore him. I clench them into fists and tuck them beneath me, head spinning.

Bastian's hazel eyes sharpen as he closes the space between us and takes a seat on the corner of the bed. There's less yellow in them today, the stars dimmed. Ferrick remains behind him, as if uncertain whether he's welcome to do the same.

"It's because my curse was broken, Amora." The words are hardly a whisper as Bastian tries to lean in to catch my stare. As the breath catches in my throat, I let him have it. "When you burned those charms of his, you freed me. *Keel Haul* is a regular ship, again. And my magic is back, too." The words freeze me, seizing hold of my heart. For a moment there's hope, but it sizzles sharply away.

"It's . . . not exactly working," Bastian admits. "But I know it's there. I can feel it, like a fire inside me. I can't reach it, yet; I've forgotten how. But my magic is back, and I promise we're going to get yours back, too."

I sharpen my gaze into daggers that pierce into him. "Don't come in here spewing false hope when Visidia's in danger. I've failed, and now my kingdom will pay the price. I left those people for dead back in Zudoh."

"It's not false hope." The voice belongs to Ferrick, who finally moves to stand beside me. "We should have time for Bastian to relearn his magic. Kaven was severely injured; he'll need a while to recover before traveling. We can warn the king, and then if Bastian can learn to use magic against his brother, we could still win this fight."

I toss my head back and a vicious laugh escapes me. "Because it will be that easy? Because someone who hasn't had magic since they were a child can take on someone who's mastered it? Whose curse magic goes beyond anything we've ever seen?"

"Kaven won't be in great shape after that fight," Bastian argues. "We can use that to our advantage, to overpower him, or—"

"It doesn't matter what shape he's in!" The harshness of my words causes both boys to tense in surprise. "He won't give us time to prepare. He'll strike the second he's able to."

Bastian starts to say something, but Ferrick grabs his shoulder. "There's no point talking to her like this." There's a cold judgment in his words that snags my skin and caves my insides. Even bundled in the sheets and curled into the warmth of a bed, I shudder.

"I have no idea who you are, right now." Ferrick's glare

traps me. "I don't know who this fearful, empty thing is, but you're better than this. You were cursed, not killed. You made a promise back in Zudoh, and those people are trusting you not to give up. We can still do this."

When I turn my head away, Ferrick brushes past Bastian and grabs hold of my hands, ignoring the blood on my palms. He ducks his head until he's staring at me, face stony and impassive.

"You are Amora Montara," he says, awakening something inside me. A tiny match still waiting for its flame. "Now it's time you stopped hiding down here, and start acting like the ruler you are. Tell me what you want us to do."

I reach for that flame, but it snuffs out the moment it's in my grasp. I rip my hands away from him.

"Without my magic, I'm useless." The words tear through me. "I have nothing. I *am* nothing."

These boys want me to stand tall and proud with the belief that we'll win. But they don't see how badly I've already failed. How I fled my home to save my people from the lie of practicing multiple magics, but am returning only with their destruction.

I've nothing to offer, and no way to save Visidia. I should have stayed home and accepted my death. Perhaps then, Kaven never would have had a chance to assemble a fleet.

"I can't be the girl you two want me to be." I push myself from the bed, hands stinging with a sharp pain as they brush against the sheets. "Not anymore."

I make my way to the stairs, far away from the pressure of their fantasies, because I can't take it.

One more look from them is all it would take for me to crumble.

CHAPTER
THIRTY-TWO

I find no solace in the early fall breeze that snakes around me, seeping salt into my pores. The end of summer has finally arrived.

I've cleaned my hands, but the briny air bites into my palms and stings. It's a sharp reminder of the darkness I can't seem to claw my way out of. The sea may be helping, but when I clamp my eyes shut and breathe, there's still emptiness where my magic should be coiled, waiting to spring.

A presence stirs behind me, and though I know I'm safe on *Keel Haul*, instinctively I reach for the satchel and dagger I keep at my waist. But my hands come up empty and the hollowness in my belly inflates. I suck in a breath and shove my fisted hands into my sides.

Casem is beside me. He keeps his head low and his shoulders slouched forward, as if he's already being scolded. Over two weeks have passed since we were in Arida, but it's as though, instead of providing him with life, the sun has leached it all from his body. His once-large frame has thinned and withered with the exhaustion he carries on his slumped shoulders. He wears the pain of it in his cool blue eyes.

"I'm sorry," he says without prompting. He grips the ledge of *Keel Haul* to support himself, knuckles turning white from the pressure of his grip. "When my father suggested I come with him, I was doing it because I wanted to find you and make sure you were safe." He turns to me, but I keep my focus on the sea, watching as turquoise waves crash against the ship and morph into a soft white foam as they recede. Casem draws his hands closer together on the ledge and scrapes at the cuticles of his right thumb, worrying at the skin.

"What good would that have done?" I huff. "I could have been executed if I stayed."

Casem's face twists. "You never heard? Amora, they were going to give you another chance. We all pleaded your case, including your aunt; she told everyone she wasn't fit to be Animancer. They were planning to bring another prisoner up, for you to try again. But none of us could find you."

I expect his words to gut me. To shred me and destroy any light I had left, because what's one more knife when you've already been stabbed by a dozen?

Instead, the words make me pause as realization strikes—my people were going to give me another chance.

The weight of that knowledge sears hot in my chest. I dig my fingers into the ledge of the ship, steadying myself.

Not all of them wanted me dead, or thought me too dangerous. They were going to give me another chance.

"I had no idea what my father's real plan was when I left to look for you, I swear," Casem continues when I say nothing. "I found out on the way to Ikae. If I'd known sooner, I would've never gone with them. I would have told the king. I care too much about you to do something this cruel. And not only you, but Mira. I would never want to put her in danger. You *know* this, Amora. I just . . . I need you to believe me."

I recall Casem's face behind the window in Ikae, and the panic in his expression as he chased after me on the docks. Then I think back to the soldiers accompanying him that night.

I can understand the Kers who joined up with Kaven. But my own soldiers? The father of my friend and guard, who helped train me for years?

The fact that these people want me dead hurts more than they'll ever know.

"I believe you were clueless," I say, recalling how hurriedly he'd tried to get the others away from me and on the wrong path. "But why did you do it? You could have left. You could have found a way to warn me, or stop them."

"They would have killed me." He dips his head like a scolded pup. "I don't think even my father would hesitate to. I knew he always envied your father's power deep down, but I guess I never realized the extent of it. He presented me with the truth after you fled Arida, wanting me to join him. I figured that if I did, it would at least give me a chance to learn their plan and attack when the time was right. Or wait for an opening to escape. I knew it was a risk, but by the gods, I never thought it would end up like this."

The idea of their soul magic alone has me grinding my teeth. To be able to curse someone's soul for an eternity is a far crueler punishment than ending their life or causing temporary pain.

Kaven must be stopped, but how? Without my magic, I'm useless against him.

"How many are we up against?" I ask. "How strong is their magic?"

"We're up against nearly half of Kerost and Zudoh," he answers honestly. "And as for their magic, they're strong . . . but there's some good news I think you'll like to hear."

I draw back at the small, hopeful smile on his lips.

"The curse in Montara blood isn't meant for others," he says. "When people try to learn it, it slowly destroys their souls, warping them. Most who trigger soul magic are unable to use it, and are destroyed in the process. Though there are a rare few who have managed to learn it, like Kaven, he stopped forcing it on his followers years ago, because it kept failing and his numbers were dwindling. People only try to learn it by choice, and there are only a handful who have succeeded."

I press my lips together and from the corner of my eye catch sight of Bastian descending the rigging. The sight of him strikes my heart fierce as a knife.

He moves to the ship's helm and grips it tight in one hand, steering. Glancing down at a compass, he adjusts the helm, again, purposely avoiding my stare.

Vataea leans over the ledge behind him, chanting over the waves as if trying to work her magic on them. Her lips are pursed and her sweat-slicked brows fret with annoyance. Every now and then she manages to lift a wave a little higher than normal, but it's nothing like the magic I hear she pulled off back in Zudoh.

Ferrick's between them, trying to do whatever it is that needs to be done, and I jerk my focus away from them as a knot of bitterness coils within me. Everyone is trying except for me.

"The pirate's still adjusting to his curse being broken," Casem says. "And we don't have much of a crew, especially with you and Vataea both having been out for a few days. I've been trying to use my magic to manipulate the air and bloat the sails, but this ship is too heavy for me to move. We all thought Vataea would be able to help us sail faster when she woke up, but saving us back in Zudoh took a lot out of her. She was . . . incredible." His eyes wander to her for a moment, and in his awe, I remember vague flashes of the sea parting around us. Of being surrounded by walls of dead fish and algae, but never touched by it. I know I should thank her for saving us, but there's a kernel of bitterness that wishes she'd left me behind to sink.

"We're finally on the right track. It's taken a while to get anywhere." Casem points to the vibrant water, and to the school of yellow and blue fish that flank us. With water this clear and bright, we must be somewhere between Mornute and Arida. We'll be home before nightfall.

A wave of relief fills me, but I smother it quickly. Casem notices, frowning deeply.

"Amora?"

I shake my head. "I've no right to return home."

"That's exactly what I used to think after I first left Zudoh." The words stop me cold. I've no idea when Bastian appeared behind me, but he stands there now with his chin lifted high and his eyes hard.

"For years I refused to return to Zudoh because I was afraid to face everyone," he says. "I felt responsible for the destruction of my home. For the murder of my parents and so many others, all because of my brother. It ate me alive. I hid because I was afraid, and if you turn your back on Visidia now, you'll be doing the same thing."

Bastian's words are like needles as I swallow them down, because every single one of them is true.

Slowly, hesitantly, he draws a step closer. When I don't flinch away, he takes another. My hands ignite when he takes them in his, and it's like I can breathe again. "You helped me face my fears, and showed me not to run. So don't you dare say you or I shouldn't be here, Amora. This is exactly where we need to be. There are people counting on us. We can do this." They're nearly the same words I said to him, and they strike hard.

I see Raya's angry face, older and wiser than it should have to be at her age. I see the time-warped hands and exhausted wrinkles of those back in Kerost. I see Sira, who showed me the way my kingdom is meant to be.

Finally, I see the people in Zudoh who dipped their heads to me and, for the first time, offered me their trust.

If we don't hurry to warn my people, it could be the end for my kingdom. And it will certainly be the end of those Zudians.

The match in my soul catches the flame, considering it. It doesn't flare, but it sparks—just once—with a promise that perhaps one day it might burn brightly again. When I reach out for the warmth this time, it's distant, but it's there. I have to cling on to it.

The loss of my magic is a void that I'll never be okay with. But I can't hide from my fate. My life is Visidia's, as it has always been and will always be.

Ferrick and Vataea stand close, listening. I turn my attention to Ferrick, who offers a small but wavering smile. My lips don't feel right mirroring the movement, so I nod instead in silent thanks for his support. Then I look up at the pirate, whose jaw is a hard line as he stares down at me. When I wrap my fingers around his hand and squeeze once, his shoulders fall and his body relaxes. He drops his forehead onto the top of my head, words muffled in my curls. "We'll do this together."

I press my head against his chest, keeping my eyes shut tight so that no tears can escape. But no longer is it just his arms around me. It's Ferrick, too. Then Vataea. Casem. All of them hug me tight, and I'm rendered useless against the tears.

Bastian once asked me why I didn't just find a crew and save myself. But what he didn't realize was that I'd already found them—this is my crew, and I hold them tight. "We'll do this together. All of us."

The others peel away, and I'm left looking up into Bastian's hazel eyes. He's warm and smells of brine, and for a moment I wish I never had to move. That we could stay like this forever, pretending my kingdom wasn't about to be in a war. Because when he touches me, it's like I'm myself again, if only for a moment.

But there's no time for fantasies, and I'm not sure my soul could handle another broken one. I peel myself away, square my shoulders, and force myself to become Amora Montara, the Princess of Visidia once more.

"We'll need to hurry," I tell them. "Kaven's likely already on his way."

Keel Haul's sails bloat satisfactorily as we're pulled windward, but even the ocean's heavy breeze can't carry us as quickly as I'd like.

Head still dipped and his shoulders caved nervously, Casem awkwardly clears his throat. "Does this mean—"

"By the stars, Casem, yes. I forgive you." I roll my eyes, letting them wander to Vataea. "But I do have a question for you."

She arches a brow, face sallow and sunken. It's clear that whatever magic she used to split the sea back in Zudoh did a number on her.

"Why didn't you tell me that one of the curses you sensed on *Keel Haul* was from me?"

Vataea puckers her lips and answers easily, "It felt ancient. I didn't think you should have to worry over something beyond your control."

I sigh. She was trying to be kind, then. "Well, what about this new one? Surely I have to be cursed to something nearby, because I don't feel ill. Can you sense it?"

She shakes her head, fists tightening at her sides as if angry about it. "I've tried. Mermaids can't see curse magic, we sense it;

it's a skill my kind developed centuries ago, to protect ourselves from early poachers. Makes my gills all prickly." She points to the scars on her neck. "Yours is making *everything* prickly. I don't know if it's because it's so fresh, but your curse feels like it's surrounding me. Like it's in the very air around us."

I lift my chin to *Keel Haul*'s mast. Kaven was so far from this ship, and yet . . . Could it be *Keel Haul* that my soul is attached to, after all? If Vataea feels the curse all around her, that's the only thing that makes sense.

"We're going to figure it out," Bastian offers, drawing my attention forward again. "Remember, Kaven has to keep your blood in order for the curse to exist. When we face him again, we'll find where he's kept it and destroy it. You'll have your magic back."

I nod and wait for the familiar heat of my magic to warm my skin and agree with this plan. But it never comes.

"Set sail straight for Arida, then," I tell Bastian. "Full speed ahead. We've magic to collect."

And the entire kingdom of Visidia to protect.

CHAPTER THIRTY-THREE

The sea quivers as thunderclaps explode from the sky.

Arida is a smudge in the near distance, veiled in rain and billowing gray mist that blooms from the water and lightens into milky wisps the farther it lifts.

I stand at the edge of the bow, Bastian at my side as harsh wind snarls at my clothes and lashes at my soaked curls. His hand rests over mine; the only warmth to be found. The sharp air has sunk into my bones and numbed my core.

Bastian's careful not to touch the cuts in my palm as he curls his fingers around my hand. He squeezes it, just once. A soft pulse to remind me that he's there.

I allow my fingers to do the same, lacing around his so I might draw some of his strength. I search again for the familiar thrumming of magic in my body, but inside I remain hollow. There's not even a spark.

"Be careful." The pirate has to lean close for me to hear his words. Even against the rain, the warmth of his breath prickles my ear. "I know I can't stop you from fighting, but whatever you do, please be careful. I quite like having you in my crew."

I draw back at the feeling of cool metal in my palms. My dagger.

"I think you're ready to have this, again." His smile is small, forced. "I hated having to take it away." He carefully hands me Rukan, too. I revel in the tiny pulses of magic that whirl up the weapon and heat my hand.

I can still be strong. With Rukan, I can still fight.

"Thank you." My voice is weaker than I want it to be, trembling with emotion I force myself to swallow down.

"Of course, Princess," Bastian teases. "It's not really my weapon of choice, anyway—"

"No, Bastian." I sheathe the blade and take his hands in mine, squeezing them. "*Thank you*. For warning us about Kaven. For standing up against your own brother. For getting me off Zudoh. For you and Ferrick reminding me I still have a duty. For all of it."

Both his hands close to encompass mine. He brings them up to his lips and kisses the tips of my fingers.

"Thank *you*," he says, his eyes warm as his hands. "For believing in me. And just know, Amora, that no matter what happens today . . . I don't want this to be where our journey ends."

"Neither do I." And I'm surprised to realize I mean it.

He lets go of my hands to cup my face instead, and draws my lips to his.

All our adventure. All my dreams of protecting my kingdom and family. It's all led to this moment.

I'm closest to my old self when I'm with Bastian. Never has a man had such a hold on me, and never did I want one to. But I can't deny that when I'm with him is the only time I'm calm.

It's the only time I feel ready to take on the challenges ahead of us.

I pull him tight, seeking solace in his lips. In the hands that graze my face and warm me from the sheets of rain and the air's harsh bite. I hold him as close and as tightly as I can, a part of me wanting nothing more than to live in this moment forever. To not have to show the kingdom and my people that I've failed them by losing my magic.

But there are too many lives at stake for me to be selfish.

It feels like hours pass before we pull away, and a smudge in the distance draws my attention.

Ahead of us, Arida is a hazy outline. The closer we get, the darker my home grows, and as I squint, I realize why.

The dark smudge of my island isn't formed by clouds. It's formed by the deep amethyst sails of ships that shroud Arida's docks, and plumes of smoke from cannons. Fire devours the cliffsides, tearing its way through thickets of plants and trees. Destroying my beautiful home.

Kaven's already here. We've no crew, and with Bastian's broken curse, we were too slow.

"No!" My heart spasms and I jerk away from Bastian. I clutch the hilts of my daggers tight, trying not to stumble on my unsteady legs. He grabs my waist to steady me.

Behind the sails, on the shoreline, there are figures I can barely see. They move in a way that almost looks as though they're dancing until they stumble to the ground or into the hungry ocean.

Bastian sets a hand on my shoulder, but I rip away from his grip.

"VATAEA!" I scream her name like I'm chanting to a god, and our eyes meet briefly before she whips her head to the water, knowing what must be done. She throws herself over the ship without hesitation, and hits the waves with a slap and a burst of golden light. Her tail fin smacks the water once, and then she's gone.

"Drown them!" I yell as she races toward the shore. "Ask who they fight for, and drown anyone who stands against us!"

Zudoh has declared war, and Visidia's survival is all that matters. No matter what I have to do to ensure it, my kingdom must remain standing.

The thunder and rain are ferociously loud, meaning Vataea will have to get close to the attackers in order to charm and lure them. I don't need to worry about those on this ship being affected.

"Amora! Calm down, breathe."

I grip the weapons so tightly at my sides that my palms threaten to rip back open. I ignore the voice, not caring to decipher which of the three boys it belongs to. A brief flash of Casem's profile in my peripheral vision tells me he's here, but I don't *see* anyone. All I see is a world covered in the scarlet blood I'm about to pour.

"Go to the helm," I growl at Bastian. "Get us to the docks."

He doesn't question me. He moves swiftly, and I step forward to squint at the scene unfolding before me.

Vataea's made it. Figures on the shore become more distinct as we close in on them. They've stilled from their erratic movements and saunter toward the water, letting the churning sea swallow their bodies as they try to claw their way to Vataea and the glowing gold ring surrounding her. I don't hear her song, but I know it works when I see men and women dunk their heads into the water she dives into.

They never resurface.

My shuddering breaths come a little easier. She's clearing the shore for us, giving us time to move.

Keel Haul closes in on Arida. Once we're past the reef, it's as if the island desperately sucks us into it. The ship spasms and I grip the ledge tightly as we slam into the docks, scattering broken planks of wood into the sea.

Casem runs to anchor the ship while I dart for the ladder. I hold my steel dagger in my mouth and use my free hand to toss myself down, ignoring the sharp burn from the rope that sears into my already wounded palms.

There's no time for trivial injuries. I glance over my shoulder to see Ferrick and Bastian hurriedly using a blade to cut strips of fabric from their shirts and stuff them into their ears to avoid hearing Vataea's song. Casem's a few paces behind them, but I don't wait for him to catch up.

"Ferrick, help the wounded!" I yell, hoping he can understand what I'm trying to tell him.

Sand kicks up at my feet and gnaws at my ankles as I dart across the clearing shore toward the group of Aridians who have been fighting off the invasion. I don't look to see if Ferrick listens.

Bodies lay littered across the ground in pools of blood the sand soaks in and feeds from. A palace guard I don't recognize drags herself toward the sea on her stomach. Her legs have been severed and she's bleeding out quickly, but Vataea's song holds her tight as a lure.

Only a few men and women are left standing. I press a palm to my heart to steady its relief when I see Aunt Kalea's among them, alive and holding her own with a sword in one bloodied hand. The other forms a fist.

There's a girl charging her with a sword drawn and poised to attack. The girl's eyes are gone, consumed by shadows, and blood trails in rivulets down her cheek. She's blind with rage and magic, and Aunt Kalea looks ill. She wavers with her sword, rusty from years of forgotten training. When the girl strikes,

Kalea barely manages to avoid the full force of the blade. She stumbles back, clutching her wounded arm with a grimace. Her hand is still fisted, carrying something I can't see.

The girl raises her sword again, and my heart seizes. I run as fast as I can, but it's not enough. I won't reach her in time—I can't protect her.

Just before the sword falls, Aunt Kalea tosses her weapon and drops to the sand. She twists out of reach, narrowly missing the blade, and tips her head back. With trembling hands, she drops a small bone into her mouth. It's coated in blood.

I lunge to stop her, but it's too late. She swallows the bone, and I stumble back like I've taken a fierce blow to the gut.

Her opponent's sword clatters to the ground and the girl falls to the sand, screaming. The acid in my aunt's stomach gnaws at the bone, destroying it inch by inch. The girl's skin peels back and melts away as she claws at herself, trying to stop the pain and smack the rotting skin back into her body.

It will never work. The girl's death will be a slow, painful one.

Aunt Kalea has forever bound herself to soul magic. This whole journey, and I couldn't spare even one person from a life they never wanted to have.

She chokes on it as it etches itself into her soul, grabbing desperately for her throat. Her stomach. She lurches as if about to retch, her entire body shaking uncontrollably.

When I accepted soul magic, it was a vicious, monstrous thing that took hard work and Father's help to tame. I was sick for weeks with the curse, just as Aunt Kalea will be.

May this magic be every bit the beast you are . . .

The group of Aridians behind her stir with panic as Aunt Kalea's eyes roll to the back of her skull. When they spot me, it's through blood that drips into their eyes. Some of them need medical attention immediately. I'm glad to see Ferrick tending to some of them in the distance, but we need to get more Suntosan healers here as soon as possible.

"Get her inside!" My voice cracks when I yell at the women, full of a thousand apologies I wish I had the time to say. But I've wasted too much time already. "All of you find a weapon and get somewhere safe!"

There's a man in my path whom I don't recognize. An enemy soldier dressed in white, whose iron spear reflects the flames that devour my home and glints a violent red. A small collection of leather bracelets smudged with blood sits on his wrist, and my rage burns white-hot.

This man has the same magic as Kaven. He's one of the few who's learned cursed soul magic, and I will not let him have anyone else's blood.

I don't falter. I continue my charge, leaving Aunt Kalea to the others. When the man tries to block my path, the pain and rage that has been building within me flares and bursts. I duck under the attack of his spear and stab my dagger deep into his abdomen, twisting it. The spear falls from his hand, and I draw back only to rip Rukan across his throat and watch the blood fall like freshly corked wine. He gargles on it, choking as I press forward.

More attackers block our path, but Casem's arrows fly from behind me. They slice through the air too quickly to keep track of, hastened by his Valukan air magic, and he takes all four of them down before they can become a threat. Bastian covers me from behind as I tear Rukan cleanly through the neck of another woman who lunges for us. I hear her head *thunk* to the sand, followed by her body, but I don't look back.

"Keep going!" Bastian yells. "We'll cover you!"

I leave Ferrick behind with the wounded, never having planned to stop.

An earth-affinitied Valukan stands at the edge of the

cliffside, sending giant boulders spiraling from the cliffs at two invading Kers attacking him. When he sees me, his eyes light with recognition and he grounds his feet in the dirt, crouching low. He makes a sweeping motion with his arms, and the mountain trembles and cracks, splitting down the middle as a makeshift staircase takes shape. It's a direct path to the palace, only about a half mile up.

"Go!" he yells, grunting as one of the Kers attacks, moving too fast to avoid. The Valukan pulls the earth around him like a barrier, shielding himself. Before the Kers can follow, the Valukan tears his hand through the air and the beginning of the staircase collapses after us.

The Kers turn back to him, angry, but we can't help him fight. We have to keep climbing.

This far from the shore, Casem and Bastian remove the fabric from their ears and toss the scraps to the ground. The rain has slicked the cliffside, and in our haste, I trip and slam my knee on the ground. Searing pain stabs through my thigh and up my spine until I see white.

Someone grabs me beneath the arms and hauls me back up. My leg tries to give out, but I grit down the pain and force myself forward.

The palace is in sight.

Just a little farther . . .

Pain tears through my shoulder, and I cry out. I turn to see a knife embedded in my skin. It drips with an oozing black liquid that spreads through my arm and forms a web of thin black lines over my shoulder. My attacker is a Zudian who has rushed us from the side of the palace and is drawing another throwing knife from their belt.

"Casem!" Bastian yells as I clutch my numbing arm into my chest. The next thing I hear is the familiar thump of a falling body as Casem shoots the attacker down. His shots never miss.

Bastian's by my side within seconds. He snatches the bone dagger I took from the woman I killed in Zudoh and, without warning, grinds it into my shoulder. I scream out, gripping on to his soaked shirt and balling my fists into it.

I want to curse. I want to call him the most vicious names. But as he slices into my shoulder and draws blood from my arm, sensation trickles its way back into my fingertips. Slowly, but it's something.

"You're going to be fine," he tells me, voice gruff as he rips at his cape and tears off a sliver of wet fabric, tying it firmly around my arm. I grimace against the pain, tears threatening to sting my eyes.

But we have to keep moving. With a searing knee and a numbing arm, I'm battered and magicless. But we've no other choice.

Supported by Bastian, I make my way through the doors of my home.

CHAPTER THIRTY-FOUR

The palace is empty. Likely evacuated, as most of the guards fighting for or against Arida are near the shore. Slick marble floors screech against our wet and muddied footsteps, telling us we do not belong here. Warning us to leave while we still have the chance.

I clutch Rukan close and slip out of Bastian's hold. My body is ghostly, limbs tingling with the slow threat of increasing numbness. My legs tremble, and with every step agony stabs up my thigh from where I've shattered my knee. But still, I will walk.

Still, I will fight.

The screech of our footsteps echoes against the overly bright walls of the palace, filling the dense and soundless void. A pressure in my chest draws me forward and toward the throne room, where, somehow, I know Father waits.

I'm heavy with rain and crusted blood as I force myself up

each sapphire step. I cling to the pearl railing, gritting my teeth against pain. Behind me, Casem and Bastian keep quiet, following the awful pace I've set. I'm halfway up the flight when an earsplitting scream shakes the walls. Behind me, Casem inhales a sharp breath.

"Mira," is all he whispers before he pushes past me and bounds up the staircase at full speed. I curse my brittle knee and follow. Sweat layers my face and coats my neck from the effort.

I reel back when a black-robed Curmanan woman bounds out a door, followed by a Valukan royal soldier. They spin to face the three pursuers, two white-caped Zudians and a time-wielding Ker in deep amethyst.

In the back of my mind I remember something Father said long ago: *Those who practice time magic make some of the finest soldiers. They'll have their sword deep in the enemy's gut before anyone can blink.*

I know I need to help—to distract the Ker and slow them down as best as I can—but Bastian grabs my wrist when I try to step forward.

He pulls me back the moment the Ker touches the shoulders of one of her Zudian partners—a male whose movements speed up dramatically. I can barely keep up with the strikes of the Zudian's blade, but fortunately the Curmanan is prepared for them.

She ducks and falls back, using levitation to tear her opponent's sword from his hands. The Zudian lunges in a quick counterattack, so fast that his body is a blur thanks to the aid of his companion's magic. But the Curmanan has reversed the sword in the air, so the tainted black tip points toward the Zudian.

She pushes her hands forward, and because the man is moving too quickly to stop himself, he falls with a yelp as the sword pierces through his chest, body spasming as thick lines of poison lick their way across his skin and paint it gray.

Meanwhile, the Valukan man runs his hands through one of the torches that lights the hall, now wielding its flame in his grasp. When the remaining attackers strike, the Valukan shoves the fire into their opponents' chests.

"They've got it handled," Bastian says. "Let's keep moving."

We bound around the fight and head into the washing room, where several Valukans with the affinity for water stand ready beside the basins. My breath hitches when I see Mother is among them.

Rarely have I seen her use her Valukan magic offensively; she's never had a reason to. Yet when the Valukans see us approach, water lashes around Mother like a hungry, fierce weapon. I reel back at the vicious tides, cursing the pain in my knee. Only when she sees my face does Mother suck in a breath, the water slamming back down into the basin.

"Amora!" She rushes forward and throws her arms around me tightly. I grit my teeth against the pain her touch elicits, and bury my face in her thick curls as she drags me into her. "You're safe." Her body trembles with the sobs she's holding in, trying to keep strong for the others. "By the gods, you're safe."

I clutch her tightly, breathing a sigh of relief into her neck. She smells of blood and brine, and her touch is as desperate as mine. I have to force myself to pull away; she doesn't want to let go, and I wish I didn't have to.

"You need to get to the safe room," I tell her as I draw back. "Take as many with you as you can, but don't try to fight unless you have to. You need to go hide—"

"Princess?" a voice says weakly.

My knees nearly crumble as I turn to see Mira, who lies against one of the basins with a white-knuckled hand clutching the corner of it. A Suntosan healer in an emerald robe is on his knees beside her, his hands covered with blood as he presses them against her stomach. I know Ferrick's busy helping those who fought on the beach, but I immediately wish him here to help her. I can barely breathe when I look at her.

She's been stabbed, as have several other servants who lie beside her. One of them doesn't move.

Casem is on his knees beside Mira, cradling her head in his hands. Her skin sheens with sweat, and the Suntosan healing her wears a grim expression of tight lips and worried brows.

"The throne room," Mira whispers feebly. Her eyes are glazed when she tries to look at me, and it nearly kills me. She touches the healer's hand and shakily points to me. "Her knee."

"Touch my knee and you'll be sorry," I snarl when the healer makes a move toward me. Mira opens her mouth to protest, but I fix the healer in a firm glare and nod back to Mira. "You heal her. Now."

The light in Mira's eyes is dimming, and I won't let her die. My injuries are bad, but they're not life-threatening. I can still move. I can still fight.

When I turn to her, Mother's lips press together. Her eyes are wet, and their emotion betrays her. She doesn't want me to go, but we both know there's no choice. As far as she knows, I still have my magic.

"They have your father," she says, her words tight. "Go, Amora. Hurry. I'll get as many as I can to safety."

I nod, but no matter how quickly I need to go, I struggle to pull my eyes away from the thin veil of sweat that sits atop Mira's skin and pools in the tiny crevice below her collarbone. The fear that knits Mother's brows and her shaking hands nearly destroy me.

What have my people had to suffer, because I could not stop this attack back in Zudoh?

When I face Kaven again, I won't make the same mistake twice.

I turn so the healer can focus on Mira, and kiss Mother's cheek.

"Protect them," I tell her. "And stay safe, no matter what that takes. I'll be back soon."

I can't linger any longer. I drag Bastian behind me and snatch a torch from its holder on the wall, leaving Mira with Casem and my mother.

We ascend the staircase to the highest level, panting and exhausted, but never stopping. Not until we reach the ornate gold doors that lead into the throne room and hear the clap of an explosion behind it. The ground shakes from the impact and I grab hold of Bastian's shoulder to stabilize myself. My shoulder seizes from the pain of the movement, but I bury it down somewhere deep beneath my adrenaline to be dealt with later.

Magic. The only thing that could cause that big of an explosion is magic.

Bastian's throat tightens as he swallows. His gaze slips to me, asking an unspoken question: *Are you ready?*

I nod, and we throw the doors open.

Hot air welcomes us like death. My torch is unnecessary; the room is bathed in fire. Thank the gods for the rain outside, for it's likely the only reason Arida is still standing.

Flames lick the walls and feed on the plush sapphire rug, burrowing into it and consuming it whole. My throat aches, struggling to find oxygen that's been stolen by the ravenous fire. The windowless back wall is the only reason we can still breathe.

Father's positioned in the corner, and relief floods through me when I see he's still alive. His broad chest heaves with gasps, and one side of his face is stained crimson from the blood that spills from a profound gash on his forehead. His trembling hands wrap around a handful of bones, and when he spots me at the entrance, his chest caves. His head shakes furiously.

"LEAVE!" he yells, voice desperate.

I refuse. Wielding both daggers in either hand, I charge inside.

Kaven's shirt is stuck to his bloodied chest, telling me Father's put up a good fight. His dark eyes are rimmed with silver sharp as steel when he whirls to me. In place of the arm I took from him, he has bandages wrapped tight at the stub of his elbow.

"Have you come to see the king atone for his sins?" The question snakes its way through my skin and makes me shudder. "Poor little Montaras, so focused on being stronger than everyone else. Always so worried about being overthrown. For centuries you've put yourselves ahead of your people, destroying our homes and hoarding magic. That ends tonight."

Kaven holds his sword by the blade. It slices into his palm and blood coats the metal quickly. But it's Father who screams as his palms peel open, bleeding. I stand frozen, numb.

As Bastian was anchored to *Keel Haul*, Kaven's cursed my father to be anchored to him.

It's for protection; without the cursed bands I destroyed, his power's been weakened. By binding my father to him, Kaven's guaranteed I'll never touch him; killing him would mean destroying Father's soul.

The pain in Father's scream spears through me, but I force it away to focus. Kaven's magic may be strong, but it's not limitless. I summon my strength and brandish my daggers, closing the space between myself and Kaven. I eye his wrist for a bracelet—for his connection to my curse and Father's—but his skin is bare.

Bastian shifts to my side, tense as he eyes his brother. He

grips his pommel tight. "We're going to do this," he whispers, more to himself than to me. "We're going to end this."

"We're not going to do a thing until we break his connection to my father," I tell him. "I need you to stall."

He nods as Kaven turns to us and spits blood onto the floor. "Hello again, little brother." His teeth gleam red. "How's the new curse treating you?"

Bastian falters, forehead wrinkling. But when Kaven grins, Bastian shakes it off and points his sword ahead of him.

"There's still time to back down, Kaven," Bastian says, his grip firm and sword unwavering. "No one else has to die."

His brother shakes his head, half of his face shadowed by the flames. "I've come too far to let it end here. Visidia deserves better than a monarchy of liars and thieves. You're the one who still has time to back down; we can end the Montaras together, and share this magic with all. No more laws. No more division."

My hands shake as I clench Rukan tight, though I know I can't bring myself to use the blade. Not while Kaven still uses Father as his shield.

Bastian steps in front of me, putting himself between me and his brother. "Get your father out of here."

Kaven's lips flatten as his silver eyes narrow. "That's your decision, then? After everything the Montaras did to us, you choose to protect her?"

"She's more than her blood," Bastian growls. "And I am more than mine. You're the reason our parents are dead, Kaven. You're the reason our home is destroyed. I spent years dreaming that things could return to normal one day, and that you might realize your mistakes and put an end to this chaos. But you killed that dream, and buried it deep as those whose blood you've spilled. It's time we end this."

Bastian strikes.

CHAPTER
THIRTY-FIVE

The clash of steel roars through the air.

The further the flames build, the more my vision blurs and my throat squeezes. Fire licks at my feet, nipping my leather boots. I kick the flames away and run to Father, who chokes on thick smoke.

If we want to stay alive, we need to get out of here.

Father's satchel has fallen beside him, scattering bones onto the floor. He's clearly tried his magic against Kaven, and I don't need to ask to understand the outcome. It's like Bastian and *Keel Haul*—hurt the ship and Bastian feels it, but hit Bastian and the ship goes on as if nothing's happened. Just like the ship, Kaven is immune to the effects of the curse while Father suffers.

Father isn't strong enough to grit through the pain of harming himself when he tries to attack Kaven. It's likely he's holding back, because anything Kaven feels, Father feels. Where

Kaven bleeds, Father bleeds. Part of Father's soul lives within Kaven.

I crouch down beside him and try to wrap my arms around Father's broad body, throwing all my strength into helping him straighten.

"Go," I yell, pushing him toward the door. "Go! We need to get you somewhere safe."

Every breath he takes comes in a tight wheeze. I try to push him away, but Father snags hold of my hand. His eyes are molten brown, fearful and earnest. They pool with tears as he blinks through the smoke and looks up at me.

"I've failed you," he begins, though his words are cut off by a vicious cough that rattles his entire body.

"Later," I tell him. "We don't have time." My chest shakes with the effort of trying to drag Father away; he's dead weight.

"You're right," is all he whispers. I'm ready to yell. Ready to jab my dagger into the back of his leg and force him out. But the moment our eyes meet, my vision clouds white as Father strikes his palm straight into my chest.

I reel back, lungs emptying.

Somehow, the two of us are no longer in the throne room, but standing alone in a tainted white-gray void. There are no fires in this strange, endless space. No smacks of steel, and no bleeding bodies. Only Father, who stands tall before me.

I peer down at my palms. The blood that stained them has disappeared, as have my injuries. I've never seen magic like this. "What did you—"

"As you said, we don't have much time." Father reaches his hand out and I step toward him, letting his calloused hand cup my chin. His rich brown eyes search my soul, brows knitting as he seeks something he will not find.

"Kaven told me what he did," Father whispers, "but I never believed it could be true."

I draw back, and his hand falls to his side, still. All of the rage I've buried festers, boiling within me until I can no longer contain it.

"We could have stopped him." The words tumble out of me, knotted with rage. "You knew the truth of our magic years ago, and you did nothing. Why? We could have prevented all of this."

This strange place agitates my skin and strengthens the rage within me. Gray smoke curls around a plane of white, as if choking it. It's airless, still and suffocating.

Sorrow holds Father by the shoulders. I struggle to look at his pain. It's too raw. Too overwhelming.

"That's why I've failed you. I never wanted you to see me as a fearful king." Somehow his voice is calm. "But that's precisely what I've been. As strong as our magic is, we're no match for the kingdom as a whole, and we'd be even less of a match if Arida's magic was divided. I tried to quiet Zudoh and keep them at bay without Visidia realizing what I was doing."

Part of me wants to cover my ears, or cover his mouth so he can't say another word. Because all my life, I've wanted to make my father proud. I wanted to be just like him.

The King of Visidia. The High Animancer.

My father.

But he's not the man I thought he was. The man before me is a coward, not a king.

"My father often told me that, one day, someone would try to come for our power," he continues. "He taught me to prove myself as an animancer, just as you were meant to do the night of your birthday, and then to never draw too much attention to my magic again; to practice my skills, but only ever demonstrate them to the prisoners executed late at night when all of Arida sleeps. He taught me to be strong, but to rule from afar, just as his father did before him. If I didn't interfere with

Visidia too much, the islands were supposed to take care of themselves. I was only to step up and be loud when there was something I could easily do to further my glory."

Like protecting the mermaids.

"What about Kerost?" I ask. "I've been there, Father. I've seen the damage done. If you knew, how could you not help them?" A moment ago I was hot with rage, yet my body has thoroughly numbed in this place. The echo of our voices is the only sound to fill the abyss, and slowly I begin to understand where Father's taken me.

This is soul magic far beyond anything I can do. Somehow, he's tamed his magic enough to bring me here, into the personal space of his own soul.

I stare around the abyss—at the stark white plumes that seek to shred his soul apart and leave nothing but emptiness in their wake—and wonder if this is what my own soul looks like. Shredded and peeling, but still pretending to be whole.

"They wanted to learn Valukan magic, Amora. If we permitted that, then others would begin to practice whichever magic they'd like." His voice trembles on its hinges, as though he's struggling to maintain a hold on his words. As though he's struggling to maintain belief in them. "The people would grow stronger than us. We'd open ourselves up to anarchy."

"We could learn other magics, too," I argue. "If our family has always been worried about not being strong enough to rule, then perhaps we're onto something." I grind my feet into the solid nothingness beneath me, hating what he admits. Hating that, despite it all, I'd still hoped that he would have had an honorable reason for what he had done. That he could still be who I believed he was.

"You told me we kept Arida's magic to ourselves because it was dangerous." Each word grinds out of my throat, raw and painful. "You said we were supposed to keep others from studying multiple magics because it would corrupt their souls, not because we're afraid of our own people being strong. How much of my life was a lie, Father? Tell me the truth—did you know all this time how Aridian magic truly came to be? Did you know about Cato?"

Finally, he looks at me, but it's not with the harshness I was expecting. Father's lips lift into a smile, though the ends of them wilt with sadness he fails to hide.

"I did," he admits. Two words, and it's like he's struck me across the face. "I told you already, I've been a fearful ruler, avoiding issues until they knocked on my door. This is why I kept you on Arida for all these years. I never wanted you to see what I had done.

"You've always been dutiful," he continues, "and smart as a whip. I knew if I took you with me to travel, it wouldn't be long until you figured out my secrets. And I was right." All traces of a smile are gone. Father closes the space between us and takes one of my fallen curls, tucking it behind my ear. "The only thing I've done right by Visidia is give them you—my fearless, relentless daughter. I gave them a powerful animancer; a princess who will rule this kingdom with the bravery I could never find."

"No." I shake my head. "Kaven cursed me. I'm magicless. Visidia deserves someone who can take care of them. Who will keep them safe. They deserve better than either of us."

He laughs. It's a gentle sound that tears through the abyss and eats at its corners. The edges of our constructed world begin to fade. Heat prickles at my skin.

"My brilliant girl, magicless or not, you are here. You fight for this kingdom. You bleed for this kingdom." Father touches my hands, and I draw them back with a wince. Blood once again mars my scarred palms. "They deserve more than me, you're right. But you? You were made to rule Visidia, as I was made to give you a kingdom."

"I don't want it." The words rip out of me, as though they're tearing my own soul. I don't know if they're a lie or the truth, but they burn deep in my chest. "Our blood destroyed Visidia! How am I to rule a kingdom we've built by destroying others?" My voice falters. "I can't forgive you for this."

Father's shoulders wither, though his gentle smile holds firm. "I have not been a fair king, but now it's time for me to be a good one." Tilting my chin up, Father presses a kiss to my forehead. The touch sears into my skin as if branding me. "I know you'll take care of this kingdom, and I know you'll be brave. I love you, my daughter, more than you will ever know, and I am sorry this burden must come to you so soon. But there's only one way to help you win this fight. It's time I finally did something right.

"Tell your mother I'm sorry," he whispers. "And take care of her, please."

I still, trying to process the words even as Father draws away from me. But there's no time. Our makeshift world blurs, and fire claims my peripheral vision as I'm thrust back into the blazing throne room, where Bastian and Kaven duel through the smoky haze.

My eyes are drowned in sweat and smoke as I watch Father lift his sword from the ground. He twists it to press the tip of the blade against his stomach, and I buckle as horror freezes my limbs.

"Father?" It's like I'm back on Arida's beach, begging him to turn and look at me. But he shuts his eyes instead, a single tear rolling down his cheek. "Wait, please!"

Arida's High Animancer, the King of Visidia, plunges the sword deep into his stomach. I barely catch him in time to help his body to the ground. His shoulders heave beneath my fingertips, just once, and I feel the very moment breath leaves his body and his soul disappears to the gods.

He did this to break his connection with Kaven. So that I could kill him without worrying about hurting Father or destroying his soul.

He did this because of me.

Somewhere behind me, Bastian's yell slices the air. But I can't look at him.

All I see is Father's blood pooling over the marble, surprising the hesitant flames around him. All I see is how his body sags deeper into his blade and his hands fall limp at his sides. Fire makes its way to him, burning through his cape and plaguing his skin.

Even amid the flames, I'm cold as frost.

My chest constricts with breaths I do not take. Father's blood slithers around my boots. I stumble to my knees beside him, staring until my vision goes as red as his blood.

There's no point in looking at his chest—it doesn't move. Or his eyes—which stare unblinking into the space ahead of him. He's gone.

Dead.

And he's left me the responsibility of an entire kingdom I cannot fail.

Rukan is heavy in my hand, pulsing with hunger I have every intention of feeding.

A monster stands before me with a vicious smile and eyes that shine silver as a full moon as they stare down at Father's blood. It doesn't realize that I am a monster, too.

"I've won." Kaven's words are as firm as a prayer. He presses his palms to the blood, looking at it like it's a gift from the gods themselves. He raises his palms to his lips and coats his tongue in the very thing he's desired most.

In Kaven's distraction, a breathless Bastian draws a bone and quietly coats it in his brother's blood. He must plan to curse Kaven to it, but when he raises the bone to try, he stumbles back with a hand to his throat, then his stomach. He's choking, gagging, reaching for something I cannot see. Blood coats his lips and trails down his chin, though I see no wound.

Not another one. He can't leave me, too.

Kaven turns to him, surprised, and smiles.

"What did you do to him?" I snarl, readying my dagger as Bastian drops to his knees and lets the bone clatter at his side. As he falls, I stumble back, throat constricting as it searches for air. My body seizes and shakes as warm blood glides down my own chin, as well. I've no idea how or when it got there.

Kaven says nothing. He keeps staring at Father's blood, and his awe snatches my breath until I'm nearly suffocating. It takes all my power to force myself to stabilize, chest shaking as I lunge for him. All I see is red.

Red. Red. Red.

Red as the blood Father bathes in.

Red as the blood Bastian falls to the floor and chokes on.

Red as the blood that will forever stain my soul.

Red like the coat of blood I will weave over Kaven's corpse.

I thrust Rukan into his leg and bury it in his skin with a twist. Kaven doesn't even scream. He pulls me back by my hair, but I rip my dagger free and slice through the strands until his grip falls with hair no longer mine.

"Tell me what you did to him!" I scream it this time, movements erratic, vision spinning. I think I strike him again because there's blood on my hands. Mine, his, Father's. It all falls the same. There's no keeping track of whom it belongs to, anymore.

Bastian slaps his hand against the ground and wheezes for air he cannot find. My vision blurs, and Kaven's face flashes across it.

"The curse," he whispers. *"The moment you harm another creature, may this magic eat you from the inside out."*

My throat tightens with recognition. Those are Sira's words, the ones she used to curse Cato.

"What are you talking about?" Bastian's eyes are rolling into the back of his head, and I can barely focus.

Because I know the answer. My temples throb as my own eyes twitch back and forth, threatening to roll into the back of my skull.

"Bastian just triggered the Montara curse." Kaven's fingers dance along the hilt of his blood-crusted sword. He holds his chin proud, as if he's thrilled by the blood we bathe in. By the chaotic destruction he's caused.

My vision pulses black. I can no longer keep track of all my wounds, or the amount of blood that drains from me. I think back to Zudoh—to the tiny object Kaven cursed me to, almost impossible to see.

Bastian's hair.

Then I think back to *Keel Haul*, where until Bastian grabbed my hands, I felt empty. Like a shell. He was the only thing that made me feel even a little like my normal self.

I was right to believe no man could have such a strong hold on me. It's not Bastian himself that makes me feel whole, again. It's because he's the missing piece of me. My magic and half my soul are cursed within him.

There's no denying the truth in Kaven's words. As *Keel Haul* held claim over Bastian, Bastian now holds that over me. Where *Keel Haul* held his magic, he now holds mine.

My feet sway beneath me, and my slowing heartbeat reminds me of after I'd fought the Lusca.

A smudge of something bright orange flickers at the front of the room, near the door. It dances through the flames, a trick of my bleary eyes. The smoke that fills the room with thick plumes is taking its toll. I struggle to grip Rukan in my shaking palms as my injured knee seizes. It betrays me, bringing me to my knees.

"It's time for balance to be restored to Visidia." Kaven steps over me and lifts his sword above my head. "I will lead these people into a better future."

Pain is the fire that fuels me as I ready both daggers; we'll strike at the same time. If I'm to die, then I'll drag him to death at my side.

Kaven swings, and I thrust upward and pour everything left within me into the two blades that tear through Kaven's chest. I wait for his blade to come down on me, but instead it clatters to the floor, and blood rains onto my face.

Kaven's blood. The silver glow of his eyes winks out as he falls. His hand is gone, scattered a foot away and on the floor.

Ferrick stands where Kaven's body has fallen, a guard's sword in his hands. His chest shakes when our eyes meet, and he tosses the sword beside him. He drops to his knees as I fall and catches my head before it smacks the marble.

Icy blue lines eat their way across Kaven's skin as Rukan's poison eats through him. The moment his chest stops moving and he lies face-first on the ground is when I smile.

Then I shut my eyes, too.

EPILOGUE

Sometimes I think about how it would've been better if I never woke up. I think about what it would've been like if Ferrick had left me on the floor beside Father's body, and if Suntosan healers weren't on our island that night. I would never have had to deal with the bodies. Hundreds of them, Zudians, Kers, and royal soldiers alike. I wouldn't have to deal with imprisoning Aridians I once thought of as family, like Casem's father, or see confused and broken families.

I wouldn't have to answer so many questions with lies.

Did you defeat Kaven with your magic? Did you disappear to protect the kingdom? Did the High Animancer know about the attack? Did you?

I wouldn't have to exist as only half of myself, and rely on a single man to sustain my existence.

Sometimes I think it would have been easier that way, if only Visidia would have let me die.

But every time I think this, I remember Mother's face when I opened my eyes. It was warm like the sun with tears that fell from her eyes like stars. I remember the way Vataea hugged me fiercely, and how Ferrick cried in my hair as I held him and cried, too. I remember the way Yuriel whispered his thanks to me like a prayer, and how Casem fell into a bow at my feet. Mira hasn't left his side since he stood back up.

I also remember Bastian, shaking, bloody, and scared, but sighing relief into my skin as he held me. I remember the unspoken promise when he took my hand, and the way he refused to let go.

I turn my head, watching the soft rise and fall of Bastian's chest as we lie in the gardens, the place where everything first changed.

This man has a piece of my soul. I'd wondered whether that might be the case someday, but now that decision's been made for me, and the idea of it curdles my stomach. Because how can I be sure that any of it's real?

I try not to think about the hold Bastian has over me, because that hold won't exist for long. I refuse to allow a curse to dictate who I must spend my hours with, or who I must keep close. Though I care for Bastian, I don't want it to be because of a curse. I want it to be because I choose him.

He shakes as I watch him, tremors roiling through his chest every so often. While he's mostly stable now, his body is still weak and struggling to process both the sudden reawakening of his curse magic as well as the Montara curse.

Bastian's head turns, hazel eyes opening slowly to the golden sunlight of early fall. When he spots me watching, he casts a lazy grin and draws himself to his feet. Carefully, he reaches out to take my hand. Giving it to him is the only thing that makes me feel whole again, and I hate it.

I will break the curse on the Montaras, reclaim my soul, and ultimately restore proper soul magic—Sira's version—to the kingdom. But there's something else I must do, first.

"Are you ready?" he asks.

Nerves gnaw my bones as I look toward the waterfall, imagining everything that awaits me behind it. Bastian squeezes my shoulder.

"You were born for this." He steps forward and presses a kiss to my forehead, where Father's final kiss still burns.

My eyes sting. If only we'd been quicker to return to Arida. If only I'd ended things back in Zudoh. Father would still be alive.

If only.

If only.

I clamp my eyes shut and run my fingers over the sapphire necklace that sits heavy around my neck.

Today, I do not wear only the color of Arida. I wear a sleeveless dress of solid white to represent Zudoh's reintroduction into the kingdom, adorned by two anklets of matching strung pearls. They clash magnificently with Rukan, sheathed on one side of my hip, and with my steel dagger on the other.

"I'm ready." I take hold of Bastian's hand, and he laces our fingers together as we head toward the main gardens.

The crowd before us is a shifting wave of black, pinks and reds, greens and blues—and even white—that stills as we approach. But there's no amethyst. The only Kers here are those employed as royal soldiers and palace guards; we've still much to do if we're going to earn back Kerost's trust.

Raya and Zale are some of the first I notice among the crowd. Looking at them, with their stomachs full and their eyes glinting, eases the pain of this day some. Though there are far fewer Zudians here than there ought to be, it's a start.

It doesn't change that the crowd is half the size it was for the execution, nor does it change that I'm only here because Father is dead. Nothing will ever change that.

My stomach coils tight, reminding me that while Kaven is gone, the kingdom is more fragile than ever. And it likely will remain that way for some time, because today, for my first act as queen, I'll be reinstating the right to practice multiple magics. It's time for everyone to be given their freedom.

Though I anticipate many will welcome this change, its success will depend on whether Visidia's people believe me when I tell them that the beast is no longer a concern.

Visidia's restoration depends wholly on my people's trust in me. And for that reason, they cannot know about the curse on the Montara blood.

No one can know I've lost my magic, or that Bastian holds it. No one can know of Aunt Kalea's treason, or that the soul magic within us is corrupted because of Cato. Nor can they know of Kaven's followers who are being kept in the prisons far below, or of the strange mix of curse magic and soul magic some of them possess.

At least not for now.

I won't be like Father, or the rest of the Montaras. My people will learn the truth one day soon, after I break the Montara curse and make soul magic available to them.

But until then, they need someone to lead them into this new future. They need a ruler they can look up to while the foundation of our culture shifts, even if they might consider that ruler a fraud.

I don't deserve to sit on this throne—how could I, after all the damage the Montaras have done to this kingdom?—but someone has to repair Visidia, and I'm the only one who knows the secret to how.

Mother's gaze is soft as I approach. She bows her head to me, and though it's not customary, I bow mine back.

A throne of burnt ivory and charred whalebone waits for me on the same stone slab where my performance took place half a season ago. Though it was suggested I have it remade, I demanded the scorched throne be kept. It's a reminder not only to my people—who will look at it and know exactly what I've done for them—but for myself, as well.

This throne killed Father. And it might one day try to do the same to me.

Aunt Kalea stands at the left corner of the throne, her head bowed. When her eyes lift to find mine, my chest constricts, forcing breath from my lungs.

I see more of Father in her now than ever before. I see him in her molten eyes and firm jaw. In her sun-kissed olive skin, and the thin wrinkles at the corners of her tired eyes, which are dimmed by the weariness of mourning we all feel. Aunt Kalea may never be comfortable with the magic coiled around her soul, but slowly she's adjusting.

I tried everything I could to ensure her life remained in Ikae, but in the end, it didn't matter. I may have spared her from having to sit on the throne, but soul magic has claimed part of her. Her only hope is that I'm able to find a way to break Sira's curse.

I pass Ferrick as Mother guides me to the throne, where he stands tall at my right side. He's had his outfit personally tailored, again—an emerald-green blazer with sapphire cuffs and gold trim. Though I'd never put the outfit together myself, Ferrick's grin is broad and his chest is proud as he waits to accept his new position not as my fiancé, but as my top adviser.

The faces of my people lift as they inspect not their new heir, but their new queen. I clench my fingers on the arms of the throne as Mother offers me a crown. The skeletal eel with jagged teeth sits above my brows, and a spine of bone and jewels curves down my back—the High Animancer's crown.

Father's crown.

My crown.

She fits it onto my head with shaking hands while draping

a cape that shimmers like an opal over my shoulders, and all the while I bite the inside of my cheek, willing myself not to tremble beneath the weight of it all.

"Bow." Mother turns to address our people. "Bow to your queen, who has saved this kingdom from those who sought to destroy it. Bow to your High Animancer, who offered her own life in order to save yours, and who lives to tell the tale."

I dig my fingers into the cape, pulling it closer as I lift my chin high.

If there's one truth I know, it's that I will make things right for my kingdom. That is my fate, and I will do whatever I must to see it through.

"Bow," Mother says in a voice that booms across the too-small crowd. "Bow to High Animancer Amora, your new Queen of Visidia!"

And everyone does.

ACKNOWLEDGMENTS

Holy crud, I can't believe we're here and that I finally get to write this. It's an official Book!

I've been blessed throughout this process to work with the most incredible people. As someone who believes everything happens for a reason, I first have to thank God for paving this path for me and putting those people in my life. Publishing is no easy feat, and looking back, it's clear that every hardship I faced was to get me to these incredible people.

First and foremost, Mom and Dad. Thank you for always supporting and believing in me, and for telling me I could accomplish whatever preposterous dream I had. You're definitely responsible for my overconfidence, but hey, look, it worked! Because of you, I was never afraid to put myself out there and try. I know there's a lot of blood and stabbing in this book, but please don't lock your doors when I come visit. And I really hope you skimmed over the kissing scenes, let's never ever talk about them. I love you!

Josh, my wonderful boyfriend. Thank you for telling me to write this book, for helping me be able to do so after the accident, and for all your love and support. I'm glad you looked past the purple lipstick.

To all my siblings—Steven, Stefanie, Spencer, Bryan, Maryanna, CJ, Kristin, Sarah, and Rich—because I know I'd never hear the end of it if I didn't put your names in the book.

Hillary Jacobson, literary agent extraordinaire, for always believing in me and this book. Thank you for all the calls, the emails, the weekends, and the million hours you put into reading and supporting this book so that it could be the best possible version of itself. This story would not be the same without you.

Jenny Simpson and Tamara Kawar over at ICM, who offered excellent notes and early first reads.

Roxane Edouard, foreign rights wizard, for your work to get this book shared all over the world.

Josie Freedman, for handling the film rights for this book, and for reading and providing wonderful notes back in its early query form.

Everyone at Macmillan, you're the greatest publishing team an author could ask for. Thank you, Dawn Ryan, Melinda Ackell, Lois Evans, Raymond Ernesto Colón, Kristin Dulaney, Jordan Winch Molly Brouillette, Kathryn Little, Mariel Dawson, Lucy Del Priore, and Allison Verost for all your wonderful work.

Morgan Rath, fellow Sun Devil, for being an amazing publicist. I have no idea how you all keep up with your emails and schedule. You're a total wizard.

Allegra Green, Olivia Oleck, Melissa Croce, and Julia Gardiner for all your amazing work on the marketing and promo for this book.

At Imprint, thank you first and foremost to Nicole Otto, genius editor extraordinaire, for taking a chance on Amora and her story. I could travel all the way to Mordor and back (with hobbit-size feet, even!) and still not find an editor who just gets this story like you do. I'm eternally grateful to have you on my team, and for all of your support.

Erin Stein, thank you for being an all-around fabulous publisher, and for being the one who brought that still of Jacob into existence. My teenage self appreciated it.

Natalie Sousa, for bringing the world of this book to life with your incredible designs, John Morgan and Jessica Chung for all your work and support.

Linda Minton and Ilana Worrell, for helping get this book polished and ready to be read!

Gemma O'Brien, for a beautiful cover even better than the ones I've spent years dreaming about. It's absolutely spectacular.

Dave Stevenson, for bringing Visidia to life in the most gorgeous map I've ever seen.

The incredible sensitivity readers who read this book, for your invaluable notes and feedback on this story.

I also couldn't have written this book without my incredible friends and support system.

First . . . TOMI ADEYEMI AND SHEA STANDEFER!!! AHHHH!! I will forever be grateful to Pitch Wars for bringing you two into my life. Sometimes I think back to that first day we all met, where we were dreaming of agents and book deals over Thai food. I appreciate the two of you so so much, and am eternally grateful that writing brought me two of the greatest friends I could have asked for. Shea, thank you for being my friend without constraints. Tomi, thank you for eventually deciding it was okay to be my friend, even though you initially hated me because I reminded you of Azula. I appreciate you.

Haley Marshall, for still being an amazing friend despite how many times I've made you read this book. For helping me with a million rounds of edits, and for all the adventures and great times. I lucked out getting you as a friend, Rita Skeeter.

Megan McGrath, for being a huge part of why I fell in love with writing. For your years of support, your friendship, the stories, and for Kion, Couper, Izen, and Lierre. <3

Isabel Ibañez, for sliding into my DMs and demanding that I be your friend. I know I'm very stubborn, so I'm very glad your tactic worked (even if you do make me watch a bunch of "old" movies!). Thank you for feeding me arroz con pollo when I visit, and for being one of the most fabulous, sweetest humans I've ever met. Glad we get to go through this debut year side by side.

The Angelz—Sabina, Astrid, Mel, and Tomi. I look forward to screaming with one another and freaking out about exciting things for years to come. I'm so glad to have you all to navigate this weird industry with. Thank you to Mel Howard especially, for your invaluable thoughts and notes on multiple drafts of this book.

Akemi Dawn Bowman, for being my first critique partner and being so ridiculously supportive. For so (sooo) many reads, brilliant notes, and for writing books that make me cry.

The Pitch Wars '16 crew. Brenda Drake for creating the contest that changed my life, Brian Palmer for taking a chance on my old sci-fi manuscript and being a wonderful mentor and friend, and all my sprantz buddies.

I appreciate everyone who took the time and energy to provide early reads and feedback—Kelsey, Erin, Julia, Meghan, Nova, Emmy, Julie, Sam, Jennifer, Elesha, Kara, Gabrielle, Margaret, Ian, Amaris, Alexandria, Lisa, and Kendra. Your feedback was invaluable.

Thank you to every incredible author who took the time to read and blurb this book.

Kristin Dwyer, because you read my copyedits and then forced me to add you to my acknowledgments. But also for helping me choose my BTS bias.

Adrienne Young, you didn't ask to be in this, like Kristin, but thank you for all the advice and for deciding you liked me back at Yallfest.

Ashley Hearn for your incredible editorial notes on the first draft of this book, and for casually answering all my frantic "but what does this mean?!" publishing questions.

Lacey Gunnell for the adventures, the lip synch videos, and for reminding me that my head doesn't always need to be stuck in the publishing clouds.

Ally Crooks for so many years of reading and support.

Nikki and Sasha for all the writing memories, and for making me fall in love with stories in the first place.

Novel 19s for making me an honorary member, and to the Roaring 20s for being such a fabulous debut group.

Pookie, Rowdy, and Mooka, for being cute and for the cuddles.

Neopets, for being awesome fifteen years ago, when I first got my start writing on the roleplay boards. If you've ever participated in a story about a wolf named Shaikoh or a vampire slayer named Perce, that was totally me.

Stephenie Meyer. You'll probably never read this, but Twilight's the reason I fell in love with YA and reading. My wall was literally painted with Edward's and Bella's faces, so thank you for that! #TeamJacob.

Keel Haul's Sea Crew, for making me so hyped to share this book with the world. Thank you for being so invested in this story from the start, and for all your time and support.

To everyone who has read this book and made it this far, you are incredible and I appreciate the heck out of you.

Finally, I want to end this with a note that every single person involved in the development of this book (my agent, editor, publisher, designer, and cover artist) were all women. I think that's pretty dang cool, and couldn't have asked for a better team for *All the Stars and Teeth*.